A PRINCE SHOULD DO GREAT THINGS

The fact that since Crown Prince Aeid's birth twenty-five years ago, he had, in his own estimation, done exactly *nothing* was a constant aggravation to him. What had he done? What *could* he have done in a country hemmed in by mountains, seas, drought, and (he almost blushed at the disloyal thought, though he had harbored it often enough that he should have been used to it) the reactionary policies of a king so shortsighted that the lands he ruled would die or be conquered or, worse, be completely and fatally and irrecoverably ignored before he noticed that anything was amiss.

And that king of reactionary policies was Aeid's father. . . .

GAEL BAUDINO

O GREENEST BRANCH!

BOOK I OF WATER!

A ROC BOOK

ROC
Published by the Penguin Group
Penguin Books USA Inc., 375 Hudson Street,
New York, New York 10014, U.S.A.
Penguin Books Ltd, 27 Wrights Lane,
London W8 5TZ, England
Penguin Books Australia Ltd, Ringwood,
Victoria, Australia
Penguin Books Canada Ltd, 10 Alcorn Avenue,
Toronto, Ontario, Canada M4V 3B2
Penguin Books (N.Z.) Ltd, 182–190 Wairau Road,
Auckland 10, New Zealand

Penguin Books Ltd, Registered Offices:
Harmondsworth, Middlesex, England

First published by Roc, an imprint of Dutton Signet,
a division of Penguin Books USA Inc.

First Printing, May, 1995
10 9 8 7 6 5 4 3 2 1

To Salman Rushdie
Give 'em hell, guy!

LIGHTS! CAMERA! ACTION!
—Contemporary religious sentiment

ACKNOWLEDGMENTS

Special thanks to A. E. R. Gill, who, I am sure, had not the faintest idea that he was creating the Sacred Texts of the Panasian religion when he contributed Appendix B to Edward Johnston's *Writing & Illuminating & Lettering*.

The hundred-letter word in Chapter 15 comes from James Joyce's *Finnegans Wake*. No, I haven't actually read the thing. Has anyone? Really? *Why?*

Chapter One

   ... kill myself one of these days, there is no telling
what will happen if Father (Panas? No: I cannot find those
goods of any worth anymore, so I will remain with sperm
only.) does not come around; petrified as old Quarry-stone
the old man is, yet if he does not come around, I simply
do not want to be here to see what happens. Stone yields
eventually, given strain, but the stone here has turned rot-
ten and sandy and good for nothing except pounding into
gravel ... or maybe pavement ... and ...

   ... and what will become of those people out there in
the mud dwellings when everything falls? Take them all
with it, I suppose, but I cannot really say because I believe
they are less inbred than these fools who surround me—
Topaz and emerald!—but I see them every day in the market place squatting on their ten square cubits as though
they would spike it to the bedrock and the priests are no
better: run their temples like money changers ...

   "Land ho! Deck there! Land ho off the weather beam!"

   ... but it would not matter any more (my but it is hard
this morning punch it straight through a pillar of basalt if
I wanted maybe that is why they like me and better get off
my stomach before it breaks and I have to piss here too)
rather think about Sabihah—Hammer and chisel! Those

breasts! And that ambergris she puts in her—wait . . . wait
. . . is that Sabihah? Or is it Huda? Or Najmat? I cannot
keep track of them and all muddled now—get up eventually and go to prayers (piss first) everybody loves me but
would not if they knew what I really think but I will never
tell them no not ever because I am the dutiful son and the
first (and only) born (I wonder about that sometimes but
then they keep telling me that the best stone is scarcest in
the quarry) and someday I will inherit the Three Kingdoms
(I really believe that of course I do) and then I will change
things as I wish, just as I will juggle the paving stones in
the Great Temple of Nuhr twenty thousand kils apiece if
they weigh a scruple . . .

*"Yes, Mr. Turtletrout. I can make out the port now. Here,
take my glass and have a look."*

. . . get up oh, by Panas (in whom I no longer believe
but what of it?), that wine is foul after it sits in your
mouth all night. Did I vomit? A little. It will be clean
by the time I have bathed. And what if I had decided to
shit? They would clean that up, too. Out here. Aeid, darling of the Three Kingdoms, can do no wrong. The . . .
what did they call it in the *Journal de Paris*? The *cyno-
sure*? Odd word. We would sound strange to them, too,
and we will if I ever get a chance, but of course I will not
get a chance until we are all speaking French only it will
not be us who are speaking French but all the French and
with Bonaparte making for Egypt—

Get up, fool! Go and piss or you will blow up!

And what is this—?

*"The Three Kingdoms! Mr. Crane! Bring her about.
We'll have to beat in while the wind's from the shore . . ."*

"Ow!"

Aeid jumped up and down on one foot, holding his
other in one hand while his other (hand) thrashed back and
forth in a futile search for something to grab hold of. His

brain, still fuzzy with sleep, persisting in tipping the alabaster floor of his chambers slowly from one side to the
other even though he knew perfectly well that it (the floor)
was perfectly motionless ... and horizontal. But if he
could not trust his brain, he could at least trust his hand,
but where was something he could grab and what had he
tripped on anyway and oh dear here was a low table—

"Ow, ow, ow! Pumice and rottenstone!"

" ... but the tide will be turning in another hour."

"That'll give us a hand, then, sir."

Distracted for the moment from his thoughts about
willed non-existence, his father, his society, his society's
women, and French incursions into Africa, Aeid went
down, aiming as best he could for the carpets that covered
the floor close to the window. There were at least three
layers of them, and they were thick and springy: the best
wool. Pre-drought. He only bounced once.

Maumud was not speaking to her this morning, but, in
fact, Maumud had not spoken to her for weeks. Sari could
not remember how long it had been, neither could she recall what she had done to cause him to subject her to such
unremitting silence. As usual, the change had come on
abruptly, with a sudden darkening of his face as though a
thought had struck him. He had gazed at her, his gray
brows drawn together, his mouth turning hard, and then
the silence had begun. He ate and drank, went out, came
in, ate and drank again ... wordlessly.

Throughout fifty years of marriage to Maumud, Sari had
become accustomed to these bouts of silence. It was his
way. But these days, as they doddered through their old
age, the silences had been increasing. She had begun to
believe that he hated her, that, indeed, it would be better
if he never spoke to her again; but yet she felt at times that
she, housebound by Panasian law, hardly able even to look

out a window save by her husband's leave, would soon begin to scream if she did not hear a human voice addressed to her.

Now, on this indeterminate day of unbroken marital silence, it was early morning: away to the east, the dawn was throwing the distant Mountains of Ern into sharp silhouette, and the dark masses looked much like an immense wave that stood up between Sari's village and the sun, a rising wave, a wave ready to crest, topple, and inundate everything. The sky was the color of a twilight sea (she had seen the sea, once, when she was young), and as she cautiously peered from behind the woven lattice of the window, it lightened, turning from deepest ultramarine to a soft, cloudless azure as the black mountains became, in contrast, even blacker.

Steps in the street outside. Sari recognized Maumud's shuffle and slip, the product of last year's shattered ankle bone. He was coming home from the market square for another rug. Old as he was, he insisted upon setting up himself, carrying one rug at a time, even though he had a son who was very willing to help him.

Again Sari looked at the mountains that, even at a distance of fifty leagues, rose a third of the way to the zenith. A wave that high! What might it do? But the shuffle and slip drew closer, and she turned from the window. Waves? Sea? What thoughts to have in the midst of a drought that had lasted three centuries!

Squatting down by the cooking fire in the middle of her house, as dusty and gray as the pad of ash beneath the burning wood, she picked up one of the sticks that her son had brought to her the previous day and shoved it in, feeding the small flame.

Motion, a rustle of the hanging at the door. Maumud entered.

Glance: *Why are you wasting that wood?*

They had lived together, husband and wife, for fifty years: she did not need words to tell her what he thought. His expression was enough. "I am cooking your breakfast, husband," she replied, and her old, cracked voice sounded loud and abrupt in the morning silence.

A glare: *Waste.*

"Husband, the fire will die without wood."

A flicker of his eyes, a flash of anger at her impertinence: *Waste. You women are all alike.*

He turned away as though expecting no reply. That was just as well: Sari had none to make.

But on this morning, with the incongruous image of water in her mind, his last opinion seemed to her to be both gratuitous and, at root, inaccurate. All women? *All?* Even a priest would not utter such a generality, for there could be no mistaking the great difference between herself, dried and withered, and one of her daughters who, still in the plump bloom of early middle age, served her man in Nuhr or in one of the other coastal cities. No: women might well be quarries for the production of the stones of issue, but there could not but be a great difference between a working quarry and one that had been emptied of everything useful.

Lifting the lid of the pot that hung over the fire, Sari stirred the steaming grain as she looked at her gray, wrinkled hands. Emptied. Emptied of everything.

Well, she had been warned. The priests had told her what to expect when she had left her family—left her Goddess, left everything familiar—and given herself to Maumud, his God, and his patriarchs. The priests had told her everything. Like the great and holy Quarries in the mountains, women were a source of raw material for the future, giving into other hands what would be shaped by other hands. And Sari, bowing to the tenets of Panas as she had bowed to the impelling demands of love, had taken on her role of passive, inert, giving quarry, had taken on the face cloth and the head cloth, had gone so far (For Maumud! For love!) as to allow the sharp, priestly blade to apply to her body one further mark, one indelible and inescapable brand of emptiness—

Her hand, stilled by her thoughts, was no longer stirring, but she felt the impatient movement behind her, sensed the thoughts that went with it. *Where is my breakfast?*

She had offended him. She knew that she had offended him, even though she did not know exactly *how* she had offended him. Perhaps, though, her very existence was an offense that had, with the passing years, grown increasingly pronounced, increasingly intolerable. Stone, once spoiled, was good for nothing, even though it might be pretty enough on the surface. Cracks, flaws, impurities . . . all these things could render it useless, whether for the men who found in its shaping their holy vocation, or for the God Himself who had, in the beginning, carved the earth and all that was in it out of stone, forever sanctifying thereby the sharp chisel and the passive rock, forever dooming flawed specimens like Sari.

Did Maumud hate her now? He had, long ago, loved her. He had yearned for her as she had for him, had convinced himself that a Naian, a Goddess worshiper, could be transformed by vow, by veil, and by knife. And, indeed, Sari had thought so, too. But they had both been wrong, and just as the long and increasing drought had slowly withered the land, so had the years turned their love to ashes.

My breakfast!

He was furious with her. She spooned a bowl full of cooked grain, garnished it with dates and bread cakes, gave it to him. He ate rapidly, glaring at her as he shoved the food into his mouth.

All women are alike. Wasteful. With wood at three set-

tles a kil, you go throwing it into the fire as though we had a mountain of it.

Sari nodded. She had to nod. There was nothing she could do but nod.

I work every day for you, and you . . . you do nothing.

He hardly had to look at her, or she at him: she knew his thoughts.

You play with your herbs and you practice your quackery with Naians—

This was too much. "Husband!" she burst out. "Maumud! That is not true! I have not seen people of my own religion since . . ." She suddenly realized her unfortunate choice of words, and the rest of the sentence died in her mouth.

Maumud threw the half empty bowl across the room. It buried itself in a pile of cushions and sent its contents slopping over the embroidery in a pale wave. "You . . . your *own* religion?"

She had made a fatal error. Panas was a jealous God. Or maybe it was that Panas' priests were jealous priests, or Panas' men were jealous men. It did not matter. Her inadvertent lapse in speech—brought on, perhaps, by her meditations on the past—could result in her losing considerably more than the bit of flesh that had been pried out of her fifty years ago. "I can explain," she said. "Really. I mean—"

"You have already explained, Naian," said Maumud. He was speaking to her for the first time in many days, addressing her directly, but Sari was now wishing desperately that he were not.

A terrible moment of building resolve, and then his hand darted out and ripped the veil away from her face. "I will send you outside without your wrap and allow the priests to punish you properly, Naian whore. Where is your medallion? Your Naian medallion? You have kept it, have you not?"

She had. It was in the small bundle of her childhood treasures, the bundle she kept hidden. Tucked away, buried deep, never looked at for years at a time, it was, nonetheless, still in her possession.

"Have you not? Answer me: the stone responds to the chisel! From the beginning it yields to the impelling blow!"

Feeling naked, ashamed, vulnerable, she was fumbling for her face cloth, trying to fasten it again. Would he divorce her now? He could: a word from him would suffice. And then she would be on her own, to shift for herself as best an old woman could ... an old woman whose place among the daughters of Panas had been taken from her, whose place among the children of Naia had long since been filled by others.

"But ... but is it not written that the best blow is a tap instead of a bang?" she managed, her fear putting an edge of panic into her aged croak.

"And now you all but quote the Sacred Texts aloud! How dare you—?" But as though he suddenly realized that he was speaking to her, Maumud caught himself, closed his mouth, and turned away. Without another word, he went into his shop, picked up another rug and, staggering under its weight, carried it out of the house and down the street toward the market.

Obadiah Jenkins was a thin gray man whose obvious reluctance to part with even the most trivial revelation about himself or his plans apparently extended to his choice of clothing, for in contrast to Puritan custom Jenkins (*Ambassador* Jenkins, Captain Elijah Scruffy reminded himself for the forty-third time that voyage, which averaged out to at least once per day) was clad in gray from the top of his (gray) beaver hat to the soles of his (gray) buckled shoes as though he were unwilling to make so definite a statement about himself as he would have had he garbed his gaunt frame in stark and uncompromising black.

Accompanied by his (black-clad) assistant, Mr. Mather, Jenkins stood at the lee rail of the quarter-deck as the double-frigate *Seaflower* came about and continued clawing its way in toward the harbor of Nuhr. Jenkins, his arms folded, was gazing ahead levelly, and with his gray eyes, gray hair, and gray clothes, seemed to want only a heavy morning fog to complete himself, for then—gray on gray—he would have been not only invisible, but so non-committal as to subside, perhaps, into virtual non-existence.

Scruffy adjusted his own white neck cloth: the only non-black article of his uniform. *Seaflower* was a Puritan ship, a godly ship. The officers of Old Papist England might deck themselves out like gutter drabs, but Americans were made of sterner—and more devout—stuff. From admiral to runny-nosed powder monkey, black was good enough for all, and so this gray man—nebulous and non-committal—bothered the bluff, affable, and (with but a few exceptions) very direct Scruffy, and he was glad that the ambassador and the ambassador's assistant kept to the lee side of the quarter-deck.

"Mr. Crane," he called abruptly to the ship's master. "Come to my cabin with those charts of yours. I want to look at them again."

"Immediately, sir."

With short, stocky feet that fit his boots as though they had been extruded into them, Scruffy—himself short and stocky and fitting his uniform in much the same way—plumped down the steps to his cabin. Unlike many captains in the American fleet, he did not have to duck his head in the slightest in order to avoid the deck beams above him. Mr. Crane, though, was a tall, gangling fellow, and had to bend almost double to clear the lintel when he arrived a minute later with a set of rolled charts.

In the course of a voyage whose uneventfulness had been marred only by the appearance of two tiny French sloops that, having somehow escaped the British blockade, fled the moment they had seen the Cross and Stripes, Scruffy had looked at Crane's charts many times, studying them, poring over them, committing them to memory. In fact, among the reasons that he did not keep them in his cabin (leaving aside, for the moment, the fact that Jenkins, his assistant, and his secretary had taken over fully one half of the already minuscule cabin of the *Seaflower,* thereby necessitating that Scruffy cram his possessions into substantially less space than had barely contained them in the first place) was exactly that: he *had* memorized them, and, consequently, needed nothing by way of paper and colored inks to augment his internal record.

And so, while Scruffy might well have examined Crane's charts in his mind's eye while strolling the weather side of the quarter-deck, looking at them in what was left to him of his cabin would give him a chance to remove himself for a few minutes from Jenkins' gray presence, and that was certainly something to be wished for. At least by Scruffy.

"They're not very good, I'm afraid, sir," said Mr. Crane.

"They weren't very good yesterday, Mr. Crane," said Scruffy affably. "And they weren't very good when we left Boston. It can't be helped. These heathens can't make good maps to save their souls, and as for those frogs and dagos who've been here before us . . . well . . ."

Crane, bent to keep his head from the upper beams, was attempting to face Scruffy and meet his gaze at the same time, and this was requiring him to present to his captain most of the top of his head while he rolled his eyes up toward his forehead as much as he could.

"But," Scruffy went on, "all this shouldn't be much of a problem for a master who took his ship all the way from Tahiti to Boston without sighting land once."

Crane attempted to smile, but, as he was still bent over, the expression was, unfortunately, obscured by his nose. "That was *Jehovah's Hammer,* sir."

"Yes, yes. *Jehovah's Hammer.* Seventy-two guns. Fine ship."

"But, in all honesty, we did sight land once, sir."

"Really?"

"At the Horn, sir."

Scruffy kept his affable smile. "But only once. And you came in on time to the hour, I heard."

"Yes, sir."

Scruffy nodded. He had known about the sighting at the Horn, but had decided to take the opportunity to test Crane's integrity. He was pleased by the result. "Good. I'm glad we understand one another, Mr. Crane."

Crane nodded as though wondering just what, on his part, he was supposed to understand, and, with obvious trepidation, he moved to spread the charts out on the tiny table that was already cluttered with a number of what Scruffy called his "curiosities."

Gingerly, he nudged a miniature Leyden jar and a set of polarizing lenses to one side, obviously trying to leave the more delicate apparatuses (microscope, static electricity generator, hygrometer, miniature steam engine) strictly alone. The engine, though, which Scruffy had fired up at breakfast for a quick, wheezing run about the table, took that opportunity to emit a disconsolate hiss from one of its tiny cylinders, and this caused Mr. Crane to jump back and straighten, bringing the back of his head into abrupt and violent contact with one of the overhead beams.

"Have to watch that, Mr. Crane," Scruffy said without looking up from the charts. "Perhaps you ought to consider shipping as one of the topmasts next time."

"Uh . . . yes, sir. Very good, sir," said Mr. Crane as he nursed his head and attempted to keep himself from pitching dizzily into the crowded museum cases that were packed so closely around the walls of the cabin as to take up every inch of free space save for what was occupied by the elaborate feather bed that Scruffy affected.

"Mr. Turtletrout is on watch, is he not?" said Scruffy.

"Yes, sir," said Mr. Crane. "He'll be off shortly, sir."

"We'll have our game of chess, then," said Scruffy. "The high point of my day: a game of chess with Mr. Turtletrout. Very good. Now, Mr. Crane, let's take a look at these dago charts again so we'll stand a chance of coming into Nuhr harbor properly, like a godly ship worthy of frightening the heathen bastards of the Three Kingdoms."

nied by a fluttering of the stones and of their glinting reflections: a shadowing and unshadowing so rapid and fluid that for a moment all of Nuhr appeared to lie beneath the waters of a wind-stirred pond.

It was, perhaps, not only a singularly ironic illusion, but a stupid one as well, and Aeid, son of Inwa Kabir and therefore Prince of Kaprisha (below), of Kalash (to the south) and Khyr (even farther to the south), could not but reflect on it: the illusion of water in a land which had almost none.

Standing on the topmost balcony of the highest tower of the King's Palace, his elbows braced thoughtfully on the marble railing, his hands cupping his outthrust chin (which, being outthrust as far as it was, had almost five hundred feet of empty air between it and the ground), Aeid examined the distant mountains. Up, far up among their impossibly high peaks was the whiteness of perpetual snow, lower down were the thick veils of dark clouds. The calendars of Kaprisha, Kalash, and Khyr said *Month of the Chisel,* the calendars of Europe and America (and so great was the isolation of his lands that Aeid assumed himself to be alone in the knowledge) said *mid-June,* and yet the Mountains of Ern, the impenetrable wall that isolated the Three Kingdoms from the rest of Africa (as the sea, and law—and, occasionally, weapons—isolated them from the rest of the world), were brilliant with the presence of frozen water and shadowed with the prospect of rain.

Water. Aeid brought his gaze closer, to River Forshen. Proceeding from the mountains, it had flowed across the breadth of Kaprisha, and though it appeared weak and worn out from its journey, it had, in actuality, never been anything else. Having started out a comparative trickle in the mountains, Forshen was still a comparative trickle here at the coast. For all the rain and snow witnessed by the peaks and highlands of the distant mountains, there was no corroboration on the part of the lowlands or the rivers that watered them.

Again, Aeid wrestled with the problem. Like his fellow *philosophes* (Aeid liked to think of himself as a *philosophe*), he believed in a rational world. Cause and effect. And if there was an effect, why then, there had to be a cause somewhere. But to have that much water up in the mountains, and to have rivers that came down from the mountains, and to have almost no water in those rivers . . . why, that was insanity.

Aeid struggled with the problem for a time . . . and then, as usual, gave up. Obviously, since he could find no solution to the paradox, he must have been suffering from a simple lack of information. He had, though, been suffering from that lack for a long time, and it did not seem within his power, despite his best efforts, to remedy the deficiency.

He examined again the trickle of the river. A prince, he thought, should do great things, and the fact that, since his birth twenty-five years ago, he had, in his own estimation, done exactly *nothing* was a constant aggravation to him.

Oh, there had been tremendous pomp and celebration at his birth. The priests of the temple (led by Abnel even then!) had lined up to pay their respects to the new prince, the people had thronged the streets, musicians and acrobats and thieves and cutthroats had come from as far away as Aizen. There was even one mountebank who had wandered in from Algiers (though there was still debate as to whether he had come for the festivities or had merely blundered into the city in order to sell a number of odd-colored rocks to the Naians . . . who, as was well known, would buy almost anything that was odd, strange, or even marginally crystalline). Food had been plentiful, wine had flowed like . . . well, not at all like water, for it had been abundant, and the holiday had lasted for weeks.

Aeid knew all about the festivities surrounding his birth, to be sure, for an official description of it had been noted down in excruciating detail in the official records, and one of the official duties of a prince—one of the many official aspects of his officially limited education—was a careful (and official) reading of those same official records. Oh, yes: assemblies and huzzahs and then, two days after the block of royal stone had been pried out of the properly purified royal vagina, the chief minister, standing before the king, the king's family, the councils of the priests, the ministers and overseers and counselors and officials down to the petty collectors of the temple tax levied on all good Panasians, and even the gathered population of the city (including, for once, the Mud Dwellers who lived outside the walls), had unveiled a golden tablet. *I can only record the date and the time and the place,* he had said as he had brandished a golden chisel. *For the rest I must leave blank in order to provide room for his accomplishments—and I foresee many!—which if it please the mighty Panas (blessed be He!) and the All Highest King, it shall be my pleasure and my duty to record!*

And what had he done? What *could* he have done in a country hemmed in by mountains, seas, drought, and (he almost blushed at the disloyal thought, though he had harbored it often enough that he should have been used to it) the reactionary policies of a king so shortsighted that the lands he ruled would die or be conquered or, worse, be completely and fatally and irrecoverably *ignored* before he noticed that anything was amiss.

Aeid slapped a hand to his forehead in frustration, winced as a large gold ring cracked against his brow bone.

And that king of the reactionary policies was Inwa Kabir. Aeid's father.

"Pumice . . ."

Far away, the mountains kept their snow. At their feet,

the land lay brown and desiccated and fit only for an increasingly nomadic life. Below, the city awakened to another dry day, the stunted date palms waved, the impaled bodies of the women who had been found adulterous, immodest, or contemptuous by the priestly courts attracted early and optimistic flies.

". . . and rottenstone."

But was it really just the king? Or was it the king and the priests who advised him? Or was it the king and the priests who advised him and the ministers who toadied to him? Or was it all those things combined with a dying, drought-stricken land, cities which themselves were, quite literally, graven in stone so deeply that they offered not the slightest opportunity for change, and a population that collaborated with it all, even encouraged it, because it provided an intelligible framework for their lives, their hopes, and their ambitions?

It was morning, and Aeid was already developing another installment of his daily headache; but when, looking for relief, he turned his face away from the white mountains and the brown deserts and toward the blue sea, he saw not only the endless water and the curved horizon and the faint trace of haze that had not yet burned off (tantalizing and cool it looked this sixteenth day of the Month of the Chisel), but also something else. Something unexpected. Something that . . .

He leaned out, straining his eyes. Just coming over the horizon was a patch of white. No, several patches of white. Rectangles of white, in fact. Minute and tiny they were at this great distance, but they appeared to be approaching.

Aeid squinted into the haze and the distance. In violation of the official strictures upon him, he had read widely (albeit secretly), and therefore he knew what he was seeing: topsails, topgallants, two . . . no . . . three masts, and the dark line of a ship beneath them. And was that a second cluster of light and darkness beside the first?

He wished that he had a telescope. In fact, he *did* have a telescope, but by law and by custom, he was not *supposed* to have a telescope and therefore he certainly could not be seen *using* a telescope without causing a major upheaval in the priestly council, deep embarrassment for his father, and a profound uneasiness among the general population.

It was yet another opportunity for a resurgence of the constant frustration that had infected his life. He could only sigh, strain his eyes, refrain as best he could from adding a second bruise to his brow bone, and wonder whether there were any high rooms in the tower private enough to contain himself, the glass, and a view of the sea.

The morning was growing, the haze was burning off: the ships, though still distant, were becoming remarkably clear. Aeid knew nothing of intuition—that was, to be sure, for women . . . and maybe some of those Naian men who prided themselves on such irrational and effeminate things— but he had the sudden hunch that they were American.

Describe the seagoing conveyances that were approaching the coast of the Three Kingdoms—specifically, the harbor of the city of Nuhr—on the morning of 16 June 1798.

Two vessels, ships of the fleet of the Righteous States of America. To wit: *Seaflower,* a double-frigate, and *Speedwell,* a sloop of war.

With what warlike appurtenances were the two aforementioned ships supplied?

Seaflower: 54 guns (24 pound), arranged on two decks. Two bow chasers (18 pound), occupying stations to either side of the bowsprit, and two stern chasers (12 pound) positioned on the quarter-deck so as not to encumber further the already doubly cramped cabin.

Were there any indications—?

In addition to the aforementioned heavy guns (the smaller being in no wise inferior to the larger owing to their longer throw), *Seaflower* was also possessed of four carronades (36 pound), designed for close-in fighting. These were strategically mounted at four widely-spaced stations of the ship's deck: starboard and larboard of the foremast, starboard and larboard of the mizzenmast. On board was also the customary assortment of cutlasses, dirks, pistols, and various other weapons and heavy objects that could be used as weapons. An adequate supply of muskets was in the care of a company of Marines (Lieutenant Daniel Cuttle, commander) that was stationed on board *Seaflower* for both defense in battle and discipline in case of desertion or mutiny. To—

Very good. Were there—?

The provisions of *Speedwell* remain to be enumerated. They are, to wit—

Were there any indications—?

—22 guns (14 pounds)—

Ah: *Were there any indications*—

—arranged on one deck (there being, in the case of a sloop, —

Damn you! WERE THERE ANY INDICATIONS—?
—)— . . .?

—*that* . . . ah . . . that the aforementioned ships were in any way apprehensive of what might occur upon their reaching the aforementioned foreign port?

Being that the ships themselves (inanimate objects down to the last nail and scantling) were incapable of human emotion, the question more rightfully should be put in terms of the crews. Granting this rephrasing, the answer would be very much in the affirmative.

Enumerate these indications.

Upon their entrance into the mouth of Nuhr harbor, both ships would have been observed to have had their gun ports open and their guns run out. Upon closer examination, the gun crews would have been observed standing ready at their weapons, which from all appearance, looked to be loaded, primed, and ready to fire. The members of the ships' crews were individually armed with various combinations of hand-to-hand and close range weapons, including, but not limited to, dirk; cutlass; pistol; dirk and cutlass; dirk and pistol; cutlass and pistol; pistol, dirk and cutlass—

Were the members of the ships' crews able to discharge their weapons with any alacrity?
Which ones?

Were the crews able to discharge the aforementioned 24, 18, and 12 pound guns with any alacrity?
On a good day, without unforeseen mishap, the crews of *Seaflower* and *Speedwell* could fire repeated broadsides with a delay of only two minutes between discharges.

Could this rate of fire be maintained indefinitely?
No.

Explain.
Given repeated explosive detonations of gunpowder within the confines of the guns, the metal which formed

the containing fabric would, by necessity, experience a rise in temperature. In time, this rise, whether expressed in terms of degrees of Fahrenheit, Celsius, or the yet-to-be-invented Kelvin, would prove sufficient to detonate prematurely the gunpowder cartridges which, in accordance with the level of technology then current among the artillery engineers of the Righteous States of America (or, for that matter, the artillery engineers of any of the European or Asian states, their dependencies, territories, possessions, or colonies), were by necessity introduced into the gun via the aperture afforded by the muzzle. Any such premature detonation would invariably cause damage to the physical being of whatever member of the gun crew happened to be positioned less than fortuitously—this condition being very likely, indeed almost unavoidable—and would possibly and simultaneously damage the fabric of the ship itself, which by nature could not but be positioned less than fortuitously.

Were the crews aware of this?
Yes.

Were the captains?
Yes.

Speaking of the captains, were there any public indications that Elijah Scruffy, captain of *Seaflower*, harbored anything more than a strictly platonic attachment to his first lieutenant, Mr. Turtletrout?
There were no indications, either by public deportment or public speech, that anything of the sort was harbored.

None?
None, whatsoever.

Returning to the ships. What prompted such warlike preparations as were exhibited by both *Seaflower* and *Speedwell*?

The close proximity of a foreign port which might prove hostile, the lack of any ready information as to the reception likely to be offered to the two ships upon their arrival, the unknown alignment of the government that controlled the port.

Specific possibilities of alignment?
British, French, American, neutral.

Expound upon the likelihood of any of the four alignments being currently maintained by the foreign government.
British: unknown but unlikely. French: unknown but unlikely. American: unknown but extremely unlikely. Neutral: unknown but very likely.

Was the captain of *Seaflower* aware of these possibilities?
Very much so.

Speaking of the captain of *Seaflower:* were there ever any *private* indications that his relationship with his aforementioned first lieutenant was anything other than platonic in the strictest sense of the word?
In that such private indications would have been exhibited exclusively in private, there were none.

Speculate.
Insufficient data is available for speculation.

Intuit, then.
Possibly.

Explain.
Explanations might prove embarrassing.

Why were the unlikely alignments discussed above unlikely? Why was the very unlikely alignment discussed above very unlikely? Why was the likely alignment discussed above likely?
The unlikely alignments were such because of the known aversion on the part of the government of the foreign land in question to any form of intercourse—

Speaking of intercourse—
—with outside cultures whatsoever. The very unlikely alignment was such because those in authority on board *Seaflower* would have been aware of it. The likely alignment was such because of the known tendency of isolated governments that are determined to be isolated to ignore any current or ongoing affairs outside of their isolation. Hence, without knowledge, there could be no intercourse, without intercourse, there could be no alignment.

Speaking of intercourse, did Captain Elijah Scruffy—?
The roots of this isolation—

Enough of the isolation. Did Captain Scruffy ever—?
The answer to that question is not known.

That question has not yet been asked.
Even if it were asked, the answer to it would not be known.

But Captain Scruffy—
What about Mr. Mather, assistant to Ambassador Obadiah Jenkins?

Why do you mention Mather?
Why indeed?

At ... at ... at any rate, were there any reasons, besides
the isolation of the government of the foreign land in
question ... for those in authority on board the ships—and
that *includes* Captain Elijah Scruffy and Mr. Turtletrout
and Ambassador Jenkins and Mr. Mather, thank you—to
expect any belligerent action on the part of those in authority upon the shore?
Yes.

Enumerate them.
Tradition, history, apprehensiveness.

Explain them.
Tradition: the hostility of the Three Kingdoms to representatives of other cultures was well known. History: previous ships attempting to anchor in the waters of the Three
Kingdoms had been boarded by stealth and put to the
torch. Apprehensiveness: the standard caution on the part
of brave but cautious men to enter cautiously into those
situations which demand caution.

Were there any women on board either ship?
No.

Concerning Captain Elijah Scruffy and Mr. Turtletrout—
What about Mr. Mather?

Had there ever been any women on board either ship?
No.

Scruffy—

Mather.

. . .

!

Did the captain of *Seaflower* have any assurance that his crew—and that of *Speedwell*—would be able to avoid the unfortunate fate that tradition and history ascribed to previous ships that had entered the waters of the Three Kingdoms?

The captain of *Seaflower,* knowing the strengths and weaknesses of the crews of the two ships, did have some such assurance.

Did the captain of *Seaflower* show such perspicacity in all facets of his life?

The general opinion at the time was that he did.

Was this the reason that he had been given overall command of the ships that constituted the American expedition to the Three Kingdoms?

The general opinion at the time was that it was.

Is general opinion invariably correct?

It is frequently correct.

But is it invariably correct?

No.

Did there exist in the Righteous States of America or in the Three Kingdoms any cultural or legal disadvantage associated with non-platonic relationships between men?

In both the Righteous States of America and the Three Kingdoms, the penalty for such relationships was immediate death.

For the life of me, I do not know what I ever saw in her. That craven thing! Old and flaccid she is now, and the way she bobs her head at me and fawns—a sterile dog, that is all, fit for nothing but a good kick. Oh, she would feel it still, but I for one would never sully my hands again with impure flesh.

A Naian! Still! Blasphemy and more blasphemy! And all these years—what? Did she contaminate the children? But no, I have never noticed anything. But perhaps they keep it secret? I have no way of finding out.

And now she makes my dinner. And soon she will serve it to me. Craven. Keeps her head down. Were she a young one, she would hold it a little higher perhaps, but they are always that way and she would have to bend it to me because I am a man, and that is what Panas has decreed. Were she proud, it might be necessary for me to beat her. But she is not proud.

I do not know what I did before this, but to be sure it was a terrible thing I have done now. And I must submit. I must bend my head and bob it at him in the manner of a good Panasian wife, for surely that is the only way left for me to appease him, and what if he struck me? I would have no one to turn to. But what if he simply ignored me for the rest of my life? I could not bear that.

Why did I keep that medallion? Regret? To be sure, I raised the children without Naia. He could find no fault with me there.

Well, I will make him the dinner he likes best, and then perhaps he will forgive me and love me even though I am old and good for nothing. It could be worse, I know. There are some who suffer and who cannot leave. I see them in the market place, and even their face cloths cannot hide the bruises and the swellings and what is broken, and it could be worse than even that, for the

Or perhaps she is proud after all, but she is a Naian. Yes, I can see that. All these years, and she is still a proud Naian. And so I must beat her. Yes. And it will feel good, the strong thopping of proud bones. Yes, just like the heft of a good carpet. Yes.

priests are willing to condemn, and a spoiled stone is worth nothing, fit only for putting on a stick, or hanging from a noose, and oh, he is rising now, perhaps he will forgive me and we can (please) spend our last (please) years in (please) peace.

Chapter Three

Well, what shall it be today, then? Boy . . . or girl?

The face that looked back from the mirror was pretty by any standards: an immaculate complexion, large eyes the color of jet, high cheekbones, well-formed lips that held just the slightest pout . . . all framed by a fall of hair that swept down like liquid night and cascaded over smooth, brown shoulders.

Bakbuk turned from side to side, examining the reflection, debating. Choosing to be male would give him the advantage of free movement, and he would not have to endure the startled expressions of the court: the upcast eyes, the occasional gasps of horror or—in the case of Abnel and his silly gaggle of priests—of anger. Oh, yes, he thought, it was very easy to be male. To stare one's fellow men (he giggled at the thought) straight in the eye, flail about with one's hands as one talked, brandish a fist if necessary, swagger and crotch-hitch and puff one's way about . . .

Actually, Bakbuk greatly enjoyed tormenting the court and the priests, and, in any case, she was rather attracted by womanhood today. Face cloth and head cloth and shoulder cloth and skirts, eyes cast downward and small, mincing steps that hinted at ankle fetters even when the ankle fetters were not there. A small, simpering voice. Perfumes and eye makeup ... and asking a man to accompany her if she wanted to go out into the streets so as not to attract the brutal attentions of the religious police (not that she ever asked, or that it would do even the religious police any good to complain).

She turned about, took up her hair and piled it atop her head. Naked and smooth, without a hint of breasts or genitals, she swayed her hips slowly and stared herself in the face with studied insolence.

All that. Yes. And then there was the distinct pleasure of having one fool or another grope out ... and then shriek as his hand was slashed to the bone. And (as always) the fool would complain, and (as always) the fool would then find not only that absolutely nothing would be done— because the woman was no more a woman than she was a man, because the woman was, in actuality, the king's eunuch sworder—but also that any attempt at vengeance or satisfaction on the fool's part would result in either quick death (and Bakbuk would enjoy that) or the laughter of the king and his court (and Bakbuk would enjoy that, too ... though not quite so much).

She suddenly dropped her hair and whirled like the women of Khyr during their marriage dance. Darting glances in the mirror, she noted that she had at last gotten the knack of it—for her long hair whipped out in a broad fan while her hips remained thrust forward. Setting her feet and halting abruptly, then, she let her hips swing out to the side while her hair wrapped itself about her torso like a veil.

"Perfect," she said. "I will have to go down to Khyr during the wedding celebrations. The men will surely fight over me."

She repeated the movement. Spin. Stop. Wrap. A woman's face peeped coyly and invitingly from behind a web of jet black strands.

"Until," he added, "I find it necessary to kill them."

And once more.

"What fun!"

Swaying his hips, feeling his own gracile movement, perhaps even aroused by it (though arousal would have been pointless: that had been taken care of when he was a boy) Bakbuk considered. "And so shall it be a fetching little girl today, Bakbuk?" he said to his reflection. "Shall we wear a different costume this time so that the counselors will not recognize us? Some new beads and bangles? A new silk face cloth? A hint—just a hint: we are not immodest, after all—of a foot showing from beneath our hem? Shall we be a girl?"

She played with her hair, watching the expression on her face change from the defiance of a pseudo-man to the slightly acid sweetness of a woman manqué whose eyes were perhaps a little too calculating. But only Bakbuk noticed such things ... as she noticed also that no man ever looked into a woman's eyes deeply enough to see the shifting emotions and the caution and the fear—

She made herself start back, hands pressed to her cheeks, eyes wide (yes, the men liked the eyes wide: it gave them a sense of power), lips parted (she had gotten the knack of that, too, and she often reflected that it was too bad that no one could see that perfect little moist mouth beneath her face cloth) just slightly, as though uncertain whether to clench, smile, or open receptively to whatever mixed horror and pleasure was about to be forced between them.

For a moment he stood thus, and then he dropped his hands and laughed. And the fear. Yes, the fear. It was perfect, absolutely perfect. Better than perfect, really, for it was not reality that Bakbuk imitated (and he knew it), but rather fantasy. Observing objectively from the vantage of his enforced separation, Bakbuk had seen the truth, the lies, and the fantasies. And Bakbuk adapted them all, used them all, manipulated them all.

But just then there was a shout from the market square outside and below Bakbuk's window, and, almost at the same time, another shout from the hallway of the palace outside the closed door. Startled, she whirled, one hand on her belly, the other pressed to her just-parted lips. The shouts continued, and those from the hallway resolved into words:

"Ships! Ships approaching the harbor! Foreign ships!"

For a moment, Bakbuk wondered what had happened, why foreign ships had come to Nuhr, what might be required of the king's personal sworder as a result of it. And then he caught a glimpse of himself in the mirror: hand to belly, hand to lips, body curving *just so,* preparing to yield to whatever might come, whatever might thrust itself . . .

Her laughter was bright—bright and bright edged. A woman! A perfect woman! Skirts and bangles today, Bakbuk! Skirts and bangles . . . and knives!

Aeid ran up the steps of the main staircase of the palace, not caring in the slightest that two of his father's counselors were nearby. Let them wonder about his actions. But, then again, what with two foreign ships preparing to anchor—

Take in the fore and main topsails and headsails!

—in the harbor and the people of the city suspended somewhere between terror of the ships' guns, anger at the uninvited intrusion into the holy waters of the holy city, and greed with regards to the traditions of burning and looting applicable to the situation, they were probably not wondering at all. Of *course* the counselors knew what

Aeid was doing and why he was taking the steps two at a time, trying for three, and—

Oops!

The two counselors ran to help him as he came to rest in the middle of the flight of marble stairs, a brightly-colored and princely heap of robes, jewels, and bruises. Kuz Aswani (who was short and had a pointed nose) reached him first and, after kneeling as best he could and kissing the steps between his hands (almost knocking out a tooth on the juncture of tread and riser) rose again, caught Aeid under the arms, and began attempting to haul him to his feet.

This effort, though laudable, was hampered by Kuz Aswani's lack of height. His head, in fact, came up only to the level of Aeid's shoulders (when Aeid was standing, of course), and therefore, after lifting the prince partway to his feet, the short, pointy-nosed counselor found himself unable either to lift him any higher because of a decided lack of leverage, or to lower him back to the ground because such an action would have drawn perilously close to insult, and it was well known—the point having been made in everything from the Holy Texts Themselves to Zhag Me'redig's incomparable "Tale of Shibli Bagarag"—that it was a foolish man indeed who would insult, even obliquely, his prince.

As luck would have it, though, Nash Shar (who was tall and had a snub nose) arrived just at that time, and sizing up the situation as best he could (which was, in fact, not very well, he being unable to see anything of Kuz Aswani's face, which was buried in the folds of the back of Kuz Aswani's prince's robe) decided that Kuz Aswani, being exceedingly worried about the health of his prince after such a fall, was doubtless now in the midst of endeavoring to carry his prince either up or down the stairs so as to bring him to a more comfortable resting place.

Understanding, then, not at all, Nash Shar knelt, kissed the steps between his hands (fortunately avoiding any mishaps regarding his teeth), and thereafter rose and seized Aeid's ankles, lifting them off the floor (and Aeid, still fuzzily wondering what he would say to his father with regards to the foreign ship in the harbor, now found himself swinging like a hammock between a short man (Kuz Aswani) who was nearly stifled by an overabundance of princely robes, and a taller man (Nash Shar) who thought that he knew what he was doing, but, in actuality, did not).

"Up or down, Kuz Aswani?" said Nash Shar.

Kuz Aswani gave a muffled yelp that appeared to indicate that *up* was the direction most on his mind; and in response to this, Nash Shar lifted Aeid's feet higher and, to Aeid's fuzzy horror, began to move in the direction of the head of the stairs, thus threatening with a major collapse the precarious equilibrium that had so far existed among the three men.

At this, Kuz Aswani not only yelped, but uttered a dismayed chitter that finally cut through the fuzziness of Aeid's mind. Unfortunately, the yelp and the chitter also convinced Nash Shar to immediately reverse his estimation of the previous order and begin attempting to drag both Aeid (wide awake now, and suspended) and Kuz Aswani (bewildered now, and tottering) toward the bottom of the stairs.

"Will you both—!" started Aeid; but then he checked himself for fear that the two men, if sufficiently startled, would drop him, thus adding to his bruises and possibly causing a repetition of the whole sorry scene. Clearing his throat, therefore, he presented his sentiments in a tone of princely moderation. "Kindly put me down, most august counselors."

Both Nash Shar and Kuz Aswani began lowering him at the same time.

"On my feet, if you please."

For a moment, the two counselors seemed unsure how to effect this state of affairs, but then, finally, Aeid found himself upright, free, and only slightly rumpled by his adventure.

"Thank you," he said.

"To hear is to obey!" said Kuz Aswani and Nash Shar in unison. They dropped to their knees and started to kiss the steps between their hands, but Aeid did not remain either to receive their homage or to see what fortune befell their teeth: he was already on his way up the stairs, settling his headcloth, his robes, and his sword as he ran.

Hard a-starboard!

But maybe, he reflected as he gained the upper corridor and began to become increasingly aware of the bruises inflicted by his fall, Kuz Aswani and Nash Shar actually had not the faintest idea why their prince was hurrying so determinedly to meet with his father. After all, who ever asked Aeid for advice about anything? Who *would* ask Aeid for advice about anything? It was Aeid's job to be suave and charming, to be handsome and noble, to manfully and secretly bed the wives of nobleman and potentate alike, to be the perfect, public fantasy of a dashing Crown Prince. Advice? What could such an unreal confection possibly offer by way of advice?

But today, Aeid was determined to make Inwa Kabir listen to him, and he reproached himself bitterly for not having gone directly to his father when he had first sighted the ships. Instead, he had wrapped his telescope up in a cloth, found a room that possessed both privacy and a view of the sea, and spent hours staring through his glass as the vessels had tacked their way toward the coast until, just at the entrance to the harbor, they had both unfurled the Cross and Stripes.

American. He had known that they were American.

But only then had it finally occurred to him that this was an opportunity that he could not afford to waste. What if Abnel got to his father first? It was, in fact, very probable that the Gharat was even now filling Inwa Kabir's ears with the most reactionary pronouncements, all of which were, of course, sanctioned by none other than the Divine Sculptor Himself.

Aeid pressed his lips together. Yes, of course. And was it not odd how the will of Panas always coincided so neatly with the will of a certain High Priest?

Let go!

The marble floor beneath Aeid's feet gave way to ivory inlaid with bands of polished emerald, and the prince smelled incense and coffee as he approached a golden door.

The soldiers to either side of the door snapped to attention. "The soldiers of the All Highest wish the Prince of the Three Kingdoms a long life and a happy one."

Aeid sighed. Despite his title of prince, despite (and here was the bitterness again, as dark and brown as a cup of the unsweetened coffee that the All Highest preferred over the candied liquid that everyone else consumed) his unspoken and ignored title of *son,* the door before him was locked, and would remain so until the proper, polite, insulating, and artificial courtesies had been exchanged.

Aeid cleared his throat. "The Prince of the Three Kingdoms acknowledges the wish of his most faithful subjects and orders them to present his compliments to his father, the All Highest King of the Three Kingdoms, Inwa Kabir." *And may your souls find a hot place under a flat rock in the desert.*

The reply came instantly. "It would give the soldiers of the All Highest the greatest of pleasures to carry out the orders of the Prince of the Three Kingdoms. Would it please the Prince of the Three Kingdoms to have the soldiers of the All Highest carry out his orders immediately?"

"It would give the Prince of the Three Kingdoms the greatest pleasure . . . . . . *if you stuck your swords up your assholes and sat on them until the points entered your brains and by Panas where is Abnel?*

And so on and so forth while the American ships swung to their anchors in the harbor of Nuhr, their guns run out, their carronades (charged, doubtless, with canister shot: Aeid had read of that particular technique for discouraging boarders) at the ready, their boarding nets hoisted. Finally, though, after the last compliment, after the last prostration of the soldiers, after the last, elegant wave of a princely hand indicating princely benedictions lavished unconditionally upon the honorable individuals who so safeguarded the person of the All Highest King of Kaprisha, Kalash, and Khyr, the door was unlocked and thrown open with yet another flourish.

"The Crown Prince Aeid, born by the grace of Panas to be King of Kaprisha, King of Kalash, King of Khyr, Sacred Priest of Nuhr, Sacred Priest of Katha, Chief and Unassailable Minister of Runzen, Inviolable Gharat of Kanez, Monarch of the Great Waste, Prince of the Quarries of the Mountains of Ern, Grand—!"

"Shut up," said Aeid, who suspected that he would remain a Crown Prince until the end of his miserable life. He pushed past the soldier and entered.

Ivory floor, jasper walls. Windows of amethyst lit the room with the softest and palest of purples. Everything was fringed, gilded, carved, scented, flowered, and colored. The mosaics on the wall shimmered with gold and gems. Here, in the king's chambers, everything was royal, imperial. Only the thin pad of cloth that lay on the floor in a corner—a soldier's bed—seemed out of place, but Aeid knew that his father would sleep upon nothing else.

There was a throne beneath a canopy to one side of the room, but Inwa Kabir, stout and mustachioed and robed in cloth of gold and silk, was not sitting on it. He was, instead, at the window, looking out toward the harbor of Nuhr.

Aeid looked around, mildly surprised to find that Abnel was not there. That was unexpectedly good ... albeit very odd. Under normal circumstances, the High Priest of Panas would have been the first person summoned to the side of the king at the unexpected appearance of a pair of foreign ships. Well, perhaps Abnel had been and gone already. Perhaps the king had already made up his mind ... or had had it made up for him.

In fact, Inwa Kabir's only companion at present was a woman who stood to one side of the king, her hands clasped loosely and submissively before her. As Aeid entered, she turned to look at him, and the prince caught sight not only of a pair of dark eyes above her silk face cloth ... but also of the bulge of a dagger beneath her skirts; and despite the seductive set of her hips that brought a tightening to his groin, he realized that the woman was Bakbuk.

Aeid shook his head. Had Bakbuk not been such a phenomenal sworder, his excesses would have been brought to a very quick and very permanent end years ago. But Bakbuk could do anything with weapons, Bakbuk was loyal to the king with all the dispassionate objectivity that sardonic irony could bring, and Bakbuk was quite capable—both by temper and by temperament—of killing anyone who tried to interfere with his recreations. And so no one interfered. Inwa Kabir was amused, Bakbuk was amused ... and that was the end of it.

Now Bakbuk looked up, eyes widening just as a girl would have widened them (And where *did* he get that unnerving skill with eyeliner?), and, hips softly swaying as though he (or she: Aeid never knew quite what to think when Bakbuk was like this) would have liked nothing better than to be thrown onto the nearest pile of cushions and brutally raped right then and there, came toward Aeid.

"Oh, my prince!" she (Aeid gave up) said, her voice soft and lilting, "perhaps you have heard of the strange ships in the harbor of Nuhr?"

The tone, the pitch, the inflection—everything was perfect. And so was the sentiment. A woman would never have phrased the matter as anything save a slightly apprehensive question that managed to ask without actually asking: *Will you protect me?*

Inwa Kabir did not turn around. Aeid passed a hand across his face, found that he was sweating. Of all the times for Bakbuk to . . . "Yes . . . yes," he said. "They had come to my attention."

"They are American ships," said Inwa Kabir very deliberately. Then, equally deliberately, he added: "I think."

Aeid did not think that they were American ships: he *knew* that they were American ships; but he was not *supposed* to know that they were American ships, and so he joined his father at the window, pretended to peer out, pretended to examine the vessels, pretended to be properly perplexed by the Cross and Stripes (and the perfume that Bakbuk was wearing was making him quite dizzy: ambergris and musk. Bakbuk! Really! That was what Rahina wore . . . or was it Rahania? Matiera? He had lost track. Perhaps he should be keeping records . . . writing things down . . . it really would not do if . . . and oh, by Panas, here he was getting an erection . . .), and finally made a harrumph in his throat that befitted (he thought) a monarch-to-be (if he lived that long), and said, "Yes, Father. I think that might be so."

Inwa Kabir looked some more, furrowed his brow, made

a harrumph of his own. Deliberately, then: "They have violated our holy city."

Aeid felt a dryness in his mouth that was only partly caused by the close proximity of Bakbuk's slender body. Yes, Abnel had doubtless been here, and Abnel had doubtless told the king exactly what to do. Board the ship. Loot the ship. Burn the ship. Very simple. And then the Three Kingdoms could stagnate for another three hundred years . . . if anything that was as dry as the Three Kingdoms could possibly be said to stagnate. "That is true, father. But perhaps . . ." He groped. ". . . perhaps they are strangers and have lost their way. Perhaps they have simply made a mistake. I think it would only be a matter of . . ." He looked around. No Abnel. Bakbuk was smiling at him with a look that said *I want you . . . now* that was perfect in every nuance. ". . . of . . . ah . . ."

His father was not looking at him. Out in the harbor, the ships had anchored. The Cross and Stripes fluttered from two spanker gaffs.

"Has Abnel been here?"

Bakbuk replied. "No one has been able to find the Holy Gharat . . . ?" A simper that turned into a question. Yes, Bakbuk. Perfect. Very nice. Now get the sandstone and pumice out of here.

Aeid, aroused in spite of himself, had the feeling that Bakbuk was laughing at him. But then, no one really knew whether Bakbuk was laughing, or at whom, or . . . or . . . or what else Bakbuk might be doing. Another princely harrumph, then. "It might be a matter of common courtesy."

"It might," said his father. "I will have it thought about."

I will have it thought about. His father's standard reply. The country could be burning down or, drying up, or, perhaps more fittingly, inundated by a tidal wave, and his father would have it thought about. Meaning that nothing would be done. Meaning that nothing would ever be done.

"Father," said Aeid, and it struck him that his father had *not* summoned his counselors, had *not* thought at all about what to do beyond standing aside and awaiting the destruction that would eventually come to the ships of its own accord . . . or rather of the accord of people who, given time, could become very used to the thought of a pouch full of settels, "the crews of the ships might need our help. It might be best to offer them the hospitality of a cultured people."

"I will have it thought about," said his father again, and Aeid, turning away in frustration, found himself belly to belly with Bakbuk. Dark, kohl rimmed eyes looked up shyly, and then Bakbuk pressed ever so lightly against him.

"May Panas protect the Prince of the Three Kingdoms," she said. There was no question in her voice, Aeid noticed, and that was some relief, but he still found himself reacting instinctively to the facade of willing womanhood that Bakbuk was presenting. He wanted . . . that is . . . she wanted . . .

He swung quickly back to his father. "Why not let *me* think about it for a change, Father?"

"You?" said Inwa Kabir.

"Me," said Aeid. "I have been thinking about it . . . ah . . . for some time. And I think that . . ."

"You?" Inwa Kabir was not stupid, nor was he foolish. He was no more gullible than any other man of the Three Kingdoms . . . and perhaps a good deal less so. In spite of the threats and even outright violence offered by the independence zealots of Khyr and Kalash, he had maintained his throne, he had held the priestly Council of Katha in careful and hostile balance with the priestly Council of Nuhr, he had managed even to keep the question of Naian tolerance very carefully off to one side where he thought that no one would notice it. In short, Inwa Kabir had kept the Three Kingdoms much as the Three Kingdoms had always been kept, which was saying both very little and a great deal.

And yet, for all his demonstrable canniness, Inwa Kabir seemed rather thunderstruck by Aeid's suggestion. His mouth worked silently, much in the manner of a grouper about to devour something tasty. Aeid had seen the expression before. Many times. Usually just before someone was given the sentence of death.

But then the king smiled. "Ah, my son. You are so impetuous."

"Humor me," said Aeid, thinking despondently of the drought, the stagnation, the horror of a country condemned forever to be a global backwater.

"And what would you suggest we do with these ..." Inwa Kabir bent forward stoutly, peered again at the Cross and Stripes. "... American ships?"

"I would ..." Aeid chose his words carefully. It would not do to say *Make them welcome,* or *Ask them if they knew how to end this demonic drought,* or even *Trade with them.* No, anything like that would be going much too far. "I would ... at least find out what they want."

His father considered. "Very well. We will find out what they want." He glanced at Aeid, gave Bakbuk a wink. "And then we will burn them and use the men as slaves." A short nod. "Very good, my son. Very good."

Chapter Four

Light. Light. Light.

The harbor of Nuhr was ringed with it. The buildings and towers of Nuhr were aglow with it. The quays and wharves of Nuhr were shining with it. The small boats of Nuhr—riding at their moorings, seemingly abandoned— were brilliant with it.

Flame flickered everywhere, reflected everywhere, and *Seaflower* and *Speedwell,* rocking gently upon a liquid mirror, seemed to float upon light. Indeed, so universal was the radiance that the watch in the frigate's maintop— had he been able to take his nervous eyes from the shore or found it possible to think about something other than imminent attack—might well have been astonished to look down and see, surrounding the pale deck far below his feet, a seething, coruscating mass of reflected fire.

Darkness. Darkness and cold. The desert wastes cooled as soon as the sun set, and, barren as they were, offered no shelter to the old woman who lay wrapped in a blanket, her head pillowed only by the sand. She did not sleep. It was too cold. She had not slept. She was too frightened.

No one slept on board either ship. Scruffy, considerate of his men and confident of his lookouts, had given half the crew leave to go below, but they had not gone below.

No: sleep, even simple rest, was out of the question to-night, and, therefore, those who had stations kept them and watched; and those who did not have stations stayed out of the way . . . and watched.

Scruffy paced the quarter-deck, mindful of the light, mindful that a movement or a sudden shout from the shore might be instantly followed by an attack, mindful also of the presence of the American ambassador. Jenkins himself, though, did not pace: that would have been too much of a declaration of some sort—nervousness, perhaps; perhaps impatience—and such things as declarations, Scruffy had long ago concluded, were out of the question insofar as the ambassador was concerned.

The captain cast his eye the length of the ship, examining, inspecting. Boarding nets were up. Cutlasses were ready at hand. Cannon were loaded. The carronades were double charged with canister shot.

It was on these last that Scruffy's eye stayed the longest. Capable of throwing the equivalent of several hundred musket-balls at one time, they would be the first line of defense against any concerted effort to board the ships, and probably the second and third as well. Some of the up-and-coming fellows at the military academy were, in fact, already calling them "anti-personnel devices", and were speaking in enthusiastic terms of using them against the last pockets of Indians and even the few remaining Quaker villages that still clung to a clandestine existence in the foothills of the Rocky Mountains. Scruffy had doubts about that sort of thing—the effectiveness of carronades on land had never been tried, after all, and Scruffy was too cautious a man to put his trust in something that had not been tried—but he had no doubts about their effectiveness at sea, whether against men or against the fragile, lateen-rigged boats that were all the Three Kingdoms had to offer.

*Even the slightest breeze was biting out here, and Sari
stirred, shivered, turned onto her back and stared at the
brilliant stars that glared down like so many accusing
eyes. She clutched the blanket about her old shoulders,
feeling the ache of bruises and cuts. She knew that she was
going to die alone, die in darkness.*

Scruffy looked back to the shore. Light. And no more.
No people. No movement. It had been that way since the
hawsers had roared out that afternoon. *Seaflower* and
Speedwell were being watched.

Jenkins spoke up suddenly from behind him, his voice
as gray as his dress and his manner. "It'll be when they
put out the lights that we'll have to worry."

Scruffy was glad that he had not been facing the ambassador, for his eyes and mouth had both turned into large,
startled circles at the sudden comment out of the prolonged, brilliant silence. "Aye, Mr. Ambassador," he said,
gathering his wits. "They'll douse the lights before they
attack."

Jenkins nodded. "Cowardly heathens," he said. "This is
more than likely exactly what they did when the *Frères
Marseillaise* tried this some years back. Unlike the frogs,
though, we're ready for them . . ." He eyed Scruffy.
". . . unless I'm greatly deceived."

Scruffy was startled again, this time by the man's sudden expression of something akin to an actual opinion.
"We're quite ready, Mr. Ambassador."

"I'm sure we are, but they'll try it again this time,
doubtless. They'll . . . how did you put it, Scruffy? *Douse*
the lights?"

"Aye, Mr. Ambassador."

"Douse the lights . . . *douse* the lights. Hmmm." Jenkins
appeared to consider Scruffy's choice of words, but, then
again, perhaps he was only appearing to appear to consider

them. Scruffy was not sure. It was hard to tell. Sometimes it made him dizzy.

Oh, give that good captain facts any day of the week, and he would be happy! There were so many facts in the world—facts about steam, facts about electricity, facts about light and magnetism, facts about gravity—and they were all proper facts: right out there in the open, with none of this perpetual reservation and caution and reluctance to commit to anything. Scruffy found himself wanting very badly to descend to his half-size cabin (which had been made quarter size by the appropriations of Jenkins, Mather, and their secretary, Mr. Wool) and fire up his miniature steam engine, looking to find, in its predictable course and laborious chugging about a carefully circumscribed area, a sense of rightness and directness that was most decidedly lacking at this time of possible attack (on the part of Nuhr) and undeclared course of action (on the part of the ambassador).

Her last beating, her approaching death: she could think of nothing save these, and therefore she relived constantly the events that had brought them about. Once more, Maumud's fists came thudding down upon her shoulders, and once more she bent her head and hunched, hoping that womanly submission would bring an end to the blows. But submission had done nothing for her then, and submission would do nothing for her now.

Jenkins stood, silent. Suddenly: "Have you read your sealed orders, Captain Scruffy?"

Another surprise. Scruffy was again glad that he was, just at that moment, facing away from the ambassador. After taking a moment to compose himself, he turned and replied, "Why, no, Mr. Ambassador. I warn't given any sealed orders. I warn't aware that I had any other orders than to bring you to Nuhr."

"Ah, Captain Scruffy, but you do." Jenkins contemplated him for a few moments, then turned toward the companionway that led down to the aft cabin. "Come to my cabin . . ."

Despite his surprise, Scruffy sighed inwardly. *Jenkins'* cabin!

". . . and I will give them to you."

And, a few minutes later, Scruffy was examining the canvas-wrapped bundle that Jenkins had put into his hands. Everything seemed to be in order. In fact, everything seemed to be more than in order. There, fastening the cords in four places, was the seal of the Synod. That was to be expected. But at the center of the four was another—the seal of President Winthrop himself—and the package was weighted with what was obviously more than enough shot to take it to the bottom of the sea before its security could be in any way compromised.

Scruffy stared at the package, his mouth a little dry, then held it closer to the cabin lamp and examined it again. Winthrop himself! And all this had come to him! To Elijah Scruffy!

For a moment, he was almost dizzy with the thought that along with such officiality might come that much more official scrutiny; but then, ever the captain, ever the skipper who could order a man flogged for impertinence, shepherd a ship through a hurricane, or even read an unrepentant crew member out of Christian communion, he shook himself free of his concerns and read the instructions that had been inked upon the wrapper.

". . . *upon reaching, in the name of God, the waters of the harbor of Nuhr,* it says here." He looked up. "Was I supposed to open this in your presence, Mr. Ambassador?"

"If you please, Captain Scruffy. Its contents are no secret to me, I assure you. I was present when it was assembled, and present also when President Winthrop put his seal to it."

Dizzy ... mouth dry ... Winthrop himself!

Maumud ... beating her, kicking her. And all that she had learned to do among the women of Panas (an outsider despite her sacrifice of her beliefs, her people, her body) had not stopped him. But then something had made him stop, and she had looked up to see his glazed eyes. His face, beneath its darkness, had held a tinge as of green water. His mouth, opening crookedly ...

Scruffy cut the cord, peeled back the strings and the seals, slit the canvas. Inside was a thick bundle of papers, and he sorted through them quickly. Most had to do with the conduct of the ship, the litany of cautions that were included as a matter of course. There was a copy of the Holy Scriptures, but that also was nothing unusual. On the top, however, was a letter to him—the orders themselves—and Scruffy recognized the hand in which it was addressed.

"Winthrop!"

"Himself," said Jenkins.

"But ... the president? Wrote my orders?"

"The president." Jenkins had reverted to his grayness, but the yellow light of the lamp glittered in his eyes. "Open it."

Scruffy was already doing just that, but it took him only a moment to read the few lines that were within. "I don't understand," he said.

"Ah, but I do." Jenkins turned toward the window, his hands clasped behind his back in the manner of a midshipman. Scruffy noted the gesture, added it to a few other observations that he had made, and came to the conclusion that Jenkins had, in his youth, spent some time on board ship. "As of this moment," the ambassador continued, "I am in charge of these two ships. I am no longer a passenger. I am ... authority. I'm sure that, as a God-fearing man and a Christian, you have no difficulty with accepting authority from an ordained minister. Do you, Captain Scruffy?"

Like all dignitaries of the Righteous States, Jenkins was a minister, and Scruffy—who was indeed a God-fearing man—was puzzled by the needless question. "Of course not, Mr. Ambassador."

(Bronze by gold, the sconces held the torches up and away from the polished walls of veined jasper and inlaid rose quartz ...)

"Good," said Jenkins, "And now I'll tell you what we are going to do here, and I'll even tell you a little about why we are going to do it." He turned back to face Scruffy. "We are here to open the Three Kingdoms to trade, Captain Scruffy. American trade. Christian trade. For too long, these lands have remained in isolation, and while for a great many years that posed no inconvenience to anyone, the situation has changed." Another glint of his eyes. "You're aware that the French fleet has sailed?"

"He got out of Toulon?" Scruffy was surprised yet again.

Jenkins appeared not to notice. "He?" he said calmly. "Who?"

"Why ... ah ... Napoleon ..."

"Oh ... you mean Citizen Bonaparte." There was a hint of a sneer in Jenkins' voice, and, worse, the faintest touch of probing accusation.

"Uh ... yes. Yes."

Jenkins reverted to noncommittalism. "There were storms. Admiral Nelson was delayed. The French fleet escaped."

Scruffy looked at the orders in his hands. *Assist, in the name of God, Ambassador Jenkins in any and all ways possible, in accordance with his wishes.* A few more lines—*Hereof nor you nor ...* and so on and so forth ... *at your Peril*—and that was all. Jenkins was in charge, indeed! "I wonder where he ... I mean, they ... I mean. . . ."

"The French fleet is bound for Egypt," said Jenkins.

(... and he lay in a bower of rose petals and fresh-cut hyacinths, his eyes outlined in kohl, his lips reddened. The device that was strapped over his groin pinched, but the discomfort reminded him that the device was still there, and the reminder was a pleasure in itself.)

Scruffy glanced at the stern windows. Out there, heralded by the light that poured in from the watching city, was Africa. And there also, according to Jenkins, would soon be Napoleon.

Egypt! What a bold stroke! Now *that* was Napoleon Bonaparte! Why ... he was probably going to take Malta first! What a man!

"The cursed, degenerate papist," he said properly.

"Yes," said Jenkins. "And apostate, too, along with all his countrymen. But with French presence in the offing, Africa is now something to be contended over, and there are many people in Africa—whether they are heathens or not—who stand to be in need of protection. We are here to make agreements and treaties, Captain Scruffy, and in exchange for their good will, the people of the Three Kingdoms will find in the people of the Righteous States of America a strong, ready ally against French aggression."

The light was lapping against the ship, flowing in through the window, flooding the cramped cabin. Scruffy frowned doubtfully. "They don't want us here, Mr. Ambassador. If the past shows us anything, it shows us that they'll try to be rid of us any way they can manage."

"True," said Jenkins. "But that is why the Synod sent a double-frigate and a sloop of war with fine Christian captains."

And then Maumud had fallen, striking his head on the cooking pot so that he was burned and gashed both, and

*then he had been lying beside the fire, his skull open and
fountaining blood and his face twisted and his mouth
agape and his breathing stopped.*

Scruffy felt himself grow warm, and it had nothing to
do with the temperature in the cabin. Scrutiny! And Jenkins and his colleagues had been right next door! What
if . . . ?

"My task," said Jenkins, "is to negotiate the agreements."

Scruffy nodded.

"Your job is to keep us all alive while I do."

(He wondered what it would be like if it were real, *to
feel that pumping within, to feel that onrush and thrust
and be held helpless in large arms while a face was
pressed against his and a flood, yes a flood, and oh, do
not stop my beloved—!)*

But Scruffy's worried nod was cut short by the sound of
a distant explosion. For a moment, his heart lurched at the
thought that his ship was being attacked while he was below, but not a moment had passed before he realized that
the sound could not possibly have come from a cannon.
No: it was something else . . .

*And she had run. Run away. She was not a Panasian.
She had tried, and she had failed. She was but a woman
who had disguised herself as something that she was not,
and the magistrates and bailiffs would know without a
doubt that she had killed him. The afternoon had sunk into
evening, she had crouched terrified in a corner of the
house that had been her home and her prison for fifty
years, and then, when the brief twilight of the tropics had
yielded to the onslaught of night, she had fled.*

Scruffy shoved the orders—such as they were—into the
pocket of his coat as he rose, then pounded up the companionway to the quarter-deck, leaving Jenkins to stare out
the window. After the hot stuffiness of the cabin, the air

outside was comparatively cool, but there was no visible change on the shore: the lights were the same, the port was the same, the towers and buildings were the same. But now the lingering echo of the dull, crunching roar that had so startled him was mixed with something akin to a grinding, as though boulders were slowly being mashed into gravel by some immense, infernal machine.

(He stirred. There had been a sound. He had left orders that he not be disturbed, but there had been a sound, and, bronze by gold, the sconces had trembled, and bronze by gold, the light they threw on the jasper and the rose quartz had vibrated in response to a dull concussion more felt than heard.)

Mr. Turtletrout was already on deck, and from the look of him, he had been sleeping in his clothes . . . if he had been sleeping at all. A nod from the first lieutenant. "It came from the southeast, sir."

Scruffy nodded his reply. It would probably be some time before he and Turtletrout again had the leisure for a game of chess. Too bad.

"There's some smoke . . ."

Sari shivered again. There was nothing behind her but pursuing death, and there was nowhere to go to escape it. She lay exposed on the sand, miles from her village, and the stars looked on accusingly as the fugitive from an imaginary crime wondered whether, impossibly, there was anyone who would look upon her and not consider her guilty.

Scruffy turned to the southeast, peered hard. Yes, just as Turtletrout had said, there was a dimness out there that was rising, growing. Stars were flickering out even as he watched, and as though to add yet one more hellish detail to the sense of apocalypse that grew within Scruffy's Christian mind, a voice, distant but clear, burst out in an unintelligible language, the syllables—partly sung, partly chanted, partly screamed—rising and falling as the smoke spread and the grinding continued.

Turtletrout looked shaken. "In the name of God . . . what is that?"

(Something had disturbed him against his express orders. Something had awakened him. "What is that?" he called, trying to pitch his voice high and sweet like a woman, but his words came out full and deep. "What is that?")

"What is that?" came Jenkins' voice. "If you wish to believe a heathen voice in the night, that's the vengeance of Panas."

"You understand the words, sir?"

"It's Kap . . ." Jenkins frowned. "No. It's Khyrling. The speaker is claiming that those who dwell in the vicinity of tyrants, heretics, and miscreants have quite justly paid the penalty by being either buried or blown up."

Scruffy squinted at the smoke that was visible only by virtue of its rendering other things invisible. "Come again, sir?"

"There is . . . political dissension within the Three Kingdoms," said Jenkins. "At one time, there were actually three separate countries here. Kaprisha, though, proved itself the strongest by conquering its southern neighbors. There are factions in Kalash and Khyr, however, who still refuse to acknowledge that fact."

And then she thought of Naia. The Mother. The Mother who did not accuse.

"Do you mean, sir," said Turtletrout, whose sloping forehead was glistening with sweat, "that we've come into port in the middle of a revolution?"

"Hardly," said Jenkins. "The conquests occurred some five hundred years ago. Matters have been comparatively stable since then."

Now Scruffy could hear screams and moans drifting

across the night air. A distant crash as something collapsed or toppled. He sniffed the air. "Gunpowder," he said. "Well, they can't be *that* isolated."

"Been doing some trading, sir," said Turtletrout.

"Yes," said Jenkins. "Indeed. Trading. Hmmm."

A second crash silenced the screams, and the realization suddenly struck Scruffy. "Do you mean, Mr. Ambassador, that some renegades just blew up a number of people over something that happened five hundred years ago?"

(Another sound. He started up, blinked at the (bronze by gold) torchlight. "What is that? Come here and tell me!")

Another crash. The screams started up again. "A number of people?" said Jenkins. "Quite a number of people, I should imagine. And, yes, Captain, that is exactly what I mean."

Turtletrout was leaning on the rail beside the hammock netting, and he had thrust his pointed nose toward the sounds and the screams as though it were a weather vane pointing out the winds of destruction. "Bloody fu—"

"Mr. Turtletrout!" Jenkins interrupted. "This is a Christian ship!"

"Begging your pardon, Mr. Ambassador." Turtletrout straightened, cleared his throat. "Filthy savages."

"Yes," said Jenkins. "Exactly." He examined the smoke. "Filthy savages. But they need protection, and we want trade, so protection and trade they will have."

Naia. And Maumud had accused her of being a Naian still. But could she, made a woman of Panas by affirmation, marriage, and knife, call upon Naia now? She had no illusions: she would die whether she embraced Naia or not . . . or whether Naia embraced her or not. But still, a single, sympathetic face in the midst of so much horror would be comforting . . .

"Mr. Ambassador! Mr. Ambassador!" A pounding of short legs along the deck, and Mr. Mather, stout and acne-pocked, came into view. He was clutching a number of papers. "I finished the calculations! Those mountains in the distance: if the maps are right, some of them are over forty thousand feet high! It's absolutely amazing!" Seemingly oblivious of the continued screams, the crashings, and the presence of Scruffy and Turtletrout, Mather skidded to a halt before Jenkins and waved his papers so violently that Scruffy could not but notice that they were covered with painstaking calculations. "Forty thousand feet! Forty *thousand*! I do believe I'm getting gravitational deviation! Even here! On a ship! We've seen the same thing in India—the Himalaya, you know—but never—" He suddenly became aware of Scruffy and Turtletrout, caught himself, colored even in the already ruddy light of the city's torches. "Ah ... that is ..."

(And a slave—blind and mute—came in response to his cries, and, misunderstanding, or perhaps so accustomed to other demands that he could understand in no other way, removed the uncomfortable, pleasurable device, filled him until he cried out, and then left him to sleep again.)

Scruffy stared at Mr. Mather. Mountain elevations and gravitational deviation (Gravitational deviation?) were very odd things to hear coming from a diplomat's assistant. But the captain's bewilderment was increased when he turned to Jenkins and saw in the ambassador's face a white fury that, had it been capable of taking independent action, would surely have trampled the hapless Mather into a mixture of dust and jelly.

"We will talk about this ... later, Mr. Mather," said Jenkins, and the fact that, despite his obvious anger, his voice remained calm, controlled, and noncommittal was perhaps more terrifying than any outburst. "I'm sure you understand."

"Yessir." Mather nodded quickly, turned, and vanished down the companionway to the cabin.

"Geology," said Jenkins. "His . . . hobby, you know."

"Yes, yes," said Scruffy, forcing himself to be affable and agreeable. "His hobby."

Naia. Who would not accuse. "Will you take me back, Mother?" she whispered softly, wondering whether exhaustion, cold, or perhaps simple fright would end everything for her even before the priestly tribunals would have a chance. "Will you take me back after all this time? After all these years?"

Turtletrout turned back to the smoke and the sounds. More screams. "Bloody fucking savages," he said, but Jenkins was apparently too preoccupied to notice.

Chapter Five

The Mountains of Ern, high as they were (and it was not without good reason that the inhabitants of the Three Kingdoms referred to the interior plateaux of the range as *The Airless Places*), seemed even higher out here in the open. Framed only by the morning light that washed the stars from the sky, they stood seemingly on the edge of the world, remote and distant. And they themselves were an edge, a boundary, for no one had ever crossed them.

Sari herself stood at another edge: the edge of her life. About her, the wastes stretched away, but had she turned and looked carefully into the distance behind her, she might have seen a bit of indistinct haze in the rising light: her old village. But she did not look back. She had left. She had run away. She had her clothes, she had her blanket, and she had the small bundle that her husband, on the last day of his life, had so criticized her for keeping. No food, no water—just herself and her private treasures: a silly old woman who had gone out to look for death. Doubtless, she would find it today.

The mountains bulked black before her, piled high, one on another, mounting hugely even at a distance of many leagues. No one had crossed them. "No one," she murmured, but there was nothing behind her, and so she had

Hungry, thirsty, cold, she nonetheless looked at the mountains for a long time . . . remembering . . . wondering.

So, here we are: the morning of a new day, *Seaflower* and *Speedwell* still anchored in the harbor of Nuhr, and the inhabitants of the city still dithering over plans that involve (in various combinations) diplomacy, death, lust, and profit. Pretty much a typical day anywhere in the world on this 17th day of June, 1798.

Here is the morning then, and here is Prince Aeid looking out his window. Yes, Aeid, the ships are still there. Yes, Aeid, father will speak to . . . well, to someone from them today. Yes, Aeid, if you have any say in the matter, the ships will still be there tomorrow, and Abnel and his reactionary priests will have to chew that bit of mutton gristle for a good long time.

No, Aeid, you have no idea whether you have any say in the matter or not, do you? But you sense that you have no say at all, right? That is the way it has always been, correct? Frustrated? Yes? Provoked almost to violence? Good! No, no, let us not speak of suicide: that is too easy. Rather, what would you give for a chance to smack that bloated spider of a Gharat right in the face? To tell him that he and his maggoty ilk are destroying what vestiges of the Three Kingdoms have been left intact by three centuries of drought? With impunity? Really? That much? Oh, my. . . .

Let us see if it can be arranged.

And over here, down the hall, across several courtyards (assuming that we are not bound by the usual restrictions of gravity, because if we were, we would have to deal with stairs, too, and I am sure you do not want *that*), down another hall, down several more halls, in another wing of the palace (and need I mention again that it is *all* jasper and carnelian and onyx and chalcedony and marble and alabaster?), Bakbuk has decided to be a boy today, and now that he has finished winding his waist-length hair about his head, he is in the process of covering it with skullcap, red cap, and head cloth. A minute later, he dons (all by himself: for he hates the ministrations of slaves and eunuchs), a robe and jacket of white, polished cotton. Both are edged in gold and gems, and he arranges them so that they bare a precise V of his smooth, immaculately complected chest. He looks remarkable: boyish and handsome. And, yes, he thinks so, too.

It might be noted that there is a certain gleam of satisfaction in his black eyes as he takes up his sword and girds it on. It might also be noted that, just for fun, he flashes it from its sheath, whirls it about himself so fast that it blurs even to his own eyes, and then slides it back into its covering without another glance. In his mind, he has beheaded seven men, gut-stuck another, and carved the legs of yet another down to the bone, and were there indeed nine men in the room, they would indeed be lying at his feet even now.

A boy . . . today. But when he looks in the mirror and gives himself a wink, there is something of a certain vicious femininity both in the wink and in the face from which it proceeds. Bakbuk may fool many, it appears, but he does not fool himself.

Maybe.

On the other hand, Abnel, the Gharat, may well be fooling himself and everybody else, too. As Bakbuk dons his splendid sworder's garb and shows off with his blade, Abnel is attempting to make himself look impressive for the first formal reception of a foreign ambassador since the legendary time of old Abramelin, and in the privacy of the High Priest's chambers, he is being robed by slaves. His white reflection gleams dully in the walls of polished jasper and rose quartz, and in that uncertain mirror he floats like a large, pale ghost as the robes go on and a golden razor takes the stubble from his scalp.

He aches a little. He shifts his weight. He must have gotten a bruise yesterday. Was the device too small? Valdemar, though, has always shown himself to be a careful man, whether in his embroidery or in his other merchandise, and as the guns were of the proper size, Abnel is confident that the device was of the proper size, too.

The razor removes the last of the stubble. The golden fillet goes around his skull. The hands of the slave are dark and cool, and they were dark and cool, too, when they . . .

Abnel shifts again, lifts his arms so that the sash can go around his middle. He will have to look to see if there is a bruise.

Later.

Then there is King Inwa Kabir, who is also preparing for today's almost unprecedented reception, and if you were wondering, he is, yes, thinking about that explosion of the previous night. Or rather, he is having it thought about. By Haddar. (And please do not feel that you now have to begin flipping back toward the beginning of the book: you have not met Haddar yet, but you will.) Somehow, it seems, though his network of bailiffs and spies has succeeded admirably in keeping Prince Aeid under surveillance (Inwa Kabir is being just a little uncharacteristically naive here), it has failed him miserably with regards to such things as explosions and freedom fighters, and he wants the names of the men responsible for the failure. Actually, he wants their heads, but he is having it thought about by Haddar, and Haddar understands what having it thought about means in this case.

To be sure, a small part of Inwa Kabir's thoughts are turned in the direction of the actual perpetrators of an act that dismembered or buried alive at least three hundred of his subjects. Appearances have to be kept up, after all, and if renegade Khyrlings can go about blowing people up right outside the walls of the Holy City itself (even if those who were blown up were only Mud Dwellers), then the reputation of Inwa Kabir—and, by extension, that of all the Three Kingdoms and even (Oh, sandstorms!) Panas himself—cannot but suffer.

They must be found, then. Inwa Kabir can have Haddar think about the ministers and bailiffs first, and then he can have him think about a more thorough investigation.

He frowns thoughtfully as he holds out his arms for a golden shoulder cloth. And where *did* they get that gunpowder, anyway?

"Is the garment not acceptable to the All Highest?" asks a frightened slave, backing away with the ornate, supposedly-offending shoulder cloth clutched in her hands as she doubtlessly remembers that people, particularly women, who displease the All Highest do not have to worry about the infirmities of old age . . . or even the comparatively minor distractions of youth and beauty.

"Hmmm?"

The tunic problem is sorted out more by Inwa Kabir's silence than by his actions or words, which is, perhaps, pretty much the way all problems in the Three Kingdoms have been sorted out for a very long time.

And what then of the ships whose appearance has initiated all these preparations?

What indeed. Captain Elijah Scruffy is on the weather side of the quarter-deck even at this early hour. He wears his best uniform today, and has donned silk hose for the benefit of the surgeon, Mr. Squibbs, under whose care (not to mention saw) he might well come if matters take an unfortunate turn. To be sure, Scruffy is not at all enthused about his formal apparel, he being the sort of captain who has at times been known to don, in preference to more confining headgear, a very unconfining and rather disreputable straw hat (and only the presence of Mr. Jenkins and his staff has prevented this latter article of clothing from appearing during this voyage, not so much because Mr. Jenkins and his staff might disapprove, but rather because, with his belongings crammed into considerably less than their usual space, Scruffy simply cannot *find* it).

But Scruffy is not thinking of his comfortable straw hat this morning. He is, rather, preoccupied with other things. One of those things is chess, and following directly from chess is the fact that the state of constant alertness that prevails on board the American ships has interfered with his nightly game with Mr. Turtletrout ... and probably will interfere with it for a good many nights to come. He is also thinking about Mr. Squibbs and his saws and hammers and knives, and of what unpleasant things all of them (Squibbs included) can do, particularly when their arrival has been preceded by the attentions of a people who do not appear to mind blowing up their fellow citizens *en masse* in the name of liberty. But uppermost in his mind this morning are his thoughts regarding the strange interchange that took place last night on the quarter-deck.

Scruffy is a slow, methodical man whose interest in scientific curiosities betrays something of his admiration for the sort of rational, technological progress that advances ploddingly, inexorably, step by step. He has, from his readings of the forbidden books in his locked chest—books by Gibbon, Diderot, Voltaire, and other enemies of the Righteous States of America (and of most of the rest of the civilized world as well)—come to believe in such progress, and he attempts to order his thoughts and his intellectual activity in the same way, struggling to reduce the unintelligible to the reasonable, the obscure to the lucid.

Jenkins, however, will not be reduced. He is standing at the rail at present—motionless, gray, and non-committal—and nothing in his face or in his demeanor betrays the slightest hint about his true mission ... which, Scruffy is beginning to guess, has to do with something more than trade and treaties.

Movement on the shore. A lateen sail lifts, swings, catches the breeze.

Jenkins stirs out of his gray non-commitment. "How is your French, Scruffy?" he asks.

Were Jenkins to ask him his opinion of Johnny cake and bounceberries, Scruffy could not be more astonished. "French?"

"French is a second language here," says Jenkins mildly, without inflection. "As it appears to be everywhere else."

He takes off his hat for a moment and wipes his brow. The day is already growing quite warm, and Scruffy almost thinks that he can see steam rising from the ambassador's gray head.

"We must make sure, though," Jenkins continues, "that it doesn't become compulsory."

He glances at Scruffy, resettles his hat.

"Aye, sir," says Scruffy in prompt agreement, not knowing what else to say.

The sail is moving toward them. Jenkins would straighten up, but he is already straight. He appears never to be anything *but* straight. He holds out his hand for the speaking trumpet, and Chips, the boatswain's mate, puts it into his hand.

Dearly beloved brethren, it is truly a humbling observation to make that, sinful as man is, and loathsome as he therefore must be in the spiritually perfect sight of the Divine, he is nonetheless preserved from the pains and fires of hell from day to day ... nay, from moment to moment. You did not go to hell last night, did you? You did not go to hell a moment ago, did you? And yet surely, brethren, all of you who have not felt within yourself a conversion, all of you who have not experienced a regeneration, all of you who have not passed under a great change of heart are all worthy of this fate, and therefore, brethren, this mercy, this great, great mercy of your continued existence can be attributed only to the undying and limitless fire of a Divine Love so profound that It can look upon what must seem to It the most hateful, venomous serpent and still have such hope that even so craven and bestial a thing can be saved that It preserves it ... ah, I mean the serpent ... from immediate destruction.

And if such love is necessary to shield man at his worst from divine punishment, then how great must be the divine joy at the sight of man at his best. And surely, brethren, there can be no better sign of man's share in God's wonderful grace than the demonstration of love and concord, the civil and brotherly exchange of courtesies, and the pledging of mutual aid and loyalty.

It therefore cannot but be an honor to witness this first cordial expression of the affection of nations. Entering at the door of the Council Chamber, the Very Reverend Mr. Obadiah Jenkins advances with all the dignity of a most learned Christian minister to pay his respects to a king who might be construed by some who should know better as heathen and simple, and who might even be looked down upon by those same individuals; but I must remind you all that man was heathen and simple before the Word came to him, and so this offering of the light of spiritual knowledge and civilization to the ignorant must be, and ever shall be, fraught with greatest of eternal ... ah ... importances.

Sandstone! They are wearing wool*! Of all the stupid things to do, they must walk into the presence of the king wearing the most unclean of fabrics. They are going to undo everything. Father will nod and smile, and then he will burn their ship. Is this a deliberate affront? No: the one who is the ambassador carries himself with the greatest respect. Amazing! But I never expected this: the journals say that wool is popular up there, but if I can read their journals, then they can read our histories . . . no . . . they do not have our histories. No one has our histories. We are an island. A sinking island. Sinking? In a drought? Who is the fool now!*

Oh, yes, and here we go again. I will bow to you and you will bow to me and perhaps we will smell one another's haunches to see if we have the proper odor. And look at how that one with the pocky face minces along: he has been practicing, I can tell. I wonder what they do, whether their women are as absurd as they. Probably. Breeders, all of them. And it is all sex, rutting and being rutted, sex . . . sex that I do not—no . . . no . . . such fine suits—(idiots they are to wear wool but they probably do not know any better)—and such fine manners, but I see what is real. I must listen as they are presented. Hmmm . . . he is called Mather, *then?*

And the Very Reverend Mr. Jenkins thereupon succinctly states (for Truth is always succinct) the reasons for his coming, describing the mutual profit that cannot but be a consequence of the forging of fraternal bonds between two nations. The nations in question. I mean America and Africa. I mean . . . America and Nuhr . . . no . . . the Three Kingdoms . . .

I will have this thought about. It is impossible, of

Falsehood and heresy! (Ow! Must have pinched

course, that these savages have come to my realm for anything good, but it is indeed astonishing that they can put such an innocent face upon their obviously nefarious plots. I will have it thought about. And wool! Pah! And yet ... and yet Aeid says that I should deal with these men. I will have it thought about. But what does Aeid know? I will have it ...

myself yesterday.) Ravenous dogs, coming into my ... I mean, this realm and it is certainly a good thing that they are keeping their sailors on board the ships because ... I wonder, what is it like, all that pale skin? Their women: what would it be like? Any woman ... oh, to be held down ... not like those Naians. Why, they sit astraddle on their men and ... ow!

Now, I lay this before you, my brethren, to consider in your heart of hearts, your inmost forum of interior conscience, wherein the godly light shines most brilliantly: what could there possibly be within the purview of sinful human endeavor that is greater than this? Surely the love of man for woman, good and necessary though it is, is a transient thing. Surely the affection of fathers for their sons, immutably decreed as the finest expression of manly hearts, cannot last. But here, imperishable because it is an imperishable ... ah ... because it is a true manifestation of that Other Love that so preserves us against all possible harm, is sweetness, concord, and felicity!

Now ... come to me, my man. I want you (and I must not forget that little lift to my breasts (I wonder if I could grow some breasts if I found

... thought about, but Aeid did say. Well, he is but a boy, a stripling. I will have Haddar attend to it. We will burn the ships tonight, I think, and

Too bad that we will have to burn them. But wait ... wait. That look. Oh, that creamy flesh! I can ... and perhaps they can tell me things like

the right herbs?))	*the men will*	*Valdemar has*
when I do it. Oh,	*make fine*	*told me. I wonder*
my!	*slaves.*	*whether . . .*

And lo! A miracle happens, for the grace of God works upon the company, and despite violent precedent, despite the centuries of unmitigated hostility shown by a backwards, primitive people toward men from distant lands, the simple and heathen king of a barbaric people confers with the High Priest of a barbaric religion, and, upon opening themselves to the Light . . .

. . . they accept the delegation of the most Christian and Righteous States of America.

Asses!	*He wants*	*. . . it*	*No, I . . .*
Pumice!	*me! Oh! he*	*thought*	*I mean we,*
They will	*is looking*	*about, but*	*will listen. I*
ruin every-	*away. He is*	*Haddar will*	*sense that*
thing with	*ashamed!*	*know.*	*there is*
their clumsy	*Well, per-*	*Haddar*	*profit to be*
buffoonery!	*haps you*	*knows every-*	*had here.*
And Father	*would prefer*	*thing. But*	*And we can*
will not lis-	*me as a*	*the Gharat*	*always burn*
ten to me	*woman,*	*accepts*	*the ships.*
again. I am	*then? A*	*them, and*	*But I saw*
surrounded	*sweet little*	*the Gharat*	*that glance*
. . . by . . .	*girl? I can*	*knows best,*	*at Bakbuk*
fools!	*oblige.*	*of course.*	*. . . ow!*

Chapter Six

Haddar, Jenkins realized very quickly, was *the* man in Nuhr. Haddar was skilled, adept, cunning. Haddar could get things done. Haddar missed nothing, thought of everything. Haddar knew every important detail of every important plot, rumor, or planned action. Haddar was stern, implacable, excruciatingly loyal, and peered into all things with a kind of penetration with which Jenkins felt an instant kinship.

And Jenkins decided that he would have to be very careful around Haddar.

The seating protocol of the Three Kingdoms (which, like the matter of the gunpowder, had escaped the diligence of American research) put Jenkins beside Haddar at the banquet that the king gave that night in honor of the arrival and acceptance of the American embassy. On Jenkin's other side was the Gharat himself, Abnel, but one look at his shaved head and ornate vestments—not to mention the odd light that hovered about his eyes—made Jenkins sit down on his embroidered cushion with the feeling that he had been placed next to a particularly large specimen of the tarantulas that had been discovered in the southwestern deserts.

Touchy business, this. Jenkins was a man caught in a

finely meshed web of duty and circumstance, and as might be expected of a career diplomat with many successes behind him, he was determined to seize that web and shape it to his own ends. But in order to bring that shaping about, he would not only have to win the trust of a people that, seemingly by nature, was prone to distrust, but he would also have to perform actions that, were they to become known prematurely, would add to that distrust a distillation of anger and lethality that was well known throughout the civilized world.

Not an easy task. No, indeed.

"Minister Haddar," he said in perfect, perfectly neutral French, "I cannot but tell you how delighted I am to have been privileged to be the first foreign ambassador to be received at the court of Nuhr for many years."

Haddar's eyes were as neutral in their blackness as Jenkins' were in their grayness. "Is there any other?"

Jenkins suppressed a frown. He had heard of the unsettling ways of Africans, had, in fact, experienced some of them firsthand in Egypt and in Algiers. "Ah ... any ... other?"

"Any other court." Haddar examined Jenkins as he had been examining Jenkins throughout the pre-appetizer sweets, the appetizers, the post-appetizer sweets, the pre-first-course sweets, the first course, the post-first-course sweets, the pre-second-course sweets, the second course, the post-second-course sweets, the pre-third-course ...

Had they gotten that far? Or, rather, *only* that far? Jenkins (suddenly possessed by visions of meals that went on for hours and hours, perhaps only breaking up with the dawn) was not sure. He was certain, however, that the amount of sugar that diplomatic courtesy had forced him to consume might well affect his mind. Win these people? God in heaven! "Of course not," he said. "I am simply honored that we ... ah ... that we ... were not killed upon our arrival."

"We could still kill you," said Haddar. Noncommittal. Objective. Unsettling. But he dropped his eyes to Jenkins' garments with an expression that made the ambassador feel as though the gray wool were going to crawl away of its own volition.

"Of course you could," Jenkins agreed, but as Haddar's remarks were beginning to make him a little worried, both for himself and for his colleagues—there were, after all, many stories about the insidious and occasionally crippling practical jokes that the people of the Islamic kingdoms delighted in playing upon everyone from Christian missionaries to credentialed ambassadors (and Jenkins recalled with a start that he was *both*), and the Panasians of the Three Kingdoms might share the trait in their own pagan way—he cast a quick look up and down the long table. Some distance away, Scruffy (Why the devil had that idiot been allowed in here, anyway?) was holding forth in bastard French and pidgin English about the wonders of American technology (*See! Chuggee-chuggee all by self. Big fella firesnake one-fella man tall,* comprendez-vous?) while Turtletrout nodded in his slope-headed way, now and again picking up bits of the food put before him as though he were examining glass beads in a shop in Cairo. The six Marines stood at attention by the door, their (black) dress uniforms utterly eclipsed by the silks and polished cottons and gems and gold of the thirty or so palace soldiers who kept them company. Close by, but just out of range of an unobtrusive nudge, Mather, apparently overcome by fatigue and wine, had fallen asleep with his head in his hand; but courtesy in the Three Kingdoms apparently dictated that no one notice this definite smut on the American nose, and the officials on either side of him went on with their meal and their conversation.

"Now, class, it's time for geography. I assume we've all been studying very hard for our little oral examination today. Haven't we studied hard . . . Master Mather?"

Mr. Jefferson is tall and thin, with a regal face and a nose upon which a mischievous boy, taken by an extreme fit of impertinence, might attempt to impale a melon. He bends down towards Master Mather, and his nose wavers invitingly inches from the boy's eyes.

Master Mather rubs a face prematurely pocked with acne and tries to look attentive. "Yes, sir!"

A suety voice on Jenkins' other side, though, prevented him from considering the matter any further for the time being. "I trust that the Ambassador from America finds nothing distressing about my country's hospitality?"

Jenkins turned away from Haddar's examination and turned toward Abnel's . . . well . . . something else. Something about the High Priest repelled everything that was staid and Puritan in the ambassador, but he could neither put his finger on it (and was not sure, in any case, that he wanted to) nor, for the sake of his mission, allow it to bother him.

"Oh, everything is perfectly to my liking," said Jenkins, trying for a smile and coming up with an arid thing that would not have fooled a fish. It fooled Abnel, though. Or (Jenkins reflecting, perhaps, a little more than was good for him) perhaps it only appeared to fool him.

Abnel, though, smiled, nodded in return . . .

"Sure you've studied?"

"Very hard, sir."

"Sure?"

The nose waggles back and forth. Mather watches, fascinated. Melons! "Yes, sir. Absolutely, sir."

"Very well, then, tell me about the towns of Kaprisha."

"Kaprisha, sir?"

The other children in the room titter. Mr. Jefferson's nose turns insinuating. "A-ha! Gawd-a-mercy, but I was under the impression that you said you'd studied."

. . . and cast a sly glance in the direction of the unfortunate Mather.

Just then, the musicians at the side of the room struck up another one of their wailing, cacophonous songs. Jenkins suppressed an undiplomatic wince, continued proffering the arid thing to Abnel, wished that what passed for music in the Three Kingdoms might at least awaken Mather. But the assistant continued to sleep.

"I am rather surprised at you, though," continued Abnel, whose French was all but flawless.

"I do not understand," said Jenkins, matching him, French for French.

"Well . . ." Master Mather is confused. Kaprisha? Why, he has never even heard *of Kaprisha. And the towns? There was nothing in the book about towns in Kaprisha!* "Well . . ." *he tries again,* ". . . that is to say . . . I mean . . . it's . . . it's . . . its . . . uh . . . not . . . uh . . . in the . . . uh . . . book." *He looks up at Mr. Jefferson.* "Is it?"

Mr. Jefferson, carrying his slender frame with great dignity, strides to the bookshelf and picks up the heavy geography book, then returns to Master Mather and drops it onto the table directly beneath the boy's pocky face. With astonishing precision, the teacher flips open the book and—horrors!—there it is, a whole (Oh, dear God!) chapter of the book devoted to the Three Kingdoms, Kaprisha in particular, with subheadings on Kaprishan towns and local color.

"Well?" *Mr. Jefferson slams the book closed.*

Master Mather struggles, decides upon a desperate stratagem. "Well, they're small."

"Very good." But there is terrible accusation in Mr. Jefferson's voice.

Abnel fixed Jenkins with a glance that reminded Jenkins that, on his other side, Haddar was still examining him, still, perhaps, nursing thoughts of doing away with the entire party of Americans when it suited him ... or suited the king, or suited Abnel, or suited whoever happened to be in charge of this little pagan horse turd of a country.

And, despite his acute discomfort, Jenkins paused for a moment at the question of who might actually be in charge of the Three Kingdoms. He perhaps did not yet know who was in charge, but he would find out, and, indeed, he knew who would *eventually* be in charge in any case.

But Abnel was going on in that suety voice, the golden fillet about his head gleaming in the light of the torches, his small lips coated with sugar from the candied pomegranate seeds heaped in the dish before him. "You say you do not understand? I will tell you, then. You, a minister of your people, did not invoke your Gods before our meal. I was very surprised. I had heard that it was the custom in your country."

"Small and ... well, mostly made out of bricks of dried mud. A-and, a main street up the middle. No paving like we have here, you know, but just dirt. Sand, I mean."

"Indubitably," But Mr. Jefferson's nose, sharp and waiting for an opportune melon, is quivering with doubt.

"There are always two sections to the towns in the Three Kingdoms," continues Master Mather, finding that he is becoming increasingly desperate and, paradoxically, increasingly aroused by this crisis. There is, indeed, a firmness in his breeches that he wishes would go away ... or perhaps increase. "There's the Panasian section—that's the better-off people, and it's up by the main gate and around the main square—and then there's the Naian section toward the back."

"All right."

"The Panasians are the upper class and the educated people."

"Like the Christians in our country," says Mr. Jefferson.

"Well . . . yes. And the Naians are lower class and un-educated. They have a little ghetto in each town. It's got a wall around it, and there are Panasian guards at the gates to watch over who goes in and out. The Panasians are worried about their women escaping and becoming Naians."

"Would they want to do that?"

"Oh, yes. The Naian women can go where they want to, even own property and businesses. The Panasian women are veiled, and are kept shut away . . ."

Mr. Jefferson was nodding approvingly. *"Like the Christians in our country!"*

". . . so they might like to join the Naians." Master Mather shrugs, looks at Mr. Jefferson's nose, feels something in his groin tighten. *"They're killed if they try, of course."*

"Oh," said Jenkins, reminded uncomfortably of the story of Saint Francis and the crosses in the carpet. But Saint Francis had been a degenerate, ass-kissing papist, whereas Abnel was dealing with a staunch and doughty Puritan: there was a considerable difference. "Allow me to explain. It is also the custom in my country to be respect-ful and thoughtful guests, and as the customary, fifteen minute prayer to—" He forged ahead in spite of the tacit blasphemy. "—to our God—" Well, at least he could let the benighted heathen know that he was dealing with monotheists here! "—might be repugnant to our illustrious hosts—" And he glanced at Haddar, who was examining him as though he were a nice, cooked brisket of beef. "—I gave my companions a general dispensation for this eve-ning."

*Master Mather, frightened and aroused both, has be-
come caught up in his own tale. "What's really important,
though, are the mountains."*

*Dead silence in the classroom. Mr. Jefferson clears his
throat. "That's enough. Thank you, Master Mather."*

*"But . . . the mountains." Mather, inspired, warms to his
elaborations. "They're high. Incredibly high. Forty thousand feet if they're an inch. And they're impassable.
Supposedly."*

"That's quite enough."

"But, you see, we think there's a way—"

*Mr. Jefferson turns away, lifting his voice into peda-
gogy. "Which just goes to show us all, class, the stultifying
effects of paganism on the human spirit. Why—"*

*Master Mather stands up. "I'm not done," he says
firmly.*

"Oh, yes you are."

"But . . . Bonaparte . . ."

*"Do you want to be flogged?" Jefferson whirls toward
Master Mather again, and the boy sees a greedy, almost
eager look in the teacher's eyes. "Do you?"*

"A dispensation . . ." Abnel nodded his bald head, the
pale flesh of his face at once flaccid and taut. "How interesting. And they saw nothing unusual in this?"

Jenkins was puzzled. Or maybe (Jenkins was losing
track, was not even sure of himself anymore. Drat that
sugar!) he only appeared to be puzzled. "Of course not,
my dear Gharat. The people of America are firm and un-
swerving in their faith. They would never think of questioning any decision made by a minister, who is, of course,
their direct and only link with the divine."

For an instant, Abnel appeared struck. He considered,
murmured something in his own language, and then, in
French: "Amazing. And this includes revelation?"

Revelation. Such a strange word to hear coming from

the mouth of a fat, bald man in outlandish vestments. "Well, yes."

"Amazing."

"I do not understand, Honored Gharat."

Abnel waved a perfumed hand. "It is nothing. A thought only."

A hesitation that seems to drag on and on. Master Mather looks at Mr. Jefferson. Mr. Jefferson looks at Master Mather. Then ...

"Yes!" shouts the boy. "Yes! I want it!"

He is jumping up and down now, eyes clenched, fists balled, shrieking:

"I want it! I want it! I want it!"

And Jenkins continued to feel Haddar's black gaze. *We could still kill you.* Yes, indeed, they could. After all, there were only two ships in the harbor. If Inwa Kabir's soldiers—and there were many of them: Jenkins had not missed that—made a concerted, prolonged attack, even carronades, cannon, and muskets would eventually fail.

"And no one ..." Abnel resumed in French after another wave of his hand, "... no one questions your authority?"

"Of course not. America is, without exception, a righteous land." This, of course, was not the exact truth. Jenkins knew of many incidents involving forbidden books by the notorious *philosophes,* shipments of erotica, clandestine printing presses that churned out the persistent scrofula of Quaker tracts, secret meetings of Free Thinkers and Universalists, even (God help them all!) a few witches ... though the latter plague had been largely ended after the entire Seven Town area in Rhode Island had been fired. A few hundred charred bodies, a few hundred hangings, and no more witches. If they could only pin down those dratted Quakers the same way!

And the children, at a crook of Mr. Jefferson's long fin-

*ger, have risen as one, are clustering even now around
Master Mather, are peeling away his clothes to reveal his
plump, little-boy body as Mr. Jefferson takes up a switch
from the well-stocked rack at the side of the room. There
are labels on the switches:* Boys, Girls, Young Ruffians-
In-Training, Plump Little Wenches, God-Fearing-
Ministers-To-Be, *and so on. The one that Mr. Jefferson
has chosen, though, says only* Playmate. *Mr. Jefferson flexes it, and then, incredibly, with a motion that Master Mather cannot fathom (It looks like no more than a
flick of his wrist), the teacher divests himself of his
clothes, and the glory of the approaching rod is all but
eclipsed by the magnificence of his erection.*

No, it was not the truth at all, but Jenkins knew that the
truth was not always the best friend for an ambassador to
keep at his elbow. Far better for him to present the Righteous States as a united and devout Christian people rather
than to have this heathen priest conceive of Jenkins'
homeland as harboring even the slightest trace of hetero-
doxy.

"I am a minister," Jenkins continued. "I tell the people
what to believe, and, in accordance with Scripture, they
believe it. Their faith is internal, integral."

Abnel nodded slowly, seemed about to respond with another *amazing,* but seemed to consider against it. He took
up a scented cloth and wiped some of the grains of sugar
from his lips. "Well, I trust that your dealings with our
country will be profitable and holy, Mr. Ambassador."

*And Master Mather is bent over a desk, elevating his
pale, round rump for his teacher's convenience, offering a
tempting option that, he hopes, might be included in today's bill of fare. And then the blows begin to fall, each
one harder and firmer than before, and Master Mather,
awash in a sea of erotic heavings, loses track of who is*

*flogging who, or with what, and a hot fire in his groin is
rising, rising, rising—*

"Oh," said Jenkins, thinking of Haddar, "I am sure
they . . ." He suddenly glanced around, was met by two
black, calculating eyes. Inwa Kabir was obviously one of
those monarchs who governed at a distance, who had long
ago given over the reins of power to trusted ministers and
underlings so that he himself could pursue more kingly
amusements. He had, in fact, not even bothered to attend
this dinner: his place at the head of the low table was con-
spicuously vacant.

". . . ah . . . they . . . ah . . . will," he finished limply.

He looked down the table. Mather was still slumped to
one side, his head supported by his upturned hand. What
a sorry sight to present to the chief minister!

Scruffy was still holding forth—*"Man belong far away
place. Man-a-wee-wee bugger-im-up-im with talk he-hide.
But he-no mow yet."*—about something, to the obvious
amusement of the officials about him. Irritably, Jenkins
caught the eye of Lieutenant Cuttle, nodded in Mather's
direction.

But, "Yes, sir! Immediately, sir!" Cuttle bellowed in fine,
loud, completely-inappropriate-under-the-circumstances
American fashion, and, to Jenkin's horror, he proceeded to
execute a right face, a presentation and shouldering of arms,
and then a ceremonial march in the direction of Mather,
who, still asleep, was now being cooed over by a young
woman in an ornate veil and head cloth.

Jenkins stared at the woman. A woman? Here? With
men? Very odd.

"You are perhaps wondering about the girl who is so so-
licitous of your assistant, Mr. Ambassador?" Abnel said
with great blandness.

"Why . . . I was under the impression that women and
men were not allowed to mix in public."

"Oh, yes," said Abnel. "That is so. Women, in fact, are confined to their houses. Some protest, of course. For the first offense, they are fettered. For the second ..." He smiled, shrugged.

Servants were bringing tureens containing pieces of lamb cooked in a dark sauce that obviously involved grapes. Jenkins looked at the Gharat. "For the second?"

And, yes, Mr. Jefferson has found that little rosebud, has, now that Mather is completely aflame with passion, plugged in, and even now his bristly face is scraping Mather's cheek as his thin lips twist frantically to the side to mouth the tender succulency of boy-flesh.

Abnel reached into one of the tureens, extracted a grape. He popped it into his mouth and chomped down with a deliberate gesture that told Jenkins everything.

"Ah ..." Jenkins fumbled for a moment: unpardonable sin in a diplomat! "... why, we do the same."

"Oh?"

"But ..." Not to lose the contest that he sensed was going on beneath a veneer of courtesy, Jenkins reached a little too far. "... but there are no protests."

Abnel's eyebrows lifted, then resettled. "Because you are ... a minister ..."

"Because the people of America carry the words of their God within their hearts," said Jenkins, relieved that Cuttle was at least approaching Mather so as to end the hideous absurdity. "But ... that woman ..."

"Oh ..." Abnel seemed distracted and amused both. "That is not a woman. That is Bakbuk, the king's sworder. Bakbuk is a eunuch. A clean eunuch. He has somehow been saved the usual lot of obesity, and it pleases him to play these little charades sometimes. It amuses the king to allow him his pleasure." The Gharat regarded the sleeping Mather, the cooing Bakbuk, the approaching Cuttle. "He *is* amazing, is he not?"

"Ah ..." Jenkins felt even more repelled by Bakbuk than he was by the light that gleamed faintly about Abnel's eyes. Gleamed faintly, and (as Cuttle, upon reaching Mather, gave him a polite shake ...

Huh? What? Oh, God ... must have dozed off. Hope no one noticed.

... and Mather awoke with a start and glanced uneasily up at the officious Bakbuk with a look that Jenkins would have sworn was something very close, if not identical to lust) grew.

Abnel allowed the servants to transfer a portion of the contents of the tureen to his dish. "I find myself increasingly intrigued by your people, Mr. Ambassador," he said. "And increasingly delighted that we have at last ended our long isolation." He eyed Mather, who was accomplishing something rather superhuman in being so obviously, so simultaneously, and so equally attracted to and repelled by Bakbuk.

Jenkins was not sure what to do.

Abnel indicated the tureen. "Please be so kind as to try this lamb with grape curry, Mr. Ambassador. That it is being served to us indicates that you have acquired the king's highest favor."

"Oh ..." Jenkins was distracted. "... really?"

"Oh, my, yes," said Abnel. "Grapes need water to grow, and water is so lacking in our country ..." A meaningful pause to which Jenkins could assign no meaning whatsoever. "... that there are very few grapes." The Gharat reached again into the tureen, extracted another grape, popped it into his mouth. "Very few. Consider yourself very welcome in the Three Kingdoms. I would like to speak with you. A great deal. Later."

Chapter Seven

It was a little village, smaller even than the one Sari had lived in for five decades, but it was a village, and there were people in it, and therefore, along with people, there had to be water, food, and shelter.

She had walked all day. Her eyes were rimmed in red from the heat and the dust, her feet bleeding with unaccustomed travel. It was, in some ways, a miracle that she could even perceive this village at all, and her mind was so numb with exposure that she would not have been greatly surprised had she been confronting nothing more than a product of delirium.

But it was not delirium. It was a village. Sari could see mud buildings, dusty streets, prowling dogs and stray cats, Panasian boys tumbling one another over in rough play, newly-veiled Panasian girls sitting just outside their doors with their knees pressed together and their heads bent. It was all common. Very common. Delirium, she was sure, would have forgotten the cats and the dogs. Or perhaps it would have made the Panasian boys look less dirty, or the girls a little more cheerful. But this was not delirium (She had to keep reminding her stumbling mind of that fact, just as she had to keep reminding her stumbling feet to continue to walk), this was real, this was a village, a place where she might be able to live a little longer, where she could possibly stay for a time. At least until the news of Maumud's death arrived.

But before she approached further, the thought came to her that, dressed as a Panasian woman—head cloth and face cloth and arms wrapped to the wrists—she would find no solace in this village, for a woman of Panas did not travel alone, could not even buy food alone. For Sari to walk boldly and unaccompanied through the weathered gates would be for her to risk, at best, overt suspicion and hostility. At worst, she would find herself immediately arrested by the village bailiffs and brought before the priests for questioning. And then . . .

She had seen what happened to the women of Panas who ignored the laws of Panas.

But here she was, with nothing, and there was the village, with, comparatively, everything. And where else could she go? To the mountains? With nothing? She would not last another day. She would probably not last another hour.

In the distance, the mountains swam in the evening light, their clouds and snow-clad peaks pale and cool, their rugged slopes a fantasy of high relief. Those were the mountains that others had crossed, and among their foothills were the Caves of Naia where others (Others!) had worshiped. Others. But not Sari. No, she would never reach the mountains, and she would never see the Caves. She would, doubtless, not even reach this village, because . . . because . . .

No—

No. Wait.

She stood a moment longer, fighting through the hunger and thirst that turned her thoughts to dry wind, and then she dropped to her knees and began pawing through her bundle.

Her hands found it before her eyes did, but when she held it up and squinted at it out of old eyes made infinitely older by a day's unprotected journey through the desert, she felt at once cold and hot, empty and full, hungry and satiated. For a moment, she traced the twin, interlocked circles on the front of the medallion with a gnarled finger, and then she turned it over and read the legend that was graven so deeply on the reverse that, unlike the love of her heart, fifty years had not been able to erase it:

Sari, daughter of Mesthia

It was real, then. She had it still. Daughter of her mother, child of her Goddess. Maumud had cursed her for keeping it, but Maumud was gone, and now this palm's breadth of bronze was all she had. But did Naia allow one who had so denied Her to wear Her symbols?

She could not consider any answer save an affirmative one, but as she started to drop the cord over her head, she found that her bulky head cloth was in the way, and, with a sudden rush of horror at the betrayal that the garment had come to represent, she jerked it off. Her veil came with it, and she threw them both on the ground.

Wind on her face. The cord slipped over her head easily now, and she pulled the fastenings from her gray hair and let it tumble loosely down her back.

Her head bare, her face feeling strangely naked, Sari rose as a Naian. The medallion rested just over her heart, and though it marked her as a member of a despised minority, it was also her passage to freedom, for unless the laws of the Three Kingdoms had changed terribly in the course of the last five decades, those women who wore the emblem of the Goddess were tolerated in their violations of Panasian custom. True, their freedom made them an easy mark for any passing man with violence or rut on his mind, but, officially at least, they were safe, and Sari—

old and withered and of no use or interest to anyone—
knew that her own security was virtually absolute.

Sari, daughter of Mesthia, tottered forward in the brief,
African twilight, reaching the gates of the village just as
the solemn gong from the tiny temple of Panas announced
the close of another day. Far behind her, tumbled in the
sand, lost in the falling darkness, were her head cloth and
her veil.

Aeid knotted the end of the rope about one of the orna-
mental spires that decorated the west wing of the palace.
He put his weight on it. It held.

Sari was in luck (if luck could still be said to have anything to do with one who had, in the space of a day, lost
her husband, her home, and her people): the gates of the
town were still open, and the gate keepers hardly gave her
more than a sneering glance as she passed through.

She entered the town, allowed the encircling walls to
enclose her as Maumud's house had once enclosed her, allowed the buildings with their slit windows and their sad,
mud parodies of the jasper towers and agate pinnacles of
the great cities to hem her in as once the laws of Panas
had hemmed her in. Now, however, she walked the sandy
streets of this nameless town of the central desert of
Kaprisha not as a humble Panasian wife whose husband
claimed her as property, but as a Naian woman, one who
stepped freely, one who walked alone, one who worshiped
the Goddess who brought joy to human endeavor and fruc-
tification even to the most arid land.

Free. Free to make a new life. But she could not but
wonder what that life could be. Could it be anything? She
remembered herbs and their uses, but where her skills had
given her a certain exotic and even desirable distinction
among Panasians, they would be held of little account by

Naians, for almost every Naian woman knew something about herbs. It was simply part of being a Naian. Sari would be no different from anyone else, and probably considerably inferior to most.

For a moment, her resolve was shaken, but then she steeled herself and went on. Naia had brought her this far. Naia would take her even farther. And when Sari lifted her blurring gaze above the surrounding roofs that, tall as they were, could not hide the topmost peaks of the distant mountains, she suddenly wondered how far Naia might eventually take her. Perhaps all the way to the Caves of Naia. Perhaps, in that place of living water, an old, worthless woman might find a renewal of her life that would go beyond the end of a marriage and the resumption of long unused skills.

And then he (Aeid, remember?) took hold of the rope and swung his leg over the sheer drop. There was no moon. The only light was what spilled from the thousands of palace windows: mingled torchlight and lamplight as yellow as the hair of one of those northern girls he had read about in forbidden books and journals.

Aeid actively hated this part of his life. Oh, to be sure, there was a certain sense of release inherent in it, but it was a constant annoyance to him that he was, as far as the kingdom was concerned, as far as his father was concerned, just a frisky young stallion, appreciated for the erectile properties of his penis ... but for nothing else.

Descending skillfully, keeping to the shadows, he approached the latticed window of the lovely Sabihah, prized wife of Kuz Aswani.

The street took Sari through the center of town. The shops in the market square were all shuttered for the night, and even the ubiquitous water vendors had gone home. Sari's mouth was parched, her stomach had long since given up any hope of food, and her feet were still bleeding; but so intent was she upon the white wall ahead that she hardly noticed.

There it was: the boundary-wall of the Naian Quarter. Sari had thought that she would never again approach such a wall, but here she was, unveiled, a Naian again, coming home to the place of the Naians after a lifetime's absence. Yes, she had lost her heart (for it had died years ago), and yes, she had lost more than that (for though the Naians did not mutilate their women, the Panasians did), but she tried to forget both as she stumbled toward the gateway into the Naian ghetto.

The priestly guards obviously thought that she was attempting to beat the curfew, for they waved mockingly at her. "Run, Granny," said one. "Run. You will not reach your house tonight if we have anything to say about it."

But the laws established by the kings of long ago apparently still held, and so, while it was still possible to tell a white sheep from a black sheep without the aid of a lamp, Sari was free to pass into the Quarter. Still, the guards delayed her, making a great show of examining her medallion.

"Hmmm . . . I do not recall seeing you before, Granny," said the guard who had taunted her.

Sari said nothing. To speak would mean further delay. To argue would mean a quick trip to the magistrates. She felt a momentary twinge of fear: the news of Maumud's suspicious death might have already reached this place. Even if it had not, though, the guard would more than likely remember her if he were ever questioned.

"Get on your way," said the second guard brusquely. He eyed his companion, shifted the weight of his sword. "I want to go home, Basfani. I am in no mood for games."

"Awww . . ."

The second guard jerked a thumb toward the dark opening of the gate. Sari bobbed her head appreciatively and ducked through it . . .

. . . into another world.

The houses were mud, the streets, sand. But a scent of incense hung in the air along with a tinkle of wind chimes. Off in the distance, she heard the sound of drumming, and the thudding beats were punctuated by cries, whistles, and a chant that sounded like *Hunna-hunna-hunna-ho!*

She stopped, listening. She had never heard anything like it before. Well, it had, after all, been fifty years.

Aeid dangled just outside the lattice, swinging back and forth at the end of his rope (his period, T, of course, being equal to $2\pi\sqrt{\frac{l}{g}}$). Within, he could see Sabihah, her veils dropped, her headwrap undone. In the glow of the oil lamps, she was a soft presence of long hair and smooth skin, and despite Aeid's disinclination to be thought of as nothing more than the chief stallion of his father's household, he found that his lips were dry, his heart racing.

She turned toward the window as though sensing his presence. Wait a moment. That ruby at her throat. Wait . . . Sabihah hated rubies. Or was that Huda? Wait . . .

Suspended a hundred and fifty feet above the marble pavement of the courtyard, swinging $\left(T = 2\pi\sqrt{\frac{l}{g}}\right)$ just out of reach of the light of Sabihah's lamp, Aeid sorted through his mental lists. Huda liked . . . ah . . . diamonds. And hyacinths. Yes. But Sabihah . . . did not Sabihah *loath* rubies? What then was she doing with a ruby at her throat? Had her husband found out about her nocturnal trysts and, unable to do anything about them (Aeid was, after all, the prince), had decided to shame his wife and put a little stamp of ownership on her?

But was this even Sabihah? Well ... yes ... Aeid thought that it was. Maybe.

The woman (and it *was* Sabihah, he was sure of it, ruby or no) approached the window, released a catch, swung open the lattice. "Aeid?"

"Sabi—" Or was this Huda? Or maybe Najmat? He was losing track. Damn this ridiculous game he had to play! He would have to risk it. "Sabihah?"

$T = 2\pi \sqrt{\frac{l}{g}}$

"Yes. Yes, beloved, it is I. Come in. What are you doing swinging back and forth like that when you know that I am waiting for you?" Her eyes gleamed in the starlight. The ruby (Ruby? *Ruby!?*) at her throat was a glowing presence. Her lips ...

Aeid was breathing faster. "The ... ah ... ruby ... ?"

"What ruby?" she said, laying her hand absently upon the ruby.

Aeid gave up. "What about your husband?" (Swinging past the window again, trying to time his reach (and T *still* equaled $2\pi \sqrt{\frac{l}{g}}$ so that he could clasp her hand, missing and adding still another vector to his oscillation ...)

"Oh, he will not bother us. He was with Umi Botzu all afternoon, and now he has locked himself in his chambers. Just before we parted, I noticed that he was trying to scratch himself behind the ear with his foot."

"His ..." $T = 2\pi \sqrt{\frac{l}{g}}$ "... foot?"

"Well, you know about Umi Botzu."

"Has he been telling him ..." $T = 2\pi \sqrt{\frac{l}{g}}$ "... stories again?"

"Has who been telling whom?"

"Umi Botzu tell ..." $T = 2\pi \sqrt{\frac{l}{g}}$ "... ing your husband."

Sabihah sighed, spread her hands. "My husband is now perfectly convinced that he is turning into a ferret. I cannot talk any sense into him. But, then, what do I know of sense? I am but a woman."

Hunna-hunna-hunna-HO!

Sari stood, wondering, her face naked in the dry desert breeze. Incense, wind chimes, noises. A woman laughed, loudly and freely. A man laughed even more loudly.

Hunna-hunna-hunna-HO!

She was frightened. Suddenly, the fifty years came back, bringing with them estrangement. She was no longer a Naian. She was no longer even a whole woman. By what right did she stumble now into the Naian quarter to ask for shelter?

Hunna-hunna-hunna-HO!

But her stomach was empty, her mouth dry as the sand beneath her feet, and when she heard footsteps and the jingling of a woman's jewelry, she decided to ask for help whether she had the right to or not.

She turned toward the sounds, saw a shadow. "Wife—" she started, but the Panasian term died on her lips.

Hunna-hunna-hunna-HOOOOOOO!

And then the drumming stopped, likewise the shouts. "Sister," said Sari, feeling suddenly as naked in her voice as she was in her clothing.

The shadow stopped. "Who?" came a voice, at once formal and imperious.

Sari struggled with old memories. "Naia's peace to you," she said as the silence grew and the darkness sifted down.

The woman turned, approached with a swish of skirts and the clank of heavy jewelry. And, yes, there was the medallion of Naia, glinting a dull bronze just over her heart. "And to you," came the reply. "To whom do I have the honor of speaking?"

All very formal, all very polite, all very . . . wrong. Sari recalled the unabashed friendliness of the Naians she had known in her youth. "My name is Sari, sister. I . . . I need shelter." She offered her hands, palms up, in the old Naian gesture.

The woman examined her for a moment, ignored her hands. "Come," she said. "Naia provides, and as Her direct channel, I shall provide in Her place." And with that, she turned as though to indicate that Sari should follow, and with a continuous clanking from her jewelry, she proceeded up the street.

Sari was startled by her brusque and formal manner, but the street appeared to be otherwise deserted. She had nowhere else to go, and so she followed.

Small as the Naian quarter was, its streets formed a very convoluted maze, and the shortest distance between any two points was, as far as Sari could tell, most certainly not a straight line. Even the houses seemed to partake of the quality, for they spilled, shambled, and dribbled into one another, their walls flung out seemingly at random; and as the dusk deepened, the roofs and roof ornaments formed a dark jumble against the stars, looking to Sari like nothing so much as a pile of broken toys heaped together by children who had been thinking of other things to do at the time.

The woman she followed did not look back, and Sari struggled to keep up as the growing darkness finally left her blundering along, fuzzily trying to navigate by the sound of nearby footsteps and clanks. At last, though, her guide paused before a door, lifted a hand, and waited. Moments passed. There was a sigh of wind.

Suddenly, as though her action were fraught with meaning, the woman knocked three times, paused, knocked again, paused, then knocked once more. But no one opened the door in response: she herself reached for the latch and pushed into the dim light of the interior. Mildly surprised, Sari attempted to follow, only to have the door slammed in her face.

The ground seemed to be bucking and whirling beneath Sari's feet, but she struggled to remember the sequence of knocks. Although she could not understand why she, a guest under the protection of the woman in question (whoever she was), should have to go through the formality of knocking, she knocked three times, paused, knocked again, paused, and knocked again.

Almost instantly, the door was thrown open. A figure was silhouetted against the dim, interior light. "You!"

"I ..." Sari struggled for words. "I thought that ..."

"Oh, in the name of Naia, I had forgotten about you, and now you have ruined everything! How can you go repeating a knock like that!"

"Like ... what?"

"Come in. Come in." A hand reached out, caught Sari's sleeve, and pulled her, stumbling, into a room that was as thick with incense smoke as it was cluttered with physical objects. "You cannot make it any better now, so you might as well come in."

Sabihah moved beneath Aeid like a warm snake, the ruby at her throat glinting in the lamplight. Yes, of course. He remembered now: it was Huda who liked diamonds, hated rubies, and enjoyed being tickled by peacock feathers. Sabihah liked opals, adored rubies, and did not like feathers of any sort, only scented oil and flowers. And then there was Najmat, who adored pearls, could not understand anything that did not have to do with food, sleep, or sex (odd that she should be the wife of the excruciatingly competent Haddar), and Halwa, who ...

Well, no matter. Aeid had it all sorted out for now. Kuz Aswani was still locked in his private room, still attempting to groom himself with his feet and his tongue

(What had Umi Botzu done to him anyway?) and Aeid (who was of the decided opinion that Umi Botzu was going to find himself impaled in the city square one of these fine, hot days) was nestled between the thighs of the lovely Sabihah.

Somewhere else, though, the dinner with the Americans was progressing, the dinner to which he had not been invited. To be sure, it was a great (but not unexpected) honor to be considered of too exalted a rank to eat with the wool-wearers, but Aeid could not shake the nagging suspicion that he had been excluded not because of his rank but because his father (who had also stayed away) did not want him to come into contact with Jenkins and his men.

Sabihah moaned softly. "Do not stop, sweetest. Kuz Aswani only wants to drag me around the house by the scruff of my neck these days. Treat me like a woman, O my magnificent stallion!"

Obviously, Sabihah preferred horses to ferrets. Wincing, sighing inwardly, Aeid fulfilled his duty.

"But what have I done?"

Sari's head was spinning, and the clutter in the house was not helping matters at all. There seemed to be at least one representative of every kind of object she could imagine scattered on the floor, piled on stools, heaped on shelves, hanging from baskets. Clothes. Toys. Bottles. Pots. Pans. Sandals. Knives. Unwashed dishes. Plaster statues. Collections of tiny cards. It was rather overwhelming.

Sari squinted through her whirling vision, the dim light, and the clutter that magnified both in the worst possible way. The woman who had brought her to the house, slammed the door in her face, and then dragged her ungraciously in was not only weighted down with great heaps of bead necklaces, chain bracelets, and wide metal earrings, but had also festooned her clothing with a multitude of tiny crystals and stones. Cluttered and haphazard herself, she seemed the perfect embodiment of her house.

"I have been trying to keep the demons away all this time," she stated, drawing herself up to her full height. "And now you have broken the spell. That knock can only be used once every day, at the hour of Mercury and the day of the moon. Only once. But you have added a second knock to the first! And now . . ."

She suddenly straightened, folded her arms formally, lifted her chin, fixed Sari with another imperious glance. ". . . now . . ." She all but intoned it. ". . . I do not know what might . . . transpire . . ."

From nearby came the sound of a child fussing, and, with a cry, the woman unfolded her arms and ran to a small bed in a dark corner.

"Oh, sweet," she said, "it will be all right. The drummers will come in the morning, and . . . and . . ."

Her formality had abruptly evaporated: she seemed suddenly frail and worn. A young mother, Sari guessed fuzzily. A young mother with a sick child.

She tottered forward, tripping repeatedly over the clutter on the floor. When she reached the side of the bed, she found her head enveloped in a cloud of suspended crystals that bounced off her forehead and tapped her cheeks like playful fingers, but her attention was taken up by the tiny child who lay among the sheets with unclosed eyes.

Hollow eyes, skin so flushed that Sari could see its reddened dampness even in the pervasive dimness of the cluttered house. "Fever," she said. "I . . ."

"Oh," said the woman, "I strung these crystals all day, and they have not helped. And the drummers will come no sooner than tomorrow morning. They are practicing to-

night, and they tell me that they must practice or else . . .
or else . . ."

"I can help," Sari managed. "I am a herbalist. I know
. . . I . . . oh, dear . . ."

The exposure and fatigue finally took her, and she
sagged against the wall. A pot tumbled to the floor, and
there was a bright splash of scattering beads. Sari saw the
woman's wide eyes, heard the child start to cry.

"Water . . ." she said. "Please . . . some water . . ."

Chapter Eight

... and it is surely amazing that he could just sit there in his stinking wool and tell me about dispensations and absolute authority but then again it really has nothing to do with authority because if what he said is true (and I know that it is true because I saw it in their faces) it is the words that his people carry about within them a minister in their heads though he did not put it that way and what do I have but cynical and conniving men who would gladly tell me whatever they think I want to hear and the priesthood is the same I see them (ow!) in the streets and in the temple and even in the Councils when I was last in Katha they are probably up to all sorts of deceit because they think themselves educated and above we of Nuhr who do all the work and have to get our hands dirty while the effeminate *scholars* they give themselves such airs sit up and build cloud castles with words and do nothing but drink coffee I wonder if they even mind the pumps anymore it would be terrible if three hundred years of work went to rottenstone just because of a few arrogant nose-in-the-air priests can I do anything about it at all and they do whatever they want to when they think that no one is looking and the women probably even take off their headwraps *in the house* the whores best to keep them in chains (ow!)

all the time instead of letting them run about loose and
they enjoy it I know because I can feel just like that and
by Panas it is wonderful to feel that looseness and be
pinned down but the women do not look at me because I
know their secrets and they know it and they want to be
slaves I know and so I will be glad to oblige them because
I know and I do not want to call someone to take care of
this (ow!) right now because I want to think about Jenkins
and what he said and most of all I want to think about the
one who looked at Bakbuk he wants it too I saw it in his
eyes and I know that they think us savages but I will show
them who is the savage and who is the cultured *man* and
if I can catch Mather then perhaps I can find out that
sweet pale flesh no that is not what ... what ... was it
(ow!) how they do it with their people so obedient that we
have not been able to manage in three hundred years and
it all has to be internal but how to get it people memorize
the Sacred Texts but they cannot repeat any of them out
loud but that cannot be it either and oh how do they do it
I really (ow!) should call someone but for now I would
rather think and whatever can Aeid be thinking of he is
just another example of what I have to work with he ...

> And here is Bakbuk,
> lowering himself
> hand over hand down
> a long rope that,
> like Aeid's (see
> previous chapter)
> dangles from a solid
> bit of ornamental
> masonry on the roof
> of the palace.
> Bakbuk, clad as a
> boy, his hair tucked
> up, is fulfilling

his role of sworder
here: he is
interested in these
strange American
guests, and is
determined to find
out more about them.
Hand over hand he
goes, then, down
toward the window of
their chambers.

. . . says he is obedient to the laws of Panas but he fucks
other *men's WIVES* and I cannot say anything because he
is the prince (should have been me) and because he might
know something about what I do in these chambers and I
cannot risk it but how can I get Mather in here he would
be willing of course but not until he saw what I wanted
and then he would go along with it but not before oh the
color of gold on his arms if I put those chains on him and
I wonder what he would think of the device (ow!) it still
would hurt but to have someone like Mather see me that
way and maybe I could convince him to go along with everything and then he would be mine and he would tell me
about Jenkins and sometimes I wonder whether the pumps
will really do the work properly because nothing seems to
be changing sometimes though one lifetime is surely not
long enough to see the . . .

And on his way,
he notices Aeid,
who (see previous
chapter) is too
busy hauling himself
up a similar
rope to pay much
attention to the

                    strange boy/girl
                    who is lowering
                    himself/herself
                    down. Bakbuk is
                    intrigued, but he
                    (a boy today) has
                    a good idea of
                    where Aeid has
                    been and what he
                    has been up to.
     Still, though, he waits until Aeid is out of sight and then
                    begins angling over
                       across the face of the
                       palace to go and
                          take a look. Here
                          he is not a sworder,
                             but rather just a
                                curious boy ... ah ...
                                girl ... ?
... effects the old chronicles say the land was green
then but it certainly is a long time to wait those headwraps
off *in the house* they will be leaving them off to run out
to the market place next thing I know to find out if the
judgment of men long dead was correct but maybe it was
not correct because no one pays any attention to the laws
if they think they can get away with it just like Aeid and
I would wager that Kuz Aswani's wife does not leave her
headwrap on *in the house* (ow!) and then they will be all
acting like Naians and if I had one wish I would wish
those Naians right off the face of the land and they get
away with it only because of old laws and maybe the first
thing is to get rid of those laws but the king would not
agree and everything runs by money and so I wonder
whether a tax or something like a tax but it would be difficult to gain the king's approval because he does not care

any more than Aeid about the laws of Panas *in the house* because his wife is a whore and goes about like a Naian *in the HOUSE* and those chains should be on everyone and if I could get everyone to *think* (ow!) as I want then the problem would be over but I will have to find out how Jenkins does it and I will have Mather's help to do that . . .

And Bakbuk peered into Kuz Aswani's chambers to see Kuz Aswani leaping and bouncing across the floor on his hands and knees while uttering a soft *chuckle-chuckle-chuckle,* and just then the door opened and Sabihah (looking somewhat rumpled) entered, to be immediately pounced upon by the counselor. Bakbuk stayed only long enough to see Sabihah dragged across the room by the scruff of her neck before he turned away.

"Breeders," he whispered in disgust, and then began to make his

> way back across the
> face of the building
> to the windows of
> the Americans.

Mather sat behind an extravagant apparatus of brass lev-
ers, steel rods, pendulums, wires, plumb bobs, engraved
verniers, calibrated screws, and gears. This bob went up.
That bob went down. This pendulum precessed slowly in
a plane carefully defined and delimited by magnets and
bronze bumpers. That pendulum hung motionless, awaiting
the influence of invisible forces.

Mather was intent, his concentration perfect as he manipulated screws, turned gears, and adjusted verniers, but
in the dim light of the oil lamps in the room, the combination of pocked flesh and gleaming metal formed a
strange bio-mechanical fantasy, and this bothered Jenkins
greatly because Mather looked so comfortable, so *at home*
in it.

But Mather reached up and, with a deft hand, adjusted
the height of a plumb bob. Swinging a magnifying glass
and a tiny alcohol lamp into place, he squinted at the minute markings on a vernier and then made a note in pencil
on a tablet that was already covered with similar markings.
Suddenly, a catch released somewhere, and with an abrupt-
ness that made Jenkins start, another pendulum began
swinging with a quick *tick-tick-tick*.

It was precise, nerve shattering work, and it was all the
more nerve shattering for Jenkins, who, knowing nothing
about the operations of the apparatus that they had so carefully smuggled into the guest chambers of the palace,
could only stand aside and fidget. Mather's nap during
dinner had obviously done him some good, though, for he
had been able to assemble the complex equipment in the
dark hours after the banquet had broken up, and he looked

reasonably calm and rested as he slowly coaxed it toward the measurements for which it had been designed.

Tick-tick-tick.

He jotted another note. A stray breeze made the lamp-light flicker, and Mather looked up at the window with a combination of worry and annoyance.

"Do you want that window shuttered, Mather?" said Jenkins.

Mather seemed suddenly to come to the realization that there was someone in the room besides himself and his mechanical paramour. "No . . . no, sir. We'd suffocate in a trice. It's just that a sudden change in temperature can throw all these readings off. I'm trying for a level of accuracy that exceeds one part in ten thousand."

"Do you want to wait for morning?"

"No, sir. During the day there'd be the problem of vibrations caused by all the commotion out in the street. And, besides, the temperature is more stable at night."

"Day unto day uttereth speech . . ." intoned Mr. Wool from behind a writing desk on the other side of the room. With pen, ink, and paper laid out before him, the secretary had been sitting there silently all this time, his bony knees sticking well up above his ears because Kaprishan custom dictated that desks, like tables, should be no more and no less than twelve inches high. ". . . and night unto night sheweth knowledge. *There is* no speech nor language *where* their voice is not heard."

Jenkins closed his eyes, sighed. "Thank you, Mr. Wool."

"He that eateth, eateth to the Lord, for he giveth God thanks; and he that eateth not, to the Lord he eateth not, and giveth God thanks," came the solemn reply, and Wool's eyes, protected from direct scrutiny by thick spectacles, seemed to gloom into an uncertain future.

Jenkins, who had eatethed considerably more than he

had really wantethed to at the banquet, winced at the unfortunate reminder of the lamb curry with the grape sauce. Honor indeed! But he noticed that, true to form, Wool had taken down, in shorthand unintelligible to all save himself, the entire conversation about windows, temperature, and vibration.

The thought of the banquet and the terrible curry made Jenkins peer closely at Mather, who was still adjusting verniers and timing the swings of pendulums with the aid of an elaborate chronograph. What *had* passed between Mather and the strange individual named Bakbuk? Jenkins had been under the impression that Bakbuk had thought the entire matter a very large joke, and Abnel, pursing up his sugar-coated mouth, had assured him that such was the case. But that look from Mather . . .

Mather made another note. "Fascinating," he said. "Amazing."

Tick-tick-tick.

The sounds of the mechanism seemed very loud in the silence. Mather watched the pendulums as though hypnotized by them, and again Jenkins was reminded of the strange look that had crossed the engineer's face when he had been confronted by the stunningly seductive Bakbuk.

Strange person. Strange customs. Man/woman sworders, enigmatic high priests, explosions that destroyed hundreds of lives because of a difference in politics that had lost all meaning centuries before. . . . Jenkins suddenly felt very alone and out of place in this ornate box of a room.

> Bakbuk swings down
> towards the window
> of the Americans'
> chambers. What in
> Panas' name is that
> ticking sound?

Nerves, he reminded himself. Keep control of your nerves. It's nerves that do in diplomats a devil of a good deal more than knives or guns.

"Aha!" said Mather. He grabbed his pencil again and scribbled madly. "This looks like it, all right."

"Looks?" said Jenkins. "Looks like what?"

And from Mr. Wool came a low intonation: "But the Lord said unto Samuel, Look not on his countenance or on the height of his stature; because I have refused him: for *the Lord seeth* not as men seeth; for man looketh on the outward appearance, but the Lord looketh on the heart."

Jenkins turned to Wool in annoyance. As before, Wool sat with his knees up around his ears, oblivious of everything save the paper before him and the black marks thereupon. "Looketh . . . I mean, looks like what?" said Jenkins cautiously, ready to cut off any second attempt at interdiction on Wool's part.

"Well," said Mather,

> Bakbuk finds here
> that he has made an
> unfortunate
> miscalculation:
> though he is fluent
> in French, he is
> ignorant of English,
> and the Americans
> stubbornly insist
> upon speaking their
> own language among
> themselves.

"the gravitational deviation is definitely there. Well over five magnitudes on the Franklin scale. We're definitely dealing with a double crustal layer."

Jenkins glanced at Mr. Wool, but aside from noting

down the conversation, the secretary remained inert. "And . . . so?"

"So? Mr. Ambassador! We're dealing with a mountain range that exceeds anything else the world has to offer!" Mather pulled out a handkerchief, fluttered it loose, mopped himself. "You see, the crustal plate that carries this section of the globe—"

Jenkins lifted an eyebrow. Science was science, but correct science was, after all, correct science. "And how long have these crustal plates existed?" he asked. "Are they Ante-Diluvian or Post-Diluvian?"

Mather's mouth, caught in an open position by Jenkins' words, remained so for an instant and then snapped shut.

Jenkins' voice was mild. *Very* mild. "Well, Mr. Mather?"

A word to the wise being sufficient, Jenkins had used several for the benefit of Mather, and Mather cleared his throat and mopped himself with his handkerchief once more. "The mountains, sir, are extremely high. Forty-thousand feet or more. And since we're definitely dealing with a double crus—"

Jenkins lifted an eyebrow again. Given his dual status of minister and ambassador, no more comment than that was needed.

"Well," said Mather, flushing and apparently growing very warm very quickly, for he required yet another application of the handkerchief, "it means that the mountains go on for some distance. A thousand miles, perhaps. I'll be able to say more exactly when I'm finished with these readings and the polar calculations, but I'd estimate a thousand miles at the very least."

"A thousand miles . . ." Clasping his hands behind his back, Jenkins took a turn toward the window. "It would take a long time to cross a thousand miles."

"True."

"A thousand miles."

"Yes."

Jenkins stared out the window. Bakbuk
                                 stares
                                 down
                                 at
                                 Jenkins.

"Think of the casualties, Mr. Ambassador!"

Jenkins chuckled, but not at the casualties. No, he was
not concerned at all about casualties. Not, at least, about
American casualties. He was thinking, rather, of French
casualties, of British casualties, of Spanish casualties . . .
and of American casualties that might, by virtue of those
other casualties, be avoided. "But think of the surprise if
we succeed, Mr. Mather. Just think of it. Bonaparte tied
down in Egypt, as President Winthrop and the Synod think
he soon will be, and the best hope of the French rotting
among the sand dunes and the Pyramids. Rotting among
them, mind you, but nonetheless defending them against
all comers. That is, until . . ."

Jenkins leaned forward, examining the last lights of the
evening in Nuhr, while Bakbuk examines
                                 him in turn and
                                 notes that the
                                 ambassador's gray
                                 head is getting a
                                 little bald on top.

". . . until the Americans arrive. Out of nowhere. And
then *we* will have the French, and *we* will have Egypt, and
we will have the key to the British possessions in the Far
East, and the world will have to deal with the Righteous
States of America!"

A moving pendulum cast a moving shadow on Mather's
face. Back and forth. Back and forth. *Tick-tick-tick.* "But
that assumes . . . a great deal."

Jenkins stood before the window. His arms were folded as though he were surveying a personal fiefdom. "It does, Mather. But perhaps not as great a deal as one might think. I've already learned a few useful things about this heathen place. More than Inwa Kabir thinks. More even than Haddar thinks. Silence sometimes speaks more eloquently than words."

"I was dumb with silence: I held my peace, *even* from good; and my sorrow was stirred," intoned Mr. Wool.

Annoyed, Jenkins swung around to find that Wool, holding doggedly to his vocation, had written down everything he had been saying. Mather knew about the plan, to be sure, and so, probably, did Wool (though it was hard to tell exactly how much Wool knew about anything). Still, it would not do to have a written record of it, even in Wool's indecipherable shorthand.

"Destroy those pages," he snapped.

"Egypt *is like* a very fair heifer, *but* destruction cometh; it cometh out of the north," said Wool, writing his commentary even as he uttered it.

Jenkins strode to the table and snatched the pages from beneath Wool's pen. While Wool singlemindedly continued writing the closing phrase of the quotation from Jeremiah on the smooth surface of the table, Jenkins thrust the incriminating pages into the flame of one of the lamps until they took fire; but though they were burning fiercely in a few moments, the ambassador suddenly realized that there was neither hearth nor brazier in which to dispose of them.

"Damnation!" he muttered, and as Mather looked up, startled at the terrible oath that had come from the lips of his minister, Jenkins, his fingers beginning to prickle and sting from the heat, returned to the window and tossed the flaming pages outside. Doubtless, he thought as he turned away, they would burn up before they hit the ground; and

118   *Gael Baudino*

even if they did not, they would either consume themselves quickly or start a larger conflagration that would do an even better job of obliterating their contents.

But Jenkins did not see the thin, dark line of the rope that suddenly flicked across the window, nor did he see the lithe, girlish shape that passed through the field of view too quickly for all but the sharpest of eyes to detect.

> The papers do
> not start a
> fire. They
> do not even
> reach the
> ground.

Chapter Nine

Maumud was beating her.

Sari's old arms could offer no defense, and she writhed weakly beneath him, his fists pummeling her, the impacts turning quickly from a series of blows into a shattering environment, of pressure and trauma that came seemingly from all sides, compressing her, turning her from a woman to a small, withered thing that had, after crossing deserts, crept into a convenient shelter to die.

. . . *DUM-dum-DUM-dum-DUM-dum-DUM-dum* . . .

And the fists seemed now to strike *within* her, battering and rebattering her, shaking her.

. . . *DUM-dum-DUM-dum-DUM-dum-DUM-dum* . . .

Sari opened her eyes from her dream, but the battering continued, a hideous, sustained pounding. But to her surprise, the agency that so abused her was not a physical one. Or, at least, it was not of flesh and blood.

. . . *DUM-dum-DUM-dum-DUM-dum-DUM-dum* . . .

The house was hot, stifling. She blinked through a haze of thirst and hunger and saw that the room in which she lay was full of men who, crammed side by side, thigh by thigh, and hip by hip into the tiny space, were stripped to the waist and bare from knee to ankle. Sweat ran down from lank hair and beards, soaked into waistbands, dripped

from foreheads, flew from arms as they rhythmically
pounded on the great drums slung from their shoulders.

. . .*DUM-DUM-DUM-DUM-DUM-DUM-DUM* . . .

Confined by the thick walls, seemingly amplified by the
heat and the odor of what seemed to be at least fifty male
bodies, the sound was as much an oppressive presence as
the men, and as hands blurred with motion and chests
(concave, convex; thin, broad; naked, hairy) heaved with
strain, the drummers' eyes stared ahead glassily, their
owners as much victims as perpetrators of the massive,
sonic bombardment that seemed on the verge of shaking
the house apart.

. . . *D U M - D U M - D U M - D U M - D U M - D U M -
D U M* . . .

And Sari writhed on a thin pallet that seemed compounded of equal parts dust, rags, and cat urine (and, yes,
there was a cat now . . . no, two cats . . . hunkered down
on a refuse-crowded shelf that overhung the foot of the
bed, their eyes intent upon her as though they were waiting for something).

. . . *D U M - D U M - D U M - D U M - D U M - D U M -
D U M* . . .

"Naia," she whispered in a voice like dust, a voice she
herself could not hear for the pounding. "Naia . . . oh,
Naia, I am thirsty."

And the drumming quickened, grew, turning into a sudden crescendo of pure noise that Sari felt must surely
pound her into nothingness.

. . . *DUMDUMDUMDUMDUMDUMDUMDUM* . . .

"Naia . . ." She could hardly speak. She could hardly
think.

. . . *DUMDUMDUMDUMDUMDUMDUMDUM* . . .

"Naia . . . where . . ."

. . . *DUMDUMDUMDUMDUMDUMDUMDUM* . . .

Harder, faster, louder. The drums peaked, peaked again, and yet again, each surge of aural climax followed swiftly by another. And Sari, all but suffocating from sound and heat and thirst, clenched her fists and opened her mouth to add to the shuddering, heaving drums a cry of helplessness and despair that was in itself an expression of absolute impotence, for just as the drumming rose to a final crest and then fell away into a silence marred only by the screaming wails of a child in distress, her utterance, caught and held by her parched throat, guttered into nothing more than an arid gurgle.

A man spoke. "That was good. We all ended together. Very good. We started together, and we ended together. I see that I am doing a good job."

The child continued to scream.

"You see, Masstab, there is a reason for all that practice."

And the child screamed.

"She is not any better," came another voice. It was the woman who had brought Sari into her house. "Not . . . any . . . better . . ."

Seemingly heedless of her words, the man continued. "Starting together is good," he said, "but ending together is the most important, for by ending together we focus all the power that we have raised. You see, Masstab? That is the difference between a powerful ritual and a common ritual. I, for one, am tired of these insignificant rites that everyone practices. We are all adepts. We are all priests of Naia. Therefore, we should do powerful rituals."

And the child continued to scream.

The woman was distraught. "She is not any better . . . not *any* . . ."

And Sari finally remembered where she was and how she had gotten there. And she remembered, too, the flushed, fevered face of the child in the bed below its sparkling firmament of suspended crystals.

Child-fever. Sari knew it well, had nursed her own children through it, her motherly skills eked out by the knowledge of herbs that she had acquired during her Naian girlhood. And she shut her eyes and grimaced when she recalled how often Maumud had cursed her herbs and her Naian knowledge.

"And it is very important . . ." continued the man.

The woman's voice edged toward hysteria. "She is not better! *She is not better!*"

The man's prattle broke off for an instant, then, "Well, Zarifah, you must understand that Calieh decided to have this fever, and if she does not decide to get better, then there is nothing we can do."

"My daughter is dying!"

The man's voice turned patient. "If she is, then it is a decision that she made before she was born."

Zarifah finally broke down into incoherency.

Obviously, Zarifah, consumed with worry about her daughter, had dragged her unexpected guest across the room, laid her on the pallet, and then forgotten about her. But Sari flailed out and managed to turn on her side. "Please . . ." Her brain was smoky, dry, her vision so faded that she could make out only indistinct shapes. She was going to ask for a mouthful of water to take away at least a bit of the parched agony that possessed her, but the thought of the child—the child who was dying—silenced her personal request. "Please . . ." she managed. "She needs herbs. I . . . can help."

Zarifah rushed to the pallet. "You can . . . ?"

Sari bleared up at her, noting with a small particle of objectivity that Zarifah's imperious mannerisms of deportment and speech had thoroughly deserted her. "I . . ." Her mouth was so dry that she could barely form words.

". . . can help. I know herbs. Bring me earfeather and sweetstraw. Boil some water quickly."

"All right, men," came the male voice that had advised Zarifah that her daughter's ills were of her own making, "we have done all that can be done. Practice is tonight at dusk. The girls will be there, too. I will see you all then."

With a murmur and a stab of sunlight from the opened door, the men began leaving, but Zarifah was already dribbling water from an almost empty skin into a pot which she then put on a hook above the low fire. "Earfeather and sweetstraw," she said to Sari. She bent and blew on the embers, and the flame came up with a glow. "Those are what you want?"

The two were common herbs that grew almost everywhere, staples of any Naian herb chest. Sari was puzzled by Zarifah's question, puzzled also by the fact that she sounded as though she had never heard of them before. "Yes, those."

Zarifah looked disturbed. "Will not something else do?"

"What?"

"Well. . . ." Zarifah shrugged helplessly. "They are weeds. We do not keep weeds in our house."

Sari blinked at the filthy room that, if it did not have weeds, surely had to contain almost everything else in the world that was useless, broken, or cast off.

"I have some gem elixirs, though." Zarifah indicated a tumble of small glass bottles of the sort peddled by Panasian physicians.

For an instant, Sari fought for words, fought for her temper. Then: "In the name of Naia, and for the sake of your daughter, go out and get some earfeather and sweetstraw!"

As she spoke, though, she realized that the child's screaming had stopped, that the room was now terribly quiet. Staggering, she swayed to her feet, groped her way across the room, put her hand to the girl's cheek. It was cool, almost clammy. With a deep feeling of unease, she picked up a limp arm, felt for a pulse, found none.

And then she realized that the child's eyes were open, that they were staring sightlessly at the roof beams.

"Zarifah . . ." she managed. "I think . . ."

She could not finish the sentence, but Zarifah caught the meaning of her tone and rushed to her side. Amid the rattling of the dozens of crystals that still hung above the bed, the mother bent, looked. . . .

From outside, the man's voice drifted in: "You see, Masstab, this community needs a strong, male leader, and I think that I have been chosen to be that leader. This community needs focus, and I can bring it. Do not forget practice tonight: it is very important."

"But what of Calieh?" said Masstab.

"We cannot become too involved in her fate," said the man, "because she chose it freely before she was born."

At Sari's side, Zarifah began to sob, her emotion so deep and racking that it could not at first find utterance. Her face twisted, her eyes clenched, the mother leaned on the edge of the child's bed, her silent tears streaking down her face and beading her clothing as brightly as the hundreds of tiny crystals with which she had adorned it.

The man outside continued: "It is not our business to meddle with the fates of others. Calieh did not meddle with ours, and it would be foolhardy and dangerous to meddle with hers."

"That is true." Masstab sounded unsure. "But we worked magic for her."

"That is a different matter. You see—"

But Sari finally flared. Going to the window, she shoved the shutters open and, despite nearly being blinded by the bright sunlight, cried out: "In the name of the Goddess, hold your tongues! The child is dead!"

Her voice, untouched by water for over two days, was no more than a croak, but the men heard. Sari glared at them sightlessly, then turned back into the dark room and sagged against the wall. She felt the roughness of the dried mud against her back. "Is there any water, sister?" she managed. "I . . ."

Zarifah looked up. "Water?" she said. "You want water? You come to my house, arouse the anger of the demons against my child, curse my husband, and now you want water?"

Husband? Sari—dazed, dizzy—stared at her.

"Get out of my house!" Zarifah screamed. "Get out! The curse of the Goddess upon you! Go out and die, for that is your fate!"

Sari found herself unable to move. Weakness? Astonishment? She supposed that it was some combination of the two.

"And do not think that you will involve me in your fate," Zarifah continued, "for you have taken yourself out of the law!"

"Please," said Sari. "I just need some water. A mouthful . . . no more . . ."

"Get out!"

Stumbling, Sari groped her way toward the place where she vaguely recalled having seen a door. Behind her, Zarifah was torn between sobs and anger. Outside, the man—Zarifah's husband—was continuing with his instruction: "I could have told you yesterday that she was going to die, of course. I cast the lots and read the cards, and it was obvious. But I went along with the drumming for Zarifah's sake . . ."

Sari gained the street and fell face forward into the dust.

1) Inscriptions are carved in stone for many uses: for Foundation Stones and Public Inscriptions, for Tomb-

stones and Memorial Inscriptions, for Mottoes and Texts, for Names and Advertisements, and each subject suggests its own treatment.

Hearken all ye to the words of Panas, the Builder of the World, the Raiser of Cities, the Ordainer of Municipalities, the Shaper of Society. May His blessings be bestowed upon His people for all time, and in all nations may there be great and endless praise raised to Him.

It is indeed fitting, just, right, proper, and helpful that the most Holy Words of Panas (blessed be He!) begin with the most fundamental pronouncements upon the role of man in society and upon the orders of men all the way from the king, who is the very foundation stone of all endeavor and who is forever in the eye of the public (and fittingly so, for it is from him that the public derives its luster or its tarnish, its evenness or its roughness), to the basest of commoners whose garb and mannerisms cannot help but reflect their baseness.

But it is to the plurality of the creation of Panas (blessed be He!) that our attention is first brought. There are indeed many uses for men, and all, from highest to lowest, from first to last, are worthy of mention in the Sacred Text of Panas (blessed be He!). Here, the highest mysteries are already hinted at, seeing as it is only in context that the lives of men are judged. And should there be any doubt in a man's mind about his inclusion in the creation of Panas (blessed be He!), such doubts are certainly swept away by the enumeration provided by Panas (blessed be He!) immediately before the words of supreme power and ultimate mystery themselves, for surely among even these few there is a place for all men.

Is not the father the *Foundation Stone* of the house? Is not the merchant the *Foundation Stone* of his business? Is not the soldier the *Foundation Stone* of all the endeavors of his superiors, just as his superiors are the *Foundation*

Stone of the soldier's orders and provisions and strategies? Contradict this anyone who dares, but surely the scoffer will be confounded!

And as the *Foundation Stone* shall be deeply graven and signed with signs of its honor and its superiority to all other stones, he who is himself the *Foundation Stone* of others shall not hide his status beneath false pretense or humility, but rather shall trumpet it forth loudly and unceasingly. There is no place for the humble in the eyes of Panas (blessed be He!), either within or without. *Woman knoweth not Woman, but Man knoweth what Man is,* goeth the old saying, and surely these words, hallowed by time if not by the lips of the God (blessed be He!) Himself (blessed be He!), has much truth in it (though not as much truth as the words of Panas (blessed be He!), the God (blessed be He!) Himself (blessed be He!))!

Therefore, let the man who is the foundation of others constantly remind those whom he supports that he is their foundation. Let those whom he supports acknowledge their dependence upon him daily as all men acknowledge their dependence upon Panas (blessed be He!). Let the man who supports others be magnified by his support, and let others magnify him, for this is truly what Panas (blessed be He!) has ordered.

And though the just and honorable man dies, let not his reputation or his wishes die, for as *Tombstones* are deeply graven with *Memorial Inscriptions* so as to pronounce for all time the deeds of the living, so too should those laws and ordainments established in the past be kept for all time. Let them be changed only after much consideration, for though they be the only concrete sign of the foundation of the past that holds up the present, they have nonetheless been bequeathed to the living by the dead and are therefore worthy of preservation.

SO BE IT
ARDANE!

2) Color and Gold may be used both for the beauty of them and, in places where there is little light, to increase legibility.

Hearken all ye to the words of Panas, the Builder of the World, the Raiser of Cities, the Ordainer of Municipalities, the Shaper of Society. May His blessings be bestowed upon His people for all time, and in all nations may there be great and endless praise raised to Him.

Those who are magnified, let them be magnified with *Color and Gold,* all in their degree, for as *each subject suggests its own treatment,* the beauty and material gain of those upon whom all depends should shine forth in accordance with their degree. And thus has Panas (blessed be He!) ordained silk for the king and his family, linen for his closest nobles, cotton for his officers and those of honorable degree, and coarser stuff for all the rest. And let their magnificence shine out in *places where there is little light* for thusly are the unworthy convinced of their unworthiness and thereby prompted to better themselves, and thusly are the great honored in their greatness and thereby urged to be greater still.

SO BE IT
ARDANE!

3) There are two methods of arranging Inscriptions: The "Massed" and the "Symmetrical".

Hearken all ye to the words of Panas, the Builder of the World, the Raiser of Cities, the Ordainer of Municipalities, the Shaper of Society. . . .

Sari came to consciousness slowly, and for some time she could neither make out her surroundings (Certainly she was not outdoors, but where was she?) nor fathom the strange sensation that was upon her, a sensation that, had she found it necessary to put words to it, (and had the words been hers to put to it in any case), she would have described as an incongruous repleteness, a sensation of being full ... or at least comparatively full.

And then the reason came to her: her mouth and throat were no longer parched.

Death? She sat up, blinked. If this was death, then death was certainly a shabby little affair, with a dirt floor, heaps of rags and clothing everywhere, and a thing in the center that looked like a shambly little shrine covered with burning lamps, incense burners, strange rocks, little bells, an assortment of ill-made figurines of women in various poses, and a plethora of dust.

She lifted her eyes. Hangings—pieced, macraméed, woven—were everywhere, and had their domain been extended even a little, they surely would have made the room their own, transforming it into a grimy fabric maze of knots and faded color. But though they seemed content (for now, at least) to hang near the walls, their shadowed and ghostly fluttering made the house (or whatever it was that Sari was in) seem to undulate as though it were a stagnant tangle of floating kelp.

"Does the Goddess wish more water?" said a voice. And when Sari turned her head, she saw a young woman, clad in dirty white, kneeling at the side of the room, her form and face barely visible amid the flutter of hangings and the general obscurity. Beside her sat a young man, also clad in dirty white, also barely visible.

The man stayed where he was. The woman rose and approached. "I am Ayesha," she said. "But you may, of course, call me Goddess."

"O-of course."

"After all, we are all the Goddess, are we not?"

Deciding against pursuing that particular subject, Sari

only made an indefinite motion of her head that she hoped
would be construed as agreement. "You found me?"

"Lying in the street, Goddess," said Ayesha. "Yes. And
I brought you home. Rhydi, my husband, who is also the
Goddess (but in Her male aspect, of course), helped me
put you to bed, and I have been spooning water into your
mouth for most of the day. It is now evening."

"Yes . . . yes . . ." Sari hung, suspended, between grati-
tude and bewilderment. It was indeed true that Naia was
everything and everyone, that human beings carried within
them the divine spark about which flesh and form had co-
hered. The Hymns of Loomar said that over and over
again. But nonetheless, she found something odd, even unsettling, about Ayesha's interpretation.

"You are welcome in our house," said Rhydi. "Will you
be our guest?"

"Ah . . ." Sari attempted to rise, found that her limbs
were unwilling, for now, to support her. ". . . ah . . . I suppose so," she said, but then the memory of what had happened earlier that day returned, and with it, fear. "Do you
happen to know a woman named Zarifah?"

"Oh, yes, Goddess," said Ayesha, kneeling down at the
side of the bed. "We know her well. She is the Goddess,
and her husband, Golfah, is not only the Goddess in Her
male aspect but also the chief of the drummers of this village."

Something else seemed wrong now. Or, rather, seemed
more wrong now. Confused, Sari asked: "This village?
Where am I?"

"This place is called Halim, Goddess."

Sari struggled back to her previous thought. "Zarifah
cursed me this morning. She said that I had brought evil
to her house."

Ayesha made a small impatient sound. "Well . . . is that
not just like Zarifah? She has taken a little bit of this and

a little bit of that, and she has woven it all together into a snare that she has fallen into herself. She told you about knocks and about demons, did she not?"

"Y-yes . . ."

Another small impatient sound. "Well . . ."

"But . . ." Sari began to wonder whether she actually *wanted* Ayesha and Rhydi to turn her out, for she could come up with no other reason to be bringing up the unfortunate details of her first night in Halim. ". . . her daughter died. She blames me."

"Oh! Calieh!" Ayesha shrugged. "Well, Calieh made that choice."

"Ayesha! Calieh was but a child!"

Ayesha nodded as though Sari's own statement explained everything. "Doubtless, you are hungry, Goddess," she said, and her tone made Sari wonder whether she were being polite . . . or making excuses for her guest's obviously deranged concern about a child's death. "My husband and I have food for you. Will you eat?"

And then Sari suddenly realized that both Zarifah and Ayesha had referred to their men as their husbands, a distinctly Panasian term. Never had that been the case fifty years ago—then, married couples had called one another *helpmate*—but now it seemed to be a matter of custom. At least in Halim.

Husbands and wives: was that what had become of the Children of the Goddess? Just husbands and wives living in dirty houses? And crystals and demons and the gem elixirs of the Sculptor God . . . and no herbs from that Greenest Branch, Naia?

"The Caves . . . I will find the Caves . . ." she murmured to herself. "It will be clear, then."

Ayesha appeared to come to the conclusion that the old woman on the bed had an equally old mind that insisted upon doing its fair share of wandering, for she nodded as though agreeing with a child's benign imaginings. "I will bring food," she said, patting Sari's hand.

Sari watched her stand up. Well, at least they were kind. At least to the living. And though they might call one another husband and wife, and though some of their customs might have been influenced by Panasian society (not an overly remarkable turn of events, really, considering how powerful and influential Panasian society was), Sari had not noticed anything that resembled the blatant hierarchy of Panasian marriage.

Rhydi spoke suddenly. "Wife," he said, "I am hungry. Bring me my dinner."

"Immediately husband," said Ayesha, and in an instant she was gone from the side of the bed.

least a few of his intrinsic evil and power (Kuz Aswani, for example, did not doubt that Umi Botzu had ensorcelled him completely, and even now, on this very bright and very dry morning, the counselor was contemplating a dish of raisins—quite the proper breakfast for an up-and-coming ferret—while on the other side of the low table, Sabihah ate fruit and cheese and patiently rolled her eyes in response to her husband's occasional chitter), but for the overwhelming majority he was no more and no less than a curious and rather exotic addition to the already curious and rather exotic life of Nuhr ... something like Bakbuk, perhaps, though along more thaumaturgical lines.

He tried, though. He really tried. He made sure that his house was situated on the darkest of streets (which was, indeed, no mean feat, considering that, in any city theoretically mortared together by none other than Panas Himself, the thoroughfares were invariably broad and well-lit) and that it exuded (or at least attempted to exude) a sense of the ramshackle and the sinister that he thought very much in keeping with his declared vocation. But alas! though his house was, perhaps, ramshackle, it was not quite sinister, and, in any case, any sense of evil that might have accrued to the place was severely undermined by the small clump of purple hyacinths he had planted near his front gate.

Inside, where he endeavored to brood, he had slung a network of ropes and nets, creating something very like a dark, intricate web, but once again the effect fell far short of what he had envisioned, for though, slung in a hammock of netting midway between floor and ceiling, he tried to contemplate mazy plots and arachnidan intricacies, he could not resist occasionally seizing hold of a dangling rope and swinging from one side of the big front hall to the other, a trilling shriek of pleasure trailing behind him, escaping from the windows, and causing passers-by to either start in fear (if they did not know Umi Botzu) or tap their heads and smile (if they did).

And on this very bright and very dry morning, as Kuz Aswani took another try at frisking and chuckling simultaneously (bringing his head into a sudden and violent juxtaposition with the corner of the table and sending himself sprawling in a very un-ferret like manner), and as a special deputation of magistrates under the direction of Chief Minister Haddar looked for someone upon whom to fasten responsibility for the detonation that, a few nights previous, had leveled most of the Mud Dwellings to the south of the city, and as a group of soldiers and workers continued to probe the remains of those same leveled Mud Dwellings for the remains of those who had died in them, Umi Botzu, suspended between floor and ceiling, was considering his triumphs (few), his failures (many), and his prospects for advancement (none).

Ah, if he could only *really* be evil! Now *then* he would be someone to be reckoned with, and it would matter not a bit that his spells were shams, his incantations mere theater, his philters and his potions only admixtures of rose water, perfume, and an odd pinch of spice or two. Frauds? Of course they were frauds! But if he were truly evil, then perhaps he could make much more advantageous use of those frauds and so achieve something a little more prestigious than the duping of a minor counselor. Why, if he were indeed truly evil, the way could well be open to ... to the chief minister, perhaps, or even the king himself!

But he was not evil. He was, in fact, rather good natured, and as he looked at the netting and ropes that crisscrossed the interior of his not-quite-sinister house, Umi Botzu caught, through the open window, a glimpse of the bright colors of his purple hyacinths, and he became increasingly depressed at the thought of his triumphs (few), his failures (many), and his prospects for advancement (none).

But gradually, in the midst of his contemplation of the (few), the (many), and the (none), he began to become aware of a commotion somewhere outside. It was, indeed, a distant commotion, but it was a commotion nonetheless, and it seemed to have nothing whatsoever in common with the kind of commotion that had been produced by the explosions the other night (which had caused Umi Botzu to hide in a very unspiderlike fashion beneath the covers of his very unspiderlike bed).

Now, Umi Botzu was not familiar with lawns of the sort that were cultivated in Europe and in America, but if he were, he might have considered just then that commotions of the sort that one can hear at a distance—particularly commotions of the non-explosive variety—frequently disturb the well-tended lawn of society, thereby making it possible for certain vagrant representatives of the plant kingdom to gain a foothold in places where, under normal circumstances, they would have found any such attempt doomed to failure. And (again supposing that Umi Botzu was familiar with lawns of the above mentioned sort), armed with this thought, he might have temporarily abandoned his conception of himself as a spider and briefly assumed the persona of an opportunistic dandelion, or a particularly virile plantain, or maybe a robust spotted spurge.

Maybe. In any case, he lowered himself down from his net hammock, opened his door, and went out into the sunlight to see what was the matter . . . and what use he might make of it.

OK, so there's these two flits walking down this street in Africa. Girls with veils, lotsa local color, weird buildings, the whole magilla. The audience'll eat it up. You know, everybody's been waiting for something like this ever since that *Raiders of the Lost Ark* thing came down the pipeline a few years ago.

Anyway, so there're these flits. You know: fags. They're nice fags, though, which is real important for the plot, and we gotta make them sympathetic anyway 'cause the queers got a lobby now. But, like, these two've been cooped up on board their ship for a couple of months, and they're finally getting on shore. They're not interested in the girls, though. Get it? They're sailors, and audience wants to watch them see some skin, but they can't because the girls are all wrapped up, and on top of it, these two guys don't give a fuck about girls at all. (Hey, that's a good one, huh?)

Now the one is this captain guy. Scruffy. He's kinda fat, with a beard and a moustache. The other's his first lieutenant. Turtletrout. He's a real string bean. Laurel and Hardy all the way, by the looks of them. The crew's on board the ships on account of the honchos don't want them screwing everything in sight, 'cause it's a real anal culture down here on the African coast and it'd blow their whole mission sky high, you can bet on it. Boy, can you imagine all those randy sailors in a place like *Mecca* or something like that? With all the *Nuke the Towel Heads* flags waving like they are? We could make a bundle on it.

Well, they're not in Mecca, but it's kinda like Mecca, 'cause like I said it's all anal and everything and the girls all got clothes on (which is too bad, really, but maybe we can PG-13 it or something like that if we tone down the stuff about them getting their clits cut out and that sort of thing, but that's not in this scene anyway so don't sweat it).

OK, feature this. Real backwards place. Horses and camels time. Western technology they no got, even the 1790s kind, and there's nothing but men out on the streets (too bad about the girls, but like I said maybe we can get a PG-13) and here come these butt-fuck buddies humping along, and you better believe they keep their hands off each other 'cause queers don't last any longer where they're from than where they are right now, but they're real good at making goo-goo eyes at each other without letting on that that's what they're doing.

But they're looking at the sights today, and so we got a big chance for laughs. Ugly American stuff. "Oh, yeah," says one, "we got something just like it in Boston." Course, it's like a pagan *temple* or something like that and they couldn't possibly have one in Boston, but it'll keep the audience in stitches and they go on like that for a while. Don't know the language, so they talk to the locals real loud and slow. You know what I mean. Laughs there, too.

So it's hot, so they get thirsty, so they try a tavern. Course, you're in a tavern, so what do you want to do? Drink, of course. The locals understand that, even though Scruffy almost queers the whole thing (Hey, that's another good one, huh?) with some more of his pidgin English and bad grammar. So there's some more of that "we got one in Boston" stuff, and Scruffy gets into this argument with one of the locals about religion, 'cept, you know, the local thinks that he's talking about *camels,* see, and the sign language gets really wild, and the audience is on the floor. We can do subtitles like in *Annie Hall,* you know, where the schlep is talking to the girl and you hear what they're saying but you see what they're thinking. *¿Comprende?*

So they're in the tavern, and Scruffy and Turtletrout are playing a little footsie under the table, which is a kick and a half (OH, wow, man: I'm hot today!) 'cause the table's so low they can hardly move their feet), and Scruffy decides that he's gonna show these people what American technology is all about. So he starts dragging all this junk out of his pockets. He's got all kinds of stuff there. Magnifying glasses, and little clear things that go dark when you turn them (Whaddaya call 'em ... uh ... *polarizing* filters, yeah, that's it.) and stuff that makes static electricity, and that sort of thing, and he's showing off to the locals, doing tricks. Astound your friends, confound your enemies stuff. You know. And the locals freak out 'cause they think that what he's doing is magic. Roll their eyes a lot like that guy in the Charlie Chan movies. Remember that? *Zat yoo, Mistah Chan?* Roll, roll. Shuffle, shuffle. Wasn't that great stuff?

OK, so this is the problem. See, like I said, this is a really backwards place. The mucky-mucks don't want any magic. running around loose, and you can get in a lotta trouble by doing the old hocus-pocus stuff. Course, Scruffy isn't doing magic, but the thing is, the locals *think* he's doing it.

So Scruffy and his squeeze start getting the fish eye from some of the official types in the place, but you see, the two snugglepuppies have got the king's protection, and the mfwics don't want to raise a stink on account of the bad press that's liable to splash all over. Like, on *them*.

But Scruffy's getting fairly elaborate with his stuff. My God, he's got all kinds of shit there in his pockets. I mean, the man's a walking Edmund Scientific catalog. I mean, gyroscopes, hopping disks, tops, diffraction gratings (Hey, it's *fantasy*, right? He can have almost *anything* in there, so long as it's not an electron scanning microscope or something like that.) glow-in-the-dark stars, drinking birds, a Zippo lighter ... whatever. And the locals, see, now they're getting really edgy, because if this stuff is magic, they can get in trouble just for *looking* at it.

Something's gotta give, and, well, wouldn't you know it, something does. One of the locals does a core meltdown routine and starts screaming about magic and about eternal damnation, and he's so wound up about it that everyone else starts to get into the act, too, except for Scruffy and his squeeze, who don't understand the lingo, so they think that there's, like, a *festival* going on or something. They can Laurel and Hardy it up here, too, 'cause when the police arrive and haul them off, they think that they're gonna be guests of honor at some *party* (Yeah, that's it!) and they keep acting like nothing's wrong and like it's a big honor for them, and maybe they even give a speech or something (and no one understands *them,* either. Lotsa yucks, huh?)

Well, the crowd's up for lynching them right on the spot, 'cause they're worried that the priests are gonna find out that they've been looking at all this bad juju that Scruffy's been showing off at the tavern, and they want to cover it all up (Use subtitles here, too: it'll be a gas!) by fingering the Americans and then offing them, but wouldn't you know it, there's some law-and-order types there that want to string 'em up right, so instead of gutting them in the square alongside the whores and stuff, they take them to the magistrate that's on duty that day.

Now, this magistrate is a feep named Kuz Aswani, and he's been buffaloed by another feep named Umi Botzu into believing that he (I mean Umi Botzu) is a magician. What's more, Umi Botzu's got this guy conned into believing that he (I mean Kuz Aswani) is turning into a ferret. A couple of sandwiches sort of a picnic, both of them, but that's the way it is. Anyway, Kuz Aswani is, like, obsessive about this ferret gig, and Umi Botzu doesn't let him forget it for a minute.

In fact, Umi Botzu has been following this whole magic schtick from the sidelines, and he's all horny about it 'cause what Scruffy has been doing with the Edmund Scientific catalog looks like real magic to him, too. I mean *real* magic. I shoulda mentioned that Umi Botzu's bogus right down to the basement, but he's got his sights set a little higher than middle management types like Kuz Aswani, and so, like I said, he gets all horny over Scruffy's toys, thinking that maybe he can cop a few of them and take his show on the road.

So the last thing that old Umi wants is for Scruffy and Turtletrout to be offed, but the problem is that unless something drastic happens in the next few minutes, offed is exactly what they're gonna be.

But, brothers and sisters, salvation is at hand, 'cause it's Kuz Aswani up there on the bench, and though old Kuz is trying to lean over and look all hard nosed like that judge on *Perry Mason,* he's got to keep shoving down this urge he's got to scratch himself with his hind foot like a ferret ('cause that's what he thinks Umi Botzu's turning him into) and chitter and jump around on the floor like ferrets do, you know, and then things get worse for him when he sees Umi Botzu standing in the back of the room and he (I mean, Kuz Aswani) can't figure out what Umi's doing there just shaking his head like he's pissed off about the whole deal.

Eventually, though, Kuz Aswani gets the idea that Umi Botzu wants him to let the two queers off, which is fine with him, on account of the stink that'd be raised if the captain and his buddy got lynched. Besides that, he's worried shitless that Umi Botzu has something else up his sleeve, and that if he (I mean Kuz Aswani) doesn't toe the line, then the life of a ferret is gonna start looking pretty damned good in comparison.

So Kuz Aswani is perfectly willing to go along with letting the Americans off, but he's no dummy, and he's not turning handsprings over Umi Botzu starting to horn into his business in any case. I mean, it's one thing to have some guy turning you into a ferret, and it's another to have him dicking around with the rest of your life, too. You see what I mean? So Kuz Aswani is looking at Umi

Botzu, and Umi Botzu is smiling and nodding (Sheesh, this guy's a real shithead, you know?) and Scruffy and his squeeze are *still*, for crissake, thinking that it's some kind of party, and they're smiling and waving like drag queens at a gay pride march while all around them the locals keep getting more and more worked up.

Well, you know, someone's gonna have to bleed in here somewhere, and even though Kuz Aswani's not real sharp, he's sharp enough to see an opportunity when it runs up to him and hits him in the face with a cream pie like this one's doing now. So he gets to his feet, does a real good Bob Dole impression, works the locals up even more, and then points at Umi Botzu and says something about him (I mean Umi Botzu) being the focus of all the evil magic in the whole fucking *world*, and maybe the city'd be best rid of someone like that and he's not making any suggestions 'cause he's a magistrate but maybe there's a few good citizens around who know their duty.

Which is all the locals need, and they turn on Umi Botzu, thinking that they're gonna drag him out of the courtroom and bash his head in with a few handy rocks, only Umi Botzu gets wise to Kuz Aswani's plan about two seconds before Kuz Aswani gives him the finger and he does a *Hi-ho, Silver* out of that courtroom just in time. The locals all chase him, but he's got enough of a lead that he shakes them after the first block or so, which is all the excuse the crowd needs to go back to the tavern and drink it all off.

But that leaves Kuz Aswani with Umi Botzu running around loose, and he (I mean Kuz Aswani) knows that he (I mean Umi Botzu) is really steamed, what with nearly being killed by the crowd of locals; and since it was his (I mean Kuz Aswani's) idea to set him up for it, he (I mean Umi Botzu) is going to be hot for getting even, and boy,

I'll tell you, the life of a ferret is looking pretty good right now to Kuz Aswani.

So whaddaya think? Is it a deal? This kind of stuff is *perfect* for summer release, and can you feature the merchandising potential? Umi Botzu drinking mugs, and Kuz Aswani action figures that grow ferret tails and jump around when you pull the string, and . . .

"Well," said Captain Elijah Scruffy, "I suppose we shouldn't be expecting anything civilized from these people, but I really warn't ready for anything like this."

Perhaps, he thought (trying to be charitable), the people of the Three Kingdoms merely had short attention spans, and having been momentarily distracted from their merrymaking by something said by the keeper of the banqueting room to which he and Turtletrout had been brought, they had rushed out into the street to pursue some other entertainment. Or perhaps they had gone to find more revelers. Or perhaps . . .

But Scruffy, in accordance with his bent toward the slow and the methodical, had been disturbed by all the shouting and rushing about, and, in addition, he was nettled by the fact that the crowd's sudden decision to fete himself and Turtletrout had resulted in a number of his pocket curiosities being left on the table at the tavern.

And then for them all to turn around and run away because of a mere distraction! Imagine that! Why, there was no telling what might happen to his curiosities!

Turtletrout was looking around him in his slope-headed way, his hands in his pockets (Turtletrout had been promoted from before the mast, and therefore had not received the advantage of a midshipman's training regarding hands and pockets), nodding now and again as he examine the room in which he and his captain had been left alone save for a strange innkeeper. "It couldn't have been a very good party anyway," he said in his coarse way. "There's no eats or drinks that I can see, sir. There ain't even a kitchen."

"Oh," said Scruffy. "In great houses, they bring in the grub from other rooms."

"From other rooms, sir?" Turtletrout blinked, scratched his beard. "Tarnation, sir."

"Mr. Turtletrout! I'll have no swearing among my crew."

Turtletrout pulled off his hat and bobbed his head. "Yessir. Sorry, sir."

The innkeeper, though, was approaching them. He was a small man with a nose that was, to Scruffy's eye, almost as pointed as Turtletrout's, and the observation prompted the good captain to reflect for a moment upon the essential unity of mankind. Noses, ears, hair . . . everything pointed to unity, and the method of achieving that unity could not, of course, be anything save the most rigorously applied reason.

Except that the innkeeper's nose . . . well . . . *twitched* a little more than Scruffy thought . . . well . . . reasonable. Turtletrout's nose, was perhaps, just as sharp, but it did not (Oh, dear, there it was again!) twitch quite so . . . ah . . . *(Twitch!)* abominably.

The innkeeper halted before them and, for an instant, he made an indefinite motion with his foot as though he were going to attempt to scratch his head with it (another blow to Scruffy's theories regarding the unity of mankind); but then, as though with a sudden effort, he replaced the foot on the floor and bowed in the manner of the men of the Three Kingdoms.

"I have saved your lives, gentlemen," he said in broken French.

Twitch!

Saved? Lives? For a moment, Scruffy was bewildered,

but then he reflected that he really did not know the customs of this place very well. For all he knew, the slaying of the guests of honor might have been the high point of a Kaprishan party. And then there was still the matter of those explosions the other night . . .

"Yes," he said. "Well, that's very nice of you. Very nice indeed. I warn't expecting, you know, to be *saved* exactly, but, well, it's very nice of you to *do* it. Ain't it, Mr. Turtletrout?"

He was speaking English, forgetting that the innkeeper could not possibly understand him. But English, in Scruffy's opinion, was as good as French—better, in fact—and therefore he trusted to the innkeeper's innate intelligence to figure out what he was saying.

Twitch!

Turtletrout, his hands still in his pockets (and Scruffy winced inwardly at the thought of the impression Turtletrout was making upon these godless heathens), examined the innkeeper from beneath his sloping forehead. "Yup," he said.

The innkeeper again made as if to groom himself with a foot. Again, he appeared to stifle the urge. "I trust that the gentlemen will remember this."

Twitch!

"Of course," said Scruffy amiably. "We're Americans. We never forget a favor or a friend." He reached out, clapped the innkeeper on the shoulder with a massive, seafaring hand, and nearly sent the little man sprawling.

"Indebted," said the innkeeper *(Twitch!)*, bowing and withdrawing. "You are indebted. I trust you will *(Twitch!)* remember."

"Of course," said Scruffy, but the innkeeper continued to withdraw *(Twitch!)* until he reached the door on the far side of the room, and then, just *(Twitch!)* before he disappeared, he bounced two or three times with a soft *chuckle-chuckle-chuckle.*

"Don't understand it a bit," said Scruffy when the innkeeper had left. "Damned odd."

Turtletrout's eyebrows lifted to the brim of his hat. "Captain!"

"Oh, yes." Scruffy was abashed. "Sorry."

They went out into the sunshine together, Scruffy declaring that he was half of a mind to go back to the tavern and reclaim his curiosities. Turtletrout, however, dissuaded him, reminding him that, since the suddenness of the revelers' decision to have a celebration had prevented them from paying their reckoning, the curiosities would provide adequate recompense.

"And they might think that we're being ungrateful, sir," he added.

"Hmmm," said Scruffy. "I do believe you've got a point there, Mr. Turtletrout."

Turtletrout still had his hands in his pockets, but he nodded.

"Interested in a game of chess, Mr. Turtletrout?"

"I think I might like that, sir."

"*Without* the ambassador and his men next door?"

"Even better, sir."

Together then, in a very masculine and American way, they went down the street toward the harbor. They had not gone more than a hundred paces, however, before a short, roly-poly, rather jolly-looking man stepped out from an alleyway and bowed to them in the manner of the men of the Three Kingdoms.

"I have saved your lives, gentlemen," he said in broken French.

Chapter Eleven

Overcome by hunger, thirst, and exposure, Sari lay ill for some days. But though, as she drifted in and out of exhausted sleep, she was frequently unsure where, exactly, the boundaries between dreaming and waking lay, this was a minor point compared to her greater unsurety as to the location of the dividing line between fantasy and memory. As far as she had ever been able to tell, the recollections of Naian life that she had preserved from her childhood had been reasonably accurate; but as she convalesced and became more aware of what went on about her, she slowly discovered that those recollections corresponded only superficially both to what she saw taking place in the house of Ayesha and Rhydi, and, when she was at last able to stagger outside, in the Naian community as a whole.

And, within the roots of the Mountains of Ern, a snarl of conflicting stress vectors within the living rock— compression, expansion, shear—

There was something wrong, some subtle, underlying difference between what she remembered and what she now witnessed. Had Sari been a casual observer, she might have noticed nothing particularly amiss, but Sari was not a casual observer. She was a Naian. And moreover, she was a Naian who had returned to her faith and her people with something that, though perhaps a little less than the unquestioning fervor of the convert, was certainly more than the unquestioning acceptance of the birthright believer.

And so, when Rhydi told Ayesha to bring him his dinner, Sari noticed that Ayesha immediately put aside whatever she was doing and did his bidding. And when, in the middle of the square, Zarifah listened to Golfah lecturing her about the rightness and inevitability of the death of their child, Sari saw that she listened without complaint, with, in fact, a kind of tacit agreement that Sari, a mother herself, could not comprehend. And while to a Panasian ear the terms *husband* and *wife* that were so freely used here in the Naian quarter might have seemed mere commonplaces, they were, to Sari, a shocking departure from hallowed custom.

—*finally, under the lubricating influence of water that has been infiltrating the multiplexed strata for nearly three hundred years...*

"Oh," said Rhydi when she asked him about this last alteration, "is there something else?"

"Well," she said, "in my memory ..." Her memory! "... Naians have always simply called one another *helpmate*."

"Helpmate." He contemplated the word. "Odd. That does not make much sense, though."

"I do not understand," said Sari. She thought back to what she had learned as a child, what had been evident in the relationship of her parents. "It is a matter of equality in the eyes of the Goddess, and of the partnership that is the basis of making children and establishing a family." Her old voice almost shocked her: here she was, stumbling back to Naianism after a betrayal of five decades, and she was speaking to this young Naian man as though she were an elder of her religion!

"I can see your point," said Rhydi in a tone that indicated that he did not see it at all. "But, you see, we must always respect the complimentary powers of man and woman."

Sari blinked. "Powers." The word seemed ill-suited to the egalitarianism of a Naian relationship.

"Yes, powers." Rhydi sat down on his pile of cushions. He contributed a very small amount to the household budget by telling fortunes for clients, both (legally) Naian and (illegally) Panasian, and, to his credit, he made sure that he rested himself thoroughly between appointments. "You see, there is man's power, and there is woman's power, and each has its place. We have to respect that place, and honor each equally."

Indeed, it made a kind of sense. But . . .

"We have to achieve *balance* in all things, and so we must acknowledge one another as individuals who are different, and who have different tasks and different abilities. Husband and wife. You see?"

This was going too far. "Ah . . . no."

Rhydi shrugged and settled himself into his cushions. They were the very best cushions he had been able to find. All of the profits from Ayesha's weaving for a month had gone toward those cushions, and, to his credit, Rhydi appreciated them greatly. "Well, you probably just have to meditate on the subject."

. . . *LETS GO*.

"When I was a boy," he continued, "I had a teacher who could trace her lineage back to one of the first Naian priestesses to cross the Mountains of Ern. She knew all about complimentary powers, you see, even though she did not say very much about them." He settled himself a little farther down into the cushions that he had bought with Ayesha's money, and, to his credit, he was obviously very comfortable. "I mean, she would have had she thought of it."

Sari was reassured that a woman had taught Rhydi, but she was dismayed to find that he had not learned his religion from his mother, as was—or was that *as had been,* or maybe *as she had believed had been*?—the custom. "Did your mother die?" she said. "I am so sorry."

"Hmmm? Oh, no, mother did not die. But, well, you see, she was just a mother. I wanted to learn my religion properly, and so I went to a teacher."

Sari lifted her old hands, touched her old face. Wrinkles. Age. She was a mother, or, rather, according to Rhydi, she was *just* a mother. Her children, though, were gone: the boys to the fellowship of male dominion, the girls to rich merchants. She had never taught any of them about Naia. Just a mother. "I ... I suppose that was ... wise ..."

"Helpmate." Rhydi contemplated the word again. "Odd word. I do not think that I have ever heard it before. I will bring it up with the men at the meeting tonight." He settled himself even deeper into his cushions. To his credit. "You know, Sari, it is so wonderful to have you as a guest. All these little old ways that you can remember—why, it gives me a very spiritual feeling."

Fractures, vibrations, spread suddenly, the ripples of force reaching out across the land ...

"I would not know," said Sari. "I fear that I am just a mother."

Her irony was, perhaps, a little too evident in her voice, but, just then, the ground swayed ever so slightly. Ayesha's hangings quivered, and a pot on a shelf rattled with a brittle sound.

Sari jumped involuntarily. She was nervous these days: there was always the possibility that bailiffs from her old village would come to Halim looking for her, wanting to ask her questions ...

"Earthquake," she murmured, trying to calm herself by the utterance of a plain, factual name. Earthquakes were a part of life. There had always been earthquakes, would, doubtless, always be earthquakes. Odd, though, that they seemed to be occurring more often as the years went by.

"Naia's demons," said Rhydi. "How they rattle their great chains!" He nodded knowingly. "The Goddess will loose them upon us if we do not obey Her laws."

"But . . ." Sari felt as though more than the earth had been shaken. "But Naia is our Mother. Mothers do not send demons to hurt their children."

"Perfectly correct," said Rhydi, "but, you see, Naia has her hard, male aspect as well as her soft, female aspect. Respect for her laws—"

Sari pressed her hands to her face. "How do I get to the Caves of Naia?" she interrupted.

Rhydi stopped with his mouth open for a moment, then: "The Caves, Sari? No one goes to the Caves anymore."

Sari dropped her hands, looked at Rhydi. "No one . . . goes . . . ?"

"Because of Naia's demons, you see. It is too dangerous."

. . . *upsetting the paltry creations of human beings.*

The pot that had rattled fell suddenly from the shelf and shattered on the floor as the door swung open and Ayesha entered the house, her eyes bright. "The tapestry, husband," she said excitedly. "I have sold the big tapestry."

Rhydi nodded. To his credit, he was most enthusiastic about Ayesha's successes. "Very good, wife. Give me the money, and then bring me my dinner."

Ehar felt the ground sway as Paal and Marrak took some of the camels down to the miserable little trickle that was all that was left of the once-great River Forshen. With a long, dark finger, he tapped the gold ring that dangled from his left ear, but the genie who lived within, concerned only with sandstorms, evinced no desire to enlarge his field of expertise.

Behind him, he heard the flutter of cotton cloth as the women folded and packed their tent in the dry wind. Paal and Marrak continued to lead the camels toward the river (such as it was), but the rest of the men were preparing to load one of the beasts that had already had its drink. Understandably, it was struggling and spitting, but Oued rapped it smartly on the nose and, knowing full well that, where Oued was concerned, a rap on the nose was only a beginning, it settled down.

After a moment, the ground also settled, but not so Ehar's concerns. "Paal! Marrak!" he called, "hurry up there and let us be off."

Paal handed the bridles of his camels to his brother and jogged up to the slope to Ehar. "You felt the heaving, father?"

"Yes I did, and I want to be away from this riverbed now."

"But surely a river surge would not come so soon!"

Paal was young. Oh, he was old enough to learn the ways of the caravan, perhaps, but he was most certainly young in experience. "Maybe," said Ehar with a trader's ingrained caution. "But there is no way to predict when the surge will come or how big it will be, and this close to the mountains I do not wish to take chances. I once saw half a caravan carried off by a sudden surge." He indicated the walls of the wide, dry riverbed that spoke of better days for River Forshen. Better days now long past. "It filled a valley much like this."

Paal's eyes widened, but Ehar turned back toward the women and their tent. "Yalliah! Hurry! We must be away from here!"

"Oh, husband!"

"Hurry!"

Yalliah, heavy and shrewd, made him an obeisance that (Ehar was sure) was entirely insincere. With an inward laugh, he flicked his earring again, but the genie knew just as much about river surges as Ehar did about wives—that they were there, that they were often unpredictable, that one had to deal with them and (in the case of wives) love them—and so, wisely, remained silent.

Mr. Mather was restless.

Jenkins was off in another part of the palace, enduring yet one more game of verbal blind-man's-buff with Haddar; Wool was sitting at his low desk, staring straight ahead with his knees poking up above the level of his ears; and Mather was right where he had been for the better part of a week: in the palace chambers, fretting and trying to think of something to do. He could, he supposed, have set up the apparatus, repeated his measurements, and then broken down the apparatus and stowed it away again (which would have done away with, perhaps, two or three hours), but he had already repeated his measurements several times in the last several days, and he had received the same answers as before. Though, until now, his life had revolved about such pieces of apparatus and the measurements that they produced, Mather had reached the point at which he would do *anything* rather than face that intricate collection of pendulums, plumb bobs, gears, rods, wires, and damnable *tick-tick-tick*s again.

And why should he face it again in any case? He had done everything that he could possibly do in Nuhr. If Jenkins could get him up into those mountains—or even close to them—he could do considerably more, but for now he was finished, for now he was done, for now he had absolutely nothing with which to occupy himself, and yet for now—and for the foreseeable future—he was stuck in a set of palace rooms that seemed to grow smaller and drabber and more confining and less private every day. He had even considered asking Jenkins for permission to return to *Seaflower,* but he knew that such irregular behavior on the part of someone who was supposed to be a high-ranking diplomatic assistant would immediately be vetoed by the ambassador (and probably brutally so: Jenkins was getting nowhere at all with Haddar, and his frustration was beginning to show).

Jenkins knew that Haddar was examining him with growing irony. Well, that was to be expected: the chief minister was holding all the cards and, therefore, had only to sit and watch as the American ambassador made a fool out of himself. Haddar had to agree to nothing: the Righteous States had come begging at his door, and Haddar was making sure that Jenkins knew it.

"Father, I am simply asking you to give a hearing to the Americans. Here they have come knocking on our door, and it does not seem at all right that we leave them standing outside of our house, ridiculed in the sight of all. I can tell you that their ill will must certainly come of this, and that it is very possible that their ill will is nothing that we want to incur."

Mather chafed: was it *his* fault that all his training in engineering had unsuited him for diplomacy? Was it *his* fault that Jenkins wanted to keep him out from under the gaze of the indefatigably hostile Haddar?

In truth, though, Mather's distress was amplified and compounded by something else, something about which he had to observe the strictest silence, not because he feared yet another biblical quotation from Mr. Wool (who mournfully uttered enough of them even *without* any encouragement), and not because it might bring an angry reproof from Jenkins, but rather, because it would certainly get him killed.

Oh, it was bad enough on board ship with all those suntanned men running around without their shirts, but at least the corrosive effects of the sea air and the pervasive dampness of the ship had required him to make a constant job of cleaning and maintaining the gravimetric apparatus even while it was in storage, and, as a result, he had been able to keep himself occupied, his thoughts under control. Here, though . . .

Mather found that he was again thinking about Bakbuk, found also that his palms were sweating. Again. With a furtive glance at Mr. Wool, he clenched them, opened them, wiped them nervously on his breeches.

"In the sweat of thy face shalt thou eat bread," intoned Mr. Wool.

"Uh . . . yes . . . of course, I agree completely," said Mather, hoping that quick agreement would silence Wool.

No such luck. "If two of you shall agree on earth as touching any thing that they shall ask, it shall be done for them," came the reply.

Damnation, Mather cursed inwardly. *I've gotten him started.*

But Wool, who was also barred from the ambassador's conferences with Haddar because of his unfortunate habit of saying what Jenkins did not want said and writing what Jenkins did not want written, fell back into gloomy silence. Mather wiped his hands again . . . cautiously.

But there it was: the ache in his stomach, the ache in his groin, and he had nothing with which to occupy himself. And if he spoke or moved, then he would have to listen to another one of Wool's quotations which, annoying as they were, could not but also remind him of the fate that America meted out to individuals like himself. And, now that he was thinking of it, the Three Kingdoms were much the same, if not worse: in the course of the few official tours of Nuhr that had been allowed the Americans, the sight of women impaled or staked out in the blinding heat of the city squares had become exceedingly familiar to him, and when he had asked one of the king's French speaking attendants about their male counterparts, he had received in reply only an "Oh, it would not do to speak of it, monsieur."

They were heathens. Godless heathens. Primitive, Godless heathens.

"My son, you must understand that they are but barbarians."

And so Mather wiped his hands again and waited for Wool to make another comment, absolutely positive that he would shriek if he did.

Again, Wool refrained, but Mather, already tense, nervous, and on the verge of shrieking anyway (and now doubly angry at Wool for not having given him an excuse to shriek), jumped up and made for the door. He had to go ... somewhere. He had to do ... something. He knew what he wanted to do, of course, but that would have been out of the question even under the best of circumstances, and these were most certainly *not* the best of circumstances.

"I've got to go," he said, but even though he slammed the door behind him, he did not slam it quickly enough:

"That thou mayest say to the prisoners, Go forth; to them that *are* in darkness, Shew yourselves."

Mather ran.

But Jenkins had been in Africa before, and he understood the ways of the African mind. This was a

"We must be cautious. These people come to us without invitation, intrude upon us, and ignorantly

game, and Haddar had the upper hand, and Haddar was going to exploit that fact, enjoy that fact. It was, perhaps, a mark of the lack of culture of the Africans' lands that they took such pleasure in these matters. pollute the holy waters of our capital; and, though I must have it thought about, this demonstrates very well their lack of culture. They play games with us, treat us as children, and take pleasure in these matters."

There were guards stationed outside the Americans' door, to be sure, but as the days of the embassy's presence had lengthened, both the Americans and the guards had become increasingly used to one another, and now Mather (who, only a few days ago, had been followed to the privies and watched with a suspicious eye as though a single drop of his urine might pollute the entire land) was, despite the lateness of the hour, allowed to leave the room unmolested and make his own way down the well-lit corridor.

Distracted, and having no particular destination, he quickly became lost in the labyrinthine passages of the palace. Corridors, rooms, stairs, hallways, corridors, cul-de-sacs, wings, gardens ... he had passed by or through a number of all of them before he finally came to himself and realized that he had not the faintest idea where he was.

And, coupled with the lateness of the hour, the fact that the men of the Three Kingdoms tended to sit down and stay put until business called them elsewhere ensured that Mather was not only lost, but also that he would have no opportunity to meet anyone who could assist him in becoming unlost. In fact, he was now outdoors (with no idea of how to get back indoors), in a garden he had never seen before ... but, then, he had not seen most of the gardens before, because—water guzzlers that they were—they were reserved for the use of the king, the prince, and a few very high-ranking ministers.

He was, though, almost relieved at this new development. Here, no one would see him. Here he would have some privacy, with no penetrating and caustic observations from old gray Jenkins or annoying biblical quotes from Wool; and if he were discovered trespassing, why, he could always cry diplomatic immunity, which might, to be sure, end the mission, but would at least save him from an *Oh, it would not do to speak of it, monsieur.*

He was half of a mind to drop behind a row of rose bushes and attend to some of his needs right then and there, but a movement that he caught out of the corner of his eye made him decide against it. Privacy? Well, perhaps he had gained a little of the commodity, but his isolation was apparently not yet complete.

Moving cautiously, therefore, he made his way past the rose bushes and along the formal and elaborate paths of the garden, seeking a more secret place, a more perfect privacy. The night was cool, and here, in contrast to the dusty aridity that seemed to hold the entire city—the entire land!—in its grip, the well-watered earth turned the air moist and fragrant with the odors of a thousand flowers.

The odors, the tinkle of fountains, the rustle of his shoes in the grass: it was all quite intoxicating, and Mather, wandering in darkness, seeking always paths that would lead him deeper and deeper into this moist, fragrant place, felt almost as though he were floating, drifting along in a sea of luxury and moonlight.

And Jenkins considered the futility of the task he had been given. He and Haddar had nothing in	*"Father, these matters are not insurmountable. Surely America and the Three Kingdoms have many*

common: not religion, not culture, not even the ephemeral vocabulary that was the product of millennia of shared history. Haddar might well have been a member of a different species. And those bloody coal black eyes!

things in common, not the least of which is a desire to better themselves, which is the desire of men everywhere. We cannot continue to treat the Americans as though they are animals, even if their skins are a rather disgusting color."

But Mather was being followed. He knew that he was being followed. Whenever he looked behind him, he could see movement. It stayed mostly out of sight, but it allowed enough of itself to be seen so that he could not but know that someone was there . . . and that someone was drawing closer.

Strangely enough, though, he did not mind in the slightest that someone was drawing closer. The garden had ravished him, and when a sudden strange turning of the path took him both into absolute darkness and into a pair of strong, fleshy arms, he could do nothing else—*wanted* to do nothing else—but yield to them.

And Jenkins could not but wonder what thoughts motivated men like Haddar.

"Where are you getting ideas and thoughts like that, my son?"

Chapter Twelve

The writing made no sense.

Bakbuk was back to being a girl today, and (perhaps out of frustration, perhaps not) had gone to more pains than usual with her appearance, but the precise arrangement of her hair beneath her head cloth and the slightly-more-than-completely-legal amount of throat that she was showing below her face cloth were not at all in her thoughts (even though she *was* beginning to suspect that those new herbs were working and that she was starting to develop just a trace of breasts). She was, instead, preoccupied with the half-burnt paper on the table before her.

It was the most maddening document that she had ever seen. Not only was the paper itself of a peculiar fashion, but the writing on it seemed such a hodgepodge of squiggles, lines, and dots that it was as if someone had dumped a handful of tiny worms into a bucket of ink and thereafter allowed them to crawl across the surface of a clean, white page. She was not even sure which side was up. (Did the Americans write in columns? Right to left? Left to right? Boustrophedon?)

Was the document even in English?

She could, she supposed, have taken the paper directly to King Inwa Kabir. But Bakbuk, who, in her entire life, had never hesitated in making a transition—whether from male to female, female to male, sworder to sex object, sex object to sworder, or whatever—was hesitating now, for with the coming of the Americans, she sensed that previously unknown desires and wants were beginning to manifest in the inhabitants of the palace of Nuhr, or, rather, that motives and forces that had before been held in check were now suddenly finding avenues by which they could move forward. The Prince was looking at the Americans and seeing opportunity. The Gharat was looking at the Americans and seeing opportunity. The Americans were looking at the Three Kingdoms and (Bakbuk suspected) seeing . . . opportunity.

Under normal circumstances, her course of action would have been clear, but these were not normal circumstances. If she gave the paper to the king, the king would, doubtless, immediately show it to the Prince or to the Gharat, and Bakbuk (who, for all her predilection for sexual metamorphosis, was utterly loyal to Inwa Kabir) had seen the Prince's nocturnal escapades and had overheard his conversations with his father; and she had seen also the Gharat's purposeful stalking of Mr. Mather . . . and his tumid success the other night.

So Bakbuk, chin in hand and breasts just beginning to bud, stared at the paper, pondering the question of who could translate the unknown writing for her.

The answer came to her suddenly, and she laughed. Of course! She should have thought of it earlier. The most powerful man in Nuhr, the most powerless man in Nuhr. How obvious! And with a swish of skirts and a concealed dagger (and an appreciative look in the mirror: yes, her breasts were beginning to show), she was out of the room, making for the streets, making for the shop of Citizen Valdemar.

* * *

Bronze by gold . . .

Comment upon the serendipitous juxtaposition of intellectual judgment, emotional need, and real world event as demonstrated by circumstances surrounding the visit of one Sari to the village of Halim in Kaprisha, West Africa, located at an approximate longitude of 00°, 25′, 35″ East; and latitude of 21°, 14′, 47″ North.

The intellectual judgment, emotional need, and real world event relevant to the narrative at this point are, to wit: Sari's increasing disillusionment (intellectual judgment) with the practice of her religion (that is, Naianism) in vogue at the time of her arrival in Halim; her desire to counter that disillusionment (emotional need) with a spiritual experience of undeniable authenticity and import (that is, a visit to the Caves of Naia); and an available form of transportation (real world event) suitable for the conveyance of an old woman across 150 miles of barren desert (that is, the arrival of a caravan bound for Katha).

What interpretation might be given to the providence of this juxtaposition by practitioners of the Panasian religion?

The lay practitioners of the religion are forbidden not only to make any public interpretations of doctrine but even to quote from their Sacred Texts; however, the priests, particularly the priests of the city of Katha, being allowed both to interpret and to quote (subject, of course, to the approval of the Gharat of Nuhr), would explain at length that said juxtaposition is not at all a matter of chance, but rather a predestined and inescapable outcome of decisions made by the Quintessential Deific Force (QDF) before the world began. As the sculptor envisions the end product of his artistic endeavor and moves incrementally but directly through the steps and processes necessary to realize it, so Panas (the QDF) envisions the universe not only in its final form (which no mortal will ever know) but also in every one of the infinite intermediate states that will exist preparatory to the realization of that final form, these intermediate states being just as fixed and inescapable as the final form itself. In this interpretation, then, Sari's needs, her meeting with Ehar, and his agreement to allow her to travel with his people were all preordained from the beginning of time, determined not for the convenience of the unlettered practice of a heathen religion, but rather for the glory of Panas Himself (the QDF).

And in the case of the practitioners of the Naian faith?

This question has vexed some of the subtlest minds of the late 18th century. Do the practitioners of Naianism as a class have an opinion from which can be drawn general conclusions as to faith or doctrine? Or, given that each practicing member of the religion is considered to be, *de facto,* a member of the clergy, must the individual opinion of each discrete Naian be considered a quantum unit of belief that is unto, of, and within itself inviolable, indivisible, and incapable of being considered in conjunction with any other? Numerous arguments along both lines have been made, the most noteworthy being Joinaud's incomparable *Exegesis of Leng: Doctrine and Supposition* (Anglo-American Cyclopaedia, New York, 1917), which, though it falls outside the purview of this historical period, covers the question in depth in Section III.

That being said, some similarities of opinion regarding the subject at hand can indeed be found among sundry groups of Naians, though whether these similarities stem from general paradigms of belief or are merely coincidental cannot at this time be determined (*q.v.* Joinaud's *Exegesis*). Three of these follow:

1) Sari, as she is co-equal and consubstantial with an

immanent Goddess, has complete control over all aspects, physical and non-physical, of her life. Hence, she herself decided to marry her (late) husband, Maumud, she herself decided that she would aggravate him to the point at which he would die under suspicious circumstances, she herself decided to allow the practice of her religion to degenerate, and she herself decided to despair.

2) Sari, having existed prior to her present lifetime in an omniscient, interincarnatory state, essentially chose for herself all the conditions, circumstances, and events of her subsequent incarnation, and therefore has only herself to blame for any less than satisfactory occurrences in said life.

3) Sari's interpretation of her life is solely the product of her mindset, and therefore, any negative interpretation she might have of what are essentially neutral events—her clitoridectomy upon her conversion to Panasism, for example, or her frequent beatings at the hands of her (late) husband, or her dismay at the degeneration of Naianism—are hers and hers alone.

In general, though, it appears to be impossible to determine with any degree of certainty a characteristic Naian view of the aforesaid juxtaposition.

What interpretation was, in fact, given to this juxtaposition by Sari herself?

That of a direct, personal, and loving divine interest, as might be expressed by a mother toward a daughter, an aunt toward a niece, a sister toward a sister, a grandmother toward a granddaughter, a female marmot toward her young (both male and female), or a member of the sentient and hermaphroditic race of the third planet of the star Zeta Eridani toward almost everything (though these last two are, possibly, doubtful, based as they are upon predicted but nonetheless hypothetical future incarnations of the individual soul presently named Sari).

Did Sari herself possess any elegant and concise verbal framework into which to put her beliefs regarding this juxtaposition?
She did.

Could that framework be expressed for the benefit of the reader?
It could.

Express that framework.
Naia provides.

"Wool," said Jenkins. "Have you seen Mather?"
"I shall see him, but not now," said Wool. "I shall behold him, but not nigh."
(Bronze by gold . . .)

Bakbuk minced and simpered her way through the streets of Nuhr. Here in the capital city, the paving was good, though worn, but the desert sands (encroaching since the drought began three hundred years ago and more than likely present to some degree even before that) crunched beneath the soles of her embroidered sandals and occasionally added to her gait what she considered to be a delightfully helpless looking sideslip—though if any man had tried to exploit that illusory opportunity he would have found a very unillusory dagger thrust expertly between his ribs.

In truth, Bakbuk was taking a little more than a woman's standard risk today, for, disguised as she was in the garb and demeanor of a Panasian woman—a very attractive Panasian woman, in fact, who had added to her lengthy list of charms an obvious tendency toward a decided *looseness* (as evidenced by that hand's breadth of soft, naked throat-flesh)—she was alone, unaccompanied by a man, unescorted even by a slave . . .

(Bronze by gold . . .)

. . . and this, at least in theory, left her open to immediate arrest, summary trial, and instant punishment. Actually, Bakbuk was benefiting from her own reputation here, for as her status and position at the court of King Inwa Kabir made her immune from prosecution for either her violations of sumptuary law or her lethal retaliations for molestations of any kind—sexual or legal—the local authorities, from the highest magistrate to the lowliest municipal bailiff, were understandably reluctant to approach *any* unescorted woman out of fear that she might turn out to be the hot-tempered sworder.

And so Bakbuk found no interference as she went on her way down the Street of Panas' Benevolence, past the turning to the Avenue of the God's Love, across the Square of the Divine Statue, along the tree-lined Way of Righteous Worship (though the trees, not being fortunate enough to reside in the king's garden, had withered long ago from lack of water), through the Alleyway of Priestly Tolerance, under the Arch of Omnipotence that led into the Byway of Magisterial Indifference, and finally, into a tiny embroidery shop on the Promenade of the Justified Wealth of Merchants that belonged to one Citizen Valdemar, one-time officer of the ill-fated *Frères Marseillaise*.

On her way, though, near the middle of the Square of the Divine Statue, she passed the market stall of a certain Baroz, a rug merchant. Baroz was tall and slender, and he carried himself with a youthful grace that belied the gray whiskers that covered his face. Being something of an incorrigible flirt, Bakbuk had not been able to resist a little

extra wiggle of her hips at the aged merchant, but if old
Baroz had anything on his mind save the price of his rugs,
he gave no indication . . .

(Bronze by gold . . .)

. . . until, of course, he stepped back into the shadowed
interior of his stall, pulled off his beard, and discarded the
dusty brown garb he had been wearing. Then he was revealed to be none other than Prince Aeid himself, who always had something on his mind and who had been
carrying on this particular deception (among others) for a
number of years.

"Bakbuk," he said to himself, peering out the window.
"Hmmm, and with something on her . . ." He paused, considered. Pronouns were always a little problematical where
Bakbuk was concerned. He decided, though, to go with his
first inspiration. ". . . on her mind. And in her belt, I imagine. Hmmm."

But while he was considering what disguise might be
appropriate for following the pretty sworder through the
city, a cry came from the front part of his stall. "Baroz!
Baroz!"

"What?" said Aeid in his normal voice. He caught himself, though, and immediately assumed the cracked croak
of an old man as he grabbed for the false bard and dingy
clothing he had cast aside a moment before. "What? What
is it?"

(Bronze by gold . . .)

"Have you heard about the temple tax, you old sandstone rubbing?"

It was Shandar, his neighbor in the market. Shandar
bought dear, sold cheap, and never could figure out why
he never made any money. Despite his poverty, though, he
was an honest man . . . if one discounted tax evasion, one
or two rapes, and the disembowelment of a competitor as

mere youthful indiscretions (he had, after all, been no more than 38 at the time).

"What about the temple tax, you miserable festering boil?" roared Aeid—oops! . . . I mean Baroz as he fumbled with his beard and tried to get his dusty clothes back on.

"Come out here, you old camel fart! I want to talk to you face to face!"

Baroz had gotten his head halfway through the opening of his shouldercloth, but the fastenings of his false beard had apparently developed a sudden affinity for the fastenings of the garment. Half in and half out of his disguise, the would-be rug merchant stumbled about the room in a state of *metamorphosis interruptus,* his fingers searching frantically for some way out of his predicament. "You pile of monkey dung! Don't tell me what to do! I am old, but I can hear you just fine!"

And, in fact, he wanted to hear more, for it was for just this reason—the opportunity to hear rumor that bordered on truth and truth that bordered on rumor—that Aeid had developed the character of old Baroz and had thus freed himself from the official (and heavily censored) channels of information that wound their torturous way through the court of Nuhr.

(Bronze by gold . . .)

"You stinking heap of parrot droppings . . ." (And it perhaps should be mentioned here that Baroz and Shandar had, over the years, come to express their affection for one another through the constant employment of derogation, insult, and malefaction, this peculiar habit having something to do with the finer points of male bonding that the author, a mere woman, does not pretend to understand.) ". . . get your syphilitic backside out here and speak to me."

"All right, you malignant tumor upon the testicles of society," replied Baroz, who, finally having parted his oddly affectionate beard and shouldercloth, managed to make himself presentable and, thereupon, went out into the open part of his stall.

Shandar was leaning over the counter, banging his fist on a pile of fine Runzenian carpets which, thick and plush as they were, detracted somewhat from the effect, since the bangs were thereby reduced to something in the vicinity of −10 dB. Heedless of (or, perhaps, because of) the technical difficulties he was experiencing in the audio portion of his demonstration, Shandar was just opening his mouth to utter a fraternal endearment so ripe with obvious blasphemy that it would doubtless have gotten him something in the way of Mr. Mather's *Oh, it would not do to speak of it, monsieur* (and where *was* Mather, anyway?) . . .

(Bronze by gold . . .)

. . . when Baroz appeared, settling his headcloth in place with one hand while the other clasped manfully the antique relic of a sword that had given the old merchant the unspoken reputation of being a nobleman who had fallen on hard times.

"What about the temple tax, you phlegmy horse maggot, you?" he inquired, clasping Shandar's hand warmly as the religious police (who had been hoping for something more spectacular), gave up with a shrug and continued dragging away a woman who had been unfortunate enough not only to look completely unlike Bakbuk but also to have lifted her skirts enough that an (unfettered!) ankle had been revealed. Despite the protestations of her husband, she was already black and blue. In a few minutes, she would probably also be bloody. Panasian law was very clear about things like that.

Baroz and Shandar paid no attention: her screams were not even half loud enough to interfere with their lusty, male conversation. "Why," said Shandar, "the priests are saying that it must be collected from the Naians as well as the Panasians!"

Baroz was speechless.

"Well? Is that not something? All this time, and it has been right there in the Sacred Texts (which . . ." said Shandar, straightening as much as his years would allow and placing his hand reverently over his heart, ". . . though I memorized them as a boy I have never once uttered aloud), and they never said anything about it!"

Baroz had grown a trifle flushed.

Shandar was growing flushed, too. "Imagine that! Those heathen Naians, all these years, have been making everyone else bear the burden of the Temple Tax! And they never said anything about it!"

Baroz would have lifted an eyebrow had he not been too occupied with other thoughts. "Those fetid cankers upon the breast of our society . . ." he murmured.

(Bronze by gold . . .)

Shandar was offended. "Surely, Baroz, you cannot love the Naians as much as that!"

But Baroz . . . er, Aeid was thinking of the priesthood, and of a personal dislike for it which, as a result of Shandar's news, had just kindled into a white rage, a rage which prevented him from noticing Kuz Aswani, the magistrate to whom the unfortunate woman now in the custody of the bailiffs was theoretically being dragged, was, in actuality, walking quickly away in the opposite direction, not because he was at all concerned with the welfare of the woman (in fact, he did not even know that anyone had been arrested), but because of his increasing certainty that Umi Botzu was following him, watching him, preparing to cast upon him a spell that would make him wish that he had never regretted turning into a ferret or ever contemplated the death of that same Umi Botzu.

Kuz Aswani crossed the teeming market square quickly,

making his way via a circuitous route around the stalls and shops whose arrangement, laid out by the hand of God centuries ago and delineated by walls of granite and inlays of semiprecious stone, had not changed in millennia. Camels hissed, horses stomped, men bartered and gesticulated at one another, women stood mute beside their escorts— Kuz Aswani passed them all. He was counselor and magistrate both, and he should have been pronouncing judgment on someone or making a decision about something at that very moment, but the demands of the law did not take into account the needs of a frightened ferret, and so the judgments and decisions would have to wait.

Where was Umi Botzu? Out of what window was the sorcerer examining him? From under what shelf was the manipulating spider peering at him? Into what new snare of magic and obscene power was the sinister mage about to force him? Kuz Aswani repressed an urge to hop back and forth with a nervous chuckle as he wound among jugs and pots and rugs and bottles and lamps, doubling back, turning, twisting through the market in the hope that he could throw off the wizard's all-seeing eye.

(Bronze by gold . . .)

"Chuckle-chuckle-chuckle!" There! He had done it in spite of himself, and the merchants and the hawkers and the dealers and even the women were staring at him (modestly, to be sure, in the case of the women: Panasian law was very clear about things like that); but Kuz Aswani looked up from all fours and twitched his nose defiantly at them all. Humans. Just humans. They did not know in the slightest what it meant to be a ferret. He twitched again, chuckled again, gave a quick roll (which made him wince, for beneath its coating of dust and sand, the pavement was very hard), and, with a very ferrety hiss, went for one of the carefully arranged shelves of jugs.

Immediate chaos. Jugs went everywhere. Merchants

shouted. Hawkers yelled. Customers gaped. Women shrieked (and were promptly arrested by the religious police: Panasian law was very clear about things like that). Kuz Aswani bounced over and around the rolling jugs, hissed at the bailiffs, scampered under awnings and carts, and, with the decided sensation that (by Panas! Yes!) he was growing *fur* on his belly, bolted for an egress that had suddenly opened up between two camels and a cart loaded with the reeking liquid that passed for water in most of the major cities of the Three Kingdoms.

Fur! Yes, it had to be fur! (He jogged on through the Square of the Divine Statue, bounded along past the turning to the Avenue of the God's Love, *chuckle-chuckle-chuckled* his way up the Streets of Panas' Benevolence.) Oh, merciful Panas, was *that* how Umi Botzu was going to exact his revenge? Was this poor counselor now going to have to give up his very *form* to the wiles of the sorcerer? How would he keep up his appearances in court? How would he pronounce judgment? How would he make decisions? How would he drag Sabihah about by the scruff of her neck anymore? (She was not a large woman, but, after all, she was much larger than a ferret.)

(Bronze by gold . . .)

"Now *this*," said Captain Scruffy to an entranced Umi Botzu, "is a Leyden jar."

Bronze by gold . . .

Chapter Thirteen

Naia provides.

The words had come to rise and fall in Sari's mind like the tides of a comforting ocean—slowly, constantly, unceasingly—buoying up her thoughts and her spirits even as she turned her back on the site of her first dissillusionments and, with Ehar's caravan, rode away from Halim as the burning sun touched the western horizon and night prepared to flood the land.

No, it did not seem that Naians were at all the same as she remembered them . . . or as she wanted—perhaps *needed*—them to be. Perhaps the differences had something to do with the village of Halim itself, or perhaps they were a symptom of something more general and unavoidable that had come as the result of centuries of coexistence with Panasian ways. Regardless, Sari turned away from Halim, fixing her thoughts upon the providence of a Goddess who might well carry her away from her old life, away from everything dry and dead: the Greenest Branch that was itself the source of living water.

Outside of Halim (which, like all the isolated villages of the Three Kingdoms, owed its survival to the presence of an equally isolated well) were stony hills and gullies that had not known water for a hundred years. Sari, who had been given a seat on a camel because of her age, could see for several leagues, and it was all dry, all desert, all—hill and valley, sand and stone—seemingly as absolute and irrevocable a denial of the existence of water as the religion of Panas seemed a denial of anything female. Even this caravan with which she was traveling was emblematic of the profound alteration in the Three Kingdoms (an alteration that, decade by decade, was increasing), for, years ago, caravans had not existed. Instead, just as in Zhag Me'redig's tale, there had been rich processions of wealthy merchants through a green and living land, and though, when those merchants had stopped at the end of the day, they had caused to be set about their palatial pavilions fountains of cool, scented water, it had been the fountains themselves (gold and silver and adorned with precious gems) that had been remarkable, not the water itself.

But now, scrubby caravans like Ehar's plied their way across the dead land from village to village, from city to city. They traded and bartered, sharing their scant use of the desert's meager resources only with an occasional messenger of the king or with the nomadic herders whose lives were, if anything, even harder and more primitive than their own.

"Tents down!"

The second day. Evening. Time for travel. Sari awakened beneath a sky of thick, colored cotton, grateful that, with the protection of the caravan, she could now face the long journey to the mountains with something approaching equanimity. She had food, water, and a place to sleep: a distinct improvement upon the resources of the old Panasian widow who had staggered away from the corpse of a dead husband only a few weeks ago!

There was no one in the tent, though, save for herself, and she heard voices outside: Yalliah and her daughters were already up, already attending to the traditional tasks of Panasian women. But though Sari was flattered by their consideration for an aged traveler, she was, at the same time, a little disturbed: they obviously thought her no more than a useless old bag of bones, someone to leave to sleep in, someone to awaken only when it was time to drag her out, feed her, and stick her atop a camel for the night's march.

Annoyed, though, with herself as much as with her companions' supposed opinions of her—she had, after all, overslept—she wrapped herself in her clothes and went out to help. The heat of the day was already subsiding, and there was a hint of a cool wind that would, as the night deepened, turn chill. Already, with the suddenness of the equatorial night, the darkness was turning absolute, and the moon was beginning to make its presence known by silhouetting the peaks of the Mountains of Ern.

Ehar was adding wood to the fire while Yalliah readied the cauldron of soup, their movements, different though they were, strangely complimentary. They might have been dancers, each performing the steps given them by an unseen Master, and Sari, watching for a moment from the edge of the firelight, thought of Rhydi's words about man's power and woman's power.

She shuddered. Was this the legacy that Naia had left Her children?

But Yalliah looked up. "Sari," she said. "I had thought to let you sleep."

"I can do more than sleep," said Sari. She knelt beside the flour and water that were lying ready and, with practiced hands, began to make bread cakes. "I did not ask for passage without work like a pampered priest. I will—" She suddenly realized how insulting her comment about priests must have sounded to the Panasians and fell into an embarrassed silence.

Yalliah examined her for a moment, then went back to

her soup. She glanced at Ehar. Ehar shrugged, gave his gold earring a tap, and continued shoving sticks into the fire. It was dry wood. Old wood. The blaze crackled higher. "Your dislike for priests is understandable, Naian," said Yalliah, returning to her soup. "But I . . ." She was silent for a moment. "I heard once that all Naians considered themselves priests."

"Well . . ." Sari busied herself with the bread cakes. They were the staple breakfast of many Panasians, even when that breakfast was eaten at night, and she guessed that Ehar and the other men of the caravan could devour quite a number of them. ". . . in a manner of speaking. But it is more because we have no priests that we are all priests. I mean . . . ah . . ."

"No priests and yet all priests," said Yalliah. There was almost a catch in her voice. "How strange."

"I am not making much sense," Sari admitted.

"No," said Yalliah, shifting her heavy body to the side as she lifted the cauldron into place above the quickening fire. "Your words make sense. However . . ." She watched Sari's hands, and a crinkling of her eyes told Sari that, beneath her veil, a slow, knowing smile was spreading across her face. ". . . your hands do not. Where did you learn to make bread cakes like a Panasian wife, O woman of Naia?"

Sari flushed. Fifty years of learned habit had undone her, and she had betrayed herself. A runaway Panasian woman masquerading as a Naian was bad enough, but a Panasian woman who might have killed her husband (and she was still sure that no one would ever believe her story) was even worse. Yalliah's question could well be but the first of a series that would, eventually, bring the bailiffs and the magistrates.

"I . . . ah . . . learned . . ." she managed.

Ehar shoved another stick into place. "Sandstone and pumice," he muttered. "I am not hearing anything of this."

But Yalliah laid a hand on her arm. "Peace. Say nothing unless you wish to. There are many caravan routes in the world, some more uphill than others." She went back to her soup. "Be easy, sister."

"Sister?" said Sari, growing warm at the word. "Have you known a Naian before, Yalliah?"

Yalliah stood as though struck. Then, after more of a silence than Sari could comprehend, "Ehar's great grandmother was a Naian woman who gave up her faith for a man. I have heard something of her ways."

Sari tried to hold back her tears. She succeeded. Mostly. "I thank you, sister."

With an intent expression, Ehar was tapping at the single gold earring that he wore. After a moment, though, he shrugged. "Finish your tasks, women," he said, "I want to be off quickly."

"Worried about river surges still, husband?" Yalliah's tense silence had evaporated, and Sari heard the old, well-worn affection in her voice.

Ehar drew himself up straight, gave Yalliah a roguish grin. "I am simply reminding you both of my status, and I am very tired of hearing your babbling hen-talk. It means nothing to me, after all. I have more important things to be concerned about."

"He is as long as he is tall," Yalliah whispered to Sari. "So he thinks." It was a standard joke of Panasian women, and Sari laughed ... and felt uncomfortable because, though she had returned to Naia, she still found it funny. Perhaps it was that she had known a few Naian men who—

But that made her even more uncomfortable.

"There are men's tasks and women's tasks," said Ehar, "and as I attend to my duties, so you will attend to yours."

He fixed Sari with a glance. "And you, Naian: I gave you leave to travel with us. I did not say that you could preach."

Sari looked up quickly. "Oh, Ehar! Forgive me! I meant nothing!"

All she got in return was a wink.

IN THE NAME OF PANAS, THE BENEFICENT, THE WONDROUS, THE SHAPER OF CITIES, THE CARVER OF WORLDS, THE ARBITER OF THE LIVES OF MEN AND THE SUBJUGATOR OF ALL THINGS WEAK AND EFFEMINATE, FOR WHOSE GLORY THE GREAT WORK OF THE PUMPS AND RESERVOIRS GOES ON CEASELESSLY NIGHT AND DAY, TO WHOSE CREDIT WAS THE FIRST REVELATION OF THE GREAT WORK OF THE PUMPS AND RESERVOIRS, IN WHOSE NAME THE WRITER GREETS AND COMPLIMENTS THE READER AS MANY TIMES AS THERE ARE GRAINS OF SAND IN THE DESERT, PEBBLES IN THE DRY VALLEYS, PARCHED FIELDS IN THE WASTELAND AND HUMBLY OFFERS THE FOLLOWING INFORMATION.

Mishap: *Earthquake*
Pumps damaged: *#2374, #98, #9672, #4*
Reason for damage: *collapse of pump tunnel #456*
Slaves dead/injured: *10/32*
Reasons for death/injury: *collapse of pump tunnel #456*
Percentage drop in overall capacity: *5*
Estimated time until return to full capacity: *16 days*
Damage to dikes, dams, and retaining walls: *minor*
Collateral release of water before containment: *16000 kils*
Projected strength of repairs: *excellent*

IN THE NAME OF PANAS, THE BUILDER UP AND THE WEARER DOWN, THE MUNIFICENT AND THE

PROFITABLE, THE POWER OF THE PRIESTS AND
THE FEAR OF THE LAITY, THE HOLY AND THE
RIGHTEOUS, THE SMITER OF ENEMIES AND THE
HELPER OF FRIENDS, SO CLOSES THIS REPORT IN
THE HOPES THAT THE READER MAY BE SO MAG-
NIFIED AS TO BE GREAT AS THE CLOUDLESS SKY,
AS WIDE AS THE DESERTS, AS HOT AS THE BURN-
ING SUN . . .

"... ah, yes, my little darling, I am so glad that you
could come back today with the paper. You see, my eyes
they are not good for reading when I have been embroid-
ering for any length of time. I suppose one might say that
I am getting old. Yes! Old! And such a pretty little girl as
you coming to someone as old and wrinkled as myself,
though I tell you in complete confidence that when I was
the first lieutenant on board the *Frères Marseillaise,* I
was such a young buck, ah! the girls they would flock to
me when I was ashore, and look at me now! Old! Ah, yes!
And a pretty little thing as you, all blushes and in the
bloom of young womanhood . . . let me see the paper.

"So strange! Here is a kind of paper that, my God, I
have not seen in many years, ever since I was the first
lieutenant on board the *Frères Marseillaise* (and a strong
young first lieutenant I can tell you that I was). Ah, youth!
Pray, give me a little kiss, my sweet young girl! Ah, do
not be afraid: there are no bailiffs in my shop! Look! Do
you see any? Ah, such innocence! And such lovely soft
lips to put against the cheek of an old man who has grown
half blind with his age and his embroidery! Such a sweet
. . . but where was I? Ah, yes, the paper. Well, I have not
seen such paper in many years, ever since . . . but I repeat
myself . . . such a handsome young man I was, and such
a lovely girl . . . but I repeat myself.

"These words? You wish me to read these words? Ah,

such a pretty thing you are to trouble yourself about words. A lovely girl like you should concern herself only with flowers ... flowers and men. And surely you have the acquaintance of many young men who would wish to ... ah ... how do you say it? ... *converse* with you? Of course you do, and if I were as lusty a young man as I once was, I should wish to *converse* with you, too! But I repeat myself. Here are the words. Let me see what they say.

"Ah, but, you see, I cannot read them! Ha-ha, you think to play a joke upon me! *Old Valdemar,* you take the thought into your pretty little head (and if I were as young a man as I was when I was the first lieutenant on board the *Frères Marseillaise,* I would be sure that you would never have such thoughts, for I would shake them out of you the moment they came into your pretty little head), *I believe that I will play a little joke on Old Valdemar,* you say, and surely you have the acquaintance of many young men (as I was once a young man on board the *Frères Marseillaise*) who might keep you occupied so that you might not play such jokes on an old man, and surely they would *converse* with you. Yes! Converse! And they would keep such thoughts out of your pretty little head, for pretty girls like you should not bother yourself about such things as papers and words, but only about, yes, flowers, and young men, and silks, and pretty underwear, yes, and devices of leather and steel ..."

Jenkins and Haddar had met every day for the last two weeks, and they had finally reached the point at which, for the duration of their conference, they did no more than hunch wordlessly on either side of the low table, glaring at one another like two baboons preparing to fight to the death over a moldy onion. True, Haddar had finally lost his hostile indifference to Jenkins' proposals, and now and again the ambassador reflected that he might well have congratulated himself for that accomplishment, but the fact that the chief minister's hostile indifference had been replaced by hostile belligerence warranted, perhaps, something less than outright applause.

And so they met, and so they glared. And since by now they had gone well beyond the ability of words to express their conflicts, their dialog, by necessity, took the form of the expressions of eyes, the twitches of mouths and nostrils, the slight, almost subliminal gestures of hands. Through the agency of these martial mudras, then, the diplomacy continued:

Why don't you just surrender your sickening little piss hole of a country to us and let a real government take over?

Bah, your women dress like prostitutes, your clothing smells, and your body odor is of soap and scents. Disgusting.

If I had my way, I'd have those twenty-four pound cannon trained on this palace, and to the devil with you all.

If I had my way, your men's foreskins would be hanging on the palace gate to dry by tomorrow morning.

Well, if I had MY way, those foreskins would be stuffed down your throats, you perverted, idol-worshiping swine.

And if I had MY way . . .

But fortunately, since this dialog took place in circumstances devoid of aural verification, very little of any permanence (or, for that matter, violence) could come of it, and even had Mr. Wool been present (and he was, by Jenkins' orders, most assuredly *not* present), the page before him would have been as blank at the end of the meeting as it would have been at the beginning, nor in the course of several hours would he have been given even the slightest cue upon which to hang the embellishment of a biblical quotation.

Trade? Jenkins by this time would have been more than glad to settle for trade. Or fishing rights. Or an exchange of navigational charts (entertaining, for the sake of argument, the possibility that such a backwards and heathen country could have possessed any navigational charts worth having). But though he had previously held up all of these things before the flinty eyes of Haddar, the chief minister had not risen to the bait. And, given that the negotiations for trade or rights or charts were, in actuality, but a prelude to the real plans of the Righteous States of America, the marked failure of those negotiations not only boded extremely ill for those real plans, but was in itself so excruciatingly frustrating that at times Jenkins, in response to a particularly maddening curl of Haddar's lip, found himself half rising out of his seat with a fully formed intent to beat the man senseless ... which was very humiliating for a diplomat (and a minister to boot) with a long career of successes behind him.

It was after a particularly frustrating specimen of one of these meetings that Jenkins, accompanied, as usual, by guards in bright uniforms, musicians braying on brass horns, and several barefoot boys with powdered faces whose function he had not yet been able to determine, returned to the embassy's rooms to find Mather sitting intently behind the swinging, turning, ticking apparatus.

For the better part of a minute, the ambassador stared at the engineer (who, on his part, was engrossed in the workings of the apparatus ... or maybe (it was hard sometimes to tell) he only *appeared* to be engrossed in them). Finally: "And where the devil have you been, Mather?"

"Those by the way side are they that hear; then cometh the devil, and taketh away the word out of their hearts, lest they should believe and be saved."

Wool. Jenkins stifled a very un-Puritan curse. But Mather looked up from the apparatus with a bland expression that seemed to Jenkins to be, perhaps, a little too bland. "Oh, hello, sir. I was just finishing up a few . . . observations."

"Blessed *are* they that have not seen, and *yet* have believed," intoned Wool.

But Jenkins had noticed that the slight pause in Mather's greeting was accompanied by a slight shift in the engineer's posture, as though something pained him. A pulled muscle, perhaps. "A few observations? But you made all those before—"

"That's true. I did." And another slight shift . . . almost a squirm, really. "But it's becoming ever so much more important that I check them now."

Jenkins considered for a moment the question of why it should be so important for Mather to check measurements that he had already checked—as Mather had told him (and Jenkins was, in fact, very tired of hearing about it)—twenty times before. He could come up with no plausible answer. "As I said, where have you been?"

Mather went back to his apparatus. *Tick-tick-tick.* Jenkins was certain the engineer knew that the sounds annoyed him. "Well," said Mather, "you told me yourself that there wasn't anything that I could do, so I looked around a little."

"A little that a righteous man hath *is* better than the riches of many wicked," said Wool, pen in his hand, paper before him. (And, damn him, there he was taking *notes* again!)

But Jenkins forced his attention back to Mather. One thing at a time. First the errant engineer, whose *looking around* had doubtless imperiled everything (as though absolute futility could be imperiled), and then Wool's notes. "And just *where* have you been, as you put it, looking around?"

Mather adjusted a vernier, set another pendulum in motion. *Tick-tick-tick*. And then, to top it off, a little gear began going *wegga-wegga-wegga*. It was almost more than Jenkins could stand.

"You know," said Mather, still with that extreme blandness, "I've discovered a way to increase the accuracy of this by a power of ten."

Jenkins wanted to stamp his foot, wanted, in fact, to pitch Mather out the window. But he was both a minister and a diplomat, and so he had to set an example to these men. "Mather," he said, "in the name of God, where have you been?"

"I *am* the Lord thy God, which have brought thee out of the land of Egypt."

Jenkins could stand no more. "Wool! Damn you! Shut up!"

Wool stared at the wall, pen in his hand, paper before him. The latter was covered with vermicular shorthand.

Heavenly Father, Jenkins thought. *He's taken everything down again. I'll have to burn that one, too.* Aloud, he said, "Mather . . ."

"I've been having some meetings of my own," said Mather.

Tick-tick-tick.

Wegga-wegga-wegga.

As Jenkins had feared. How long, he wondered, did they all have to live? "With whom?"

Tick-tick-tick.

"With an official."

Wegga-wegga-wegga.

"About what?"

"Oh, about any number . . ." *Tick-tick-tick*. ". . . of things."

Wegga-wegga-wegga.

Jenkins had run out of patience. "Mather, I believe I

will have you clapped in irons for insubordination and disobedience."

Tick-tick-t—

The engineer looked up, his hand on the pendulum he had just stopped. "I can't see how you'd get any measurements out of me then, sir."

"Measurements be hanged!" (And out of the corner of his eye, Jenkins could see that Wool was still taking everything down.) "You've done all the measurements, and we're not going to be getting any closer to the mountains than this, so you most certainly won't be doing any more."

Mather blinked at him—squirmed, perhaps, just a trifle—and shrugged. A gear started up again, but he silenced it. *Wegga-wegg—.* "Oh, I wouldn't say that."

Bland. Languid. And there was something almost shifty about him, too. Jenkins was at a loss as to what might have caused the change. Maybe the water or the food. Maybe whatever intercourse Mather had had with whatever official he had had it with had caused something of the inscrutable oiliness of the Kaprishan court to rub off on him. Whatever the cause, though, Jenkins did not like its effects at all. "And why," he said, feeling as though he were only playing along with some infernal game that Mather's scientific mind had devised with as much cunning as it had amplified the sensitivity of the gravimeter, "wouldn't you say that?"

Mather went back to the apparatus. "Because we're going to be going to Katha. Up in the mountains. I'm going to arrange it. We'll be leaving in a few days." He gave a pendulum a flick.

Tick-tick-tick!
Wegga-wegga-wegga!

Chapter Fourteen

1) Inscriptions are carved in stone for many uses: for Foundation Stones and Public Inscriptions, for Tombstones and Memorial Inscriptions, for Mottoes and Texts, for Names and Advertisements, and each subject suggests its own treatment.

Hearken all ye to the words of Panas, the Builder of the World, the Raiser of Cities, the Ordainer of Municipalities, the Shaper of Society, *the Bringer of Responsibility to All.* May His blessings be bestowed upon His people for all time, in all nations may there be great and endless praise raised to him, *and may all people contribute equally to His glory.*

It is indeed fitting, just, right, and proper that the most Holy Words of Panas (blessed be He!) begin with the most fundamental pronouncements upon the role of man in society and upon the orders *and responsibilities* of men all the way from the king, who is the very foundation stone of all endeavor and who is forever in the eye of the public (and fittingly so, for it is from him that the public derives its luster or its tarnish, its evenness or its roughness), to the basest of commoners whose garb and mannerisms, *though not absolving them in the slightest from their responsibilities toward Panas (blessed be He!),* cannot help but reflect their baseness.

But it is to the plurality of the creation of Panas (blessed be He!) that our attention is first brought. There are indeed many uses for men, and all, from highest to lowest, from first to last, are worthy of mention in the Sacred Text of Panas (blessed be He!). Here, the highest mysteries are already hinted at, seeing as it is only in *the* context *of the discharging of their responsibilities* that the lives of men are judged. And should there be any doubt in a man's mind about his inclusion in the creation of *responsibilities to* Panas (blessed be He!), such doubts are certainly swept away by the enumeration provided by Panas (blessed be He!) immediately before the words of supreme power and ultimate mystery themselves, for surely among even these few there is a place for all men *and for their responsibilities toward Panas (blessed be He!) Himself (blessed be He!)*

Is not the father the *Foundation Stone* of the house? Is not the merchant the *Foundation Stone* of his business? Is not the soldier the *Foundation Stone* of all the endeavors of his superiors, just as his superiors are the *Foundation Stone* of the soldier's orders and provisions and strategies? *Are not the taxes of the commoner the Foundation Stone of the nation itself?* Contradict this anyone who dares, but surely the scoffer will be confounded!

And as the *Foundation Stone* shall be deeply graven and signed with signs of its honor and its superiority to all other stones, he who is himself the *Foundation Stone* of others shall not hide his status beneath false pretense or humility, but rather shall trumpet it forth loudly and unceasingly. There is no place for the humble in the eyes of Panas (blessed be He!), either within or without. *Woman knoweth not Woman, but Man knoweth what Man is,* goeth the old saying, and surely these words, hallowed by time if not by the lips of the God (blessed be He!) Himself (blessed be He!), has much truth in it (though not as much truth as the words of Panas (blessed be He!), the God (blessed be He!) Himself (blessed be He!))!

Therefore, let the man who is the foundation of others constantly remind those whom he supports that he is their foundation. Let those whom he supports acknowledge their dependence upon him daily as all men acknowledge their dependence upon Panas (blessed be He!). Let the man who supports others be magnified by his support, and let others magnify him, for this is truly what Panas (blessed be He!) has ordered.

And though the just and honorable man dies, let not his reputation or his wishes die, for as *Tombstones* are deeply graven with *Memorial Inscriptions* so as to pronounce for all time the deeds of the living, so too should those laws and ordainments established in the past be kept for all time . . .

Inwa Kabir listened carefully to the words of Abnel, the Gharat, the High Priest of Nuhr, and, when Abnel was finished, Inwa Kabir nodded into a lengthening silence that was, for the time being, broken only by the distant screams of the woman who had lately been convicted of the serious crime of exposure . . . and had therefore been impaled in the square that morning. "I will have it thought about," he said finally.

"O All Highest," said Abnel, "may Panas (blessed be He!) reward you. I am sure that the God will be perfectly willing to wait while your counselors debate the finer points of His words and apply their human understanding to His decrees."

Inwa Kabir debated, caught between the reactionary convenience that had, until then, been the prerogative of kingship and the words of the God Himself. It was odd that he did not recall the particular passages that the Gharat had been quoting, even though, like all good Panasian men, he had in his boyhood committed most of the Sacred Texts to memory. But that was nothing unusual.

Over the years, Abnel had recommended many courses of action based upon words in the Texts that Inwa Kabir had not remembered. That was why laymen, no matter how lofty or regal their status, were forbidden to quote the Texts aloud. Errors of one kind or another were inevitable, and the words of Panas were nothing to be trifled with. The priests studied long and hard to be priests, and part of that study was devoted to the right, complete, and error-free knowledge of the Texts. That, along with a rigorously upright way of life, was what made them priests. Still . . .

"What of the priestly Council of Nuhr?" Inwa Kabir asked suddenly. "I assume that you have consulted them?"

"I have, All Highest," said Abnel. He nodded, and though Inwa Kabir noted the nod, he also noted a certain odd . . . well . . . squirm . . . that ran through the Gharat's body. "They have arrived at the same conclusion about the tax."

Still, Inwa Kabir looked for a way out. Finally: "Have you consulted the Council of Katha?"

If Abnel felt any irritation, he gave no sign of it. "All Highest, the meaning of the texts is very clear. I have no doubt that the Council of Katha will arrive at precisely the same conclusions as has the Council of Nuhr."

Abnel had, in fact, quoted the Texts just a few minutes before, and their meaning was indeed very clear, even to a royal layman. The temple tax—the prop and support of the priesthood of the entire Three Kingdoms—was, fittingly, and in accordance with the wishes of Panas, to be applied to all inhabitants, regardless of whether they were Panasian believers or Naian heathens. Still, though, Inwa recalled the passages in the Texts about respecting the judgment of the dead and preserving laws made in the past. He said as much to Abnel . . . without, to be sure, quoting anything directly.

"Let them be changed only after much consideration by

the priests," Abnel quoted, *"and particularly the Gharat, for though they be the only concrete sign of the foundation of the past that holds up the present, they have nonetheless been bequeathed to the living by the dead and are therefore worthy of preservation as the priesthood, particularly the Gharat, deems it fitting."*

And, to be sure, since Abnel was the Gharat himself, his memory and his words could not but be correct.

But Inwa Kabir did not like the idea of changing anything. His entire reign—like that of his father, his grandfather, his great-grandfather, and all his other grandfathers, regardless of how many greats dangled before them—had been built upon the principle of not changing anything, and he was not about to change that now. "It is the will of Panas (blessed be He!) that the taxes be imposed," he said. "But it is the will of the king that you consult first with the Council of Katha. The priests there are all scholars, and their judgment is, perhaps, superior to that of the priests of the Council of Nuhr. With, perhaps, the exception of the Gharat himself." Inwa hesitated, decided against adding *But I must have it thought about.*

"All Highest, it would appear disrespectful to disagree," said Abnel, "but I am certain that Panas (blessed be He!) Himself (blessed be He!) would feel the same way."

"Meaning?"

"Meaning that as the All Highest does not wish his will contradicted, the God (blessed be He!) of the All Highest might wish His will contradicted even less." Abnel nodded. Again, that little squirm.

What is the matter with the Gharat? I must have it thought about, thought Inwa Kabir. Aloud, though, he said: "I suppose that you are right, though I must have it—" He caught himself just in time. They were not, after all, talking about the peculiarities of a deranged counselor like Kuz Aswani. They were talking about the decrees of Panas.

"May I order that the taxes at least be collected in the city of Nuhr so that the will of Panas (blessed be He!) may be made at least partly manifest?" (Squirm.)

Abnel's squirms were making Inwa Kabir nervous. He desperately wanted to be rid of the man, his office, and his demands. Aeid, at least, did not squirm. But Inwa Kabir suspected that Aeid had greater vices in his life than squirming. Where *was* he getting those ideas? Skin color! Why, he sounded like a . . . like a . . .

(Squirm.)

"Very well," he said quickly. "Collect the taxes in Nuhr. But at your earliest possible convenience, journey to Katha and consult the Council. That is my will."

Abnel bowed. "All Highest, may it be as though it has already been done."

The Sari who walked into the village of Kestir was very different from the Sari who had stumbled into Halim, for while the latter, a former Panasian wife, had been most concerned with the possibility of being accused of her late husband's murder, the former, though still partly laboring under such fears, had turned a nagging worry about the basic fabric of her spiritual life and heritage into something approaching an obsession. She had left Panas . . . was, in fact, not sure that she had ever really gone to Him. But could she now, after so long, return to Naia? Or, better (and, given what she had seen over the last weeks, even more fraught with terrible uncertainty): was there a Naia to return to?

When the caravan reached Kestir, Sari attended to her share of the daily chores, and then she entered the city and went directly to the Naian Quarter. The priestly guards at the gate gave her only the most cursory of examinations: an old woman was obviously of no concern to them.

But as Sari stepped into the Naian Quarter and took a look around to orient herself, she wondered about the allurements that the Panasians invariably attributed to the Goddess worshipers—the allurements that necessitated the presence of a wall and two guards—for here in Kestir was the same sense of tawdry haphazardness that she had seen (and been dismayed by) in Halim. Houses, in contrast to the prim and rectilinear Panasian dwellings outside the wall, were ramshackle, their corners chipped away as though they were rat-gnawed pieces of cheese. Weeds that could find a purchase in the terrible drought were growing up everywhere—between paving stones, in cracks in foundation walls, along the borders of the sandy street—and everywhere, too, were the sounds of windchimes, the gaudy colors of cheap paint (itself cracked and flaked and ill kept), and the heavy thud of drums and men's voices.

Hunna-hunna-hunna-HUN!

Allurements?

She stood for a moment at the edge of the market square, wondering what, exactly, she was doing here. What had she come for? Reassurances? But she had only just arrived, and she knew already that there would be no reassurances. Perhaps she should simply return to the caravan and to Yalliah's matronly wisdom, make her way to Katha in the silence and obscurity of an old woman, and then, alone, turn her steps northward toward the Caves. Maybe there would be something for her at the Caves. She hoped so. She needed something.

But as though unwilling to admit failure and defeat or to accept the concomitant despair, she set off across the square, threading her way among the little stalls and shops whose owners were just now throwing open their shutters and lifting their awnings. With a sense of unease, Sari noticed that, even here, the owners were all men, and, with a greater sense of unease, she saw that almost all were Panasians.

"Oh, old woman! Oh, old Naian woman!"

Since it seemed too early for Naians—old or not, female or not—to be up and about (indeed, the market was almost devoid of customers), the words were obviously meant for Sari, and, turning, she saw small, dingy stall occupied by a man and a woman.

By their dress, both appeared to be Naians, but Sari was uncertain as to whether she found that reassuring, for not only was the woman's stringy hair plaited in a multitude of randomly situated braids that themselves contained a multitude of randomly situated beads, crystals, and colored stones, but there was also, perceptible even at this distance, a disturbing vagueness to her eyes. The man at her side was huge, stout, and bearded, and his hair—as long as his partner's, and exhibiting the same disarray (but without the addition of braids and lithic ornamentation)—hung down below his shoulders. But what was most odd, most remarkable, and, perhaps, most unsettling about him was that he was wearing a crude copy of the medallion normally worn only by Naian women.

"Naia's blessings on you, old woman," called the young woman, waving.

"A-and on you, sister," Sari replied, wondering not whether there were a catch in her voice, but rather how much of one and whether it were completely obvious.

But not having anything better to do, she passed through the jangle and clank of chains and shutters that went with the setting up of shops and the arranging of goods, endured the patronizing stares of Panasian merchants who saw in her only an old woman who could not possibly have even a single settel to spend, and walked up to the counter of the Naians' stall.

Within—arranged on shelves, suspended from hooks, leaning against the walls, standing on the floor—was an assortment of wares that defied categorization . . . and, in some cases, definition. Strange collections of knots that might have been weavings dangled next to shelves containing vague earthen shapes that might have been pots. Wooden boards with carvings on them might have been plaques, but then again, since Sari could discern no apparent pattern to the carvings, might not. She dimly recognized a table and a stool, though if the box with strings stretched across it were supposed to be some kind of musical instrument, she could not guess what kind it was, much less what sound it might be induced to make.

"We are so glad to meet you," said the young woman with the vague eyes.

"We do not often see strangers in Kestir," said the man with something like an annoyed glance at the woman beside him. "My name is Aruhn, and this is my wife."

Sari stared. "Naia's blessings," she managed.

Aruhn smiled broadly. "I let her help out in the store sometimes. Of course, according to the *old ways* . . ." The emphasis he gave the words was unmistakable. ". . . she has much more important things to do than to help me."

Old ways? Or, rather, *old ways*? What old ways? "Ah . . . yes . . ." said Sari.

The sunlight seemed too harsh now, the indescribable wares and the vague eyes and the counterfeit medallion too confusing: Sari wanted to go back to the caravan, to the soft shade of a cotton tent, to the muted color and comforting softness of thick rugs. She wanted to find a quiet corner by herself. Yalliah, she knew, would leave her alone. Yalliah was wise . . .

"Where are you from, old woman?"

Old woman. Wife. Sari cleared her throat, cursed inwardly at her cracked, crone's voice. "I am from Ouzal," she said almost defiantly, realizing only when it was too late that she really should not have been revealing her origins. There was the matter of her dead husband, and of questions likely to be asked by the village magistrates.

But here she was in Kestir, staring across a wooden counter at a broad-faced man with a greasy beard and a fake woman's medallion—and at his wife—and she was suddenly entirely unable to find any connection, real or imaginary, between herself and a certain Panasian woman who had staggered away from Ouzal.

"My name is Sari," she added.

Aruhn's wife brightened. "Oh, what a wonderful name. Did you know that it means *dove* in the ancient language? Aruhn and I know that because we are experts in all the *old ways*." Again, the unmistakable emphasis. "We know all about them. In fact, we have dedicated our lives to bringing back all of the arts that were lost when the Panasians invaded our peaceful land."

Aruhn jumped in. "Now, now, Nuzhab, I am certain that Sari does not want to be wearied with tales of our craft." He looked at Sari meaningfully. "Does she?"

Despite her belief that her old life had been left behind, Sari's response—the product of five decades of Panasian living, of deferring to men, of sensing and responding to the needs of others without regard to her own—was instinctive. "Oh, do tell me about it." *No*, she thought. *Please . . . no . . .*

Too late again: Aruhn had already started, and over the course of the next hour, he recounted a history that Sari had never heard before, a history of violent Panasian invasion, of the destruction of a peaceful, enlightened, matrilineal Naian culture and its priceless cultural treasures, of the deliberate suppression of knowledge about that previous civilization and its achievements. Fortunately, as Aruhn explained at length, he and his wife (and Sari suddenly realized that she could not remember the woman's name, even though Aruhn had uttered it, even though she was standing right there, smiling and nodding as her husband (How Sari was beginning to hate that term!) droned on and on) had been given spirit messages that guided them to the ancient secrets, and they (that is, Aruhn and his wife, whatever her name was) had resolved to rescue as many of them as they could from complete oblivion.

"And so, here we are," Aruhn finished up, sweeping his hand out at the collections of knots that might have been weavings, the earthen shapes that might have been pots, the carved boards that might have been plaques, the box with strings stretched across it that might have been some kind of musical instrument. "We have educated ourselves and studied everything that remains of the *old ways,* and now we have finally reached the point at which we would, in ancient times, have been considered masters of our crafts." He smiled broadly, regarded his handiwork with satisfaction.

Sari managed an "Oh . . . how nice."

"It is a sign of these times—" Aruhn's voice shifted momentarily into a snarl . . . "—*Panasian* times—" . . . and then resumed its normal, booming resonance. "—that the old ways are not recognized and appreciated."

"When they create things that are so greatly superior to all of the other things that are bought and sold," added Aruhn's wife (whose name Sari *still* could not remember) with a nod and a clicking of beads, crystals, and rocks.

And again, faintly, Sari heard the sound of drums and chanting:

"Hunna-hunna-hunna-HUN!"

Aruhn saw that she was listening. "Now, I know all about the ancient arts of drumming . . ."

"As well as everything else," said his wife, and the vagueness about her eyes, if anything, increased.

"Please, Nuzhab, you interrupt me."

Nuzhab! That was the wife's name. Sari vowed to remember it this time ... but ...

"I beg forgiveness, husband," said Aruhn's wife.

... but ...

"As I was saying," said Aruhn, "I know all about the *old ways*. I could instruct them in the proper way of doing things. But they persist in their errors.

... but what was her name again?

Sari was nodding, wondering how she could get away. But what could she get away to? To the caravan and the company of Panasians? Did she secretly crave to don the veils of Panasism once again?

"Hunna-hunna-hunna-HUN!"

Aruhn was shaking his head. "Terrible. Terrible. They might as well act like ..." And again, his voice shifted into a snarl. "... Panasians."

"You ... do not like Panasians, then," said Sari, half to take her mind off her uncertainty, half to find out whether her former status would be seen by Aruhn and his wife (And what *was* her name, anyway?) as a reason for spurning her.

"Terrible people," said Aruhn. "Terrible. Their history is nothing more than a series of murders and rapes."

His wife was nodding.

"They destroyed our civilization when they invaded our peaceful land."

His wife was nodding more vigorously.

"And as for their religion—"

His wife could nod no more vigorously, and so she broke in. "It is an absurd mass of contradictions and does not further the growth of anyone's spirit or individuality!"

Aruhn's voice turned stern. "You are interrupting me again, Nuzhab."

Nuzhab!

"Forgive me, husband."

Nuzhab, Sari repeated to herself. *Nuzhab. Nuzhab. Nuzhab.*

"But you are quite right," Aruhn continued. "Absurd. Absolutely absurd. And not only that, but a relative newcomer when compared with the long history of . . ." And, again, he indicated the collections of knots that might have been weavings, the earthen shapes that might have been pots, the carved boards that might have been plaques, the box with strings stretched across it that might have been some kind of musical instrument. ". . . Naian accomplishment."

"Of course," said Sari, trying to stifle a grimace.

"Hunna-hunna-hunna-HUN!"

"Is something wrong?" said Aruhn's wife.

Sari stared at her. She had forgotten her name again. To cover her failings—and her dismay—she shook her head. "I . . . ah . . . was just listening to the chanting. They did it differently in Halim."

"Really?" said Aruhn. "How do they do it in Halim?"

"It was . . . ah . . . *Hunna-hunna-hunna-Ho!* as I recall."

"Hunna-hunna-hunna-ho . . ." mused Aruhn. "Hmmm. It would work so much better if they only did it *right*."

Chapter Fifteen

In Nuhr, the matter of the temple tax proceeded as though it had indeed already been done. Which it had. In fact, the tax collectors had received updated lists three days before, and both classes—true believers and heathens, or (depending on one's sympathies) heathens and true believers—had already been notified by bailiffs and messengers and criers that all who wished to fulfill their responsibilities to Panas (regardless of whether they wished to believe in Him or not) should present themselves at the collection tables in the market square ... or be faced with some appropriate version of *Oh, it would not do to speak of it, monsieur.*

Parasites upon the body politic ...

Understandably, this turn of events provoked some distress in the Naian community. Some advanced the theory that the misfortune had been part of an inter-incarnatory, communal-growth project of the group-mind variety—in other words, that the ecumenical application of the tax had, in fact, been decided upon by the Naians themselves when they were very safely between lifetimes (and very safely dead), and therefore, like a child who had decided to die or a woman who had decided to be raped, they could put the blame on no one else.

Jean Jacques said it best, of course: "Laws are always useful to those who own, and injurious to those who do not own."

Others in the community attributed it to the work of the demons who lived in the growing desert wastes—particularly in the vicinity of the foothills of the Mountains of Ern (Everybody knew that, did they not?)—imperiling travel as well as emitting, periodically, the noxious odors of damp and decay that sometimes manifested in those regions. Doubtless, Naia—who was a dark, evil mother as well as a bright, loving mother (Everybody knew that, did they not?)—had unleashed some of those malign forces against Her children in order to teach them a lesson. What the lesson was supposed to be, however, remained the subject of much debate.

Yes, and everything is good when it leaves the hands of the Creator, and everything degenerates in the hands of man. Jean Jacques, you are so right! Oh, to be able to take up arms against those miserable drones!

And a small and relatively unimportant group, which had come into contact with certain absolute truths advanced by certain Naians of the central wastes, held firmly to their certainty that if everybody had only *done it right*, then absolutely none of this would ever have happened.

Arms . . . hmmm.

TICKETS! Tickets! May I see your tickets, please (thank you sir . . . uh . . . ma'am (sorry about that)) and keep your kid in his seat guy let's see your ticket thank you very much and yours thank you thank you thank you . . .

Welcome, ladies and gentlemen, kids and kiddettes, to Sari's Dream Tour of a Naian Childhood. We'll be getting started in a minute, but before we do I have to remind you all that there's no smoking allowed on the tram—of anything—and that management asks you to kindly keep your hands and arms inside the tram at all times as management cannot assume any liability for any oneiric misfortunes that result from sticking them out, and please remain in your seats at all times until we've reached the end of the tour and the tram comes to a complete stop.

OK, here we go. Coming up on your left you can see Sari asleep in the little house in Ouzal, and yeah, it's supposed to look that way. Naians don't live too well to begin with, and the government doesn't offer any incentive programs except the one called Pay Your Taxes and Keep Your Mouth Shut. Thanks very much, sir, I know she's ugly. If you wanted pretty skin you should have taken the Marquis de Sade Dream Tour that leaves just after this one. Sorry, but you'll have to bring that up with the management. Can't help you.

And I'm supposed to remind you, folks, that this is all a dream, so if it doesn't make much sense, then you'll just have to take the tour again. (That's a joke, pretty good one, huh? Well, it ought to be, 'cause my real job is writing scripts for Hollywood. Yeah, Hollywood. I've got one being looked at right now. Can't tell you about it, though, 'cause I have to protect my rights, you know?)

Where was I? Oh, yeah: the house. Yeah, it's run down, but like I said, the government doesn't offer incentives, and Naians are kinda low class anyway, particularly this dude and his squeeze. I mean, when you're trying to support yourself by selling the Three Kingdoms version of porcelain scotty dogs, you're not exactly gonna be raking in the dough, and believe me, I know all about not raking in the dough. You ought to hear what they're giving me for this gig.

But, hey, it's better than nothing, and it's a whole shitload of a lot better than the kind of bucks you're seeing here. (Sorry, you'll have to talk to management about that. OK, OK ... pardon my French. OK?) But coming up on your right is the beginning of what we drivers like to call the Big Wet One. This is what Sari's dreaming, and it's Ozzy and Harriet all the way. (Hey, I said I was sorry. You'll still have to talk to management about it.)

So here's Sari when she's five. Cute kid, huh? Big brown eyes, enough to break your heart. Hey, kid, keep your hands inside. No grabbing.

That's her mom and dad, all lovey-dovey there, making breakfast together, putting Sari to bed together, working in the shop together. See? Mom there doesn't go around dyking it up and lifting bags of concrete or anything, but she's got old dad pussy-whipped anyway. Boy-oh-boy, what a wimp this guy is. Look, there's her dad listening to her mom say that she doesn't like something, and there's her dad not doing what she doesn't like. Can you believe that? And why does he go along with it? Well, if you ask him he gives you some cock and bull story about loving her and wanting her to be happy. Je-sus Christ! Hey, sorry, sir, it's just an expression. Yeah, I respect your religion and everything, but look, it's just an expression, OK? I'm a writer, and I believe in free expression, don't you? This is America, right?

Anyway, if you ask her, Sari's mom is gonna say the same thing, and, yeah, she sticks by it, too, but look at her dad just sitting there holding her mom's hand like he enjoys it . . . doesn't it just make you sick? Whipped. That's all. Whipped.

Look, lady, I got nothing against you women's libbers, or anything, I just think you should shave more often. That's a joke, get it? 'Course, what you shave is your own business, I just don't like being all scratched up in the morning. Hey, same to you!

C'mon, kid, keep your hands inside the tram. Can't you do something with your kid, lady?

And then, when the Naians all get together, you just

won't believe this stuff. There's not one of those guys got the guts to cop a feel. I mean . . . hey guys! You *know* they want it—all women want it—so why don't you just go ahead, huh? No, they're all into this whole *respect* thing the girls have got cooked up. Look, coming up, here's a wedding party on the right again. *Helpmate* they call each other, but you know who's on top, if you know what I mean. I mean, look at the bride and groom giving gifts to one another, why you'd think they really meant it or something.

Hey, don't get me wrong, I believe in marriage and all that. Why, after I've made a bundle on this script deal, I'm gonna find a nice girl—you know, a pretty one—and settle down and let her take care of me. But you can bet I'm gonna let her know who's boss. She'll do what I say, and *that's* the way it ought to be, and I know what I'm talking about. I come from a good home, real normal all the way, and no problems, and that's the way Dad always treated Mom, and she never had any complaints. A new car every two years, five kids, her church group, and she was happy. Believe it. Lady, I'm telling you I don't have anything against your kind, just sit down and watch the show, huh?

Kid, I'm telling you for the last time, keep your hands in the tram or I'm gonna have to start kicking some butt. I'm sorry, sir, you can take *that* to the management, too.

Anyway, that's the Naians' idea of a marriage. Coming up now on the left, Sari as a teenager. This is where she was learning the Hymns of Loomar—at least what the Naians know of them. Imagine that! They think their holy stuff is, like, divinely inspired. What a riot! And you don't know the half of it, I'll tell you, but you have to take the private tour to find out about that kind of stuff, because then you can take the floating pavilion all the way out to the secret library and see it all. But that's somebody else's department.

Anyway, this is where she learns the Hymns, and already you can see that the kids she hangs out with are real Big Time Nerds who think that quoting poetry back and forth at one another is, like, a real fun game or something; but that goes for all the Naian kids. Sure, there's a few bright ones who can't be bothered with the Hymns and the namby-pamby shit that does down (sorry about the French, sir, and yes I know there's kids here 'cause I've been telling them to keep their fucking hands inside the tram for the last five minutes and same to you—yeah, go ahead and report me). Where was I? Oh, yeah. There's a few who want to go off on their own and find out all sorts of new shit, and you can bet they're gonna do it, too. Give 'em time. After all, you can't go through your life mealy-mouthing everyone with that old Stepin Fetchit routine. Nice never got nobody nowhere, and it'd sure be worth it to me to be able to see one of those Naian guys get some balls and stand up to his woman. Get it? Stand up to his woman? That's a joke. Hey, I know what I'm doing 'cause I'm a writer and yeah, bitch, you just go ahead and report me. I'll tell you, though, there's something you need and every man's got it to give, but you're such a bitch that they won't, so whaddya gonna do? Besides, I'm gonna be outta this chicken-shit tour business any day now, on account of I got this script with a *major studio,* and they're gonna pay me mega-bucks for it. Any day now. Just you wait and see!

It is just like any other day in the market square at Nuhr. Over closest to the wall, the horse traders are doing a fine business, as are the camel sellers. Closer to the center, the jewelers and the jewelry traders are casting dubious looks at one another (the former at the latter because the latter are not craftsmen, but rather only the hawkers of the handiwork of others (and not very good handiwork at that); the latter at the former because the latter consider the former something of a pack of brigands because no one could possibly charge so much for a lump of ornate metal without being something suspiciously close to a thieving scoundrel, and in any case the former's wares are not *that* much better than the latter's (in the latter's opinion) and it just goes to show that no one appreciates a bargain even when it rears up like a cobra and sinks its fangs into one's thigh).

Elsewhere, eminent doctors (and they are all, every single one of them, eminent) from distant parts of the Three Kingdoms keep booths for private consultations on cases that have perplexed the local physicians; and, with priestly approval, they dispense their gem elixirs and their powders of crushed stone while they eye the suspicious looking little booths that offer the service of astrologers, card readers, spiritual counselors, and other heterodox trades without actually advertising that fact (thereby staving off, at last for a time, a visit from the religious police and, perhaps, a fate that Mr. Mather has heard of . . . and often thought about).

There are men with monkeys (little forlorn things (the monkeys, I mean) that look as though they need a drink even worse than their masters), men with snakes of various sorts, jugglers, acrobats, even an occasional woman . . .

And over here, where the big square is bounded by the elaborately carved and polished Temple of Panas, are the tax collectors. These days, they are doing a thriving business, even considering that the Naians responsible for their increased revenue base are very much a minority in Nuhr . . . as they are throughout the Three Kingdoms. This might have something to do with Abnel's decision to make the Naians' new tax burden retroactive to the date of their birth (unless, of course, they convert to Panasism), but we should, perhaps, not be hasty in our evaluations.

Men who make leather harnesses for the above mentioned horses and camels, men who tan leather for the men who make leather harnesses for the above mentioned horses and camels, men who skin goats and horses and camels for ... unspecified reasons, men selling birds, men selling food, men selling cloth, men selling clothing, rug merchants, cobblers, copper beaters, wood carvers, knife sellers, bottle makers, pot vendors, and, over here, on the rooftops, a masked figure garbed in a fantastic suit of blue—cape and boots, tights and tatters—is flitting along between the pinnacles and crenelations with a coil of rope—

Uh ... wait a minute ...

From concealment to concealment he darts—a masked face peering out from behind a pinnacle, a flash of movement, a flutter of a cape, and then a blur vanishing behind a column—as he makes his way along the edge of the roof (shops), toward the edge of the roof (more shops) and, having reached this interim goal, continues on toward his primary objective: the edge of the roof (temple).

So far ... good. I can fasten one end of this rope at the middle (Parasitical mites!) and push off from the south end. If I give myself enough thrust outward, then I can swing directly over the (Thieving, scrofulous rogues!) tables.

Aeid (for, yes, this ultramarine unknown is none other than the crown prince about to debut yet another disguise ... albeit for reasons that have nothing to do with evading the palace censors) continues on his way along the rooftops, and it does make one wonder that no one—absolutely no one—sees him, notices him, or calls attention to him in any way.

As though their previous revenues were not enough! Well, all that is about to come to an end.

His cape flaps in the hot breeze. His mask is a glorious azure, his turban, sapphire. Yes, it does make one wonder.

A few days of this, and the tax collectors will no longer be willing to work, and Abnel will have to find some other way to finance his excesses. He does *have excesses, I assume. I mean ... why else ...*

And then Aeid's train of thought is immediately derailed by the fact that, if Abnel has excesses, then a certain Prince Aeid also has excesses. There is, for example, the matter of the counselors' wives; and Aeid, if he is honest with himself (which, devoted follower of Jean Jacques that he is, he tries to be) has to admit that at times he actually ... well ... rather *enjoys* the exploits of a palace stud.

But now Aeid is slipping along the roof of the Temple itself, which is a very dangerous thing to do, for it is a capital crime for any save the priests of Panas to have anything to do with the non-public areas of the temple, and the roof is most certainly a non-public area. Aeid is taking a great risk now, and if he took some time to think, perhaps—

Too late! No time for thoughts of prudence or wisdom now! Peering over the edge of the roof, Aeid has seen the tables of the tax collectors, seen coins passing from the hands of Naian men into the hands of the representatives of the Panasian priesthood—oh, excuse me: *money grubbing, reactionary Panasian priesthood,* seen stacks and heaps and baskets of coins lined up on the table, and his temper has gotten very much the better of him. Therefore, without pausing for further reflection, he knots one end of his rope around a likely-looking pillar and, playing out the coil, makes his way toward the south end of the roof.

I must be very sure to kick outward, else I shall wear my skin raw with scraping against the facade of the temple,

*not to mention perhaps colliding with something that I do
not want to collide with.*

And, down below, the money is still changing hands,
the hawkers are crying their wares, the merchants are selling, the vendors of food and water are doing quite well,
and the Naian men standing before the tables are debating
about whether to order their families to convert to the
ways of Panas and thereby save a great deal of money
(clitoridectomy being a relatively painless procedure compared to the torments of penury, and, anyway, it would not
be *their* problem) when—

"*SANDSTONE SUPPOSITORIES TO THE PROFLI-
GATE PRIESTS OF PANAS!*" COMES THE SUDDEN
SCR ... (oops, sorry) ... comes the sudden scream from
the temple roof, and as the tax collectors (along with everyone else) turn, stare, and gape, a splendid, dashing figure
clad in boots and cape and tights and tatters (and the mask:
do not forget the mask) described above suddenly swings
down from the top of the temple on a rope, and, T *still*
equaling $2\pi\sqrt{\frac{l}{g}}$ bears directly down on the tax collectors
and the tables they occupy.

The tax collectors, quite sensibly deciding that any en-
counter between themselves and a masked man willing to
swing down from the roof of the Temple of Panas is likely
to be less than pleasant, rise quickly and attempt to depart,
but, with a sound that, though rather milder than a good,
sturdy *bothallchoractorschumminaroundgansummuminarum-
drumstrumtruminahumptadumpwaultopoofoolooderamaun-
sturnup*,* is nonetheless quite remarkable, the masked (Do
not forget the mask!) figure (Aeid, of course) who has correctly understood his angle of attack but miscalculated the
length of his rope, does not, as he had planned, swoop

*© 1939, James Joyce

gracefully by just above the heads of the cowering tax collectors, but rather slams down onto one end of the long tabletop and then skids the entire length, sending balances, weights, records, tables, styli, counting tables, and (perhaps most important) stacks and heaps and baskets of coins flying everywhere, thereafter (having lost his grip on the rope) hurtling off the far end and crashing square into the assembled backs of the fleeing tax collectors, who immediately collapse in a tangle of bodies, robes, and sandals.

For a moment, silence. And then, suddenly, a collective gasp from the current population of the market square as it sees the shoals and sandbars of scattered coins that have been washed up, as it were, by Aeid's sudden storm. And then, immediately, another gasp, much louder than the first, as that same population realizes the implications . . .

Aeid, untangling his cape and picking himself up, lifts his eyes to see a heaving mass of humanity converging on the tables and just manages to get to his feet before the impact of the human wave topples him backward into the disheveled tax collectors, who, in turn, have just managed to get to their own feet when Aeid hurtles once again into them. Aeid, as he is going over, looks frantically for the rope, and by Panas, he sees the end of it just a few feet away.

Rippling nervelessly, (T, yes, equaling $2\pi\sqrt{\frac{l}{g}}$), the rope hovers just out of reach, but though Aeid lunges for it, there are suddenly people (grasping, shouting, scooping up fallen coins, punching one another in the face, and screaming deprecations that involve one another's grandmothers and grandfathers and great-grandmothers and great-grandfathers, all of whom apparently had various kinds of illicit liaisons with various kinds of draft animals and fish) in the way, and the rope flutters out of his grasp and his sight as he sprawls once more on the ground.

And oh! here are the bailiffs running up now with their staves, and as the sound of good, solid hardwood smacking into not quite so solid heads and ribs echoes off the temple facade, the crush of avaricious flesh eases just enough to allow Aeid to stand up. Unfortunately, his mask has become skewed, and he cannot see. Both of his eyes are, in fact, covered, and it is all he can do to shake free of the pressing crowd enough to get his hands up and re-settle it ...

... only to find himself staring straight into the face of a particularly large bailiff with a particularly long hardwood staff that looks particularly thick, shiny, and ready for use.

"Over here," the bailiff cries to the others. "Here is the one who started it all, by Panas (blessed be He!)!"

Aeid, perceiving even better than the tax collectors that certain encounters are apt to be less than pleasant, turns to lose himself in the milling crowd (which, despite the efforts of the bailiffs, is still grabbing for coins), steps on his cape (which, like his mask, has gotten quite skewed) and winds up face down on the pavement.

Again.

With a shriek of delight (the penalty for trying to escape being even more unpleasant than the penalty for whatever the bailiffs were going to make sure the magistrates convicted Aeid of), the bailiff lifts his staff ...

"By Panas (blessed be He!)!" cries Aeid, flailing out, turning over, and pointing at the bailiff, "he has collected more coins than all the rest of us together! He is keeping them all for himself!"

Which, to be sure, results in the bailiff, along with most of his fellows, being immediately buried beneath a swarming heap of humanity that (What else?) is still grasping, shouting, scooping up fallen coins, punching one another in the face, and screaming deprecations that involve one another's grandmothers and grandfathers and great-grandmothers and great-grandfathers, all of whom apparently had various kinds of illicit liaisons with various kinds of draft animals and fish.

And there is that rope again, the delimiting equation $2\pi\sqrt{\frac{l}{g}}$ bringing it back to Aeid just when he needs it most, and, this time, his ruse has cleared enough space about him so that he can actually get hold of it and, straining, begin to haul himself up.

Never ... never ... never underestimate the covetousness of the Panasian citizen. Never. But thank Panas (blessed be He!) for that covetousness!

But before he can completely escape the crowd that is still grasping, shouting, scooping up fallen coins, et cetera, a hand grips his shoulder. It is a woman, and her face cloth is as askew as Aeid's mask and cape.

"O great deliverer who has so disgraced and humiliated the tax collectors," she says, "who are you? By what name shall we call you?"

For a moment, dangling as he is half in and half out of his predicament, Aeid is tempted to ignore the question and flee, and since the bailiffs are even now getting up, swinging their staves, and cracking heads once more, he reflects that this is a very good temptation, one to which he should doubtless succumb. But Aeid is a prince, and therefore he cannot but reflect also that a good prince gives his people what they need; and as, at present, they need a name, he must oblige. "Know, you people of Nuhr," he begins in a loud voice, "that I am ... I ... ah ..."

And it is only now that Aeid realizes that he has forgotten something absolutely crucial. He is Baroz the rug merchant, Darzo the tailor, and a number of other people. But who is this masked figure he has now become?

"... ah ... that is ... I ..."

Pumice!

Thinking quickly, he puts together something ad hoc, something inelegant, something that he will, unfortunately, have to live with for a long time.

"I am the ... the ... the ... ah ... the ..."

Really, he is unwilling to utter it, but he must have a name. For his people. He *must.*

"I am ... the Blue Avenger!"

And as the woman who touched his shoulder is beaten to the ground by the bailiffs (she has, after all, touched a man, and Panasian law is very clear about things like that), and as Aeid hauls himself up the front of the temple and makes his escape ...

... so it is.

Chapter Sixteen

Strips of gold leaf. A piece of copper wire. A cork. A clear glass bottle. A bit of wax . . .

With a sensation as of a tightening in his groin, Umi Botzu bent over the seemingly random collection of parts that occupied the low table in his study. His ropes—his webs—hung vacant, untenanted, for one could not pursue the ways of high sorcery when suspended from the ceiling like a flaccid wineskin. No: as Captain Scruffy had said, "A man—" (By which Umi Botzu understood him to mean *a sorcerer,* for who else but a sorcerer could be a real man?) "—must have a place to work." And so Umi Botzu had exchanged his webs for a table, his hammock of woven ropes for a stool. And now he bent over a collection of parts . . .

You don't love me anymore.

Umi Botzu took up the wire, bent the last bit of one end at a right angle, and then, with much muttering and cursing under his breath about the softness of the metal (which *would* bend every time any force was applied to it), he thrust the other end through the cork until the width of several fingers was protruding from the far side, after which he took a pair of pincers and carefully formed the protruding end into a loop.

Sorcery! Yes!

Carefully again, making sure that he did not inadvertently breathe upon it, Umi Botzu lifted a single strip of gold leaf and attempted to hang it on the right-angle bend of the wire, but his hands were shaking so badly that he tore the first three strips beyond use. Finally, though, he got his fingers under control and managed to coax the strip into position.

Oh, yesyesyes . . .

And then, slowly, as though relishing the vitreous penetration, he lowered the end of the wire that bore the gold leaf into the bottle until the cork fitted snugly into the mouth.

Tightening . . . tightening . . . almost there!

His hands were shaking badly now, and he forced himself—"A scientist must have discipline," Scruffy had said (by which Umi Botzu had understood him to mean *a sorcerer must have discipline*)—to get up from the table and walk outside.

Under the influence of Captain Scruffy's teachings, Umi Botzu's house was already beginning to lose some of its overtly spiderish qualities. The hyacinths by the front gate, for example, now had company in the form of violets and sweet peas ("The study of Nature is very important to the scientist," Scruffy had said, by which Umi Botzu had understood him to mean *to the sorcerer*.), and the walls were cleaner and in better repair ("A well-ordered house for a well-ordered man," Scruffy had said, by which Umi Botzu had understood him to mean, as usual . . . something else).

At last, though, Umi Botzu calmed himself enough to return to his work space; and there, with unshaking fingers but well-tightened groin (really, he felt as though . . . well . . . as though . . . he just might . . .), he heated the wax

and applied it to the meeting of cork and glass until he had
formed an air-tight seal.

But of course I love you.

For a minute or two, he held the electroscope (for such
it was) up before his eyes, turning it so as to examine it
from every angle, caressing it as though it might respond
to him. (He was certainly responding to it!) But at last
(Discipline again! Always discipline!) he set it down on
the table, took a key from a pouch on his belt, and opened
a locked chest.

A square of wool. An amber rod.

Yesyesyes . . .

This was it. Sorcery. High sorcery. His hands were trembling again, but he paid not the slightest attention, for he
was immersed, obsessed, fixated upon the just-within-his-
grasp presence of his Beloved; and as he briskly rubbed the
rod with the square of wool, he felt his personal fire building
in response, throbbing, rising ever higher.

Sorcery! Oh . . . oh, yes!

It's very hard for me to tell
sometimes.

And when at last he held the rod to the loop of wire that
protruded from the cork, and when at last he saw the ends
of the enclosed gold leaf flutter, quiver, and—slowly, will-
ingly, yieldingly—spread apart within the protective confines of their glassy world, then the fire got the better of
him, rose up his belly, and consumed him utterly as,
clutching the electroscope to his breast, he screamed, over
and over:

"It is mine! Mine! Mine! And soon it will all *be mine!"*

The tax collectors are being terrorized again today.
There simply is no way to predict when the bright, dashing

figure of the Blue Avenger will sweep down from above,
scatter collectors and coins both, and then vanish back up
the rope by which he originally arrived. Bailiffs cannot
stop him. Priestly denunciations cannot stop him. Even
palace guards cannot stop him (for some have tried, only
to discover that the Blue Avenger is as handy with a sword
as he is with ropes). True, the tax collecting goes on, for
though there is but one Blue Avenger, there are many tax
collectors; but the members of that honorable profession
have lately been developing a number of eccentricities in
their behavior: strange nervous tics, rapid over-the-
shoulder glances, a tendency to jump at abrupt sounds . . .

What do you mean by that?

At present, though, someone else is demonstrating a
skill with ropes, climbing, and stealth that the Blue
Avenger himself might envy. Bakbuk (who, being no
friend of the priesthood, finds a source of continual
amusement in the Avenger's exploits), is lowering himself
(it is a boy day today) down a rope on the outside of the
palace, somehow managing to stay out of sight among the
carvings, ledges, and pinnacles, even though it is broad
daylight and all the usual guards are on duty.

Forsaking the rope at the last minute, he clings to the
cracks and crevices of the wall and descends using only
the strength of his fingers and toes until he reaches a particular window at a particular level. In a moment, he is
peering into the chambers of Prince Aeid.

You're just taking me for granted.

The prince, oddly enough, is not in his chambers, but if
Bakbuk, making note of this fact, couples it in any way
with the simultaneous appearance of the Blue Avenger in
the market square (and he can hear the distant screaming

even now: something about draft animals and fish), he keeps the coupling to himself.

Couplings aside, he is here today not for himself, but for King Inwa Kabir, and if there is any loyalty in the world, Bakbuk is loyal to the king, else he would have refused this particular assignment with harsh words, and perhaps the point of a knife. As far as Bakbuk is concerned, you see, spying on the Americans is one thing, spying on the prince himself is quite another.

But Bakbuk is loyal—to the king—and therefore he is springing the catch on the lattices that cover Aeid's window, and therefore he is swinging those lattices open, and therefore he is slipping into the room, his bare feet silent upon the marble floor and soft rugs alike.

I certainly am not! How can you say that?

Again he hears distant screams from the market square. Draft animals ... and fish. Strange.

With the lattices closed and lamps out, Aeid's chambers are shrouded in an obscurity that turns tapestries into shadowed images out of uneasy dreams, carpets into undulating passageways down to the infernal regions of the Puritans, dishes of uneaten food (really, the servants should have cleared them away long ago, but Aeid is not one to scold them: he appears to be very much the republican these days, which is one of the reasons Bakbuk is here this morning) into bouquets of carnivorous flowers ready to ensnare an unwary hummingbird.

Silently, Bakbuk makes his way into the prince's inner rooms. Touching nothing, disturbing nothing, he merely examines, looks, stands on tiptoe and peers. By Aeid's express orders, no one but the prince himself enters these rooms, and with mild curiosity tempered by a loyalty that is almost clinical, Bakbuk takes note of the locked cases of books—Western books—ranged around the room, memorizing a smattering of titles and a sampling of authors in order to flesh out the report that he will make to King Inwa Kabir.

You never take me anywhere!

Encyclopédie, Cicero, Hume, *De l'esprit des lois,* Vergil, *Dictionnaire philosophique,* Montesquieu, Rousseau . . .

"Mucus."

"I am sorry: what?"

"Mucus."

"Ah . . . just so."

Dubiously, Sari regarded the woman who sat on the other side of the low burning fire, the fire burning low, doubtless, because the atmosphere in the tiny house was about as stifling as Sari had ever experienced, the air being stifling, doubtless, because the woman kept the fire burning without great regard for the niceties of such things as ventilation.

And where could I take you?

Sari had come to Sayam, the last village before the city of Katha, and she had come to it, again, as a different woman. Where before she had managed to preserve at least a shred of hope, now she was finding that even that had been taken from her, for, everywhere she looked, the simple, elegant, trusting Naianism she had once known was gone, its place taken by a conglomeration of superstition, exploitation, and sheer ignorance so different from the former that she could not begin to fathom how the change had taken place.

Though she had tried at times to put it down to faulty memory or to the parochialism of isolated communities, the presentiment was growing on her that it was neither. Nothing could account for the discrepancies between reality and her memory save madness, (and she knew that she was not mad); and there were too many similarities between the excesses of one Naian community and the obsessions of another for her to ascribe it all to simple parochialism. No, this perversion of the ways of Naia was something that had happened—happened everywhere—over the course of several generations, as though the drought that had afflicted the entire land for three centuries had at last reached into the collective Naian heart and bled the last trances of fructifying water from it, withering what had once been the greenest of all branches.

Hmmph!

"Mucus," said the woman again. "It all comes down to mucus. Mucus in everyone. Mucus in you, mucus in me . . . though, to tell the truth (for that is what I must do), there is much less mucus in me than there is in you."

Regarding the woman across the fire—young, but exuding a strange sense of desiccation—Sari felt the hopelessness growing. This, she had been told, was the elder of the Naian community of Sayam. Everyone she had met in the street had agreed, everyone had pointed out her house. "A brilliant woman," one had said. "Oh, yes: she might as well be Naia Herself," another exclaimed.

And Sari, who had at first been disquieted because the woman was so young, had been further disquieted because the sum total of what the woman had to say appeared to have nothing to do with anything save the eradication of mucus from one's body.

Oh, tell me!

"Mucus is at the root of everything," the woman went on. "It affects everything we do. Now, you might wonder

how I know that you have so much mucus in your body.
I can tell, believe me. You look frightful. You are old . . ."

Sari, who had assumed that her sagging skin and droop-
ing breasts had more to do with age than with mucus, was
nonetheless offended.

". . . and you are ugly, and that is on account of the mucus in your system that has slowed the circulation of the
vital fluids."

Sari had difficulty believing that the woman across the
fire had any acquaintance with any kind of fluids, vital or
not, but, "Honored sister," she said, trying to be polite, "I
am over seventy. I have had five children and have been
pregnant ten times—"

"And that is something else," the woman went on, veer-
ing onto a new course as though she had been planning it
all along. "Your miscarriages. Mucus. It was only luck that
gave you the children that you had."

You get mad whenever I talk
about it.

"I was under the impression that Naia—"

The woman rolled over her protest like a dusty wave.
"You happened to have a low level of mucus in your body
at the time that you were carrying them. The others . . .
well . . ." She shook her head. "You ate unwisely. You had
too much mucus." She suddenly peered hard at Sari, her
lusterless hair falling over one eye. "Have you been excised?"

"Ah . . ." Sari was confused, uncertain, but she preferred
both to the growing certainty that now she knew exactly
what the woman was talking about.

"Have you been cut? If you have not, then I am not a
bit surprised that you lost those children. That thing you
have is an abode of worms. They breed there, and they
feed on the mucus, and they kill your babies."

Sari stared in disbelief. She had never quite gotten over her miscarriages—no woman, no matter how resilient, could ever put such things completely behind her—and now not only was this woman blaming her for them, she was also calling attention to something that, until now, Sari had been doing her best to ignore: the fact that she was, forever, marked as a Panasian woman, her very body sealed with the sign of the God.

Tell me! Anything!

"Ah, yes," said the woman, "you weep. You weep because the truth hurts. But it has been revealed to me that my duty in this life is to speak the truth, no matter how painful it might be, no matter how unpleasant, and I have taken the name Truth Teller so as to witness my devotion and dedication to my calling."

"That is ..." Sari blinked back her tears. "That is ... terrible."

The woman, Truth Teller, was unfazed: "Ah, but now you seek to interfere with my calling, and I cannot let you do that, for my calling comes from Naia Herself."

"I was told that you are the elder of the community here."

"That is so. I am the elder of Sayam. I was recognized very early on as a spiritual leader. I am a very spiritual person. Others might be mundane and boring, but I am spiritual, and I tell the truth. That is my calling, and I am happy to fulfill it."

What's the use? You'll just get mad.

Trembling, Sari stood up. "Thank you. I will go now."

"Wait." The woman fixed her with a dull eye. "I have not yet told you what to eat and what to drink. Then you will not have any mucus in your body." Again, a peering through her lusterless hair. "I can excise you, too."

For a moment, Sari stood, shaking, and then, without another word, she turned and left the house, left the Naian quarter, left the city . . . and came to the cluster of tents and camels that marked the campsite of Ehar's caravan.

Yalliah was bent over the big pot, preparing the evening meal, but she could not but look up, startled, at the old woman's rapid approach, for, indeed, Sari was running, her aged body both protesting the exertions she forced upon it and feeling with every step the mutilations of the past and the present. "Sari? Ehar says that we are leaving tomorrow morning. There is nothing to be had in Sayam, he says."

"Fine . . . fine . . ." Sari rushed past her, making for the women's tent, searching for some privacy in which she could sob out her pain.

"Sari . . . ?"

"Tell Ehar that he is perfectly right about Sayam," Sari called over her shoulder as she plunged into the tent. "There is, surely, nothing to be had in Sayam."

No. No. I promise. Tell me.

She found a number of cushions in one corner, and, in the dim, cloth-filtered light, she threw herself on them, clutching one to her belly, sobbing into another. It was but a minute or two—just long enough to give the big pot a final stir—before Yalliah, veiled and, yes, excised, came into the tent and, sitting down beside her Naian sister, took her head into her lap as though she were a hurt child; but Sari felt nonetheless that a void had opened within her that was beyond the reach of such things as kindness and compassion, and she could not help but wonder why Naia had so deserted Her children.

You keep me cooped up in here,
and we never do *anything*.

What was wrong with Mather?

Well, Jenkins cataloged, for one thing, he seemed to be in a certain amount of pain all the time. From a single, occasional squirm, the mousy engineer's repertoire of discomfort had grown into a virtual multitude of tics, jiggles, and minor spasms.

Most of them were not overly noticeable. Quite the contrary. Under normal circumstances, Jenkins might not have noticed that anything was much amiss with his counterfeit assistant. But after having shared with Mather (and, God help him, with Wool) the confines of a ship's cabin for several weeks, Jenkins had become intimately familiar with the man's behavior. His normal behavior. And so Jenkins saw the changes and additions, and Jenkins wondered.

But twitches and squirms were not all, for (And here was, most decidedly, the other thing) since his sudden and unexpected return after his sudden and unexpected (and still unexplained) absence, Mather's attitude had changed from servile acquiescence to sustained, arrogant, and almost open rebellion. Indeed, Jenkins at times had the distinct impression that Mather was only tolerating his presence and his orders, that, under only slightly different circumstances, the engineer would have gladly snapped his fingers in the ambassador's face and bid him go do something . . . something . . . well, something less than pleasant.

But what could we do?

But Jenkins had to admit that aside from a few changes that could be pinned down but not necessarily complained about—to be sure, the squirms and wiggles were only *barely* perceptible, the rebellion only *almost* open—Mather was certainly doing his job, was, in fact, doing far more than that. He had, for example, reset the gravimeter so that it did indeed work with much greater accuracy, predicting that, were he and the device transported to the city of Katha, in the mountains, he would be able to determine, once and for all, the feasibility of finding an appropriate passage to the interior of the continent ... and thereby bring closer to reality the Righteous States of America's plan to surprise Citizen Bonaparte's army when Citizen Bonaparte least expected it.

And even beyond that, Mather had somehow managed to worm his way into the good graces of none other than the Gharat, Abnel, the High Priest of Nuhr, the head of the Panasian religion. This, given the continuing intransigence of Haddar, was an unexpected stroke of the greatest kind of luck, and even though Mather's action had violated the spirit of Jenkins' secret orders (by which it was understood that Jenkins was the ambassador and Mather was the engineer), Mather was, after all, passing as a diplomatic assistant, and so, in the end, the letter of the orders had been followed.

Well, you could take me . . . somewhere.

In contrast to his opaque behavior at that first banquet, Abnel proved in the end to be a far more congenial official than the imperious Haddar (with whom Jenkins continued to fight every day ... though without revealing his new contact). Abnel, despite his bland demeanor and his fondness for unpalatable examples of Kaprishan gourmet cooking, was all smiles and courtesy, willing to talk about his country, willing—even eager—to listen to Jenkins. And, more important, Abnel had direct access to the king.

And Abnel, it turned out, was willing to escort the American embassy to Katha.

Where could I take you?

Jenkins did not understand why Abnel should be so pliant while Haddar was so stubborn any more than he understood what had gotten into Mather, but he was unwilling to let such an opportunity slip through his fingers. Here was the chance he had wanted, here was a distinct diplomatic coup. True, going off to Katha would more than likely aggravate Haddar, but, in a theocracy, the chief minister was a comparatively minor official compared to the high priest, and Jenkins was a man who was—to use a phrase much in currency in the Three Kingdoms—perfectly willing to drop a blunt chisel for a sharp one.

You could take me . . . oh, what's the use!

And so, despite Mather's twitching, wiggling, and squirming, despite his growing penchant for petty snits and condescension, Jenkins agreed (hesitantly and dubiously, to be sure, as befitted a proper diplomat) to the trip, and about a week later, just as the nameless party of Khyrling revolutionaries detonated yet another bomb that blew up yet another neighborhood of the Mud Dwellings that swarmed thickly about the base of the jasper and marble walls of the city of Nuhr, Jenkins and his companions—escorted by a large number of priests, guards, and minor officials (including, to be sure, the men in bright uniforms, the musicians braying on brass horns, and the barefoot boys with powdered faces whose function the ambassador had *still* not been able to determine), and at the side of no less than the Gharat himself—rode out of the east gate of the city.

No, please. Tell me.

Pushed forward by the shock wave of the detonation as by a hand . . .

"Good Lord!" said Jenkins, abruptly reminded that the Three Kingdoms were obviously not as closed and isolated as he had thought. Where, for example, *were* they getting that gunpowder??

"They are corrupt; they have done abominable works; *there is* none that doeth good," said Mr. Wool.

Well . . . you could take me . . .

Mr. Mather glanced at Mr. Wool and (Squirm!) looked nervous.

Where? Tell me! Anything!

. . . the party set off along the road that followed what was left of the once-great River Forshen . . .

You could take me with you when
you go to . . . to . . .

. . . making for Katha, making for the mountains.

Chapter Seventeen

"Ah! It is so wonderful to see you again, I cannot tell you how delighted I am to set my old eyes upon you, though I am sure you understand that I cannot see you as clearly as I would like ... the embroidery you know. And I am old! Yes! Old! The years have taken much from me, and I am flattered, flattered so much that you have come to see what an old man can do for you.

"The last shipment? Poor quality? Oh, I am so sorry, I cannot tell you how sorry I am that the goods with which I have provided you have caused you the least bit of dissatisfaction, but I assure you that from *here*, they seemed of the very best quality indeed! Yes! Quality! Oh my, yes. My walls shook, oh, I would say for the better part of a minute, though I cannot tell you for sure since my pocket watch stopped running a long time ago. Alas! it was one of the few things I had managed to keep as a memory of the old *Frères Marseillaise,* but as I am sure you understand, there are no watchmakers here in Nuhr—none!— and therefore the old machine stopped and has not run since. But, Panas be praised (Yes! Panas! You see I am just like you now!), fortunately this machine of mine is still working well, and is still able to—

"But the quality ... Well, I must tell you that my walls

shook for some time, and I myself went out to the gates just this morning to see what had happened, and it certainly looked to me as though the goods were everything one might wish for, but, of course, my eyes are not what they were when I was a young and dashing lieutenant on board the *Frères Marseillaise,* and, of course ... the embroidery, you know.

"But you are dissatisfied, you say, and you have come to me and said to me, *Old Valdemar, we are dissatisfied,* and therefore I must in all conscience make it up to you. Perhaps half of the next shipment should be with my compliments? Would that be satisfactory? You understand, I am sure, that I must provide for myself in my old age that is even now upon me, and that this arrangement will of course put some hardship upon me, but you have said that you are dissatisfied, and therefore amends must be made. Yes! Amends! And so I will make them!

"Until next time, then. Thank you. Thank you. Thank you. Goodbye. The blessings of Panas be upon you. Good bye. Thank you ...

"Bastards!"

Adventure was addictive.

Prince Aeid found this out quite rapidly, for, more than when he donned ragged clothes and a rusty sword and became Baroz the rug merchant, more than when he hunkered down in the dim light of a shop at the end of a twisted street and assumed the role of Darzo the tailor, more even than when, at night, he donned white robes and a face cloth and flitted mysteriously through the deserted market square as a strange, ghostly woman whom some thought to be a widow searching for a son executed for a long ago transgression of Panasian law, others thought to be the ghost of some woman who had been executed for a long ago transgression of Panasian law, and all agreed was the most remarkably tall woman they had seen in a long time (and surely there was some law against that), Aeid found that his escapades as the Blue Avenger provided him not only a release from the daily frustrations of being prince and palace stud (and, therefore, about as impotent a man as there could be in the city of Nuhr), but also with a deep, internal satisfaction that he had not experienced since that one, single evening almost ten years ago when, for the space of an entire hour, he had believed that a woman had liked him for reasons other that his status and his royalty ... that belief being abruptly shattered when she had thereafter attempted to poison him.

But—"*SCORIATIC SINUS SCRAPERS FOR THE ICHTHYOPHTHIRIUSIC INTRIGUERS OF INIQUITY!*" COMES, ONCE ... (sorry) ... comes, once more, the call from the roofs above the market square, and (Yes, well, he is at it again.) the Blue Avenger swoops in with a flutter of cape and tatters, bearing directly down on the tax collectors (whose expressions mirror sundry variations on the theme of *Oh, well, it was not a very good day, anyway,* and who make half hearted attempts to flee, obviously knowing from the start that it will be useless, that they will manage no more than two or three steps before the bright blue, anthropomorphic bolt from the heavens will plow directly into them).

And it looks as though, once again, the Blue Avenger is aiming not directly for the fleeing tax collectors, but for the table, having become hopelessly addicted (See above: *Adventure was addictive.*) to that bump, swish, and crash that come from impacting on a good, solid table, skidding down its length, and smashing not only through the stacks and heaps and baskets of coins but also directly (and finally) into the backs (the length of the table acting somewhat like a gunsight) of the tax collectors themselves (who have indeed only managed two or three steps) thus making one swoop suffice for no less than three instant gratifications.

And so it is. Bump! Swish! Crash! The tax collectors go down, the crowd closes in, and *"I am the Blue Avenger!"* Aeid roars to the sound of cheering that is, admittedly, already much adulterated with deprecations involving various kinds of draft animals and fish.

But today, as Aeid puts out a hand to retrieve his rope (that, by the magic of $T = 2\pi\sqrt{\frac{1}{g}}$, should be swinging back toward his grasp, the prince having become so used to the inviolability of physical law that he can now manage the retrieval without even *looking*), he finds that the rope is not there. In fact, looking up toward the roof from which, a minute ago, he swung down, he notices that the rope no longer appears to be attached to anything, that it, in fact, no longer appears to be in evidence at all.

And then he sees that many guards are appearing from out of the temple doors, from beneath carts and wagons, from under awnings, from behind shops and stalls—many more, in fact, than he can ever hope to overpower alone, no matter what his skill with a sword—and that they are surrounding him and beginning to close in. They have, apparently, cut his rope and obviously intend to bring him down simply by weight of numbers.

This really will not do. It is not so much a question of being caught (though Aeid suspects that his father, after having it thought about, can surely come up with something wonderfully unpleasant for him) as of future opportunities lost, for Aeid has, over the course of the last week or so, been making plans, plans in which the Blue Avenger figures prominently, plans that involve not the terrorization of simple and relatively insignificant tax collectors, but of the Gharat himself.

But as the guards close in, it looks to Aeid very much

as though all those plans will come to nothing, for there seems to be no escape. At least, none that involve a rope.

So, with a shrug, a scream, and a *yah-da-diddle-diddle-bam-bam-bam* shuffle, side-slip, and full-speed-ahead run, he flings himself directly into the nearest (and, because of its quick advance, thinnest) line of guards. He goes down immediately, of course, but this is what he intended, for he immediately begins seizing as many guards as he can—finding a wrist here, a leg there, a waistband over yonder—and, with a good hearty pull, inviting them to join him on the ground in a nice, cozy sprawl.

But at the same time as the guards are falling around him and the dust is rising in a obscuring cloud, Aeid is ripping off pieces of his blue tatters and pressing them into hands, stuffing them into shoes, sticking them into waistbands; and the flashes of blue in the rising dust cloud prove to be marvelously attractive to the guards who are beyond his grasp, for they immediately pounce on those flashes with shouts of "Here he is!" and "We have him now!" and "Do not let him escape!", thus dragging to the ground their fellow guards who, despite Aeid's thoughtful invitation, have managed to get back to their feet (and, almost invariably, joining them).

The dust rises higher, the shouts of the confused guards mix with the sound of cheering (and, to be sure, deprecations involving various kinds of draft animals and fish), and Aeid, after knotting his cape around the neck of the captain of the guards while shouting "Here he is!" and "We have him now!" and "Do not let him escape!" thrusts the bewildered officer straight into the hands (and truncheons) of his own men, pushes through an opportune thinning of the press, and sprints away—away from the temple, away from the guards—following a zigzag course through the stalls and shops of the market, passing quickly through the Square of the Divine Statue (And, by Panas, they are following him!), running full-tilt along the tree-lined Way of Righteous Worship and the Alleyway of Priestly Tolerance (And they are gaining on him!), ducking, with the sounds of many footsteps and the clatter of many swords and truncheons not far behind, through the Arch of Omnipotence and from there into the Byway of Magisterial Indifference, dithering for a moment (as the footsteps—many footsteps—draw ever closer) between two turnings before choosing the Promenade of the Justified Wealth of Merchants (and trying, as he does, to remember whether the Justified Wealth of Merchants is, in actuality, a dead end . . .

"Ah! It is so wonderful to see you again, I cannot tell you how delighted I am to set my old eyes upon you, though I am sure you understand that I cannot see you as clearly as I would like . . . the embroidery you know. And I am old! Yes! Old! The years have taken much from me, and I am flattered, flattered so much that you have come to see what an old man can do for you.

"The last device? Poor quality? Injury? Oh, I am so sorry, I cannot tell you how sorry I am that the device with which I provided your master has caused him the least bit of dissatisfaction, but I assure you that when I made it, it seemed of the very best quality indeed! Yes! Quality! Oh my, yes. He told me so himself, oh, I would say, for the better part of a minute, though I cannot tell you for sure since my watch stopped running a long time ago. Alas! it was one of the few things I had managed to keep as a memory of the old *Frères Marseillaise,* but as I am sure you understand, there are no watchmakers here in Nuhr—none!—and therefore the old machine stopped and has not run since. But, Panas be praised (Yes! Panas! You see I am just like you now!), fortunately this machine of mine is still working well, and is still able to—

"But the quality . . . Well, I must tell you that he himself told me that he thought the device excellent, and he even tried it on in the back room of my shop while I watched, and it certainly looked to me as though the device was everything one might wish for, but, of course, my eyes are not what they were when I was a young and dashing lieutenant on board the *Frères Marseillaise,* and, of course . . . the embroidery, you know.

"But he is dissatisfied, you say, and you have come to me and said to me, *Old Valdemar, our master is dissatisfied,* and therefore I must in all conscience make it up to him. Perhaps the next device should be with my compliments? Would that be satisfactory? You understand, I am sure, that I must provide for myself in my old age that is even now upon me, and that this arrangement will of course put some hardship upon me, but you have said that your master is dissatisfied, and therefore amends must be made. Yes! Amends! And so I will make them!

"Until next time, then. Thank you. Thank you. Thank you. Goodbye. The blessings of Panas be upon you. Good bye. Thank you . . .

"Perverts!"

. . . and narrowly avoiding a group of priestly slaves who are just now making their way back up the promenade), sprinting along the narrow way from which the slaves have come until, with a glance over his shoulder that tells him that the guards are, in fact, almost upon him, he takes hold of the door of the nearest shop, throws it open, and plunges in.

"Ah! It is so wonderful to see you again," begins the old merchant, a foreign-looking man (Foreign? In Nuhr?) who nonetheless wears the head cloth of a Panasian and appears to have something to do with embroidery. "I cannot tell you how delighted I am to—" And then the em-

broiderer suddenly breaks off, peers hard at the figure who
has entered his shop so precipitously (and who, despite the
loss of his cape and many tatters, is still—booted, masked,
and clad in blue as he is—rather striking), and stares,
dumbfounded.

Aeid has no time for introductions. However, as he is a
good prince, he gives his people what they want, and since
the foreign-looking merchant so obviously wants some
kind of explanation, Aeid sings out a cheery "Just passing
through, my man!" and darts through a door into the interior of the shop just as the guards burst in behind him.

"Ah!" begins the merchant once more, "it is so wonderful to see you again—" but the rapid advance and
deployment of guards causes him to fall silent even more
quickly than did the appearance of the Blue Avenger.

Aeid, meanwhile, has found himself in a long corridor
lined with doors. Knowing full well that the guards will
quickly follow him, he does not hesitate, but runs down its
length, takes a corner, takes another (How large *is* this
shop, anyway?), then takes another. Still, though, as he is
still in the hallway, and as the hallway is still lined with
doors, Aeid is forced to make a decision as a rattle and a
thud and a clash of swords and truncheons from behind
tell him that the guards are again gaining on him.

The first door he chooses comes completely away from
the wall, and Aeid discovers that it bears a price tag. The
foreign-looking gentleman is obviously both an embroiderer and a dealer in used doors. Undeterred, he puts the
door back, turns to another, which (1) proves to be real
and (2) opens into a large room filled with casks and barrels on which are stenciled (in French): *KEEP AWAY
FROM FIRE*.

Foreign? French? Fire?

But the room has no door save the one Aeid has just
opened, and so the prince must turn his back on the mys-

terious barrels, and he must turn it quickly because the guards are still advancing. A crash tells Aeid that the guards have also discovered that the foreign-looking gentleman sells doors, but, since the necessity of making a thorough search forces them to try all potential exits— attached or not, functional or not—the crash is immediately followed by others as doors and more doors come tumbling down.

Aeid tries a third door and winds up staring at Haddar. The strangeness of meeting Inwa Kabir's chief minister under these circumstances, though great enough, is, however, made greater, amplified, and compounded by the fact that Haddar is wearing no clothing. He is, in fact, wearing nothing save a peculiar device that is strapped over his groin and that resembles nothing quite so much as a rather crudely fashioned, imitation vulva.

Haddar blinks his calculating eyes. "It must, after all, fit," he says as though there is nothing particularly unusual about standing in a small closet of a room in an embroidery shop/used-door emporium/French warehouse wearing an artificial cunt.

"To be sure," replies Aeid, who is no longer so much looking at Haddar as at the door on the *other* side of the closet. "Where does that door go?"

Haddar winces suddenly. *"Ow!,"* he yelps, and he makes an indefinite motion that has something to do with the straps of the device.

With the guards coming on quickly in spite of their methodical (and noisy) search, Aeid has no time now for anything save escape. Brushing past the fully-equipped chief counselor, he grabs the latch of the door on the far side of the tiny room and wrenches it open.

To his relief, not only does the door actually open, but it opens into another hallway, at the end of which is a curtain . . .

No time now for anything but action. Aeid runs the length of the hallway and pushes through the curtain.

"Ah! It is so wonderful to see you again," begins the embroiderer (for, yes, Aeid has come full circle, and he is back into the front room of the shop), "I cannot tell you how delighted I am to set my old—" He peers at Aeid, frowns. "Oh, *Sacre Bleu!*, what is the use?" he says just as a thudding from the corridor behind the curtain tells Aeid that the guards are coming.

At the same time, however, the other door (the one by which Aeid first left the front room) flies open, and yet another group of guards comes streaming out, seeking to blockade the front door.

"Ah! It is so wonderful . . . no . . . wait . . ." The embroiderer looks again, clenches his fists. *"Merde!"*

The captain points at the Blue Avenger: "Seize him! If he is still at large when the Gharat returns from Katha, it is ourselves who will be sent to the mountains!"

Mountains? Aeid wonders. *And the Gharat . . . in Katha?*

But he has little time to wonder about any of it. Wondering must come later. For now, he beats the guards to the door, slams it in their faces, and wedges it closed with the sign that, until now, has been hanging from an outside beam, proclaiming to all who might pass by: *Valdemar. Embroidery.*

Valdemar. The name sounds vaguely familiar, but it, too, will have to wait. For the moment, Aeid is concerned only with putting as much distance between himself and the guards as he can, of getting out of the Blue Avenger costume, of resuming (at least for the time being) the identity of Prince Aeid, dutiful son of King Inwa Kabir, lover of his people . . . and palace stud.

At least for the time being. At least until he can get sufficient equipment and supplies together to make the journey to Katha himself.

Ineluctable modality of the spiritual life: at least that. Pervades everything. Diaphanous, obdurate as iron. These blocks men call houses hewn out of origins a hundred kils away. Iron chisels. Swarthy, omnipotent hands swinging a mallet like a woodcarver in the market square, a veiled wife at home (A wife? For God?) with a brat sucking at her teat (Who would that be?) who asks for settels and copper so she can buy milk. What? (Wife: maybe . . . no . . .) Hauled on His back a hundred kils (to Katha, at least; more to Nuhr), big divine feet stumping up and down the mountainsides—*Oh, wife, I have the shinsplints again today!*—up and down and dropping the stones here, kicking open doorways and setting the rooms He made in order.

God as sculptor. God as stonecutter. God as innkeeper? Doorways passing. Dogs pissing in shadows. Old men nodding off. Shaped by the Hand. Beggars. Gnarled hands reaching up. They have to go back to hovels at night and who made them? The God? Mud-toter as well as stone shaper? Someone had to make them. Houses, too. But if God made all . . .

I remember the texts. There is nothing wrong with my memory.

"Water! Come buy my water!"

Trickling over my skull while that idiot wields the razor. Cut me and I bled. Blood on the land. Blood of Naia, they called the rivers. Particularly the Caves. Ever flowing. Naia's promise. Read it in the old scrolls.

—We know more about them than *they* do! he exclaimed suddenly.

But the rivers are drying up, and so is Naia. (God's wife. I wonder. Could it be? Who does God fuck? Impure thougths, but someone has to think them.) Water. Razor. Scraping. Giggling while he did it. Novices play too much, get carried away, and there was that accident . . . slipped. Nose of a camel. Stick it in God's tent. God. Good. Everywhere. Nowhere. Paradoxes. Everywhere. Feel it now, waggling. Seal of the God. What do the women feel? Nothing. But there he is in the doorway with a brass cup, and he is sealed, too. What did they do with the novice? Send him to girls' school? *Here, walk like this*. Growing hair instead of shaving it. Never escape. Sealed for life.

Katha: guts of a beast. You can walk away from the temple but you will always come back. Never escape. Serpent with tail in his mouth. Tail in God's tent. Here, walk like this. Waggle my hips for the God and it looks like . . . oh! His toe is rotted off. Lion charges up, says *I'll have your toe,* and comes the reply *Buy my water*. And then the God loses his toe, or maybe it was just shinsplints. Better than his member. *Walk like this*.

This time next moon no escape forever. But no escape now, really. Spirituality over all. Buy my water. Buy my spirit. Let me make you a house. If you have money.

I remembered, though. The text was not all. Cannot possibly be right, but I remember. Words on paper? Shit and more shit. No escape. What would they do to me? *Here, walk like this*. Could I grow my hair? Down the back, tickling, feel some great ape of a merchant sticking it in. Nose in God's tent.

Cloacal passageway down to the city gate, then back again. Regurgitation. Odor of coffee, they said, made the old chief priest ill. Katha bad place for him. *So be it ar— uck, uck, uck* . . . Bad place for me, too, but there is no escape. Katha swallows but does not regurgitate. Or does it? What emetic must I use so that they might vomit me out but not kill me? Where is he now? Mincing and pretty? Could I . . . would they . . . ?

No ... no ...

Next moon. And they seal me. Seal my lips. Seal everything. No escape, but I remember what the text said, and I know how to keep silent.

Something is wrong.

"For the love of Panas! A settel!"

Beshur looked at the ragged, emaciated figure.

—I have no money for you, he said, I am a priest.

"For the love of Panas!"

I lie, but he does not know the difference. Does that damn me? Pure and perfect. Sealed. Novice, priest. What does he care? For the love of Panas, give me money. For the love of Panas, give me a stone house. For the love of Panas, give me belief. Mark of favor. Stone. Mud: water and earth. Cursed dwellers in the hovels outside the walls. Stone remains. Water changes. Mud changes. Only stone remains. But I remember. It *was* changed, and something *is* wrong. Why did they insist?

Would they? Really? What? Feeling ... nothing. No ...

And yet only a moon. Month of the Chisel. Month of the Strong Hand. Month of the Sturdy Stick, by which is meant something else, and so all are sealed.

He paused and looked after a woman.

All that cloth and they cannot hide the sway of their hips. Once she might have done it for herself, but now just for others. Only the numb womb remaining. Pure for the pleasure of Panas. All their attention to their men. Cut when they do not even know what they will miss. Do they know? *Here, walk like this.*

Do I know? When did they cut me?

Chapter Eighteen

"I had no idea," said Jenkins (though he had a very good idea indeed), "that we had been so honored by our reception in Nuhr. Do I understand you correctly, Gharat? Panas *made* the cities of the Three Kingdoms with his own hands?"

It was evening, and the grand progress of the High Priest, his companions, and his attendants, after having covered five miles that day, had stopped, commandeered a large plot of ground near a village for its pavilions and tents, appropriated most of the comestible resources possessed by that village for its plates and cups, and had settled in for the night (further participation by the village not required). Here in Abnel's immense pavilion, though, lamps were burning brilliantly and, after having consumed a large, elaborate dinner, the Gharat and his American guests were enjoying their meal and finishing it off with wine and conversation.

Ever the rigid Puritan, Jenkins was careful about how much he drank, a sentiment that was, he noted with annoyance, not at all shared by Mather, who swilled down cup after cup of the potent stuff as though it were nothing but perry. On, well: if the engineer kept his mouth shut, the damage would be trivial.

"My dear ambassador," Abnel replied in his flawless French, "has it really escaped you? Who else but God could create such magnificent cities as ours?"

"With his own hands?"

"With His own hands, Ambassador." Abnel was, as usual, blandly complacent.

"But what about this ..." Jenkins gestured out and around. "... this village? It is nothing more than a bunch of mud hovels, just like the ones that surround the walls of Nuhr. And ..." He paused, suddenly wondering whether he were pushing things a little too far.

"Oh, *those*?" Abnel lifted his cup, and a mute servant rushed up silently and filled it with more of the fragrant red wine that, as Jenkins recalled, came from grapes that were drinking all the water they could get their hands on ... or, rather, roots into. "Those?" said Abnel with a dismissive shrug. "Those are the work of men. Is it not obvious?"

"Man work ..." mumbled Mather, and he immediately started giggling.

Jenkins shot him a glance that, under other circumstances, would have silenced him instantly, but either because of his new-found rebelliousness or because he was simply too inebriated to notice, Mather refused to be cowed.

"Man work ... he-he-he ... man work!"

Well, Jenkins reflected, at least, drunk as he was, Mather was no longer ... well ... *twitching* the way he had—

(Squirm!)

Oh, well ...

"Made by men?" said Jenkins, forcing himself to look at Abnel, but all too conscious of Mather's involuntary and unpleasantly suggestive writhings.

(Squirm!)

"Well, you certainly do not think that God Himself would have made such shoddy things, do you?"

Jenkins pursued the subject. "Ah, and so the lower classes live in the hovels and the villages, and the upper classes live in the cities."

"The cities, built by God Himself," Abnel nodded. "Quite right."

All of which was patently absurd, for Jenkins knew quite well that God had given His official favor and sanction only to the Righteous States of America. But Abnel was looking at him, and so the ambassador had to put aside his godly thoughts and say something appropriate. "As I said. I had no idea how honored —"

"Ah, think nothing of it!"

(Squirm!)

"But surely, Gharat, the people of your nation can do better than mud hovels."

Abnel, about to reply, stopped with his mouth open, as though considering what, exactly, to make of Jenkins' comment. A servant, misunderstanding, attempted to fill the gaping cavity with a piece of fruit. Impatiently waving the man away, Abnel composed himself. "Ah . . . whatever do you mean, Ambassador Jenkins?"

Touchy business, this. Jenkins chose his words carefully. "I am dreadfully sorry, honored Gharat. perhaps I spoke in haste."

"No, no: not at all."

"I simply meant that, well . . ." It was Jenkins' turn to consider, but he very carefully kept his mouth closed.

"Go on . . . really . . ."

Mather continued to burble and writhe. "Man work . . . he-he!" (Squirm!)

Jenkins shot Mather another glance (though, in truth, he would rather have shot him with a ball), but, as Abnel seemed not the least bit perturbed by the tipsy ejaculations, Jenkins decided to continue. "I simply meant," he said, leaning forward confidentially and dropping his voice (Oh, just good fellows all in this tent, mellow with wine and fairly brimming with conviviality!), "that, with the support of a population possessing sufficient incentives, the tragedy that afflicts your country might, with effort, be dealt with."

"Tragedy?"

"Indubitably!"

"Afflicts?"

"Yes!"

"Dealt with?"

"Indeed!"

Abnel examined Jenkins, reached for a grape, popped it into his mouth. "What . . . tragedy?"

Jenkins stared. "Honored Gharat, I mean the drought."

"Oh. That."

(Squirm!)

Abnel reached for another grape, then paused, opened his mouth, and allowed the servant to do the filling for him.

Jenkins pressed his lips together, attempting to mask his impatience. Was the drought a forbidden subject? Did this benighted land consider it bad luck to talk about misfortune? But no: he had heard the problem discussed quite openly. He had, however, never heard anyone discussing possible solutions.

And yet there *had* to be solutions. Why, during fully half of the days he had been in the Three Kingdoms, the Mountains of Ern had been wreathed in clouds, and when they had not been so wreathed, Jenkins had distinctly seen snow on their summits. Clouds meant rain. Snow meant melt. It was very simple. There was water up there in the mountains, and though the fact that no one ever talked about that water indicated either a full-blown case of fatalism or stupidity of the rankest kind, Jenkins' plan demanded that someone talk about it now, for, faced with the problem of manufacturing a reason for the Three Kingdoms to feel indebted to the Righteous States of America (and, thereby, to cause the Three Kingdoms to go along with what the Righteous States of America wanted), the ambassador had given up on trade and fishing rights and had, instead, hit upon an obvious solution: if Puritan engineers could contrive some way of bringing water back to the parched land, then surely everyone in the Three Kingdoms would have reason to feel grateful, and then, if they wanted to *show* just how grateful they were . . . why, there was the trifling matter of a passage through the mountains for . . . oh . . . say, ten or twelve thousand Puritan troops.

"The drought," said Abnel in his bland, complacent, completely maddening way.

(Squirm!)

Maybe, Jenkins thought as he restrained himself from throttling Mather, the Gharat was not worried about the drought because, as High Priest, he was insulated from most of its effects. But, looking hard at Abnel (as though by looking hard he could determine whether this suspicion were true or not), Jenkins saw what had escaped him before: a palpable shudder was periodically making its way along the Gharat's trunk. A sort of a shudder. But not quite. More like . . . well . . . actually . . . a . . .

Jenkins cast
his eyes
(Squirm!)   heavenward.   (Squirm!)
Righteous
Father!

"The . . . ah . . . drought, yes," he said. "What I mean . . ." But Jenkins was suddenly unsure of what, exactly, he meant at all. Illogical droughts, men who might have been women (or might not), random detonations for unspecified political reasons,

priests who

(Squirm!)   squirmed for   (Squirm!)

unspecified

reasons,

and who seemed abominably dense when it came to things like illogical droughts and men who might have been women (or might not) and random detonations for unspecified political reasons: nothing in the Three Kingdoms appeared to work the way it should have—or at least the way he expected it to. "What I mean is that a population base such as that which I saw outside the city . . ."

"It *is* large, is it not?" said Abnel, opening up and being filled again. "They breed like maggots in a dead camel. Quantity is everything out there. They do not know jasper from pumice. *In* the cities, however, *quality* is everything. Only the best stones, you understand. The most flawless gems."

Jenkins nodded.

(Squirm!)   "But, properly

motivated, they   (Squirm!)

could do wonders."

"Properly motivated?" said Abnel with all the politeness of a man confronting a guest who had just defecated on the floor.

(Squirm!)   (Squirm!)

(Squirm!)   (SquirSquirm!)

(Sq—)   (Squirm!)

"Well, yes," said Jenkins, trying hard not to squirm himself. Better houses, for example."

(Squirm!)

Better houses? The only good houses are in the cities."

"Well, yes. But more could be built, you see."

"Only Panas can build cities," said Abnel with such an

air of finality that there was silence in the pavilion for the better part of a minute. That is, until—

(Squirm!)

"Man work," giggled Mather, who had passed *tipsy* and was now working on *dead drunk*. "Man work. Man!"

"Well . . . yes . . . of course . . ." said Jenkins, who privately admitted that he should have foreseen that particular response.

(Squirm!)

"But, as I am sure you will agree," he went on, still trying to salvage the mission, "the drought is a tragedy of immense proportions, a tragedy which should be remedied!"

"Tragedy?" Abnel was back to being bland.

Jenkins gave up attempting to elicit an acceptable response from Abnel and moved on to his next point. "A tragedy for which America might possibly be able to provide a remedy."

"Tragedy?"

(Squirm!)

"He-he! Man work!"

Jenkins wanted to strike someone, preferably Mather (although he was beginning to feel as though Abnel would do quite nicely). Haddar had been impenetrable out of hostility. Abnel appeared to be impenetrable out of stupidity. "My dear Gharat! It is destroying the entire country! The quantity of arable land is obviously shrinking with each passing year, and as for the standard of living of the majority of the people . . ." Jenkins, in truth, nearly gagged on this last, blatantly republican sentiment, but it was good for the sake of his argument, and so, true diplomat that he was, he uttered it fervently, ". . . why, the hovels and mud huts attest to that all by themselves!"

"Standard of living?"

(Squirm!)

"Why, it is falling. Is it not?"

"Oh . . ." Abnel opened his mouth. In went a piece of fruit. "I supploth tho."

It was not much of a concession, but it would have to do. Again, Jenkins leaned forward, half to appear to be speaking confidentially, half to avoid looking at Mather. "America, as I said, is in a position to help."

"Man work!"

(Squirm!)   (Squirm!)
                                   (Squirm!)
                                   (Squirm!)

"How so?"

"We can determine the cause of the drought, and we can restore water to the land." Jenkins was, of course, overstepping himself here. He was only supposed to make whatever arrangements he could for the passage of American troops, not commit the Righteous States to a decade or more of grandiose public works. But Jenkins sensed that he was close to his goal, and he was therefore willing to gamble. In any case, the necessary retractions and reneging could come later.

Abnel was looking at him, and Jenkins suddenly had the feeling that the guest had defecated once again. For a moment, he almost wished that he were back with Haddar. At least he could understand hostility!

"And how would you propose to do that?" said Abnel.

"A simple matter," replied Jenkins, fervently wishing that it were indeed simple. How would he explain all of this to President Winthrop? "A few surveying crews, some canals, some channels . . ."

"Man work!" giggled Mather.

(Squirm!)

". . . perhaps an aqueduct or two . . ."

"Man work!"

        (Squirm!)   (Squirm!)

". . . and we will have water flowing to the lowlands before you know it," the ambassador finished, striving mightily against the urge to join Mather and Abnel in their gyrations.

But Abnel was looking at him still, and, yes, there was defecation involved. Jenkins was sure of it. "You would go . . . up into the mountains?"

"Well, yes. It would be necessary."

"It would be impossible."

Jenkins blinked at Abnel. "Impossible?"

"My dear ambassador," said Abnel, "surely you realize that the quarries from which the stones of the cities were taken are up in the mountains."

"Of course," said Jenkins, even though he had surely not realized any such thing.

"And that," continued Abnel, "as the quarries were mined by Panas Himself, they are sacred."

"Of . . . course," said Jenkins, who had not realized this, either.

"Hence," said Abnel, "it simply cannot be allowed."

"He-he!"

(Squirm!)

"What?"

"Ambassador," said Abnel, "we do not allow even our own people to approach the sites of the Sacred Quarries. Allowing foreigners to do so is completely out of the question. It would be the basest form of sacrilege."

Despite the lingering heat of the day, Jenkins felt cold. "No foreigners?"

"Indubitably!"

"Out of the question?"

"Yes!"

"Sacrilege?"

"Indeed!"

        (Squirm!)   (Squirm!)
    "He-he," said Mather.

When the sun rose that morning, gained the tops of the
mountains, and threw light across the breadth of the Three
Kingdoms, Sari knew that she would remember her first
glimpse of Katha for a long time. Clinging to the walls of
living rock, an incontrovertible testimony to their divine
origins, the houses and towers of that city seemed to be
one with the stone that supported them, and the old
woman who had left her origins, journeyed across deserts,
lost her hope, and, finally, arrived at the beginning of the
last leg of her journey felt at once buoyed up by the sight
of such grandeur and crushed under the weight of the
power of Panas.

Here was a city of granite and marble, a city that put its
roots down into the heart of the mountains themselves, a
city of Panas. And what did Naia have? Dirt. Dirt and superstition. Even from here, still standing in the lowlands
and looking up through the clear air, Sari could see the
blotch of the Naian Quarter that lay separate—as though,
rightly, in quarantine—from the order and enlightenment
that surrounded it.

"You will be leaving us now, sister?" said Yalliah, who
stood behind her.

The odor of breakfast pottage was rising from the big
kettle above the fire, and Sari realized that she would miss
that odor, that she would, in fact, miss Yalliah and Ehar
and all the others. Panasians though they were, they had
accepted her as a fellow traveler in the course of these last
weeks and, though theoretically hostile to her, had become
her friends.

And Sari noticed, too, that Yalliah had once again called
her *sister,* a Naian form of address. "Yes, sister," she said.

"I will have to go to the Naian quarter, earn some money, and buy supplies for the journey north."

She looked away from Katha, looked over her shoulder. Yalliah was nodding, but her face was drawn as though with worry.

"Please do not fear for me," said Sari. "The journey is not a long one. A day or two at most. The Caves are actually quite close."

"According to the Hymns of Loomar?" said Yalliah.

"Yes."

Yalliah nodded, and, after a moment, she said:

Two suns only will see you
Following the path to Naia's grace,"

Sari quickly turned all the way around. "Yalliah? That is from the Hymns. How do . . .?"

But if it was plain that Yalliah was weeping, it was also plain that she did not want to be comforted, either by an embrace or by words. "No, sister," she said, "I have chosen this lot, and it is, after all, not a bad one. I . . . I envy you though . . ."

Sari stood, stunned, beginning to understand.

"Come," said Yalliah, taking her hand. "Before you go, I wish to give you something. Come." She called one of her daughters and handed her the long handled spoon with which she had been stirring the pot. "Come," she said to Sari again. "I must do this. Come quickly."

Her lips pressed tightly together, Yalliah led Sari into the dimness of the women's tent. There, she knelt before a small chest and opened it. Even before the Panasian matron reached in and lifted out the bronze disk graven deeply with twin, interlocked circles, Sari knew.

Wordlessly, Yalliah handed it to her. In the spill of light from the open flap, Sari could see the words on the reverse: *Yalliah, daughter of Falyiah.*

"I knew," Yalliah was saying. "I knew about you because . . ." She bent her head. "I love Ehar. He treats me well. He treats me . . ." She choked.

"He treats you as well as any Naian man would," Sari whispered, and she herself was shocked by the bitterness that came welling up along with her words. "I was not so fortunate."

"I know."

For a moment, they stood looking at one another, trying not to look: the Naian who had lost faith, the Panasian who was trying to find it.

Finally: "I . . . had thought that . . . someday, I might go to the Caves," Yalliah said softly. "And . . . and explain to Naia. But there were children to raise, and there was the caravan . . . and travel. I know now that it will never happen. Will you take my medallion to the Caves and ask Naia to remember Her lost child?"

"She remembers, Yalliah."

"Will you?" Yalliah's face, seamed by sun and wind, was streaked with tears.

Sari nodded. "I would be honored."

Yalliah put her hands to her face, wiped away the water. "It used to be customary to make the pilgrimage."

"Many things used to be customary."

"I know."

"Do you . . . do you have any idea what happened?"

Yalliah shrugged. She looked at the open flap of the tent as though it were a summons back to her duties as a Panasian wife, a summons she would obey, a summons she had no intention of refusing or even questioning. "The water went away," she said after a time. "Life became more difficult. The land became an enemy . . . and women are the land . . ." She shrugged. "I do not really know. But as the land, I guess, so the Naians."

Sari nodded, understanding, not wanting to understand.

"But there is one other thing ..." And once again Yalliah knelt before her chest. This time, she opened a hidden compartment and took out a pouch. She put it into Sari's hand, and Sari was surprised by its weight. "It is gold," said Yalliah. "The last of my bride-price. All the rest I have spent on my children and my husband. All but this. This is for you. Buy what you need in Katha, and go to the Caves. Pray to Naia for me. Ask Her to remember."

Sari looked from the pouch to Yalliah's earnest face. "Your ... bride-price?"

"My parents were Naians," said Yalliah. "They did not keep it, but gave it to me. It was customary. I give the last of it to you now, because ... because ..." Her voice grew hoarse. "Because I think of you as a sister. Because you brought back sweet memories. Because ..." She turned away, pressed her hands to her face. Save when their husbands died, Panasian women were supposed to be impassive when confronted with sorrow.

"I am your sister and your friend, Sari," she said after a time, and she did not sound impassive. "I will always remember you. I will never deny you."

And then she turned around, and for those few precious moments, they were both Naians again, and they embraced as Naians.

But the bitterness was growing on Sari, and later, much later, after she had taken up her small bundle and had said her good-byes, after she had embraced Ehar and, in defiance of custom (she was, after all, only an old woman) planted a kiss on the weathered cheeks of his sons, after she had started up the steep road that led to the gates of Katha, she felt the heaviness of the pouch that Yalliah had given her.

The last of her bride-price. Her parents had given it to her. It was customary.

Sari looked up at the gate, saw the glitter of the Temple of Panas, the darkness of the Naian Quarter. "Many things were customary," she murmured.

Chapter Nineteen

Kuz Aswani was in disgrace.

Since the day he had caused the uproar in the market-place, the counselor had been confined to a small suite of rooms in the palace, and there, to the bewilderment of all, he had continued to chuckle, chitter, wiggle, and leap about even though King Inwa Kabir had sent in everyone that anyone else could think of—including his own personal physician—to see what the matter was and what, if anything, might be done about it.

To Kuz Aswani, though, this was all silly. Physicians? Ridiculous! It was no matter of ill health or bad humors that afflicted him, nothing that could be cured by the administration of a gem elixir or even one of the barbarous herbal concoctions that even the Naians had given up. No: magic had ensnared him, and only magic could free him; but for a man (Or was it *ferret* now? How far had he come?) in his position to confess openly to having any dealings with magic whatsoever, voluntary or not, was to invite a fate that would make the life of a ferret look very good, very good indeed, even if Umi Botzu obviously had something in mind that would make the life of a ferret look not at all pleasant.

And Umi Botzu, Kuz Aswani was sure, was watching

him. In the dead of night, the counselor would start up from the pile of rags he had heaped up across from the corner of the room he used as a litter box, and he would see the silhouette of the sorcerer's head and shoulders at the window. No matter that the window was eighty-five feet from the ground, no matter that when he jumped up with a sharp *chuckle-chuckle-chuckle* and raced for the apparition, he would find only the shadow of a date palm or the dark lump of a roosting bird that, with a startled *pa-KAAW!* would blunder off into the night. No matter at all. Umi Botzu, he was sure, had been at that window but a moment before, and that the sorcerer could not only leer in through a palace window that was eighty-five feet from the ground, but also, in a twinkling, cloak himself in the comparatively innocent semblances of shadows and birds, was but a further confirmation of his incredible command of the occult arts.

But Umi Botzu's intrusions did not stop at windows, for Kuz Aswani had become convinced that someone was prowling about in his rooms as he slept. (And ferrets, as you might know, sleep a great deal, giving sorcerers with less than honorable intentions more than ample time for prowling about.) Often, Kuz Aswani would rouse himself from a nap, convinced that he had just heard his door shut. Or he would open his eyes in a half doze and stare stupidly—not asleep and yet, maddeningly, not awake—as a shadowy form moved across his field of view.

It was Umi Botzu. He was *sure* it was Umi Botzu. It *had* to be Umi Botzu.

In fact, the counselor saw the sorcerer everywhere, not only peering in through his windows and prowling through his rooms, but also staring at him out of his water dish, peeping at him through the crack between the closed doors of a cabinet, grinning at him from beneath the low table, winking at him from the flame of a lamp. And it was torture. Unmitigated, continuing torture. Umi Botzu was *enjoying* all of this, and Kuz Aswani could to nothing to stop him. He could not even confess the origins of his torments to his superiors or to his king.

He was in disgrace. He was confined. His wife had left him (with the king's blessings). And he was *still* turning into a ferret!

Disconsolately, he scratched his head with a hind foot and once again checked his stomach to see how far the fur had spread. There was nothing he could do. He was going to be a ferret.

Today, though, it appeared that his humiliation was going to be made complete, for the door opened, and Haddar entered. As usual, the chief minister's black eyes gave no hint as to what the coming conversation might be about. As usual, that meant trouble.

Kuz Aswani looked up from his bed of rags and snuffled, but no: he was not yet far enough along for scent to be of any help. So: "The blessings of Panas (Blessed be He!) be upon you, Chief Minister," he said politely, wondering how much longer he would still be able to talk.

Haddar stood over him, examining him with those black, unexpressive eyes. "And upon you, Kuz Aswani."

Kuz Aswani scratched himself with his foot.

Haddar's eyes widened for a moment, but he folded his arms with an impassive air. "The king is very worried about you, Kuz Aswani."

"My thanks to him, Chief Minister."

"He would have you made well."

"That would be my greatest wish also, Chief Minister." Oh, but for a chance to explain! But the punishment for trafficking with magicians was death. Panasian law was very clear about things like that.

Haddar stood silently for a moment, and then, as though attempting to be comradely, he dragged up a stool and sat down next to the heap of rags. But what caught Kuz Aswani's attention was the slight, almost imperceptible (indeed, only a ferret would have noticed it) ... well, *squirm* that shuddered along the chief minister's body as he planted his linen-gowned rump on the stool and leaned forward. Quite possibly, it was the result of some kind of muscle strain, but Kuz Aswani, desperate for someone to talk to about magic and about ferrets, thought ... hoped ... no, was *sure* that it meant something else.

Certainly there must (ow!) be some way to talk some sense into Kuz Aswani. It is most unfortunate that he has been felled by this strange malady (ow!) since he has been such a good minister.

Ah! So Umi Botzu has ensnared you also, Chief Minister! Of course, it was just a matter of time before he expanded his sphere of control. But the Chief Minister himself ... this is most unfortunate! Still ...

"How are you feeling today, Kuz Aswani?"

Kuz Aswani nodded knowingly, realizing that he would have to be as reassuring as he could. Haddar had obviously come for advice as to how best to deal with the changes that must even now be upon him, changes with which Kuz Aswani was intimately familiar.

(Ow!) Curses upon that Valdemar! I can hardly sit down!

That Umi Botzu! Curses upon him! And now even poor Haddar!

"Oh, Chief Minister, I am fine. Fine. It is not really so bad as all that."

"Not so bad." Haddar nodded, and squirmed uncomfortably again.

Kuz Aswani had the urge to offer him some raisins (A few raisins between two ferrets: what could be the harm in that?) but, looking around, he discovered that he had eaten them all the night before. He was disappointed, but not overmuch: he had, after all, gotten all the raisins for him-

self, and that was something very important to a ferret.

"Not so bad . . . as, say, yesterday?" said the chief minister with yet another squirm that Kuz Aswani could have
sworn was just on the verge of breaking into a full wiggle.

"One must bow to the inevitable and make the best of
it," said Kuz Aswani.

Haddar stared.

Bow to the inevitable?   *Ah! No one has had the*
Make the best of it? What   *slightest word of reassur-*
can he mean by that? (Ow!)   *ance for poor Haddar. His*
The man is sick. Gravely   *wife is probably going to*
sick. And yet . . . what if he   *leave him, too. I can show*
does not mean that at all?   *him that I understand . . .*

And, with a nod and a smile, Kuz Aswani twitched his
nose at Haddar and threw in a ferrety wiggle for good
measure.

Haddar stared again.

Does he mock me? No   *You see, Haddar? I know*
. . . he is much more subtle   *and I understand. Wiggle if*
than that. Somehow, he has   *you want to. It is a ferret's*
found out (ow!) about   *born nature to wiggle. And*
Valdemar. He knows we   *if I can find that ball that I*
might be overheard, so he   *saw yesterday, why, we can*
does not dare speak aloud.   *chase it and one another.*

"I see . . ." said Haddar.

"Really, if people were more understanding," said Kuz
Aswani, "it would be much easier."

"Well . . . I can certainly understand that."

"They would not lock us up, for one thing."

Haddar stared again. Then, with effort: "Very true."

"And they would perhaps, be indulgent about our excesses."

Us? Our? Great Panas! He does know! But how? That unfortunate (ow!) meeting at Valdemar's ... is it possible that he might be ... ?

He most certainly understands. Poor Haddar. I know well how much of a shock all this can be. But we can face it ... together ...

"Have you ..." Kuz Aswani dropped his voice. "Have you appeared in ... in public yet?"

"In public?"

"Well ... you know ... as ... something else ... ?"

"Ah ... well ..."

He knows. He most certainly knows. And, worse, he has seen me! This will not do. (Ow!) I cannot simply have him killed, because he has been a respected counselor, and killing him would require too many explanations. But still ... wait ... Us. Our. Perhaps he shares my ... interest ...

He hesitates. Poor Haddar. It is, after all, not so bad. Raisins. Water. An occasional dust bath. No milk, though. No milk at all. Terrible diarrhea. Ever. Terrible. Yogurt, though, is fine. And a bit of cheese now and then. But, oh, it is so sad about our wives!

"Possibly," Haddar admitted after a time. "Possibly."

"Everyone will just have to get used to it," said Kuz Aswani sympathetically, and there was a trace of defiance in his voice. "Seeing as it is inevitable."

"Ah ... yes ... I suppose so."

Did he see me then, too? Dressed up in Najmat's clothing? My chest padded out (It did look fine, in my opinion) and (ow!) my ... did he see? Did he ... did he find me attractive? Perhaps a little?

I miss my Sabihah, though she was getting quite tiresome with her complaints about being dragged about. Perhaps Haddar would not mind being dragged. I mean ... he could drag me, too.

"Ah . . . Kuz Aswani," Haddar began after several minutes of nose twitching, squirming, wiggling, and simultaneous (and exceedingly erroneous) evaluation on the part of Kuz Aswani, "you have always been a good minister."

"I have tried to be," replied Kuz Aswani, barely repressing a *chuckle-chuckle-chuckle* of excitement at the prospect of sharing his transformation with a friend.

He could ruin me in a moment. He has seen. He might tell. I must win his favor now.	*Haddar knows. Why should I keep myself from wiggling? In a short time, he will wiggle too!*

"It distresses me greatly to see you caged in this room like an animal."

"But, Haddar, it is fitting for such as ourselves, is it not?"

Haddar squirmed even more violently, then appeared to gain control of himself. "Perhaps. But that must change. It must."

"I am glad to hear you speaking this way, Chief Minister," said Kuz Aswani, and the urge to wiggle, chuckle, and then explode into a bouncing, dancing, ferrety expression of unalloyed joy was growing on him.

"Yes . . . well . . . I will give orders for your immediate release," said Haddar. "I trust you will . . ." He peered at Kuz Aswani, squirmed. ". . . remember this."

"Oh yes! Always." Kuz Aswani was already rising from his rags, scratching furiously at his head with his hind foot. With a frantic twitch of his nose that echoed yet another squirm from Haddar, he bounced across the room, turned a somersault, rolled over so that he faced Haddar, and approached with a rapid *pudda-pudda-pudda* of hands and feet, making as though to seize the chief minister by the scruff and give him a good drag.

Haddar fled, but, alas! he was not quick enough, for just

as he reached the door (which, according to his orders, the guards outside opened quickly, opened just wide enough for him to make his escape), Kuz Aswani was on him, closing his teeth on the back of his neck. And yet the sight of the open door suddenly banished from the deranged counselor's mind all thoughts of giving Haddar a good drag about the room and introduced, instead, the quintessentially ferretish obsession with illicit escape.

Throwing himself through the door, evading the grasping hands of the guards with a roll and a scamper, Kuz Aswani bolted down the corridor, took the first turning, and skittered down the stairs, *chuckle-chuckle-chuckling* all the way, while the guards and Haddar pelted along behind him, unable to keep up with his sinuous, four-footed speed.

Inwa Kabir would, of course, have it thought about, but certainly the fact that his son, Prince Aeid, had suddenly and inexplicably disappeared was something that he could not but think about himself ... at least a little. Haddar would attend to the bailiffs whose watchful eyes had proved something less than watchful, and, doubtless, with enough thinking about it (done, to be sure, by individuals other than Inwa Kabir), blame could be fixed upon someone who had obviously not thought about it enough; but Aeid was, after all, Inwa Kabir's son, and that alone was enough to provoke a few thoughts in the royal head, even without the question of ... other considerations ...

"I found numerous books of European philosophy in his private chambers," Bakbuk simpered, finishing her report as she thrust her hip out to the side in a manner that would have made any man who was used to thinking about things himself half mad with desire. "I did not touch them, but I have . . . ah . . . heard of the content of many of them. They are rife with republican sentiments."

"Republican sentiments . . ." Inwa Kabir was glad that the doors of his chambers were thick and well-guarded. It would not do at all for anyone save the king's trusted sworder to hear the king utter such blasphemous words. He did not notice Bakbuk's hip at all. "Frightening. So that was the source of his comments on—" He caught himself quickly, unwilling to repeat what Aeid had said about skin color and betterment. Bakbuk was his trusted sworder, but there were, after all, limits.

Bakbuk looked up at the king, and, for a moment, a hint of calculation gleamed in eyes that, a moment before, had held nothing save the vacuous blankness of a Panasian houri. "There is a possibility that he has fled out of fear of discovery." Her voice was as beckoning as her eyes were keen.

"I will have that thought about," said the king. "But Aeid is not one to flee from anything."

"As the All Highest wills," Bakbuk said with a slight lift of a bosom that assiduously consumed herbal decoctions had enlarged to a very respectable roundness.

"But . . . why?"

"I do not know, All Highest."

"I must have it thought about."

Bakbuk was silent. Inwa Kabir ruminated for several minutes, unconsciously, despite his words, thinking about it himself, but wanting so much to have someone else think about it that he finally burst out: "Where is Haddar?"

"He is with Kuz Aswani, All Highest. We are still attempting to find cure for his malady."

"Has he thought of any reasons for Aeid to have left?"

"All Highest, he has been concerned mostly with the Blue Avenger. And, of course, with Kuz Aswani."

The Blue Avenger ... yet something else that Inwa Kabir wanted someone else to think about. "Has he determined the identity of the Blue Avenger?"

"I ... believe he is attempting to, All Highest." Bakbuk allowed her shoulders to drop, and, beneath her veil, her mouth slackened into a moist invitation so blatant that mere cloth did nothing to obscure it. She was being outrageous this morning, but, as she knew quite well, Inwa Kabir did not notice. A pity. "Actually, the Blue Avenger has not attacked the tax collectors for some days now."

It was the temple tax that had brought the Blue Avenger. Of that, Inwa Kabir was certain. But Inwa Kabir himself was still not entirely comfortable with the idea of the temple tax, for he could not set at rest several reservations that he had regarding it. "I ... I must have that thought about," he said in a tone that made it clear that he was still doing a good deal of thinking about it himself, and that he was beginning to wish devoutly that the raisin compote he had ordered for his luncheon would arrive so that he could *stop* thinking about it.

Bakbuk was ready, open, willing. A crooked finger (so her body indicated) would have been all that was necessary to put her on the floor and spread her legs. "As the All Highest wills," she cooed.

"Some days you say?"

But Bakbuk suddenly found that, despite her preserved, mocking objectivity, she wanted exactly what she thought she only pretended to want. A tightening of her blank, useless groin caught her unawares, and a giddy flood of unaccustomed desire made her drop her eyes, took the curve from her hip and the lift from her bosom. "Several," she managed, floundering. "Since shortly after the Gharat departed for Katha."

"I must have ..."

Bakbuk realized suddenly that she had pressed a hand to

her breasts as though to shield them. Grimly, she clenched her fist.

". . . it thought about."

But the thought came to Bakbuk, thrusting itself through the erotic haze that had overcome her: Prince Aeid . . . gone. The Blue Avenger . . . vanished.

But Inwa Kabir turned suddenly, two halves of a complete mental whole suddenly rushing together despite his attempt to keep them apart with the raisin compote. The Gharat . . . departed. The Blue Avenger . . . disappeared . . . "He is pursuing the Gharat!"

"Ah . . ." Bakbuk was caught between mocking logic and primal urgings . . . urgings about which she could do absolutely nothing. ". . . ah . . . who, All Highest?"

"The Blue Avenger!"

Bakbuk's thoughts, already brought to a halt by a mire of unexpected sexuality, were dragged to the floor and thoroughly violated by the ripening of the suspicions she had harbored since she had penetrated Aeid's library. Aeid . . . and the Blue Avenger!

The Gharat . . . and the Blue Avenger. Inwa Kabir was also finding himself in the grip of something unexpected, but, confined as he was to upholding the rule of an orthodoxy determined by others, he could not, in this particular case, afford the luxury of having the question thought about by someone else. No, the question had been thought about already, and the answer had been determined for all time. Panas had decreed universal taxation, and therefore universal taxation would be the law of the land. Still, the king found it difficult to be as concerned as he wanted to be over the possibility that the Gharat was journeying to Katha with the Blue Avenger in pursuit.

"Bakbuk," he said suddenly, attempting to salve his conscience, "the Gharat is in danger . . ." He looked at

Bakbuk, who was standing a short distance away, her eyes wide and staring. "Bakbuk?"

"Ah ... here, All Highest," Bakbuk returned with a start.

"Go to Katha. Protect the Gharat." Inwa Kabir felt that he sounded nowhere near sincere enough. He tried again. "Protect the ... ah ... Gharat."

Oh, dear: worse and worse. Perhaps the raisin compote would come soon?

"Protect ..." Bakbuk's distaste for the Gharat was very real ... and kept very much to herself. "... the Gharat. It shall be done, All Highest."

And while Inwa Kabir and Bakbuk were both attempting, without much success, to make some sense of their feelings, the hoped-for raisin compote finally arrived, and, with a knock at the door, a blare of trumpets, and a patter of the bare feet of the boys with the powdered faces (whom Inwa Kabir, in accordance with tradition (and though his memory about the Sacred Texts might be occasionally faulty, he at least remembered *that* much), kept because his father had kept them because his grandfather had kept them), the doors swung open, and the head chef entered, raisin compote held high.

But here again was something unexpected, for there came another patter of bare feet that had nothing to do with the boys with the powdered faces—actually, it was not so much a patter as a *pudda-pudda-pudda*—and then, with a vocal utterance that sounded very much like a *chuckle-chuckle-chuckle,* Kuz Aswani exploded through the open door, threw himself on the chef, and knocked him to the carpet, thereafter rolling over twice and rising to all fours in a kind of a bouncy dance that ended only when he flung himself on the spilled compote and began to lap it up as quickly as he could.

Bakbuk, dagger in hand and ever true to her duty, was

about to spring when Haddar and a group of guards rushed in. Before she could move, they had grabbed Kuz Aswani by the arms and, despite his twists and turns and enraged chuckles, dragged him to his feet.

"Kuz Aswani!" said Inwa Kabir.

He was answered only with a hiss of frustration from the would-be ferret.

And it looked very much like Kuz Aswani would meet with the sort of fate that Mr. Mather had heard of (and was *still* thinking about), for King Inwa Kabir lifted his hand to pronounce a terrible judgment. But before he could do so, Haddar spoke up:

"Forgive him, All Highest. He is ill. But I think that, with much care, he can be cured."

Inwa Kabir looked at Haddar, who appeared to squirm—uncomfortably—and then at Kuz Aswani. Kuz Aswani, very unhelpfully, yawned widely, lifted a foot, and scratched behind his ear.

"You think so, Chief Minister?" said the king.

"Ah . . ." Haddar looked at Kuz Aswani, who twitched his nose at the minister in a comradely fashion. "Ah, yes. Indeed," he said quickly.

"Then take him out and cure him," said Inwa Kabir. "And, though I must have it thought about, I would suggest that you make sure that he remains cured."

Another twitch of the nose from Kuz Aswani.

"As the All Highest has willed," said Haddar, bowing, "so it shall be."

"And where is my lunch?" demanded the king, turning to the chef, who, still trembling from the unexpected attack, was finally managing to stand up.

The chef looked at the bowl that had contained the compote, then at the glistening smear of the compote itself . . . or at least as much of it as was left after Kuz Aswani's frantic lapping. "It . . ." he said, ". . . that is . . . I mean . . ."

The chef was punished. Panasian law was very clear about things like that.

Chapter Twenty

"Hel-*lo*! You are new in Katha, are you not? How wonderful to meet you. My name is Watersong. Of course, that is not my real name. That is my spiritual name, which I took in order to express my spiritual duty to the world. It goes with my spiritual personality, you see. And then, of course, I have a secret name, which I do not reveal to anyone. Excuse me? You do not understand? Where are you from? You *are* a Naian, are you not?"

And, once again, water having descended, infiltrated . . .

"Hel-*lo*! You are new in Katha, are you not? Well, you will find an extremely active Naian community here. We are all very devoted to the Goddess, since we are the community that is closest to the Caves of Naia. What? You plan on going to the Caves? Oh, I do not think that you want to do that."

. . . strata that have, for fifty million years, been squeezed, bent, broken, and upthrust, find their shattered surfaces suddenly filmed . . .

* * *

"Hel-*lo*! You are new in Katha, are you not? Well, may Naia bless you! A pilgrim? How wonderful! You know, we get many pilgrims to Katha, since the community in Katha is possibly the most important of all the Naian communities in all the Three Kingdoms. What? The Caves? You want to go to the Caves? What Caves?"

. . . with moisture . . .

"Hel-*lo*! You are new in Katha, are you not? Well, I must warn you about a few things. Some who call themselves Naians are not exactly . . . well, you know. They do not do things right. It would be ever so much better if they did things right, but they do not. It was a deliberate error, you know, introduced years ago in order to keep the real ways of power secret. But . . . a pilgrim, you say? The Caves? Well, that is all very well, but you really need to know about what to watch out for here in Katha."

. . . their interiors turned suddenly pliant by the penetration of lubricating fluid . . .

"Hel-*lo*! You are new in Katha, are you not? Welcome! It is certainly a pleasure to meet someone who has obviously been traveling for so long. You were very fortunate not to have run into brigands or thieves or some of those bandits from Kalash and Khyr. You cannot be too careful, that is what I say, because you never know what the future might hold if you do not go and look. Would you like to see what your future holds? My rates are very reasonable."

. . . and ionic and covalent bonds that were hitherto unyielding turn in an instant to nothingness . . .

* * *

"Hel-*lo*! You are new in Katha, are you not? Oh, yes, I have a room for rent, but what brings you to Katha? Oh, come now, you can tell me. Family? Friends? Do you need me to talk louder? *Family? Friends?* I am certainly not shouting, I am simply trying to be considerate to someone who is obviously very old and who cannot be expected to take adequate care of herself. I always try to be considerate to people who are old, since they are the elders of our community. Do you understand me? You must need to sit down. Come. Sit down. No, no: I insist. What? The Caves? Oh, you are much too old to go to the Caves."

... and the whole, ponderous weight of the mountains shifts ...

"Hel-*lo*! You are new in Katha, are you not? I am so glad you realized that the people across the street are not the right sort. You are very discerning for one so old. They are not really Naians over there, you know. Now here, we are true Naians. It is in the family, you know. Oh, we go back forever, right to the original Children of the Dawn who crossed the mountains and reached the Caves of Naia. Yes, the Caves. The holiest place in the Three Kingdoms. No, I cannot say that I have ever been to them."

... and FRACTURES.

"Hel-*lo*! You are new in Katha are you—*Look out!*"

The device of metal and glass virtually leaped from Elijah Scruffy's hands, subsequently bouncing on the cabin table and shattering on the deck.

"Mr. Turtletrout!"

"Sir!"

"Did you charge this Leyden jar?"

"No, sir!"

Scruffy was grimacing, flapping his hand as though it had been stung by a bee. "Well, I'm stumped then. Leyden jars don't just charge themselves, and that warn't charged this morning."

Turtletrout examined the pieces of metal and shards of glass in his slope-headed, uncomprehending way. "Sorry, sir. I don't know how it could have happened."

"Bit me like a mad dog ..."

"The only one who's been in here at all was that Umi Botzu. For his lesson, sir. I don't think we left him alone for more than a few seconds."

"Tarnation ..."

"Couldn't have had time enough to do anything."

"Damme ..." Scruffy suddenly left off his flapping and looked up. "Do you hear a rumbling, Turtletrout?"

"Mine! Mine! *Mine!* Ah ... what ... ?"

The owner of the shop, anxious to get out of the flimsy building as quickly as he could, vaulted the counter and shoved Sari out of the way as he made for the door. Sari, surprised as much by the sudden rumble and shaking of the earthquake as by the shopkeeper's mad dash, reeled backward and came up against a low table, which caught her just at knee height and flipped her back so that she struck her head on the far edge just as a litter of insignificant brassware toppled down on her from an overhanging shelf.

The rumbling and the shaking continued, and, stunned, she stared up at the beams of the ceiling, vaguely wondering when they were going to give way and precipitate the entire roof upon her. But though the rumbling finally died away, the shaking stopped, and the shelf apparently ran out of brassware, Sari, still unable to move, remained stretched across the table in a silence that lengthened until the door opened and someone poked his head into the shop. "Hello?"

Sari managed a faint groan. Her mouth worked, but words were still problematical.

"It is not polite to groan at me," said the shopkeeper (for it was he who had returned). "Naians respect the Goddess in all beings, and in any case I am a professional. The least you can do is speak to me politely."

Sari gathered her wits and her strength. "I am . . . hurt."

The shopkeeper made his way slowly through the scattering of insignificant brassware that now covered the dirt floor. He bent over Sari. "Well, we came through that one, did we not?"

Sari was not at all sure that she could feel her arms and her legs. Her ears were ringing, and she was desperately afraid that she had been crippled. "I am . . . hurt . . ." she said, ". . . please . . ."

"I will find someone to help you," said the shopkeeper, "but I did want to ask you before we were interrupted by Naia's expression of wrath . . ." He examined her for a moment. "You *did* know that these earthquakes are Her way of expressing Her wrath, did you not?"

Sari was disinclined to argue. "Naia is merciful," she said, partly in reply, mostly in an attempt to reassure herself. "Naia provides."

"Well that is very true, but she is a mother, after all. I am a Naian. I understand things like that. It is my business as a Naian to understand things like that. Mothers, after all, have to be stern sometimes. They have to punish their children, do they not?"

Sari gave up. "Please . . . find someone who can help me . . ."

"I wanted to ask you whether you were interested in anything in my shop. I can put it aside for you."

"Please ... I am hurt ..."

"Well, I have to earn a living, do I not? I am a professional, and it is not easy being a professional. I cannot just give away my wares. What should you have me do? Earn a living reading cards or casting zodiacal charts?"

"Please ..."

"I believe that such things should be kept of mundane commerce. Only spiritual values should be allowed to motivate such things, should they not?"

"Please ..."

"I hold to the old ways."

"Please ..."

"Some do not, but *I* do."

"Please ..."

He straightened up, his hand placed thoughtfully against his temple. "And my wife, of course. She holds to the old ways, too. I let her be my priestess. She is a very good priestess, you know."

"Please ..."

"So long as she has someone like me to advise her. Because, you see, I am a professional."

"Please ..."

He frowned. "Oh, very well," he said at last, and Sari heard him scuff away through the insignificant brassware on the floor. "I will find someone." But then he scuffed back. "Do you have a place to stay in Katha?"

Was the numbness getting better, or worse? Sari could not tell, but her panic was growing. "Please ..."

"I have a room upstairs ..."

"Please ..."

"I charge very little for it."

"Please ..." Sari's vision was starting to fade. She wondered whether she were dying, wondered whether she really minded dying very much if it meant that she would not have to listen to the shopkeeper any longer.

The shopkeeper turned back toward the door. "I *do* have to earn a living, do I not? I am a professional . . ."

"Please . . . for the love of Naia . . ."

The door slammed, and a last piece of insignificant brassware dropped off the overhanging shelf and hit Sari on the head. But by then, her vision had darkened completely, and she did not notice.

Whose footsteps? Whose? Or did He let fall a great pile of bricks just then (worldbuilding elsewhere, elsewhen, elseother, what would it be in one of the other languages . . . code?) and they tumbling over one another falling like a big rockslide and rumblebumblesidetosididdleodumble-upanddownumblefercrimptihumptydownumptyumdumpty-botharhodcarryocrack!* The earth? Or did She Herself take the world in both hands and give it a good shake? Naia's wrath? Panas' wrath (does he give it a good shake when he is done)?

Naia? Can I think of Her? Sin?

No matter. Was not much of one. Seem to be coming more often, though, as I grow older, but they say time grows short the older you get. Ha! When I am a doddering old fool the days will fly by, flickering. Hand flapping before the sun. Whappa-whappa-whappa!

Fast enough as it is. Another week. Closer. Sign me. Teach me secrets. All. All secrets. Everything. Passage into library. All. What do they really do? Supposing . . . no sin ever, pure. Walk like this.

No. No.

Naian quarter. Why did I come here? Slums. Idiots in their mud. Wearing mud as they labor. Dying in mud as their houses fall down. There is a nice one. Pile of dirt all

*not © 1939, James Joyce

that is left. Did not take much. Odd, they come closer together. I remember . . .

I remember. It changed. Everything changes. But another few weeks and—

Who would do it if I told? Panas? What, is He real
then? We all covered our faces when Dimit said that, and
we all laughed, but then we did not see Dimit any longer.
But I am not Dimit. (How he held me, hitting me, loins
against mine, did he like it?) What would they do? No one
before. All novices, all priests. One into the other. House
into rubble.

It changed. Who? What? Naian men. Buckets. Spades.
Unburying someone. Rise, you dead! But they are dead.
Panas entombs in stone, Naia in mud. But Panas' tombs
have been from the beginning. Cities. Sepulchers. What
would they do? Where would I go? Why do they not tell?
Secrets . . .

"Make way!" they called, rushing by. "Make way for
the sake of Naia!"

What brings me here? Oh, the promptings of the flesh.
The woman will come crawling out of every pore, they
say. And here I am. Shall I put a crystal about my neck?
Dance? Beat the drum?

Old woman there, dragged out of a store. Old face.
Worn out in Naia's work. Old man face. (Here, walk like
this.) Priests fatten. Women wither. Naians dwindle.
Whole women. Uncut. Lascivious. Dancing. Breasts. Loins
against mine. Walk like this. Change. Novice into priest.
Boy into girl. Why not? Would they find me?

"She is alive!" said one. "Alive!"

"Of course she is alive," said another. "She just fell
over."

"Be careful of my brassware," said yet another. "I am a
professional. That is my livelihood, is it not?"

With mud are they clothed. In mud they live. Mud they

shape. Skewed chisels from the background, says Panas, to show off the raised letters. Angle of 45 degrees. Did I remember that correctly? Is that right? What happened? Why would they not say? Why did they insist. Changes. Wait . . . what . . . ?

Gurgling. Ah! After the earthquake, flood. Rush of water down dry riverbeds. Same thing every time. Stare at water. Panas dangling a sweetmeat. Look, but do not eat. Look, but do not enter. Live, but do not like. Learn, but do not know.

Water comes, then dwindles. Naia dwindles.

Tries to sit up. Ugly thing. Naian. Old medallion. So and so, daughter of so and so. And all daughters of Naia. Odd to think of someone like that as a daughter. Mother, maybe. Grandmother, yes. Grandmother. I did not know either of them. Did they pay for me? Have heard about that, but only the priests know. Not yet.

"Help her up," cried one. "Help her up!"

"It is no use," said another. "She is too weak."

"Be careful of my brassware!" said yet another. "Will you not?"

"Well, it was her decision to fall over," said another.

"No, not at all," said yet another. "She did it wrong, did she not? If she had done it right, she would not have been hurt."

"She chose it of her own free will," cried one.

Tying their words into knots, but they have no texts, just a bunch of hymns. We have copies. Library in Nuhr. Everything in library. Cannot get in unless you are a priest. Death, otherwise. Copies of everything. Secrets. All. More Naian than the Naians. They do not write anything down. Oral tradition.

"Chchchchch," gargled the old woman. "Ugh, ugh!"

—Give her some water, Beshur said angrily. Can you not see that she needs some water?

"But," said yet another, "water is expensive, is it not?"

—She is old, Beshur insisted. Give her some water.

"You are a priest," said one. "You have money. You give her some water."

—I am a novice, Beshur corrected him. I have no money.

"Of course," said one.

Standing there picking his nose with a dirty finger. Upthrust tower. Upthrust prick, picking the nose of the sky. Thoughts like that, how can I believe? Be a priest? Where would I go?

Be a priest? And after . . . ?

"I tell you," said another, "she chose this of her own free will. We cannot involve ourselves in her fate. It is not our right."

Someone's mother. Someone's grandmother. Uncut, Whole. Lascivious. How? Old and dry. Sticking it into a termite tunnel. (Walk like this.) Water all gone. Gone from land. Old land. Useless for anything. What will Panas stick it into at an angle of 45 degrees? Best angle. Termite tunnel . . .

Someone's mother . . .

—I will bring some water, Beshur said.

Mr. Jenkins is looking at the desert.

Dearly beloved brethren, I am sure that as we sit here contemplating God's great holiness and goodness, we cannot but be moved to consider how divine Providence has equipped every living thing with the requirements of its station. The eagle, for example, has his eyes and his talons, the lion has his claws, the sheep has his wool. And I could go on and on, with many examples and many illustrations of this undeniable fact that is not only revealed to us by the words of Scripture, but is also shown forth, day by day, in a multitude of instances.

Surely, once this most important truth is grasped (as it most certainly should be, since faith *demands* that it be grasped, else the unbeliever be cast into the Pit), then it also becomes obvious that, as God has fitted each creature for its station, so He has also decreed that some shall be empowered to order the affairs of others. And, once again, lest there be any doubt, we are given, day by day, innumerable examples of this great and wondrous working of Providence. The lion eateth of the antelope, the jackal of the hare. The sheep croppeth the tender herbs, and the bee despoils ... I mean, despoileth ... the flowers of their nectar.

So it is with men, for God has ordained that some men, endowed as they are by their Creator with certain inalienable rights and privileges, shall have dominion over other men, as the ministers shall have dominion over all. We read in the Gospels about the centurion who could tell one man to come, and he would come, and could tell another to go, and he would go; and so the Gospels, being the light of true knowledge shining forth in the dark wilderness of human ignorance, are testimony to this unalterable fact of divinely-ordained authority.

Therefore, it should not surprise us in the least that, as such is the case with the brute beasts of the forest and the fields, and as such is the case with men, so such must be also the case with nations, too. Heedless of the will of God, the countries of the earth strive and contend, seeking to impose their will upon one another, and to what avail? Why, to no avail whatsoever, for if only God (blessed be He!) can confer such authority upon one beast as regards another, or upon on one man as regards his fellow men, how much more of an usurpation of heavenly prerogative could be the self-declared imposition of one nation's will—created by men, determined by men—upon many men?

Mr. Jenkins is still looking at the desert.

Vanity, saith the Preacher. Vanity! And this we know: all authority comes from God alone, whether it be manifested in the dominion of one nation over another, the dominion of a government over its citizens, the dominion of a husband over his wife, or the dominion of a predator over its prey. And God, as supreme authority, is pleased that this be so.

Now, as a friend, and as your minister, I ask you whether we do not live in a truly blessed nation. We do! Live, I mean. Ah ... in a blessed nation. Yes, and it is blessed because God has ordained that His Word shall be steadfastly kept only in these Righteous States of America, the land of the elect, the land of the Kingdom of Heaven! Here, God is the judge and the jury. Here, God is the president. Here, God, speaking through the appropriate ministers and pastors, is the word of law. Here, God has *dominion.*

And as all authority comes from God, and as our nation is so blessed as to operate so directly under the authority and guidance of the Most High, should we not assume among the powers of the earth the separate and superior standing to which the will of God impels us? It is told in the Holy Gospels that Simon Peter was called to the service of God. Did he say to God, "Wait a moment while I finish my work?" No, he did not say that. He did not hesitate. Rather, he immediately left his nets and his boats, and answered that call. And his call was, in the end, to preach to all nations, to bring the dominion and authority of Almighty God to the far corners of the earth!

And in the same way are we called. Into the darkness of the world, the Righteous States must bring light. Into the chaotic wastes of paganism, the Righteous States must bring order. Into the ignorance of primitive cultures, the Righteous States must bring truth and enlightenment! I mean, the enlightenment that comes from truth. I mean the Truth of God ... ah ... the ministers' *teachings* of the Truth of God.

And should any nation be so perverse as to refuse to acknowledge that light, that order, and that truth, why, once again, we are furnished with proof, undeniable proof—not only among the pages of Sacred Scripture, but also among the pages of life itself—that, just as is the case with the lion which eats ... I mean, eateth ... of the antelope and the sheep which crop ... crop ... crop*peth* the tender herbs, so it is God's will that such a decadent nation ... I mean the one that refuses to acknowledge that light, that order, and that truth ... should be devoured, thereby magnifying in spite of itself the glory and authority of He Who consumes it through the agency of the most Righteous States of America, in accordance with the word of divine Truth as spoken by the ministers of that holy nation. I mean the Righteous States. Of America.

Mr. Jenkins turns away from the desert and enters the pavilion of Abnel, the Gharat.

Chapter Twenty-one

The odor brought Sari up out of her stupor as though her face had been thrust over a bowl of rancid ammonia. Coughing and gagging, she sat up quickly, struck her head on the potted plant (potted plant?) that was hanging over the bed (bed?) and immediately fell back. Despite her rapid changes of attitude, though, the stench remained constant.

"This happens often," said a woman's voice. "Almost every time we have an earthquake—Naia's wrath, you know—" And Sari heard a flutter of sarcasm behind the words. "—there is a flood, and then there is a stench. It happens. Did you want to hear the story about Naia's farts? It is wonderfully grotesque."

With a sense of relief, Sari discovered that she could move her arms and her legs, and she found that her head—with the exception of the lump that had just been raised by the potted plant—was relatively free from pain. "Where am I?" she said, recalling with chagrin that she had been asking variants on that particular question ever since she had left her village and her dead husband.

Husband? What husband? She hardly remembered Maumud now.

"Well, you are in Katha," said the voice. "But I am sure you knew that already. If you want to be specific, you are in my house. I managed to take you away from a Panasian postulant (a badly-aspected Virgo: very grotesque) who was obsessed with the idea of giving you a drink of water . . ."

Sari had a dim recollection of a young man with a shaven head. He had been kneeling beside her, his eyes at once fiery and furtive. He had been holding a cup of water in his hand.

". . . and I had you brought here." A pause. "It is not often that we receive such distinguished visitors in Katha."

"Distinguished visitors?" Sari heard the obvious flattery, could not believe that it had anything to do with her.

"A pilgrim. To the Caves of Naia." Again, that flutter of sarcasm. Sari finally turned on her side, and, after taking a quick bearing on the potted plant, managed to sit up.

The woman who, with folded arms, was leaning against the wall beside the bed, was a tall, broad shouldered specimen who, after fixing Sari with a glance and nodding abruptly at the fact that her guest had apparently recovered from her mishap (and high time it was, too), left her station at the wall, set a stool beside the bed, and settled down with a mixture of coarseness and grace that gave her something of the air of a badger attempting to imitate a kitten.

"Very distinguished," she said with another instance of the flutter that made Sari doubt that she believed anything of her own words. "And a Scorpio. A double, correct? Aries rising, too. Well-aspected."

Astrology had never been much practiced by the Naians of Sari's childhood, and so she had no idea whether she was a Scorpio or not, much less anything about double or Aries rising. And so she said nothing.

"I am Charna."

"I am Sari," said Sari. "May Naia bless you, Charna. And many thanks for your kindness."

"It was nothing," said Charna. "As I said, that badly-aspected Virgo was trying to get his hands on you. I cannot see why he was interested . . ." And her tone left Sari somewhat in doubt as to whether Charna found the interest of the badly-aspected Virgo surprising because he was a Panasian and Sari was a Naian, or because he was young and Sari was old. ". . . but well, you *are* a Scorpio . . ."

Everything that Charna said appeared to have several meanings, all of which Sari sensed would prove to be distressing . . . if she could ever figure out what they were.

"Ah . . . of course . . ." said Sari.

"Can I interest you in some food?" said Charna. "I was just about to have lunch."

"Ah . . . all right," said Sari. "Thank you."

"It is the least I can do for such a distinguished visitor."

Lunch, for Charna, proved to be dried figs that had not been improved by being dried. There was also, to be sure, some dried fish soaked in water, but as it looked as though it had no more been improved by being wet than the figs had been improved by being dry, Sari was not inclined to sample it.

Charna, on the other hand, appeared to relish the meal, even though Sari found it difficult to determine just when she was actually eating anything, for she kept up a constant, one-sided patter of conversation that consisted of every possible kind of news, from neighborhood gossip about who was sleeping with whom (and it seemed, at times, that everyone in the Naian community was sleeping with everyone else, though Sari would not have been so bold as to advance that particular hypothesis because Charna's narrative included so many names, zodiacal signs, and planetary aspects that she had become thoroughly muddled), to political news about the priestly Council of Katha, to topical events such as the impending visit of the Gharat Abnel himself and the planned attempt on the part of the Naian community to meet with him.

But always, whatever she was talking about, Charna's voice held that same flutter of underlying sarcasm, as if she not only found all of the above matters to be a source of amusement, but was at the same time of the opinion that not one of them could possibly have any impact on even the most trivial aspect of her life . . . which was, of course, not a source of amusement to anyone at all.

"I was not surprised that no one paid much attention to you," she said as the last of the fish disappeared without any apparent action on her part. "They are so grotesque. They pay no attention to anyone or anything. Here they expect to meet with Abnel himself, and they ignore the arrival of the first pilgrim to the Caves in at least a decade. I do not know how they expect to accomplish anything." And she eyed Sari.

Sari understood what she wanted. "You have something in mind, sister?"

Charna gave only a slight hint that she did not like being called *sister* by anyone. "A plan?" she said. "Of course I have a plan." She gave a toss of her head, demonstrating yet again the uneasy coexistence of badger and kitten. "We must meet with them as equals. They are currently in a position that we once occupied. They have become overbearing and prideful, and they sincerely believe that they control the hearts and minds of all the people of the Three Kingdoms." Another toss of her head. "They are wrong, of course."

Sari, not knowing what else to do, nodded. Between the fish and the stench that had awakened her, her appetite had entirely fled, but now that the fish had disappeared and the stench was dissipating, she finally managed to get down one of the dried figs. She immediately regretted it.

"You see," Charna continued without noticing the nod, the consumption, or the regret, "it is all mutable water. We held the upper hand for thousands of years. And then we became just as stupid and riddled with superstition as the Panasians are now, so that when Panas came along, everyone went over to Him like a bunch of badly-aspected Libras." She nodded, gave a little wiggle of her shoulders that was more than likely supposed to look like something other than what it actually looked like. "But now the time has come for Naia to reassert Herself. Naianism is new and fresh and different. That is perhaps the most important thing. People become bored with the same old religion year after year." She yawned as though to illustrate her point. "I know *I* would. I think it is just a matter of time before people come around."

"I thought . . ." Sari started, then caught herself.

"Thought what, *sister*?"

The tone of the familiarity—which was anything but familiar—was such that Sari winced. "Ah . . . nothing . . ."

"No," said Charna, "that will not do. You are a pilgrim. You are a distinguished visitor . . ." Why did everything that Charna said sound like it meant exactly the opposite of what it sounded like? ". . . and your opinion is very important."

"Well," said Sari, not at all emboldened by Charna's words . . . or her tone, "I thought you said that the others paid no attention to anything. That they were . . . ah . . . well . . . I mean . . . ah . . ."

"Grotesque?"

"Yes." Embarrassed silence. "Grotesque."

Charna nodded as though she had just scored a point in whatever game she was playing with Sari (although Sari, up until then, had not realized that they had been playing any game at all). "Exactly."

"Ah . . ."

Charna nodded.

"Of course."

Charna, with another wiggle that tried to be something that it was not, leaned forward across the table, planted her elbows, and cupped her chin in her hands. "You," she said, "are a distinguished visitor—"

"But I thought you said—"

"Listen to me. Together, the two of us have the opportunity to accomplish something in the Naian community. Jeddiah . . ." (And Sari remembered that Charna had mentioned Jeddiah several times in the course of her opening monologue, though she had lost track of the identity of her bed partner.) " . . . can have her school and her public temple. Such things are unimportant. Just like Jeddiah. Stupid Taurus. Gemini moon. Badly-aspected. But what *is* important is the community and the respect of the Panasian authorities."

"But . . . but they do not respect us!"

"Exactly. We are going to change all that."

"We?"

"You and I." Charna nodded and sat back. While leaning forward, she had inadvertently set her left elbow in the bowl that held the remains of the water-soaked fish, and as Sari stared, she began to suck on the sopping sleeve. "You know," she continued, picking a white flake from the cloth and popping it between her lips: the first morsel that Sari had actually seen her consume, "I can see the two of us creating a nice little upheaval in this community."

If Aeid possessed binoculars, he would be using them right now. As it is, though, he does not possess them, and so he cannot be using them, can he?

Nevertheless, he peers as best he can over the sunlit edge of what would be a dune but for the fact that it is not made of sand, but rather of a tumble of pebbles and cobbles and gravel that, after three hundred years of drought, harbors not the slightest trace of vegetation—living or dead, green or dried—a perfect representative of thousands, perhaps millions, of non-dunes very much like it that interrupt the otherwise flat wastelands of the interior of the Three Kingdoms.

But Aeid, though he numbers himself among the distinguished company of the *philosophes,* is, for now, not at all interested in the wonders of the natural world. No, Aeid is looking *beyond* the non-dune, examining with a mixture of caution, calculation, and eagerness a sprawling collection of horses, camels, asses, tents, and pavilions, which, at this comparatively late hour of the morning, is finally beginning to show signs of human habitation.

As he watches, servants both tongued (who announce to one another loudly and forcefully their general dissatisfaction with their lives, the early hours, the hard work, and the insufferable demands put upon them by their masters) and tongueless (who gesticulate to one another in such a manner as to indicate forcefully their general dissatisfaction with their lives, the early hours, the hard work, the insufferable demands put upon them by their masters, and the fact that their tongues have been cut out) appear from out of the humbler tents, soldiers rise up from their blankets and wraps, and sentries appear from nowhere, these last affirming with every nuance of their deportment that they have not been sleeping. Not at all. Absolutely not. Sleep? *Them?*

It is this last group that intrigues Aeid most, for he knows well that sentries who so strenuously affirm that they have not been sleeping—(Not at all. Absolutely not. Sleep? *Them?*)—have, more than likely, been held firmly in the arms of the Kaprishan version of Morpheus since the previous evening's inspection. And if the sentries have been asleep, Aeid (*philosophe* to the core!) reasons, then there is ample time and opportunity for those who are awake to do other things. Which he fully intends to do.

Aeid, though, is neither alone in his lack of binoculars nor in his peering over the sunlit edge of a non-dune, for though he is not aware of it, he, too, is being watched. You and I, however, know very well that he is being watched, and since we not only have binoculars but also more altitude than either Aeid or the slight, girlish figure that is lying behind the cover of another non-dune about a quarter of a mile away from him, we can easily see that the latter belongs to Bakbuk, King Inwa Kabir's personal sworder.

But though Aeid knows what he is watching, Bakbuk (who, though wearing some fairly nondescript garments that would, if the Three Kingdoms possessed such a word, be described as unisex, shall be referred to using male pronouns—subject to future change, of course) is not so fortunate. He has his suspicions, to be sure, but at a distance of a quarter of a mile, he cannot make out anything more about the other watcher than that his clothing appears to be made up of a multitude of shades of blue. This is, in a way, all that Bakbuk really needs, but as Bakbuk, a complex individual, possesses several layers of suspicions—many of which prompt him for immediate action, many more of which bid him stay put—the sworder simply continues to watch. As does Aeid.

Hold on a moment . . . May I see those binoculars, please?

Now this *is* interesting. Aeid is watching the camp (which is watching nothing, being still in the process of waking up, making breakfast, and attempting to come to some sense of the reality of a day which will see no more than five additional miles of progress made toward Katha), Bakbuk is watching Aeid (who is watching the camp), and . . . well . . . from behind another non-dune about a quarter of a mile away from Bakbuk's non-dune, three men are watching the slight figure of the sworder with evident interest.

Here: hold these binoculars while I release a little helium.

Much better. But the three men are beginning to move, and now (though we have gotten a little too low to be absolutely sure) it seems that they are connected in some way with a large group of men who are even farther away. No matter. I can heave out some ballast later on and, if the winds are favorable (What is that smell, anyway?), we can go and have a look. For now, it is only the three who are doing anything at all, and it is in them that we are interested.

And they are still moving. Toward Bakbuk. And they seem to be relatively comfortable not only with moving through the ever increasing heat of the desert (And what *is* that smell?), but also with moving through that heat in great silence. One might almost suspect them of being thieves or something like that.

Bakbuk is still intent on Aeid, who is intent on the camp (which is intent upon nothing), and, as such, he (Bakbuk) does not notice that the three men are drawing ever closer to him until, as the camp, after an appropriately lengthy breakfast, begins moving eastward, and as Aeid, after rearranging his mask (which has, once again, fallen down over one eye) prepares to follow it, the sworder (who has been preparing to follow Aeid) suddenly feels a hand on his shoulder and finds himself turned roughly over onto his back.

A sword is pointed at his throat.

"A fine one," says the first man. "A very fine one."

"A high price, surely," says the second man.

"This is most assuredly an impediment to the sovereignty of Khyr, and it must be dispatched," says the third, who holds the sword.

The second looks stunned. "But . . . the high price!"

The third looks at the second. "What is money where the sovereignty of Khyr is concerned?"

"Well, is not freedom valuable?" says the second. "Should those who fight for it not be paid?"

The third contemplates this.

"A fine one," the first says again. Doubtless, he would consider Bakbuk a fine one whether the sworder were alive or spitted on the end of the sword, but as though unwilling to leave such a succinct observation alone, he says again, with a small attempt at variety, "A very fine one."

"How much," says the third, having experienced a sudden change of heart, "do you think that we can get for . . . ah . . . uh . . . ah . . . uh . . ." He is peering down the length of his sword at their prize, and their prize, it should be mentioned, is peering back at him. ". . . her?"

"Her?" says the first.

"Her?" says the second.

This new development apparently puts the acquisition of a ransomable prize in an entirely different light, for the discussion about freedom and its inherent costliness abruptly veers around to a new tack: that of who should be first.

"I saw her first," says the first man with rigorous logic. "A fine one," he adds.

"I proposed that we take her," says the second, as though with equal assurance that logic is on his side.

"Well, neither of you recognized a woman when you saw one," says the third, who seems also to believe that he is the sole possessor of that precious commodity. "I was the one who did that."

Needless to say, Bakbuk is listening to the ongoing forensics with great interest. Needless to say, the sword is still pointing at Bakbuk's throat.

"If I had not seen her," says the first man, "we would not be here."

"If I had not suggested that we take her," says the second, "we would not be standing here right now."

"If I had not recognized her sex," says the third, "we would still be jabbering about the sovereignty of Khyr."

With the sudden intrusion of political considerations, the three fall silent. Guilty looks are exchanged.

"Ah," says Bakbuk, "I am, perhaps, in the presence of the freedom fighters of Khyr?"

This remark, pointing (Give me those binoculars.) once again to the men's tacit dereliction of duty, results in a prolongation of the silence and another round of guilty looks, this time accompanied by a shuffling of feet.

"I fear I must inform you all that I am a man," says Bakbuk, but though the irony in his voice is completely missed by the three prurient patriots, the small heave of his (her?) tidy little bosom (which, of course, belies her (his?) words) is not. Nor is the simultaneous and very inviting shift of . . . ah . . . Bakbuk's hips. All of which result in the three men moving toward the sworder at the same moment.

Which is just what Bakbuk wanted. In a flash, a dagger has somehow (Did you see that?) leaped out of a hidden sheath into his hand, and has thereupon somehow been rammed straight down through the foot of the first man, who immediately finds himself not only incapable of further movement, but in great pain as well.

Bakbuk has just given up his dagger. No matter, there is another (Where *did* that come from?) in his hand in a moment, and since he is now on his feet (How *does* he do it?), he unceremoniously inserts the weapon, point first, between the fifth and sixth ribs of the second man, who subsequently falls down and does not get up again.

All this has somehow given Bakbuk time enough to draw his sword, and though the third man, after due consideration, has decided to run for his life, he does not get very far at all before he finds himself, with what fading consciousness is left to him, face down on the ground.

Bakbuk turns back to the first man. The first man, though, has managed to get loose, and, seemingly braver than the others (or perhaps merely having decided that to fight and be killed is better than not to fight and be killed anyway), he manages to lift his good foot and deliver a powerful kick straight into the sworder's groin.

For a moment, Bakbuk stands still. The first man looks at him expectantly. Several seconds go by.

Bakbuk bows. "Very sorry," he says. "Too late."

The first man's look of astonishment is something that his corpse will carry for a long time. At least until the jackals arrive.

And you may have the binoculars if you wish, for we are now close enough to see very clearly that Bakbuk, after sitting for a moment or two on the sand, indulges in no dance of victory nor even allows himself a quiet period of satisfied reflection. Not at all. Instead, he begins to abuse himself, slapping his soft face with his small and delicate hands while screaming with such unimaginable anger that his cries are actually stifled:

"Stupid girl! Stupid, stupid girl! They caught you, and you did not notice a thing! Stupid! Stupid! Stupid! You deserve exactly what they had in mind! Stupid girl!"

And then (and, I assure you, I am just as surprised as you), the sworder casts away his sword and buries his bruised face in his small hands, for anger and embarrassment have brought with them the undeniable knowledge that what the three men had in mind was exactly what she wanted.

Chapter Twenty-two

Two suns only will see you
Following the path to Naia's grace;
The dawn-shadow of the final ridge
Pointing the way to Her womb.

The Hymns of Loomar were very clear. One left Katha and followed the trail marked by the shadow of the westernmost ridge of the mountains just as the sun rose. One continued northward until one reached the stream that flowed out of the Caves. Then one followed the stream.

But circumstance and courtesy seemed to be holding her in Katha even more tenaciously than Panasian law had bound her to her house and her husband, and Sari wondered now more than ever whether she would reach the Caves at all, for to turn her back on Charna after receiving hospitality, food, and shelter—particularly after Charna had helped her to recover from what could have been a serious injury—seemed actions completely out of keeping with the spirit that Sari considered essential to Naianism. If she had learned anything at all from her parents and her parents' friends, if she remembered anything at all (and she *did* remember . . . or so she continued to tell herself in the face of steadily increasing doubt), guests shared with their hosts as much as hosts shared with their guests, manifesting through that sharing the companionship and simple affection of children, for all were children of Naia, and (as Sari well knew) mothers enjoyed seeing their children getting along with one another.

And so she stayed, trying to hold to what she remembered, trying to tell herself that she was doing the right thing; and yet her doubts could not but be increased by the fact that Charna appeared at times to be deliberately using both her memories and her doubts to hold her in Katha.

That very first day, after making sure that her guest would not fall over or faint or something else that might be considered either grotesque or badly-aspected, Charna took Sari on a lengthy round of visits to other prominent Naians (all of whom appeared to think extremely highly of Charna, which, as Sari found herself suspecting more and more, was obviously the reason Charna considered them prominent), introducing her as a pilgrim, someone who, like Charna herself (this resemblance being emphasized) was attempting to bring back some of the old respect to Naianism. But though Sari began to assume that when Charna said *respect for Naianism* she actually meant *respect for Charna,* she could not manage to raise as much indignation within herself as she would have liked. Charna was manipulative, flattering, and willing to exploit a casual acquaintance, but she was also the only Naian Sari had met who was neither completely enslaved by superstition and novelty nor subject to an almost pathological lack of common sense. Against her will, Sari actually felt a certain admiration for the woman.

"I am having a little gathering tonight," Charna informed her at the end of the better part of a week. "Some representatives of the community. Only . . ." For once, Charna's tone was without sarcasm, but the look in her eyes gave the deception away. ". . . important people. Ev-

eryone who is working on the meeting with the Gharat."
Another look. "You will be there, of course."

Sari could only nod. Just outside of Katha were the
mountains, and, to the north, among the mountains, were
the Caves. She should have left already. She might have
been there by now. Just two days' journey . . .

She felt trapped. But what was trapping her? Courtesy?
Or was it that, given what she had seen since she had left
her village, she was no longer as drawn to the Caves as
she had once been? Perhaps the Caves were just an irrele-
vancy in these days of star charts and gem elixirs, of in-
consequential brassware and Naian wives. Perhaps Naia
had provided as much as She was going to provide. Perhaps it was Sari's turn to provide, and perhaps her provid-
ing lay not in the direction of the Caves, but rather right
here in Katha.

Sari's will, seemingly, had gone to sleep, and for a
moment, she actually found herself wanting to believe
Charna, wanting to believe that she, a pilgrim, was important, that somehow, with careful, purposeful planning, the
old ways could be brought back, respect for Naianism
could be restored, and a new life for her people—and for
herself—could be established.

"We will be discussing the meeting, of course," Charna
continued.

"Of course," said Sari, but her glance strayed to the
window where the mountains—everywhere one looked in
Katha, there were mountains: the city was as much a part
of them as a daughter was a part of her mother—rose up
above the rooftops. Mountains: thick with minerals, shot
with lodes of precious and semiprecious stone. Mountains:
the aloof, remote fastness from which Panas, according to
the Sacred Texts, had hewn the building blocks of the
cities.

Mountains. Mountains that contained the holy spring. Two day's journey . . .

She stood silently for a moment, and then she turned back to Charna. "I will attend the gathering tonight," she said firmly. "But this afternoon I will be buying supplies in the marketplace and packing my bundle, for I will be leaving tomorrow."

"Leaving?" The sarcasm was creeping back.

"For the Caves," said Sari, and though she could not keep the irritation out of her voice, she managed to hide the disappointment and the encroaching despair. "As you have been telling everyone, I am a pilgrim. I must continue my pilgrimage."

Charna stared. It had apparently never occurred to her that Sari might actually do what she had said that she would do.

"Three days from now," said Sari, turning back to the mountains, "I intend to be at the Caves."

Charna found her voice. "Oh . . . how grotesque. You must have a badly-aspected Gemini moon, Sari. Nobody goes to the Caves."

Sari hung her head. "Then am I nobody," she said.

IN THE NAME OF PANAS, THE BENEFICENT, THE WONDROUS, THE SHAPER OF CITIES, THE CARVER OF WORLDS, THE ARBITER OF THE LIVES OF MEN AND THE SUBJUGATOR OF ALL THINGS WEAK AND EFFEMINATE, FOR WHOSE GLORY THE GREAT WORK OF THE PUMPS AND RESERVOIRS GOES ON CEASELESSLY NIGHT AND DAY, TO WHOSE CREDIT WAS THE FIRST REVELATION OF THE GREAT WORK OF THE PUMPS AND RESERVOIRS, IN WHOSE NAME THE WRITER GREETS AND COMPLIMENTS THE READER AS MANY TIMES AS THERE ARE GRAINS OF SAND IN

THE DESERT, PEBBLES IN THE DRY VALLEYS, PARCHED FIELDS IN THE WASTELAND AND HUMBLY OFFERS THE FOLLOWING INFORMATION.

Mishap: *Earthquake*

Pumps damaged: *#48, #33, #1398, #2134*

Reason for damage: *collapse of pump tunnels #34, #35, #36*

Slaves dead/injured: *97/183*

Reason for death/injury: *collapse of pump tunnels #34, #35, #36*

Percentage drop in overall capacity: *12*

Estimated time until return to full capacity: *80 days*

Damage to dikes, dams, and retaining walls: *moderate*

Collateral release of water before containment: *84000 kils*

Projected strength of repairs: *good*

IN THE NAME OF PANAS, THE BUILDER UP AND THE WEARER DOWN, THE MUNIFICENT AND THE PROFITABLE, THE POWER OF THE PRIESTS AND THE FEAR OF THE LAITY, THE HOLY AND THE RIGHTEOUS, THE SMITER OF ENEMIES AND THE HELPER OF FRIENDS, SO CLOSES THIS REPORT IN THE HOPES THAT THE READER MAY BE SO MAGNIFIED AS TO BE GREAT AS THE CLOUDLESS SKY, AS WIDE AS THE DESERTS, AS HOT AS THE BURNING SUN . . .

FORWARDED TO KATHA

I must think this through carefully, for a mistake at the present moment will ruin me.

Kuz Aswani knew that he was being watched. Kuz Aswani knew who was watching him.

He is, of course, insane. So he would be perfectly willing to denounce me, even (ow!) if it meant his death.

But though he had been watched before, the watching

now was more obvious, more overt. He seemed now to have no privacy at all: there was no time when a pair of eyes was not peering at him from behind, from before, from a window or a doorway, from down a hall, from under a bush in the garden ...

And yet it is so difficult to be certain. Nothing is certain. He was masked, after all, when he saw me. (And I was not! How unforgivably (ow!) careless of me!)

At times, he could not keep himself from a quick bounce and an irritated chuckle when, yet again, he turned to find himself presented with the blur of a figure vanishing around a corner, or dropping down behind a wall, or flashing out of sight in some other way. Too quick, much too quick the figure was for Kuz Aswani to identify (ferret eyesight being notoriously poor), but Kuz Aswani did not need to *see* who in order to *know* who.

But the damage is done, and I must make the best of it. Indeed, I can make the best of it, if only I am careful.

Even though Haddar had released him from his enforced confinement (And Kuz Aswani was still of two minds about that, for though he was fast becoming a ferret, he still retained enough of his human bias to be of the opinion that ferrets should not be left to run about loose and unsupervised), the chief minister (And what about the chief minister? How far along was *he*?) could do nothing about his real prison, a prison made up as much of magic as of the continuing surveillance of Umi Botzu.

Yes. I can. For if he is indeed the Blue Avenger, an active criminal (ow!) who has been witnessed attacking priestly representatives, then would his word be good for anything? Including (ow!) denouncing me?

And that it was Umi Botzu who watched him so constantly, Kuz Aswani had no doubt whatsoever, for who else would be motivated to keep him under such close observation? Only a sorcerer who took delight in his sorcery,

only a practitioner of the black arts who derived a perverse
sort of pleasure from watching the slow, inexorable
transformation of the ensorcelled.

*But, still, he might not be the Blue Avenger, and if he is
not, then his word would be perfectly adequate for almost
anything. Including (ow!) denouncing me.*

Prowling the corridors and hallways of the palace,
rolling in the grass of the king's gardens (for Haddar's rec-
ommendations had even gained for him this great privi-
lege), *pudda-pudda-puddaing* up and down the stairs as his
fellow counselors stared at him and the servants hid their
faces out of embarrassment, Kuz Aswani tried to enjoy his
freedom, but the image of the sorcerer haunted his ferrety
mind, troubling him even as he buried his face in the ec-
static pleasures of a bowl of raisins.

*It is difficult to be sure. I think my suspicions are cor-
rect. But I must establish once and for all that he is the
Blue Avenger, for to arrest him in error would bring about
highly undesirable results.*

And therefore, if Kuz Aswani was a ferret, then he was
an extremely nervous ferret. There was certainly much to
be said for being a ferret, but only if people would leave
the ferret in question alone long enough so that the ferret
in question could enjoy *being* the ferret in question.

I will have him watched ... (ow!)

Describe the general form of the residence in which was
held, on the twenty-ninth day of the Month of the Strong
Hand, a gathering of certain members of the Naian community of the city of Katha.

Its outside walls describing, upon careful measurement,
not a rectangle but rather an unequal quadrilateral of the
trapezoidal variety, the residence in question possessed a
major axis of approximately 30′ in the standard American
measure of the time, and a minor axis of approximately

23', 2½" using the same measuring system. Within, a wall roughly perpendicular to the major axis roughly bisected the interior area into two roughly equal portions, the one reserved for cooking, the other for eating, sleeping, and, under the present circumstances, the entertainment of guests.

Was the inexactness of the general form of the residence deliberate?

Not to the knowledge of anyone then living.

Why was this?

The builder having been killed when the original roof of the residence collapsed in the course of its construction, and said builder having never written down the particulars of his designs, all knowledge of the deliberate or accidental nature of his designs perished with him.

Why did the roof collapse?

While the minor but constant earthquakes experienced by the residents of Katha might well have played some not-insignificant part in the disturbance of the structure, careful and exact measurements by competent engineers would have found the principal cause of the collapse to be nothing more and nothing less than faulty building technique.

Was this faulty technique peculiar to the construction of this particular residence?

No.

Could it have been found elsewhere in Katha?

In one form or another, to a greater or a lesser degree, within certain limits, for varying reasons, from underlying causes both obscure and obvious, it could.

Could it have been found in buildings other than residences?

Yes.

Could it have been found in buildings outside the carefully delineated and circumscribed boundaries of the Naian quarter?

No.

Was this widespread faulty technique the cause of any concern among the Naians of Katha?

In that 53% of the population believed that all mishaps occurred on the basis of choices made by the victims in an interincarnatory existence, 29% believed that all mishaps were easily predicted by the zodiacal positions of the planets and were, therefore, easily avoided, 10% believed that all mishaps would be averted by the occult agency of small pieces of polished rock hung up within their dwellings, 5% believed that all mishaps could be prevented by dietary restrictions of greater or less severity, and 2% did not ever think about such things, it was not.

And the last 1%?

The last 1% encompassed a host of individualistic and varying beliefs, ranging from Naia's providence to the phases of the moon to the accumulation of mucus in the body and are, perhaps, best left unenumerated.

And therefore this instability was of no concern to those who gathered in the above-referenced residence on the twenty-ninth day of the Month of the Strong Hand?

It was of no concern at all.

What was the concern of those who gathered in one of the rooms of the above named residence on the twenty-ninth day of the Month of the Strong Hand?

There was no single concern. Rather, by the simple fact of the multiplication of discrete intelligences present within the confines of the residence, and by the mutual independence and indivisibility of the bodily integrity of those same discrete intelligences, the concerns were many and varied.

Enumerate the most urgent and pressing of these concerns.

That some way should be found to effect the meeting of appointed representatives of the Naian community with the High Priest of Panas. That some way should be found to have sexual congress with the woman who owned the house. That some way should be found to have sexual congress with one of the men who had come to the gathering. That some way should be found to have sexual congress with one of the women who had come to the gathering. That some way should be found to have sexual congress with another of the men who had come to the gathering. That some way should be found to have sexual congress with two of the women who had come to the gathering. That some way should be . . .

Ah . . . that is sufficient.

. . . found to have sexual congress with three of the men who had come to the gathering. That the sexual prowess of one of the men not be found wanting. That no aspersions . . .

Ah . . . that—

. . . should be cast upon the sexual performance of another of the men. That . . .

Ah, really—

... one of the men not be demonstrated, either by interference or by action, to be homosexual. That one of the women (Jeddiah by name) be publicly shown to be an ass licking, dishonorable whore with ...

Excuse me—

... delusions of grandeur. That the woman (Charna by name) who owned the house be publicly shown to be an opportunistic bitch who had sexual congress with a now deceased male member of the Naian community solely in order to secure her ownership of the house by right of matrimonial ...

Enough!

... inheritance. That one of the women be found dead in her bed the following morning so that she could not steal any more students from teachers who had more right to be teaching the true and proper Naian ways than her. That the woman named Sari—Oh. Sorry.

Sari? Oh ... ah ... go on.

The extent of the previous enumeration is, doubtless, sufficient.

No, really. Go on.

Given the above adjurations to cease, it would be impolite to continue.

I insist.

Out of the question.

Ah ... were there ... ah ... any concerns specifically regarding the woman named Sari?

There were.

And what were they?
Courtesy forbids—

Oh, bloody hell, get on with it!
. . .

Ah . . . please.
That . . . that . . . that . . . that Sari fall prey to a lingering but non-fatal illness that would prevent her from leaving Katha for an indeterminate but substantial period of time.

Who was the holder of this last concern?
Charna. The owner of the house.

Was Sari aware of this concern on the part of Charna?
Indirectly, unconsciously. Generally, not particularly. Abstractly, without specifics.

Did Sari suspect that Charna was capable of achieving her ends by artificial means?
The suspicion had not occurred to her.

Was Charna, in fact, capable of doing this?
Most certainly.

By what method was Charna most likely to attempt this?
By the introduction, by subterfuge, of a small amount of a little-known herb of the nightshade family into some item, potable or comestible, that Sari would be likely to ingest.

Did Charna, in fact, have the means by which to achieve this?
She did.

Was Sari, in fact, aware of this?

In the course of the gathering at the residence of Charna that evening, ocular discernment, coupled with an extensive knowledge of the properties of herbs, enabled Sari to attain a degree of knowledge that was not out of keeping with this awareness.

Explain.

Moving on a course of south by west through the room in which the gathering was held, she (Sari) observed a previously unnoticed shelf bearing flasks and vials, said shelf being situated on a bearing of 45° relative to her course. Prompted by curiosity, and yet not desirous of being perceived as bad-aspected or grotesquely curious, she approached said shelf in a casual manner and noted that on the flasks and vials were written the names of several herbs which she, an herbalist, recognized as having various properties, among which was one capable of causing a lingering but non-fatal illness.

Was Charna aware of Sari's perception?
She was not.

Did Charna, in fact, attempt the realization of this lingering but non-fatal illness?
She did.

Did Sari discover this?
Yes.

Describe the means by which Sari made this discovery.

Turning about onto a course of north by east, and still without undue suspicion, she (Sari) lifted an as of yet untasted cup of wine to her lips and became suddenly aware that there was, in addition to the customary olfactory characteristics of vinous liquids, a not-unpleasant but entirely unexpected odor which she, an herbalist, recognized as belonging to a certain member of the nightshade family whose name she had read on one of the above mentioned flasks and vials. She then recalled that Charna had been most insistent that she (Sari) take one more cup of wine from her (Charna).

Was Sari thereafter inclined to imbibe of or to dispose of the vinous liquid that had been given to her by Charna?
She was inclined to dispose of it.

In what manner did Sari dispose of the vinous liquid?
Proceeding on a course roughly north by northwest, she passed by the pallet upon which she had been lying when she had first awakened in Charna's house and emptied said vinous liquid into the potted plant that her head had encountered immediately after she had first awakened in Charna's house.

Did Charna observe this elementary study in gravity and hydrokinetics?
She did not.

What occurred directly after the guests invited to the gathering had departed for their respective residences, the structural integrity of which was discussed at length above?
Sari, protesting fatigue, retired to her pallet, carefully avoiding the potted plant that her head had encountered immediately after she had first awakened in Charna's house.

And Charna?
Charna, considering that to protest fatigue was not only

to be grotesque but also to exhibit indications of something badly-aspected, also retired to her pallet, but without comment.

Did anything occur within Charna's residence in the course of the nocturnal hours separating the twenty-ninth from the thirtieth day of the Month of the Strong Hand that was uncustomary even considering that guests in Charna's residence were themselves uncustomary?
Yes.

Describe.
At about one hour past midnight, a figure rose from a pallet that lay beneath a potted plant, extracted a bundle from beneath the pallet, and obtained egress from the house.

How was this egress effected?
Via the aperture afforded by an unshuttered window.

Was this egress detected at the time by any other than the egressing figure?
No.

What was the ultimate fate of the plant that hung above the pallet?
Withering, wilting, yellowing, drying, dying, death.

Chapter Twenty-three

. . . and I just can't believe this bullshit they're giving me about twenty-three fucking dollars and fifty cents a week. I mean, I work hard for a living, and I pay my taxes, and can you believe all this crap? It wasn't my fault that they got sore at me. I was doing my job. I can't help it if the patrons I get one day, just one lousy day, are a bunch of feeps that just got out of the loony-bin, can I? So I tell them to pipe down. So what do they do? They complain. Is it *my* fault they're feeps? Is it *my* fault they're fresh out of the loony-bin? But the boss gets sore and tells *me* to get lost. Won't even give me the two weeks and all that. Just: *Say hey, we'll get you a CMO and you get the fuck outta here.* Can you believe that? The nerve of these guys. Think they own the world. Like, who died and made them God, huh?

Well, I'll tell you, dude, this is the real pits. I mean, how am I supposed to get anything done if I gotta stand here in line with all the unwashed here (you and me excepted, if you know what I mean), waiting to see some idiot *female* who's gonna decide if I'm gonna get some money out of old Uncle Sugar. I mean, I'm an artist, see? I got things to do. Why, I've had scripts at all the major houses. Yeah, really. No kidding. Scripts. Movie scripts.

Full length, big-time movie scripts. I put in all the camera angles and everything: I'm a professional, you know. No, never got anything sold, but how am I supposed to sell anything if I gotta come down to these offices and stand in line all day to see if some *woman* is gonna give me back some of the money I shelled out while I was working? You tell me, huh? I'll tell you, that's not democracy, that's communism. Pussy-whipped communism, and you can bet on that.

Yeah, really. Movies. Oh, yeah, I got plenty of contacts. I was just picking up a little bit of cash along the way while I was waiting for something to hit, and it would have hit real big if those assholes I was working for had just stayed off my back and let me do my job. But did they? No way. Just pick, pick, pick, all the time. Your uniform isn't clean. You didn't shave. You don't fit the company image. You didn't do this. You didn't do that. Nag, nag, nag, just like a bunch of fucking women.

And when I try to get my job done ... I mean, I'm there for the customers, right? I'm there to keep them from falling out of the tram and drifting off into inter-oneiric space, like, never to be seen again and all that shit. I mean, driving for dream tours is a responsible position, and I knew what I was doing. I mean, I'm an artist. I know all about unconscious motivations and stuff like that. Like, that's my real business, see?

No, I don't have anything out now 'cause everything fell through on account of the assholes giving me bullshit and all that. But I'm working on this script right now that's gonna make my name a household word. None of this Andy Warhol fifteen minutes of fame for Yours Truly: this is gonna go right to the moon. And can you believe this line we're in? Goes nowhere real fast, doesn't it? And I can guarantee that some *woman* is gonna try to tell me to go out and get another two bit job so that she doesn't have to give me anything at all. And even if I get my twenty-three fucking dollars and fifty cents, I'll betcha a million bucks that those fuckers who fired me'll raise a stink about paying unemployment, and yeah, I know all about getting fired with cause, but they owe me, see, and I'm gonna get what's mine.

What's the script about? Well, I gotta protect my rights, so I can't tell you everything about it, but ... I'll tell you this dynamite scene that I just put down last night. You see, there's this kind of Robin Hood guy who's been shadowing this bunch of official types, but he's not exactly a Sean Connery kinda dude. See, what I'm trying to tell you is that he's human and all, 'cause, you see, audience identification is real important these days. Personally, I kinda like the old Marvel superhero types, 'cause you could believe in those guys. Like, they had *problems* like you and me. And those women: boy-oh-boy, I'll tell you, those guys at Marvel could draw women like no one's business, 'cept they can't do it as well these days because those skanky libbers have been at them and all.

But, anyway, so this guy doesn't do anything perfect is what I'm trying to say, but he really wants to scare these official types and so he's been waiting for his chance, and tonight's the night. So he waits for the ... whaddaya call them ... the guards to fall asleep, which I've already established that they do, even though they're not supposed to (Hey, get a load of that ass, huh? What a goddess!), and then he ...

Oh, I forgot to tell you. He's like, wearing this costume. It's great. I dreamed it up one night, and I had my girlfriend ... I mean, I had *one* of my girlfriends make a sketch of it 'cause she goes to art school and she can do shit like that. Not that she's gonna get too much of a chance to do any art if she marries me, 'cause I know what a woman's place is, and it's grunting and groaning under her man, right? Yeah, you and me both, pardner. But the costume's all blue. Everything's blue. He calls himself the Blue Avenger, of course, but to me, he'll always be Robin Hood. Hey, did you see that Mel Brooks film? Wasn't that a riot! Latrine! Hey, I couldn't stop laughing!

Anyway, so Robin Hood sneaks into the camp, and he's got his sights set on terrorizing this priest kinda guy who's the leader of the official types. It's like, personal, you see, and it's looking like there's gonna be some big business going on, only just as he's gonna do it, I mean, like slip into the guy's bedroom and sit on his face or something like that, there's some other guys that show up *who've got the same idea*—million laughs, you know?—except that they're not just out to scare someone, they're out for blood.

What for? Hell, it's politics. Their great-great grandfathers got ripped off by the priest guy's great-great grandfathers and these dweebs have been holding a grudge ever since. You know, like that terrorist stuff in the Middle East, or that . . . that stuff up in Ireland where they've been blowing each other away for so long they've forgotten why. Hey, Yugoslavia, too! Boy, like, I mean, this is topical stuff, ¿comprende?

Anyway, so the dweebs want to kill everyone in the camp because of something that happened hundreds of years ago, but old Robin Hood there isn't the kind of guy to want to kill anyone. Actually, he's kinda sorta on the priest guy's side, only it's this personal trip he's on that makes him want to scare him. See? But since he doesn't want to actually *hurt* the priest guy, you know, when the dweebs show up shouting about the righteousness of whoever their god is—I'll figure it out later—and about how they got fucked over by whoever-it-was's great-great grandfathers and how they're gonna have revenge for it and how God or whoever—like I said, I'll figure it out later—is on their side, Robin Hood's gotta protect the priest guy. Only by now the priest guy is convinced that Robin Hood is in cahoots with the terrorist dweebs and that *he's* out to have his balls, too. See?

And then there's this really funny part where Robin Hood's got the priest guy's guards stabbing at him from one side, and the terrorist dweebs stabbing at him from the other, and he's, like, trying to have this political discussion with the terrorist dweebs about the justice of their cause and how he's really on their side and all. Which, natcherally, convinces the priest guy's guards that Robin Hood really *is* out for the priest guy's balls, and they try to get him even harder.

Jeez: do you believe this line we're in? I mean, I pay taxes to support this shit? Just so I can get bossed around by some bitch who's like on permanent PMS or something? Hey, and the same to you, lady. All I got to say to you is that you're taking a job away from some man with a family to support, and what do you think about that?

See? Shuts them up every time. That's insight. That's why I'm a writer. Anyway, Robin Hood's talking to the dweebs about the rights of man, and the dweebs are shouting about God and righteousness, and it goes back and forth like that, with the priest guy's guards getting a lick in every now and then, and no one really knows who's on whose side, you know, and there's gonna be, like, subtitles—You ever see Annie Hall? Yeah, like that. —showing their thoughts. It's really brilliant. And the dweebs keep wondering whether Robin Hood is on their side or not, and the guards are doing the same thing, and all I can tell ya is that it's a good thing that Robin Hood is handy with a sword, 'cause if he wasn't, it'd be curtains for him for sure, on account of he's getting so many things poked at him that he's starting to feel like a cute coed at a frat party.

So the whole thing's turned into, like, this major snafu, and Robin Hood's starting to think about just one thing, which is getting out with his balls intact. But, wouldn't you know it (And listen to me, 'cause this is brilliant stuff. I'm gonna make mega-bucks with this, just you wait and see!), just as it's looking like he's gonna make it, he fucks up, and winds up pinned down with all of the dweebs and the guards coming for him. I mean, it's the Big Green Weenie this guy is gonna bite. But, OK, well, like I gotta tell you something else about this situation. The king of this place has sent his personal guard out to protect the priest guy, and this guard's a funny one. He, like, had his balls cut off when he was little, so he's not sure if he's a boy or a girl. I mean, isn't that great? The twinkies'll eat it up. (Hey, now *that's* a good one!) But whichever he is, he's still great with a sword, and he rushes in and cuts up the dweebs and holds off the guards and lets Robin Hood get away.

'Course you're wondering why he did that. Well, it's like, real subtle. You see, this guy's been wondering whether he's a boy or a girl for so long, and kinda playing at being a girl sometimes, that something's shifted a little, and he's starting to kinda get into being a she. And that means a lot of things, if you know what I mean, and the audience is gonna see the cow eyes he's . . . I mean, she's . . . making at Robin Hood.

Isn't that great? You see why I'm talking about money? Why, after that *Crying Game* shtick, the studios'll eat this stuff right out of the palm of my hand, and can you believe this line we're in? They're probably talking about . . . like . . . *tampons* or something up there. You can't trust women to do a lick of work, and have you ever watched them? They have to go to the bathroom every fif-fucking-teen minutes? Do you believe that?

Listen, I'll warn you right now, I'm a member of the

Screen Writer's Guild, and the treatment for this script is *registered,* so don't go getting any ideas about ripping me off, 'cause I'll sue your ass off, you can bet on that. You can't be too careful in this town, and people like you are always figuring that you're gonna cut the talented writers out of their hard-earned dough . . . hey, same to you!

Surveyed, quickannoyedpunish—pid! . . . chains would Avenger footfallclipper (powder worthless) candygrapethought about old croneraisinold woman . . . vessel, valve, steam, opening, spreadthought Steam? footfallsnorth Heathen lands Tap. Coy. Stupid! Onward. Disciplease...freedomcoyfightersup blankness...
brigands...doubt...up.........grape.........powder...
'Frisco...............ninety...........................
sterilitesque......................wat......................ttt...
aspected....................er....................Tap.
Check: oneoneone. Rolling tape.

Mr. Jenkins surveyed the fallen tents, the corpses already bloating in the sun, the horses milling about. "A fine mess," he said in very smooth, diplomatic French.

"Oh," said Abnel, also in very smooth, diplomatic French, "but they were driven off. And very quickly I might add."

Jenkins, annoyed still, and still further annoyed that the brigands (But had they been mere brigands? He doubted it.) had penetrated even into his own bedroom (Had these savages never heard of diplomatic immunity?) shook his head. "I would offer my distinguished and honored friend not the slightest disrespect, but I think that your sentries are somewhat lacking."

"Fear not," said Abnel. "They will be punished."

He pointed, and Jenkins saw: men in the silks and colors of King Inwa Kabir. They were in chains. They would be punished.

"Stupid girl!" And in the privacy of an unfallen tent, Bakbuk slapped his own face one again. "Stupid, stupid girl!"

One look at the Blue Avenger (and it no longer mattered who he was: he was strong, and he was (Bakbuk could tell, even through the mask) handsome, and he was . . .)

"Stupid!"

"They are all so grotesque!"

Abnel examined Jenkins in a fashion that Jenkins did not like in the slightest, a fashion that became passé only when Mather came bustling up, mopping his brow.

"Jesus, but it's hot!" said Mather in English.

The heat of the forge was tremendous, and Umi Botzu was sweating as he leaned over the counter. Across the counter was the smith: dark skinned, dark eyed. "You want me to do what?" said the smith.

"Where were you last night?" said Jenkins, also in English.

Bakbuk plucked at his long hair. He was a boy today, and he wanted to cut off the offending tresses (Cutting off again: was that not what had started him on this useless road?), but he could not bring himself to do it. Because . . . because maybe . . .

Winding, rising and falling, the trail (faint, fainter, faintest) led along the foothills of the Mountains of Ern, Sari's footfalls following it, sonic emblem of a lithic path. The day progressed, Sari progressed. The third day. Footfalls, one after another. Slow traveling toward the north. Soon now.

"Clipper ships, Turtletrout! They're building clipper ships! Not those little schooners that a man could fill up by pissing in 'em! Real ships!"

"I will have it thought about." But it struck Inwa Kabir that he had had the matter thought about for quite long enough. Still, though: "I will have it thought about."

Mather looked up, looked down, looked anywhere but directly at Jenkins. "I was . . . ah . . . occupied." (Squirm!)

Bakbuk's knuckles pressed into his eyes. There, Bakbuk! Crying like a girl, a cute little girl, and would you not like to spread your legs for him? And what would he do if you did? What would *you* do? What *could* you?

Squirm!

The desert was hot, bright, the rocks clear-edged in the clear light. Aeid scanned the distance, northward, searching for the smudge of haze that was the camp.

Footfalls. Greenest Branch. Where, though, was there any green in this landscape of sterility and death? This might have been the corpse of an old woman Sari was looking at, the withered dugs of former rivers, the sere, rocky outlines of a once lovely face.

"Such a badly aspected Scorpio. She ran off! Utterly grotesque!"

"I want you to make a vessel," said Umi Botzu. "A sealed vessel. Only one opening. And affix wheels. You will make it, and I will give you gold."

And there! Mather and that blasted squirm. Jenkins had come to dread it even more than he dreaded Mr. Wool's insufferable Biblical glosses. But Jenkins had plans, and so he could not allow Mather's gyrations to bother him.

Squirm!

Punish.

Tap.

Raisins!

"Much as I think punishment is in order, my dear Gharat . . ."

There! That smudge! Once again, the Blue Avenger closed in, though this time he would not attack. No: better to wait.

Squirm!

She plodded northward, along stones, her old bones aching, her eyes peering into the sunlit distance, looking for some sign of the stream. It was here. It had to be here. But she found only . . .

"You have mucus in your body. Too much mucus." The woman, young for an elder, nodded over the smoky fire. "Too much. Have you . . . been excised?"

(Ow!)

". . . I think greater efficiency is perhaps a better solution."

"How so, Ambassador Jenkins?"

Abnel was eating candied grapes. Sugar clung to his moist lips. Mather, Jenkins noticed, was looking at him with a curious expression.

And with a curious expression, the smith bent over the diagram that Umi Botzu now spread out on the counter. A sealed vessel with but one opening. A valve on the opening. A wheel on each side, and one in front. "What is this for?"

"It is for something you do not understand."

"Water! Buy my water!"

. . . a dry stream bed that had obviously not seen water for some time. And yet (fingers exploring, poking into sand that bore an almost subliminal odor of something fetid . . . fetid and wet) there had been water here.

Give me raisins!

And give you the blessing of Panas, which is money. Beshur folded his head cloth over his shaved skull. (Here, walk like this.) Disguised and disguised, he hid himself among the shadows of an alley. Who was she? Old woman. Pilgrim, someone said. Not long now. Then forever.

. . . kill myself one of these days . . . Sabihah? What does she like? Between her breasts? Good and stiff. That skin . . . like velvet. Pearls against her skin. Or was that rubies? Time for that later. Katha first. Will precede them to Katha. There . . .

I wonder . . . did she know about the wine?

"Ninety days to 'Frisco! Think of it!"

Bakbuk explored himself/herself, searching the blankness for something out/in, something that would put him/her down as either him/her. There must be something. Something.

"Despite your reluctance to accept the fact . . ." Jenkins was taking risks again here, trying to play both ends against the middle. Dearly beloved . . . heathen lands . . . righteousness and truth . . .

God's will . . .

Sari looked up into the glare, the stare of the sun-blinded into the distance. Wet . . . the stream had been here . . . once . . .

True and righteous believers in the true and righteous will of Panas! Exterminators of the impious! Executors of the thief-spawn of the land!

I will have it thought about.

Citizen Valdemar inspected the barrels. "This is damp," he said. "It is ruined. I will not pay you for ruined goods."

Ow!

". . . I think that America has a few things to offer you."

"America? Offer the Three Kingdoms?" Abnel popped another grape . . .

Squirm!

Punish!

Tap.

Prodding. In or out? Girl or boy? Oh, please, take me . . .

. . . into his mouth . . .

I will give you gold, I said. *A sealed vessel,* I said. And he will do it. And then it will be mine!

"I could throw this into the fire and it would not even burn, much less explode."

... and where was he getting those grapes, anyway?

Mine!

Suddenly running, her old heart pounding. Running up the dry streambed. Running across the water-smoothed rocks now dry with the sunlight, dry as the desert that had embraced them. Running.

But what had Bakbuk been doing there? Aeid peered at the distant camp. He had seen her ... no ... him ... no ... her glance at him in the middle of that fight, had seen how she ... ah ... the sworder had driven off the unprepared (Sleeping again!) palace guards and had outright killed the freedom fighters (so they called themselves) in order to give him a chance to escape. Why? That glance: lowered head, eyes looking coyly up.

Give it to me ...

Mine!

Tap.

Tap. Tap.

Driving pegs back into the ground, the tongued and the tongueless spoke and gestured.

Tap. Tap. Tap. Tap.

Raisins!

"But what about steam?"

The stream. The water gone. Sere. Running faster. Naia's grace (her thoughts coming quickly, spilling over one another). Running.

Ugh! Ugh! Ugh!

Mine!

I will have it thought about. But Aeid ... he is my son. But he is reading ... terrible things ...

Did she know?

"I confess I cannot understand what you mean."

"The army of the Righteous States of America," Jenkins continued cautiously, carefully, "thrives on discipline."

Please! She piled her hair up on her head.

Please! She ran faster, her heart laboring, aching.

Hazy distance. Haze in distance. To Aeid's eyes, the camp was no more than a blur. Bakbuk. Shift of hips. Pull tunic from those slight brown shoulders, biting bread soft thighs, tongue . . .

. . . tongue what?

Naia! I want . . .

You! I want you! Please!

"I assure you, Mr. Ambassador, that the soldiers of the Three Kingdoms are just as prepared as any in the world to fulfill their duties."

"I assure you, honored Gharat, that the army of the Righteous States would not have been caught napping."

Abnel stopped with a grape close to his sugary lips. "Are you saying that the Three Kingdoms are in any way inferior to the rest of the world?"

Hair. Pulling down her tunic. Offering herself. Breadsoftthighs. Take me!

"It will not even catch fire. Damp has ruined it. Take it away."

Tap. Tap. Tap. Tap. Tap.

"They might not have been inferior once," said Jenkins, still cautious, cautiously advancing. "But I think that they have fallen on hard times recently. The drought has caused . . . many changes."

"Oh, the drought again."

"The Righteous States could help."

Lungs on fire, she ran, dropping bundle and water behind. Running with aching heart. Running with bleeding feet. Old woman close to dying, running like a young girl after a man (so they would have you believe), coming not

upon wide caves with eternal waterspill but only avalanche, dry dust, chthonic access sealed forever.

"We need no help, Mr. Ambassador. The Three Kingdoms are great, wise, and quite self-sufficient. Why, you
yourself have seen the wonders of our land. You yourself
have seen the cities of marble and jasper. What but a thriving and superior race of men could create such things?"

Mr. Mather was looking at Abnel's lips.

"Oh, bother steam!"

Squirm!

"I thought that Panas built the cities," said Jenkins.

Despair. And so did Naia provide? And so what did
Naia provide? Nothing. Dead land. Dead people. Dead
faith. And so, in return, the Goddess who provided nothing
received curses. And more curses. And more curses.

Take me!

... thought about ...

Raisins!

I want ...

Mine!

Bakbuk?

Tap.

Curses.

Please!

"Worthless."

Boy or girl?

Take me!

... thought about ...

Raisins!

I want ...

Mine!

Bakbuk?

Tap.

Curses.

Please!

"Worthless."
Boy or girl?
Take me!
. . . thought about . . .
Raisins!
I want . . .
Mine!
Bakbuk?
Tap.
Curses.
Please!
"Worthless."
Boy or girl?
Take me!
. . . thought about . . .
Raisins!
I want . . .
Mine!
Bakbuk?
Tap.
Curses.
Please!
"Worthless."
Boy or girl?

....
....
....

Sounds like a good one. Come on up and have a listen.

Chapter Twenty-four

The dawn-shadow of the last ridge of the mountains slid across Sari's face, and, as is usually the case with such things, the abrupt transition from shadow to full light awakened her.

Opening her eyes, she found that she was looking up at a large boulder. She recalled vaguely that she had, at one time (though she was having some difficulty placing that time now), been standing atop that boulder, and that she had been shaking her fist. Her mind, though, was fuzzy (the sunlight was not helping that in the slightest), and she could recall neither why she had been shaking her fist while standing atop that boulder (which was, to be sure, a curious thing to have been doing), nor how she had come to be lying sprawled at the bottom of it (which, though just as curious, was a consideration that, perhaps, demanded more immediate attention).

Two eyes, though, were staring at her, and after she had squinted and focused and blinked several times, she realized that they belonged to a lizard that, having assumed the place that she had apparently and precipitously vacated, was now peering over the edge of the boulder. Gray and wizened (Here in the growing wastelands left by the drought, everything that was alive, it seemed, was gray and wizened ... which was probably the reason, Sari reflected, that it was alive at all, which, now that she thought about it (through the fuzz), was probably the reason she herself—gray and wizened—was still alive), it flicked its tongue out periodically as though tasting the air to see whether she had as yet been sufficiently cooked.

"I am not dead, lizard," Sari managed, and though her voice sounded odd to her, she decided that after a fall and a night (night?) spent in the open air, many more things than her voice were liable to prove to be odd. "You will have to find your morning meal elsewhere."

The lizard (and Sari could not but shudder with a kind of macabre laughter at the thought that she might as well have been staring at her own reflection as at a lizard) blinked once or twice, and then, with an abrupt scramble, vanished as, with a flutter of wings, a bird alighted in its place.

Sari blinked. This was no carrion eater. This was a dove. It, too, peered down at her.

Dove. That is what they told me that my name meant, she thought; but inwardly, she shrugged. Whether her name meant dove or lizard was immaterial at present: she was lying at the bottom of a boulder from which she had obviously fallen, and she was not sure that she really wanted to do anything that might indicate what damage such a fall might have done to a seventy-year-old body.

But her memory was starting to come back now, and despite her fears about broken bones and necks and other similar catastrophes, she managed to turn her head. Yes, she was still in the dry stream bed, and, yes, there, a short distance away, were still the fresh remains of an avalanche: an immense mass of rock, gravel, and sand that had apparently come down from the overhanging mountains and blocked the source of the water that had once flowed that way. Blocked, actually, the source of everything. Everything, at least, as far as Sari was concerned.

She let her head roll back so that she was looking up again, looking up at the dove. Yes, that was it. After a frightened run up the stream bed (And, really: had she not already known what she would find?), she had rounded the final bend and discovered what the last earthquake had left: a tumbled chaos of stone where once had opened the mouths of the caves that had led to Naia's most intimate mysteries.

Masses. Imponderable masses of stone. She estimated that there was enough rubble blocking and filling the caves to build several cities. Naia's caves were gone. The water was gone. Everything was gone.

And, worst of all, her hopes were gone.

She was remembering now. She had cursed . . . everything. Her family. Her childhood friends. Maumud. The Naians she had, with increasing disillusionment and despair, met since she had fled her village. Ehar and Yalliah. Charna. Everything. Everyone.

Including Naia.

It had seemed to her (as she recalled now) that Naia had been the source of it all, for it was Naia who had allowed her people to slip into superstition and diluted Panasism, it was Naia who had dragged her across the deserts, it was Naia who had led her on, filling her with hope—no, with *belief* in hope—when she should have realized from the beginning that both were illusory. It was Naia who had brought her to the Caves, and thereby to final despair. And so Sari had cursed her Goddess.

She remembered some of the words she had used. Those that she remembered were quite sufficient. Those that she did not remember, she was certain, were considerably more than quite sufficient. She was, in fact, rather surprised that she had not been blasted lifeless as she had stood atop that boulder (And there was that dove still up there, peering down almost anxiously at her.), waving her arms about and screaming deprecations so loudly that her voice had been echoed and redoubled by the surrounding ridges and peaks.

But perhaps that was but another destroyed illusion, for she had screamed and cursed . . . and Naia had done nothing. Nothing at all. And what could that mean but that Naia, the Mother, the Greenest Branch, was not there. Died, maybe. Gone away, perhaps. Lost interest in a world bereft of both water and faith, almost certainly.

A blur, and the dove was gone. Sari blinked. She had not noticed that the bird had moved or taken flight. It was simply gone.

But she put the lapse down to her fall and to what appeared to be adding up to a day and a night of unconsciousness. Surely, such a combination, coupled with a lack of food and water, could account for many things, of which the simple disappearance of a dove was perhaps the least.

So, she thought, she was alive. And, having lost everything, she had nothing more to lose. In fact, she began to consider that death, under the circumstances, would be an absolute pleasure, and if attempting to rise—or even to move—would give her some indication of how soon she might expect that distinguished Visitor, why, then she would try for both.

But, to her surprise, her arms responded eagerly when she lifted them. No pain. No stiffness. And when she levered herself over onto her hands and knees, she discovered that her legs were also in remarkably good order for having accompanied her on the vertical excursion of the previous morning.

"I do not understand," she said, and, yes, her voice still

sounded odd, but perhaps no more odd than her arms and legs felt . . . which was, in fact, perfectly normal.

No. Better than normal.

Kneeling now, she gave her head a shake as though to clear it, but she discovered, with something very like dismay, that if it were not clear already (which it might well have been: it was a little hard for her to tell), it was not going to get any clearer for the present. What she also discovered, though, was that shaking her head caused her unbound hair to whip around and fall over her face, and it was while she was in the process of pushing it back with the intention of fastening it in some way (though she did not know how) with something (though she did not know what), that she made yet another discovery, one that was infinitely more unsettling than the others.

Her hair was black.

She stared at it. She blinked. She stared at it again. She rose and held a lock of it before her eyes. Black. Black hair. This was indeed very odd, for her hair had not been black for . . . for . . .

She could not remember. She had started to go gray very early, the trait, apparently, having come down to her from her grandmother. Among Naians—at least (she thought with a familiar pang) among Naians as she remembered them—gray hair was a mark of distinction. Maumud, though, like most Panasian men, had thought it ugly, and had, in his crueler moments, accused her of lying to him about her age in order to trap him into marriage.

Regardless, had Maumud been alive at that moment, he would have had no complaints, for Sari's hair was no longer gray, but black, lustrous black, as black as it had been when she had become a Panasian woman and had married him. As black as a young woman's. (And now she was sorting through it, actually *looking* for gray.) As black—

Her hands.

She instantly forgot her hair, for now she was staring at her hands. To be sure, there was nothing overtly wrong about her hands. Except that—smooth, young, supple, almost uncallused—they were, most decidedly, not her hands. Except that they were.

"Oh ... Goddess ..."

And then she understood why her voice sounded strange.

Beshur rounded a corner, examined the shops that were opening, rounded another corner, examined the stalls of the market square that were opening.

And into this would I come. Round of banal commerce. Women thrusting their bodies (What shall I do?) at me, copulating with me in their minds. Husband. Husband? Could that be? How far would I get? Would they come for me? Would they find me?

"Water! I have water!"

That could be me. Scrimping a miserable existence out of coppers and demi-settels. Get up in the morning and my black-faced wife gives me a thrashing because I came in late the night before. Oh! Her thighs! Wallowing in cuntmilk (Here, walk like this ...), pretending that I do not have to go home. And then I pick up my bottles and my bowls and make my rounds ...

"Water!"

... in the city, driven out by this man, spat on by that woman. But they all come to me in the end, for water is all and everything, and I know that even those who teach me (Teach? Taught!) would abjure Panas in exchange for a cup of camel piss were they thirsty enough.

The water-seller sidled up to Beshur, rattling his pots.

"Fresh water, honored priest," he said with a wink. "For you only the best. Pray to Panas for me." He rattled his pots again, indicated the jug on his back. "This was just drawn from the well!"

And I gave her water. The old Naianess. Lying there in the sun with glazed eyes. Spittle dribbling from her mouth. But she needed water, and her people arguing over trivialities. I gave her water for nothing. I did not see her again.

Trivialities? What have *I* been doing with my life?

—Go away, Beshur said. I am not thirsty.

"Ah, honored one," chirped the water-seller, "not thirsty today, but thirsty tomorrow!"

—Go away, I say.

In another day, he might well despise me as one of the fallen and could not be bribed to give me water. It could happen that quickly.

He stopped in the middle of the street, ran a hand back across his scalp.

How long? How fast does this grow? Seems to have to be shaved every day, but they say that is because it is supposed to be shaved. How long, then? Could they find me?

The water-seller danced before him.

"Oh, water for the priest!"

—I am not a priest, Beshur said angrily. I am a novice. I have not taken my vows.

"Oh! But you will! Novice to priest! You can never escape now!"

Beshur turned, pulled his head cloth tight, and jogged off across the market square. The water-seller and his pots rattled into the distance behind him.

He mocks me, but he thinks that he is speaking the truth. Never. Novice to priest. No escape. (Walk like this.) And yet, I have examined the texts, and there is nothing in them that says I must stay. Until the stone is carved, it remains unmarked. Until I am a priest I can leave. But can I? But what good is it? Panas? What is that? Why, I am more afraid of the priests than I am of Panas. Panas has done nothing to anyone. Only His priests do things, and I no longer believe in priests, for I saw that the Texts had changed. Liars. Liars and thieves, too. They would steal even me. Shadows in the night, hands dragging me off. Oh, Beshur? He used to live here. Vanished one night, you know. Here, walk like this.

Panas . . .

What is that?

Sari was kneeling again. Off and away down the dry stream bed from the avalanche and the buried caves, she had found the waterskin and bundle that she had abandoned the previous morning—or perhaps the previous week, or maybe year . . . she did not, in truth, have the faintest idea. But like any woman anywhere, old or young, she counted a small mirror among her possessions, and it was into this bit of silvered glass that she was now staring.

It was not an entirely unfamiliar face that stared back, but it was perhaps a little more perfect than she remembered it—perhaps just a little more perfect than she could believe—and in any case, it was somewhere in the vicinity of fifty years out of date. Unlined, its eyes flashing as though perfectly willing to compete for brilliance with its lustrous hair, its complexion flawless, it was the face of a young woman, and yet, as it was very firmly attached to her head, it was, undeniably, her face.

She dropped the mirror, put her too-smooth hands to her too-smooth face, and tried to weep. What was this? A dream? A hallucination? A curse from an angry Goddess? Instinct told her that it was none of these, and yet her inability to fully grasp or believe such a fantastic change combined so inextricably with her overwhelming feeling of terror at the thought that she had been so intimately and personally touched by divine power that she believed unquestioningly that it was, in fact, all three; and therefore,

as her emotions, finding themselves in the middle of a tri-
lateral conflict, wisely decided to remain neutral, her eyes
were undimmed by tears when she again consulted the
mirror.

Still young. Still lovely. And still quite firmly attached.
She still looked ... well ... much as she had looked fifty
years ago, save for the fact that she looked even better
than she had fifty years ago. If Naia had changed her—and
Sari could not escape the conclusion that it *was* Naia who
had changed her—then She was obviously determined to
demonstrate that Her handiwork was nothing less than
first-rate.

Sari stared. She had been touched. She had doubted everything, doubted even Naia, and she had been touched.
Worse, perhaps, she had even been graced, for what could
the acquisition of such youth and beauty be but some kind
of grace?

Hesitantly, then, she put down the mirror, put off her
clothing, and, with trembling hands, explored her body as
carefully as she had explored the bodies of her newborn
children, wondering at the soft skin, the perfect fingers and
toes, the feel of muscle and bone beneath the flesh. And finally, after satisfying herself that all that she touched and
felt and saw was real, undeniably real, and after discover-
ing that the transformation that had been visited upon her
had indeed removed every last trace of the old, Panasian
woman, she cried at last, teetering precariously between a
girl's silly tears and a crone's deep grief, because as far
behind as she had left her old life when she had fled from
the house and the corpse of her husband, it was as nothing
compared to the distance which separated her from it now.

Eyes streaming, she dressed herself and gathered her
things, registering with numb, housewifely efficiency the
fact that, though her clothes still fit her, she had barely
enough water for another day, and her food was gone. And

only then did she realize that she had not really planned to return from her pilgrimage. Not at all. She had intended to reach the Caves. She had intended to die there.

Well, it appeared that what Sari had wanted, Sari had received. The old woman had indeed died. After a fashion.

"Oh . . . Naia . . ."

She wanted to deny it. She could not deny it. Naia was real. Sari's own body was living proof of the presence, the power, and (most frightening of all) the personal *interest* of the Goddess. Despite the veil of superstition that had enveloped the Naian communities of the land, despite the growing influence of Panas, Naia was undeniably *there,* and was just as undeniably determined to make Her will known.

But what was Her will? To what end was this transformation? For all that Sari knew, it could have been no more than some kind of strange, deific joke.

But did Naia joke? Or, rather, did She joke without any purpose?

Rising then (and hardly conscious now of how her gait had altered from an old woman's shuffle to a young woman's spring), Sari went back to the avalanche and the blocked caves as though she might find, at the site of her transformation, some reason for it . . . or at least a bellow of divine mirth. Standing at the edge of the tumble of rocks, she put her young hands on one of the larger boulders and sensed how difficult it would be for even many people to move it. And there were hundreds and thousands of boulders just like it . . . and some even larger.

"What . . ." Her young voice sounded like water after her former croak. ". . . what do You want, Goddess? You have preserved me. You have changed me. I know that You want something. I . . . I will do it if I can. What is it?"

No voice from the heavens answered her. No unearthly light illuminated the desert landscape. No shaft of radiance descended from a rift in a sky full of very artistic and very opportune clouds. No glimpse of God (frontside or backside). No hand writing strange words in the air. No burning bush. No angel. Nothing. But, looking up at the rocks and the debris, suddenly struck by the thought that her pilgrimage was, in effect, not yet complete—for, indeed, she had not yet reached the Caves—Sari needed none of the above mentioned theurgic histrionics in order to grasp the divine command. She simply knew.

"Yes." She did not hesitate. "Yes," she said. "Yes, I will. Yes."

"Coo-whit!" cried one night bird.

"Chukka-chukka-chukka!" answered another.

"Urrrk!" went the slowly cooling mortar and stone.

Beshur, wrapped, determined, and silent, proceeded along the corridor of the novice's house.

"Coo-whit!"

Wake a basalt statue, they would. Loud. Odd that all these years I have slept though them. The night has a life of its own. Beware the night, they say. Never say why. Women baring their bodies for their husbands. Children smucking themselves to sleep. Stained pillows, sheets. Come, tie me up. What fear is there in all that? Nothing more and nothing less that I have seen or have heard hinted at. Slept through it all. Keep myself pure for Panas. Pure for Panas! Pure for what? Get myself thrashed by a wife. (Here, walk like this.) Dragged into some rank bed by the prick of my loins. But here . . .

Nothing here.

Silently, he progressed. Footfalls silent. Breathing silent. Thoughts silent. Marble beneath his feet. Alabaster about him. Doors ahead of him.

"Chukka-chukka-chukka!"

Night ahead of him.

Alabaster gave way to granite, marble to flagstone. Through the open windows, unbarred and ungrated, he smelled the stink of the city, the bubbling sparkle of dust and sweat twinging at his sinuses.

"Coo-whit!"

Here is the first door. (Not long now. Month of the Sturdy Stick. Not long.) No locks. No keys. Never expect anyone to leave. Novice to priest! You can never escape now! But would they say anything about other escapes? Give people ideas. Little boys smucking. Did you hear about . . . yes, I did . . . do you want to . . . yesyesyes. . . Passing secrets about escape and the taste of . . . do you want to . . . yesyesyes . . .

No locks. No keys. Push on it, it opens for you. Push on a priest's hand, it opens for a coin. Give me your money or Panas will punish you. What would He do, though? Provide more priests? Flints up your nose? Pumice up your butt?

The door was of wood, and its brass hinges were silent in the night.

"Mrkgnao!"

Beshur leaped backwards. His head found in the just-opened door a solid obstacle through which it could not pass. It decelerated quickly, his brain thudding in turn against the interior of his skull.

—Mmph! he said, stifling what he really wanted to say.

Tail held high, the cat walked stifflegged toward him, rubbed up against his leg.

"Mrkgnao!" it said again, loudly.

Beshur again stifled what he really wanted to say. Re-settling his head cloth, he nudged the cat through to the far side of the open door (through which he had just passed) and swung the wood to.

"Mrkgnao!" said the cat.

The cat is bad enough, but someone is liable to wonder

about the rest. How loudly did I cry out? Did I cry out? Just a bright flash, and then that head against my leg.

"Mrkgnao!"

Why do they keep a cat? Lascivious creatures. Touch them and they put their tails up. Take me! Here, walk like this.

"Coo-whit!"

He went down another corridor, and another. He had passed one door, and that meant that there were two more to come. And yet there were guards outside the last door. He would have to find a way past them.

Priests irresistible to women. Want it from something new. Unapproachable. Mysteries. Guards to keep them out. See me leave. Drag me up before the Gharat himself. Fat man in white robes. Why did you leave? Because I wanted to. Why did you not tell anyone? Because you would not have let me go. Oh, it is all very simple, and if I can just hide for long enough . . . grow a beard . . . something . . . leave Katha . . .

"Mrkgnao!" came the sudden cry.

Beshur's head met the wall this time, and again the dark, soft head was butting up against his legs.

Thrusting . . . let me in. I hope I did not cry out. Must have gone outside, come back in through a window. Lascivious. Marked me for its own. Will be disappointed. Did I cry out? Farther from the sleepers, closer to the guards. Oh . . . the window . . .

"Mrkgnao!"

He tried to ignore the cat as he looked out the window. Below, twenty feet down, was the ground. Thorn bushes. Roses. If he descended one floor, he would be within reach of an easy drop.

Stairs here . . .

"Mrkgnao!" said the cat, following.

. . . leading me to (what?) what? Kitchen? Oh, yes.

The odor of food and decay and incense was strong, and Beshur's stomach, already nervous, rebelled at the combination. But he had descended the stairs, and the ground was now comparatively close, and so he pushed into the reek. A draft of fresh air led him to another window. Looking down, he discovered that he was now directly above the garbage pit.

"Mrkgnao!"

It was as good as anything else, and possibly better than the thorn bushes and the roses.

Foot over. Butt over. Hang on . . . drop!

Rot. Grease. Stink. Soft, fermented mucus clutching at his sandaled feet.

I am . . .

Sinking down, the pit laving him in reek, he swamsloshtumped to the edge of the mire, felt solid ground, pulled himself up.

. . . done!

"Mrk—"